RISE OF
BOOK 1

BLOODLUST
AURYN HADLEY

SPOTTED HORSE PRODUCTIONS

BloodLust is a work of fiction. Names, characters, places, brands, media, and incidents are either the product of the author's imagination or are used fictitiously. Any resemblance to actual events, locales, or persons, living or dead, is entirely coincidental.

Copyright © 2022 by Auryn Hadley

All Rights Reserved. In accordance with the U.S. Copyright Act of 1976, the scanning, uploading, and electronic sharing of any part of this book without the permission of the publisher and the copyright owner constitute unlawful piracy and theft of the author's intellectual property. Thank you for your support of the author's rights.

Cover Art by DAZED designs (www.dazed-designs.com)

Edited by Sarah Williams

DEDICATION

We've all been outsiders. We've all felt like no one else can understand. At some point in our lives, everyone knows the pain of belonging nowhere. This is the story of that struggle. It's for everyone who's been bullied, sneered at, or isolated because they dare to believe in themselves over what society demands.

But it couldn't have been possible without two people very dear to my heart. When I felt alone and abandoned, they proved just how wrong I was. They showed me what it means to have a home, a place to belong. They taught me that it's not a structure, but a feeling. Above all, they said they believed in me.

It matters.
Il bax genause.

TRIGGER WARNING

BloodLust is a complete epic science-fantasy novel, without a cliffhanger.

Some aspects may be triggering for some readers.

Because the iliri have insatiable and exotic sexual instincts, it may be unsuitable for humans under 18.

The series includes racial injustice, persecution, and various forms of discrimination - See the **Author's Note**.

AUTHOR'S NOTE

The Rise of the Iliri series is about battling injustice in many forms. Because of this, please be aware that these books may be triggering for some readers. Discrimination and hate exist. Sometimes, they are hard to read.

When I wrote this series, I wanted to address one of the main problems I see in speculative fiction. Characters are always defined by what they are, not who they are. Orcs are evil, princesses are good. Vampires and werewolves always have to hate each other. Sadly, that isn't really how it works. Sometimes, the bad guys have good reasons. Most times, the good guys are a pretty diverse group. All times, it takes an open conversation to realize who are the allies and who are the enemies.

For some readers, there will be content in this series that is triggering. It would be easy to assume that this is a story about reverse discrimination. Spoiler: it isn't. It is a story about coming together. It is a story about removing the lines and fighting our way to equality in many ways. It is a story about realizing that we all screw up, but that doesn't mean we can't get better.

Because of this, characters will say and do things that will

AUTHOR'S NOTE

infuriate you. You will love them, hate them, and then love them again. Some, you'll just hate. Some you'll wonder about, trying to decide which side they're on. Because, in a world where everything is black and white, the real truth is that nothing is ever that simple. Humanity is made up of all the vibrant shades in the middle. Some good, some not, and most are just trying to figure it out.

In the end, we all matter, and our place is what we make it.

~Auryn Hadley

MAP: OGUN - NORTHERN CONTINENT

INTRODUCTION

*S*ince the dawn of time, we've been called beasts and treated as either pets or livestock. The only things we knew about ourselves came from whispers spoken softly, far away from human ears. Even our own language was hoarded like some treasure. From mother to child, everything we'd experienced was passed down quietly, giving us some hold on our history, but it wasn't enough. Often, the stories felt more like wishes than reality.

Until she came.

Nothing about her should have been a surprise. Always, when we needed help most, one female would rise up to lead us. We'd recognize her by her scent, that of hope and dreams, and we'd call her Kaisae. In the past, she'd been just like us – but now *we* were different. Our people had been diluted, changed by generations of crossbreeding until we weren't sure what we were anymore. *She* didn't have that problem.

One look at her reminded us all of what we were supposed to be. The pride in her eyes proved that we hadn't always been property. We hadn't been created to live as slaves! Once, long ago, *we* were the ones in charge, and it had been women like her who'd kept us safe.

But that was before humans fell from the stars. Everything they needed, they brought with them – or so they thought. From the crops they planted on our soil to the animals that grazed on our hunting grounds, what had once been ours, they took as their own. It was never enough.

They wanted metal. It held up their homes, powered their machines, and made them stronger than us, but our world didn't have much. No matter what name they used, iron, copper, and even gold were things we'd never seen until humans came. They swore it existed, but it seemed there wasn't enough to go around. They decided to use us instead.

They hunted our prey, destroyed our homes, and killed our culture to make us serve them. When we objected, they twisted us, forcing us to stand taller, bleed more red, and even speak their words. Soon, we replaced their machines, and the humans were happy with their easy lives.

In only a few generations, we became their greatest tool, kept in check by our primal needs and shackled by our own minds. Our species learned to submit. Humans were stronger, so we had no other choice. We still tried to resist, always relying on the best of our women to show us the way. Over and over, we failed, forced to become meek and obedient until we eventually forgot there had been any other option.

The stories of our history became myths. Mothers gave up whispering them to their babies. Our grandchildren ignored us when we tried, and theirs called them lies. It didn't happen fast, but after many, many lifetimes, the humans had finally won. The iliri, a once proud species, had become the pets humans had always called us, tamed through generations of domestication.

And that was when she finally appeared. With her eyes locked on the ground, no one would have guessed that the worthless bitch was a threat. We'd fought for so long, biting, clawing, and killing to keep what little pride we had left, but she'd learned something new. She'd figured out how to be overlooked.

In other times, our people never would have chosen her. In other circumstances, she wouldn't have been good enough. Lucky for us, she was all we had, because that one unimportant girl was about to become the hope of an entire species – and it only happened because no one told her it couldn't.

- Excerpt from *The History of Salryc Luxx*, by Ilus Molis Cernyn, professor of iliri history at the University of Arhhawen

CHAPTER ONE

Weaving through the large, dark-skinned bodies of the soldiers around her, Sal touched the paper in her pocket like a talisman. It gave her permission to apply to the Black Blades. This was her dream. They were the best of the best, yet the last people she'd expect to take her seriously. Still, they'd given her a chance when no one else would. Now, she just had to prove that an iliri could be as good as any human.

Easier said than done.

Distracted by her thoughts, she didn't see the blue-clad shoulder until it slammed into her, pushing her against a man on her other side. Her head snapped up, craning to see the soldier's face, and a growl almost slipped out. *Stupid instincts,* she thought as the human's dark eyes glared into her white ones. The scent of his fear was pungent.

"Out of the way, scrubber!" he snapped.

Sal quickly dropped her head, hoping her blue military-issue cap would hide her pallid skin, and tried to keep her lips over her sharp teeth. "Sorry, sir."

He grumbled something and kept going. Hiking her pack higher up her shoulder, she did the same but in the other direction. Humans would never like her. Nothing she said would change that. They claimed her kind were inferior, too aggressive to be trusted. They believed the iliri were little more than animals yet used them for everything they didn't want to do. She hated it, but there was nothing she could do to change it.

At least life in the military gave her options – like becoming an elite soldier. If she could actually do this, the humans would be saluting her, not shoving her. It was the only way her kind got any real freedom, and serving as a conscript in the military was much better than being a slave.

For years, she'd been planning for this chance. Step by step, she'd worked to make this happen. Now she just had to make sure this unit took her seriously. She had to be *perfect*. She needed to prove that being iliri didn't make her worthless. Somehow, she had to convince them that she was worth taking a chance on.

Beside the main gate, a group in black clustered against the wall. Unlike the blue and gold of the common military, their dark uniforms set them apart. That was her destination – not only where they stood, but what they *were*. The Black Blades were hard and determined, the kind of soldiers no one pushed around. To be feared like that was as close to freedom as an iliri could get. Sal lifted her chin and touched the paper, terrified they'd turn her away.

One of the elite soldiers saw her. A lean, lithe man broke from the group, heading in her direction. A glance at his shoulder showed he was an officer, but before she could salute, his hand snapped out, demanding her orders. Obediently, she passed him the admittance slip, shocked to see how the stark uniform made his skin look almost as pale as hers. The corner of his lip twitched back as his dark blue eyes hit her without blinking.

"Private Salryc Luxx?" His voice was a growl, accented in a way that pleased her ears.

"Yes, sir."

"Ya will be number nine, please place yer belongings there -" He gestured to a row of numbers drawn on the ground. "- an' be at ease. The Lieutenant will be here shortly ta give ya orders."

He smelled so different from most men. There was no fear. Instead, his scent was deep and herbal, natural instead of sweet. She resisted the urge to lean closer when he handed back her papers, but when he bent his fingers to avoid contact, a flare of resentment hit. She looked back up to find his eyes still waiting.

"Pure iliri?" he asked, his gaze too intense.

She stared back. "Yes, sir."

They stood like that for a moment before he looked down to her collarbones. "Females are rare," he said softly.

"Yes, sir. So I've been told."

With a nod, he dismissed her, but his mouth twisted almost up. Had she done something amusing? Unwilling to become the brunt of his joke, Sal turned for her marked spot and dropped her pack in the allocated square. That bag contained all of her worldly possessions. It wasn't much – but was more than she'd had as a slave. Step by step. She could do this. Slave to soldier, soldier to elite. She'd get there. Maybe the Corporal's almost-smile meant she had a chance? She turned to see the Black Blades again, hoping for some hint.

The lithe man had returned to the group and leaned beside a tall, ebony-skinned human. Their mouths were still, but both men looked right at her. Instinctually, her chin moved higher, making the human's mouth break into a grin. Under her cap, Sal's ears flicked back, but with them hidden from view, she made no effort to stop it. Then the larger man lowered his eyes. The lithe man's blue ones still watched.

Sal turned her gaze onto him, shocked when the smaller man's eyes dropped to the ground immediately. Did they realize what they'd done? Of course not. Humans didn't understand. They stared into her eyes or avoided looking at her as it pleased them. While she mentally chided herself for being foolish, another Black Blade joined them, but this one halted her mental diatribe.

His hair was gold and long - not military standard. He was taller than the soldier who took her papers, but not by much. The black man towered over them both, but this new man's coloration marked him as crossbred. No one had hair *that* shade without iliri ancestry. It wasn't blonde; the color was too yellow. When he leaned beside the lithe Corporal, Sal knew she was right. The new guy's eyes were amber, one shade darker than his hair, and they never met hers.

It was hard not to smile, but she wasn't about to show her teeth. The last thing she needed was to be accused of snarling at a superior officer, yet now she had hope. If they'd take such an obvious crossbred, then maybe she actually had a chance?

Wrenching her eyes away, the smile finally won. That one thought was enough to distract her from the scent of humans clustering all around. Each minute, more came, filling in the grid of numbers until there were no empty spaces left. It didn't take long. Their arrival time had been clearly noted, and none of them wanted to be late for this chance.

A bag hit the ground beside her, making her ears flick, but she refused to look. By the scent of his emotions, the recruit had noticed her. Fear and disgust were always distinct. Sal kept her eyes locked on the hard-packed dirt. She wasn't here to make friends, not with her competition, at any rate. She just had to make a good impression on the officers choosing the next member of the Black Blades.

"Hey Odi," the soldier hissed loudly.

"What?" This came from a guy in the row before her.

"You see this shit?" The man in spot ten chuckled. "Guess they're hard up for recruits this time."

Around her, the gravel crunched as men turned to stare. Sal didn't move. Humans had gawked at her for as long as she could remember. Keeping her face calm, she reminded herself that she was still a soldier, whether they liked it or not. All soldiers – both conscripts and volunteers – had the right to apply for special operations with the elite units after two years of service. Sal had served three. There was no reason for the Black Blades to excuse her, and the opinions of these men didn't matter, even if they did hurt.

"You scared she'll beat you out of the running, Bardus?" Odi taunted.

"Fuck that." The man beside her stepped closer. "Hey, bitch? You bite me, and I'll send your ass to the kennels, got it?"

Sal blinked slowly, but that was the only reaction he got.

"Too fuckin' stupid to even speak Glish," Bardus grumbled, making a few men around them chuckle.

The men standing around her smelled wrong. The looks on their faces were hard, even behind the smiles. Thankfully, before things could escalate, the Black Blades suddenly called out, "Attention!" making the syllables into two distinct words.

Sal snapped into position with the other candidates, glad for the distraction as the Lieutenant cantered through the gate toward them. The man rode well, making a show of it as he directed his horse to the front of their block. Dramatically, he spun his black steed to a halt. It pawed, then he patted its neck before dismounting. One of the Blades – the dark-skinned man – stepped up to hold the animal for his commanding officer.

The Lieutenant made an impressive sight. Custom resin armor covered him from his feet all the way up. The dark material soaked up daylight, turning him into a walking shadow. At his back, a quiver full of arrows peeked over his right shoulder, an acrylic sword over the left, and a strange set of tubes were strapped to his leg. Reaching up to his throat, he unfastened his helm and peeled it from his head.

Smoldering green eyes looked over each soldier before him, both applicants and elites alike. While the Blades met his gaze with a smile or a nod, the recruits seemed to melt under his pale green stare. Sal felt the weight of it. His face didn't have a single sign of age or any scars to mar the angular beauty. His shoulders were broad and strong, and his waist had to be trim to fit behind that tight plackart. When he got to her, he paused, lingering in his inspection.

She felt like a weed in the garden.

"Welcome, applicants," he said, moving on to the next man. "I know all of you are excited to show your strengths and prove that you're made for the Black Blades, but I want to make one thing clear. I do not owe any of you a position in my unit. I will not take anyone that is not a good fit with my Blades. I chose you all because I hope to find *one* of you that will be what we need, but I have refused entire groups before, and I'm not afraid to do it again. A weak link is more likely to kill us than help us. None of you is guaranteed a position."

As he spoke, the Lieutenant walked through the ranks, addressing his comments to all of them yet none of them. "The first row will go with Razor, the second with Shift, and the last with Arctic." He gestured at the men as he named them. "The officers will assign barracks for the duration of our trials and a time for me to speak with each of you privately. You may be at ease."

Then he turned to retrieve his horse, leading the animal away while a dusky man stepped forward. Their eyes naturally turned to him.

"I am Sergeant Dico," he said. "Call sign: Razor. Please place your baggage in the wagon being brought up behind you, into the space corresponding with the number you're standing on. We'll have your luggage moved to your cabins. Once your items are stored, make your way to your assigned officer, post-haste."

The applicants began to scramble. They grabbed their bags and tossed them into the wagon before the horses were even fully stopped, caring little for the marked boxes they shoved out of alignment. The others were all men, most of them *large* men. At half their weight, Sal would never force her way through, so she waited, amused by their impatience.

That was when Bardus turned his attention back to her. "Just take that shit home, bitch. We don't need your type thinking they're worthy of elite ops."

"I thought the females were just myths," Odi said, his eyes roaming across her small body. "Maybe we shouldn't run her out quite yet. Heard they have tricks."

She was tired of being treated like she was too stupid to understand the sexual nature of the insult. "I'll leave when the Black Blades dismiss me," Sal told Bardus, glancing at his shoulder before adding, "sir."

"A fucking iliri? You're joking, right?"

She slid her bag into the proper spot, then turned to find her assigned officer.

"I didn't dismiss you yet, Private!"

She stopped. The first man was a Lance Corporal, the second a Specialist. Both outranked her. "Sir, I've been ordered to report."

"Fuck your bleached ass. You can just stand there a bit." Lance Corporal Bardus evidently thought she had to obey.

"I'm sorry, sir, but the Sergeant's orders override yours." Sal tried not to smile as she leaned toward him. "You both should be reporting to your assigned officer as well." The words were barely out of her mouth before she knew she'd gone too far.

Bardus backhanded her across the mouth, making her head snap back. She growled, her muscles tensing as her eyes found him. She was a conscript; he had the right, she reminded herself. Then he hit her again. His fist slammed into her temple – and the ground came up fast.

"Don't you dare bite me!" he yelled, even as the man beside him tensed.

Her tongue flicked out, tasting the blood on her lip as her eyes found her prey. The growl rumbled, growing louder, and her lips pulled back a split second before she lunged. How dare he touch her! She'd make the bastard pay. He was too weak and slow to evade her, and his throat was begging for her teeth.

She pushed hard, intending to knock him to the ground, but a pair of strong arms caught her, yanking her back. The scent of a Black Blade wrenched her out of her frenzy, reminding her why she was here. It was the same elite who'd checked her papers.

"Enough!" Another Black Blade moved to stand between them. "Explain this!" He glared at the humans.

Sal submitted to the tone of authority, her anger quickly dissipating into shame. She hadn't even lasted ten minutes before losing control! What was she *thinking?* When her head dropped, the arms holding her loosened slightly, never touching anything but her uniform. Across from her, two other Blades held her attackers firmly.

"I'm sorry, sir," Sal said, hoping she could salvage this. "They gave me orders that conflicted with those of Sergeant Dico. My response was out of line, and the Lance Corporal felt it was worthy of discipline."

"The damned beast tried to attack me," the recruit jeered. "Can't trust the iliri, I tell ya. You ever see what happens when one of those fucks bites you?"

In her ear, a rough voice whispered, "I'm gonna let ya go. Do na hurt em."

A nod showed she understood and the Black Blade released her. Sal took the time to straighten her uniform, then tugged her cap tighter over her ears.

The Black Blade before her waited for her to look up. "Is that all?"

"The discipline caught me off guard, sir. I reacted instinctually. The Lance Corporal felt threatened, so he decided more discipline was needed."

"I see." The Black Blade turned to the other two soldiers. "Anything to add?"

"Yeah. The damned scrubber disobeyed orders – "

"No." The officer cut him off, but never showed a sign of emotion. "The Private was following her superior's orders. Our trials are not the place for you to throw your rank around." He shook his head. "Zep, Cyno, escort them to the Lieutenant. Razor, I think they were yours?"

"Two and ten. One's mine. The other's Shift's."

"Well, check the rest in and assign them rooms. I need to speak with the Private."

"Yes, sir," the Blades said in unison.

The man behind her moved to relieve Razor, the pair of Black Blades sharing a look before heading their separate ways. That left her alone with the officer, her stomach in knots. She'd already ruined her chance by reacting like an animal to a common disagreement. This had been her dream, and in a matter of minutes, it was already shattering.

Why hadn't she just submitted? Why did she always feel the need to fight back? Her stupid instincts were going to keep her trapped behind a desk serving humans for the rest of her life! What was the difference between that and slavery? Now, all that was left was the formal dismissal from the trials. She braced herself against hearing the words.

"Private Luxx, right?" the officer asked, ducking his head to look at her face.

"Yes, sir."

"I'm Arctic, second in command of the Black Blades." When she said nothing, he continued, "I would appreciate it if you'd answer my questions more honestly next time."

Her head snapped up, finding eyes nearly as white as her own waiting. "Sir?"

A kind smile preceded his words. "We all saw what happened, Private. In order for something to count as discipline and not cruelty, it requires disobedience. Pride is not disobedience, do you understand?"

She cocked her head to the side, trying to decide if she believed what his words hinted at. His white eyes made her want to, but turning exposed the bruise growing on her temple. Arctic grabbed the side of her face, tilting it for a closer look. She sucked in a breath, but not because it was painful. At his touch, snippets of conversations and thoughts flooded her mind.

"Private?" he asked. *She may need a medic. There's a nasty bruise on her head, and her lip was split. I can't believe those fucks thought we'd look the other way while they abused -*

Sal pulled her face from his hand. "I'm fine, sir."

His pale eyes watched her for a long moment. "Think you're up to finishing the trials?"

No matter how she tried, she couldn't prevent the corner of her lip from rising. "Yes, sir." The feral smile was taking over because it sounded like she wasn't done yet. "It would take more than a bruise to stop me, sir."

Well, she's determined, Sal heard, even though Arctic's mouth didn't move. *And I don't want to get your hopes up, but I think we have something special here. You've got to see this.*

"Thank you, sir," Sal said, shocked at the compliment.

"For?"

She swore she'd just heard him call her special. The words had been in his voice, but he acted like he'd said nothing. His mouth hadn't moved. Quickly she blurted out something plausible. "For allowing me to continue, sir. I assumed that's what you meant."

LT, I think we have a problem. "It is. Report to Shift. He already knows that you've been detained."

She snapped a salute. "Thank you, sir."

Turning to find her assigned officer, she made it a few steps before he called her name again. "*Private Luxx?*"

She turned back. "Yes, sir?"

"Shit." He gestured for her to wait. *She can hear us.* A pause followed, then, *I touched her. She's pure, and we have no experience with that. There's so few left.* Another pause. *I can't be sure. I didn't link her in to begin with. I can shut the whole thing down, but I have no idea if I can cut her line.* The next pause was longer. *Understood.* His eyes focused on her again. "So how much of that did you get?"

Years of practice kept her face expressionless. "I heard you call my name, sir."

"Bullshit." He smiled slyly. "Let's try this again, because I didn't do more than *think* your name - and you smell like lies."

Ice washed down her body, leaving her skin tingling in its wake. She'd heard, he knew she'd heard, and he didn't think she was crazy. Had she hit her head that hard? Why wasn't he surprised?

"It's only a minor bruise, sir. I'm sure I'll be fine in a moment."

He lifted a brow. "You think that's because you were hit in the head?"

"I'm an iliri, sir, not a fool." She dared him to deny it.

Arctic actually laughed. "I never thought otherwise, Luxx. Now, let me assure you that your answer will not disqualify you from the trials. How much of that did you catch?"

Defeated, but comforted by the promise that they wouldn't be kicking her out yet, Sal answered. "You called my name. I heard you say I had a bruise, that you didn't want to get someone's hopes up, and that you can shut the thing down."

"And did you hear the other person?" His eyes scanned her face. "Don't worry, I just need to know."

Relaxing slightly, Sal said, "No, sir. Just you, sir."

"At least there's that." He sighed, running his fingers through his long, dark hair. "No, you're not losing your mind. What you're hearing is a trick of my own iliri ancestry. Usually, I have to consciously allow someone to hear our thoughts. When did it start?"

"When you touched me, sir."

"Ah." He nodded to himself. "Physical contact. That makes sense. I guess you came with the switch on. Look, I can't lock you out. Not yet – since I'm not sure exactly how you got in – but I'd appreciate it if you keep this to yourself for the time being."

A chuckle escaped. "And who would I tell, sir?"

"Good point." His shoulders relaxed, and he tilted his chin

behind her. "Now go find Shift. He'll assign you rooms." Arctic turned away before she could salute.

Confused, Sal tried to push the strangeness out of her mind. She wasn't here to wonder about the mysteries of the world or believe in miracles. She just had to get a position as an elite soldier. Maybe the whole thing was some practical joke, intended to make her look crazy. That would be a good way to get her excused from the trials, but it seemed she hadn't ruined her chances yet.

Like she'd been told, Sal jogged to the meeting area just on the other side of the fountain. The man called Shift leaned casually against the fence with three soldiers in blue uniforms standing before him. Interestingly, the color of his skin hinted at iliri ancestry in him too. He looked up before she got close, pushing away from the wood rails to offer his hand. Sal took it out of habit, then fell into place beside the other soldiers.

Don't worry, Shift said inside her head, *I've already been told. I'm pretty sure you can hear me.*

I really can, Sal thought, her eyes widening in amazement.

Nice, and I can hear you easily. Looks like you're a natural. His face showed no hint of their conversation, the thought ending as he switched to his voice. "Glad they finally let you go, Private," he teased. "You almost missed getting a room. The rest of you have your cabins and meeting times. Luxx, you'll have cabin twelve. That's with the rest of the Black Blades. Being the only woman in the group, the Lieutenant wants to discourage extracurricular activities. Now, the rest of you are dismissed. Luxx, he'd like to meet with you now rather than in the morning." *Don't worry, he doesn't bite. We just need to sort out the incident earlier,* he assured her.

Sal nodded. *Am I going to be dismissed?* she wondered.

Nah, Shift thought. *Pretty sure you didn't mean to send that, but you did. Look, we're not a bunch of assholes, ok? You won't be dismissed because some damned idiots try to harass ya. And this little deal,* Shift gestured between their heads, *can't exactly be ignored.*

She nodded professionally, but her heart was hammering. She'd already been noticed, and she wasn't sure it was in a good way. This was nothing like she'd expected for an elite unit's trials. Too many strange things were happening, but she could handle strange. She just had to be very careful that strange didn't become a way to set her up.

When Shift gestured for her to follow, she fell in beside him, careful to stay just behind his shoulder. He might not be completely human, but she didn't want to cause any more problems than she already had. Obviously, they accepted the crossbreds well enough. That gave her hope. Maybe if she could convince them she was tame, they'd give her a fair chance?

He slowed his steps until she was beside him. *Don't do that. You're not in shit. We just need to sort out a few things.*

"Sorry, sir," she muttered.

And don't fuckin' 'sir' me. Look, we're not like that, ok? I don't care what some human says you should do, we know what you are. If anything, I should be walking around behind you.

His thoughts shocked her. *What?*

Shift looked over to her quickly. *You weren't raised by an iliri, were you.*

It wasn't a question, but she decided to try answering. *No. I was purchased young, as a pet and servant. I've never really met any other iliri.*

Well, that's going to make things harder. He gently touched her shoulder. *It's ok, though. You're not alone anymore. Just breathe, I'm sure you can smell it.*

Smell what?

Shift grinned. *The truth. There's so much more going on than you could ever guess. What we're about to show you is just a hint.*

CHAPTER TWO

Shift grabbed the plain wooden door before them and pulled it open, gesturing for her to go first. Sal pulled off her cap as she entered and took a deep breath, looking around. The ever-present sweet smell was faint, little more than a tickle in her nose. Instead, she savored scents that felt natural and comforting. They reminded her of something from long ago.

Across the room, Lieutenant Blaec Doll stood with his bare back to them. At the sound of the door, his head tilted, he grabbed a clean shirt from the chair beside him, and shoved his arms into the sleeves as he turned. His chest was smooth, perfect except for one pale line across his hip that vanished under the waist of his pants. She wondered how a soldier could've fought for so long without the marks to prove it. When her eyes finally made their way to his face, he was waiting.

"She doesn't have a clue," Shift said, leaving her side to drop into a chair before a massive desk. "Pretty good instincts, though. We've been chatting."

The Lieutenant nodded. "I see that. Any reason you didn't give me a warning?"

"Nope." Shift grinned and leaned back, the chair creaking in protest. "Brought her to the office like I was told. Not my fault you're half-naked."

He chuckled. "If you'd been any earlier, I would have been all naked."

"What," Shift teased, "didn't want to stay in armor all day?"

"Nor show my bare ass to the recruits." The Lieutenant grinned before turning to Sal. "So, Private. Heard you've been making things interesting."

She wasn't sure if she was already off to a bad start but dared to hope that Shift was right. "I'm sorry, sir."

He stopped just a step away, his hard green eyes boring into hers. When she refused to look down, he smiled slowly. "I see. And how long can you keep that up, little iliri?"

He was challenging her intentionally! *As long as I need to*, she thought, but said, "Pardon me, sir?" Her ears flicked forward, locked on him, wondering what he was trying to do.

"Her mind and her mouth don't agree," Shift said. "I'm getting a drink if you're gonna start that shit."

"Pour her one, too," the Lieutenant ordered, never breaking the gaze. "She'll need it." He stepped closer, his attention back on her. "Now tell me, are you always this submissive?"

He *was* taunting her. When she refused to blink, he stared back, a smile playing at his mouth. Sal tried to ignore the sudden desire to see him look away. He outranked her, but every fiber in her body said she deserved to see him submit. While Shift poured the drink, she tracked him with an ear, never breaking her stare with the Lieutenant.

"How long can you really hold it?" he whispered.

The arrogance in his tone was too human, too sure of himself. Her ears locked back and a rumble started in her throat. When he leaned forward, she snarled, allowing her lips to pull back, revealing her sharp teeth, including the double canines humans didn't have. He was too close.

The Lieutenant only smiled. "You really think you can make me back down? Are you *really* that sure of yourself?"

"That would be improper, sir," Sal said, refusing to look away. Her tone was professional even if the growl wasn't.

He leaned even closer. "Iliri rarely care about the ranks of humans, girl. Either you're more dominant than me, or you aren't. Pick one, and prove it." His voice was so quiet she assumed Shift hadn't heard.

"Don't push it," Shift said as the door opened behind them. "She's running on pure instinct. Never met our kind before."

"Shit." The new voice sounded like Razor, the officer who'd spoken to them earlier. "Feral?"

"No." The Lieutenant's voice was a purr. "Not at all. Strong, but not feral." He leaned back, looking pleased. "Now go sit down, Private. That's an order."

Sal paused. Her instincts said she should *not* look away or she'd give him control. Her mind realized that disobeying the order would be a good way to end her trials early. Desperately, she tried to decide which would be the greater loss. Eventually, she forced herself to blink, took a deep breath to halt the growl, and then sighed before moving to the chair beside Shift. No matter how much she wanted to, Sal refused to rub her ears to relax them. She wouldn't give these men that much satisfaction. The door opened again.

"I smell that," Arctic said. "What did you do to her?"

"Made her submit," Razor told him. "She's not too pleased about it."

Sal's head snapped around, looking at the men she sat with. "I didn't say anything!"

Razor tapped his nose. "Didn't have to. Even Shift can smell that. Defeat. It's not a good scent for you, Kaisae."

"She doesn't know," The Lieutenant said, claiming the chair behind the desk.

Arctic took the chair beside her. "So I was right."

The other three answered in unison, all with some variation of yes. It seemed they'd already had a discussion about her, and Sal felt like she was playing catch up.

"Tamed?" Arctic sounded terrified of the answer.

"Not at all," the Lieutenant said. "No, not at *all*. She knows nothing, but she still has her own opinions, even though she tries really hard to act like humans expect her to."

"I'm not a beast," Sal insisted, looking at them, one after the other. "I know you think my kind are primitive, but I've studied for years, I am well versed in both military and civilian protocols, I – "

The Lieutenant shook his head, cutting her off with a lift of his hand. "Don't assume, Private. Breathe. How much human sugar do you smell?"

She shook her head, confused.

So he tried again. "That sweet scent. Do you smell it?"

"Barely," she admitted.

"That's probably me," Shift said.

Sal glanced toward the Lieutenant. "And him."

Razor sucked in a breath. "Whoa. That's perceptive."

She turned to him. "I can smell it on you, too."

Arctic chuckled. "How about me?"

Sal inhaled. "Barely. It's there, but I have to search for it. Humans never said anything about it. I thought everyone smelled sweet, except after combat."

LT laughed. "After combat, we smell even sweeter – from the human blood. According to your file, you have little experience with iliri, so I'm not surprised that you have no idea. I'm just pleased to see you're still able to think for yourself. Too many of us have lost that."

She noticed he included himself in the iliri. Blaec Doll had fair skin, but the wrong shade to be suspected of iliri ancestry. His color was no different than so many other citizens of the Conglomerate.

The Lieutenant watched her eyes roam across him and smiled.

"I'm half. Shift is a quarter. Razor is around forty percent. Arctic, you're three quarters, right?"

"A bit over, but about that."

Sal felt her heart stop. "Iliri?"

"Yes." The Lieutenant smiled and leaned closer. "We're iliri crossbreds. That's why we're so good. Now, you want to tell me how you managed to get into our mental link, Salryc Luxx?"

"Sal." She looked up, hoping she hadn't overstepped her bounds.

His pale eyes warmed, and he inhaled deeply before daring to taste her name. "Sal." It rolled off his tongue naturally.

Trying to cover her confusion with a direct answer, she rambled on, "I don't know how I heard Arctic's thoughts, sir. The First Officer touched me, and I began to hear his voice in my head. I've never had it happen before."

"And I shook her hand," Shift added. "She's a natural. Comes through clear."

Really? The Lieutenant's voice slid into her mind. *How?*

I don't know, sir. I just hear it.

And you just think back? How do you know what to do?

I don't know. She looked down, unable to hold his eyes.

Arctic broke in. "She's not leaking at all. She's locked onto her channel but receptive to all of them. I don't know how she's doing it. If I wasn't looking for her, I probably wouldn't even know she's here." He tapped his head. "Pretty sure she's piggybacking without knowing it."

The Lieutenant dragged his hand across his mouth. "But you can't shut her off?"

"Dunno. Never met anyone who could do it before. I've only heard about it, but it might help to put her into the link. That would at least let me moderate her access." Arctic shrugged. "Tethering her will be easy enough."

A deep baritone asked in her head, *So, do you have to touch each of us, or can you just hear us?* He sounded like he was talking from a distance.

Sal cocked her head slightly. "No. I hear that, but it's muffled."

Razor offered his hand, and Sal touched it lightly. *How about now?* he asked.

As clear as if you used your voice, Sal told him.

"Yep, touching clears it up, but the lack isn't stopping her any," Razor told the rest.

"But I didn't need to touch the Lieutenant to hear him." She looked over at Arctic, hoping for an explanation.

He shrugged. "LT's been doing this his whole life. He sends better than the rest of us."

She nodded to show she'd heard. "I had no idea this was even possible. I assure you, I had no intention of causing you problems."

LT laughed. "I'm pretty sure you didn't." He turned to Arctic and nodded. "Do it."

She felt a strange shift in her head, but nothing else. Beside her, the men sighed, obviously experiencing something as well. "She's in," Arctic said.

Slowly, the Lieutenant held out his hand, palm up. "Now let me show you something."

Sal didn't want to touch him but knew it was what he expected. Meekly, she reached over and laid her hand against his, hearing him inhale as if surprised. Instead of the slick, disturbing feeling she expected, his skin was warm and soft, the calluses from hours of sword work comfortable and reassuring. He closed his eyes and let his fingers wrap around the back of her hand, holding her to him. For a long moment, he didn't move, then his eyes snapped open.

My mother had eyes like yours, he thought, following with a picture of an iliri woman. *There aren't many like you left.*

Do they know? She meant the other officers.

Yes. We don't keep secrets from each other, but we also don't share them with outsiders.

I understand. She shuffled the image far back in her mind.

"Anything?" LT asked suddenly.

"Nope." Razor shook his head.

"Not a hint," Shift said.

"I got every word, and the location she stored the memory," Arctic assured him.

LT nodded, "And?"

"It's put back about as tight as she can. I can show her how to do it better, but I've never seen a novice with such control."

Sal looked back and forth between them, barely keeping up with the new line of talk. "You mean that was a test?"

"To some extent," LT said. "We can't keep you out without more work than I want, so we might as well see how far we can trust you. And if you're wondering, it's impossible to lie mind to mind. That really is my mother. I'm one of the few here who has met a pure iliri female."

"Oh."

"Now that you've seen how it's done," he continued, "can I see what happened earlier with the other two recruits?"

When she nodded, a tickle in her mind brought forth a memory. She didn't try to hide her shame, anger, or how hard she worked to control her beastly instincts. She lived each second of the encounter, hoping the memory would explain her actions better than words could. Every detail of her disagreement with the recruits Odi and Bardus flashed behind her eyes. Her fears, disgust, and concerns relived in seconds. Once the memory was complete, the Lieutenant nodded his head slowly.

"Dismiss them. They would never work with our unit, not with that much hate for us."

"Zep asked for the pleasure," Arctic said.

Razor chuckled. "That'll make a few things easier."

"Just don't let Cyno help," the Lieutenant told them, still holding her hand. "Ok, men, we're done here."

They stood, tossing back their drinks, but Sal stayed, his grip holding her in place. As the door closed behind the last man, her heart beat faster. She was alone with him. He could order her to do anything, and she couldn't refuse. That would be a death sentence. Being part iliri, he had to know she was beholden to him now, whether she liked it or not.

"Breathe," he said softly.

"Yes, sir."

"My name is Blaec. They call me LT. It's ok for you to do the same." He slowly pulled his hand away. "You're taking all of this rather well."

"Not really, sir," she said honestly. "I just got hit in the head then started hearing voices. It's just that I'd better learn to roll with it or I'll be sitting back at a desk tomorrow."

He smiled as he stood. "Fair enough. Ok, soldier. The next trial starts at 1300 tomorrow."

"Yes, sir. I wouldn't miss it for the world. And before you say it, I understand my place and that being able to hear your thoughts does not guarantee I will be chosen."

The Lieutenant moved a step closer. His hand found her shoulder, one finger brushing the skin at her neck. "There's nothing wrong with being iliri, Sal. Whether you pass the trials or not, our kind tends to stick together." He tried to meet her eyes, but she couldn't. "Do you understand me?"

She bit her lip, unsure of how to answer, so just nodded.

The problem was that she didn't understand him. She had no clue what was going on. A few minutes ago, she'd been hoping for a chance, and now she was trying to figure out if these men were playing a sick joke on her or if they were honestly iliri crossbreds. If they were, why would they tell her? Why were they being so nice? What was the catch?

She was just a mere Private in the army of the Conglomerate of Free Citizens. Not even a free one! The military owned her title, and she would serve - one way or another - until she died. She was nothing, and these were the best soldiers her country had. They should be laughing at her, not with her. None of this made sense, but she wasn't stupid enough to ask what they were doing.

"And I won't touch you again unless I have permission," the Lieutenant continued. "None of the Blades will. You are not our pet."

"I'm no one's pet, sir. Not anymore."

"No, not anymore," he agreed. "You're also not alone, but..."

The emotion she smelled was confusing. Protective? Supportive? Timid? Scared? They were all mingled together into one, but she couldn't begin to guess why the leader of the most capable military unit in the country would feel like that around her. What was going on?

To keep from showing her confusion, she finished the thought he'd left hanging. "But you can't give me an advantage in the trials. I understand, sir. You need to choose the best soldier to keep your men safe." She dared to look up at him.

He seemed almost relieved. "Yes. Exactly. That doesn't mean we won't help you in other ways. There aren't that many of us left."

"More than you know," she shot back, her ears flicking back defensively. "Serving all over the country. We're locked in cages, chained with poverty, leashed by laws... There are *thousands* of iliri in this country."

He shook his head. "I mean those who've found their place. I have to protect my men at all costs. As their leader, I have to do what's the best for *them*. Not for me, not for you, but for them. You can't hide what you are, but we've been doing it for years."

"I understand, sir," she said, turning to the door, her heart sinking. He was trying to tell her she'd never pass. That was the part she'd been missing. He'd been kind to her because he felt bad for her, but she wouldn't give up that easily. She wouldn't just walk away without a fight, but what she said was, "Thank you for giving me the chance to try, sir."

"1300 tomorrow, Private," he called after her. "Be there."

She nodded as her hand closed on the knob. Even if she wouldn't get accepted, maybe she could get a referral to another elite unit. It was worth a shot. Maybe their kindness would be good enough for that much.

"I'll be there until I'm dismissed, sir. I won't be scared off."

The Lieutenant dipped his head in acknowledgement. "Good. Have a good evening, Private."

She pulled open the door to find a Black Blade standing in the street, waiting. The sun had nearly set, and twilight turned the sky dark overhead. Most soldiers were off duty for the night, and the base was starting to quiet down for the evening. Sal carefully pulled the door shut behind her.

At the sound, Shift looked up with a smile. "Ok, little one, let me show you to your room and keep the big baddies away from you."

"Thanks, Shift," she said, appreciating the effort but hating that he thought she needed it. "I can take care of myself, you know."

He just laughed and gestured up the street. Together, they walked past the row of cabins. "I know you can," he said, finally. "Doesn't mean you should have to. This black uniform of mine gives us both a little protection that your white skin doesn't get."

"Yep." She watched the dirt pass beneath her feet, trying to ignore the ever present resentment she lived with.

Because that was the problem. She wasn't some kind of beast. She wasn't weak. She really didn't want these soldiers to see her as helpless, but because she was iliri, everyone would treat her as lesser. Her kind were little more than second class citizens - if that. That she even needed someone to walk her back to her cabin felt almost shameful.

Shift kept pace in silence for a little while. Sal made sure her eyes stayed on the ground, watching the dirt pass under her feet. This man seemed nice, and she hadn't actually expected that from such renowned soldiers. It was why she couldn't hate him, but her life was usually easier when she did. Keeping to herself meant that no one could find dirt to use on her later.

"What's going on in that head of yours?" he asked. When she made a noncommittal noise, Shift stepped into her path, forcing her to look up. "Seriously, Luxx, you don't have to play human around me. You reek of your emotions, and you can't bottle everything up like this. You'll go brerror."

"I don't even know what that means, but it's Sal."

"Shit, right." With a sigh, he moved back to her side and kept walking. "It means loner, Sal. Lone wolf, anti-social, banished from society. That sort of thing."

"Isn't..." She paused, not sure if she should just smile and nod, sticking to her role as a well-trained iliri. Deciding to give him a chance, she took a deep breath and tried again. "Isn't that what I am now?"

"No. I think you're just lonely. I think you can't trust anyone." He rested a hand on her shoulder, touching nothing but cloth. "I also think you could use a friend."

"Never really had one before," she admitted, her ears sinking lower on her head.

He saw and nodded. "Well, I'm here, if you decide I'll do. I can't give you special treatment in the trials or anything, but I've always got an ear."

"Nice flat ones," she mumbled, aware of how abnormal her own were stuck up on the top of her head like a cat's.

He heard. "They may not work as well as yours, but they're available."

They walked on in silence. At cabin number twelve, he entered first, making his way across the dark room. Her slit pupils dilated fully, and Sal could see the lantern on the table in shades of grey while Shift sought it by feel. His fingers bumped into it, then he fumbled in his pocket and brought out a striker. A few flicks later, a spark landed on the oil-soaked wick, bringing a golden glow into the tiny room.

"It's not much, but it's yours for a bit," he said.

"Thanks, Shift. I really do appreciate it."

"Welcome. Your bag's in the wardrobe. Packed between the

Blades like this, no one will give you shit. It's the best we could do to cut down on the harassment."

Another way they were being nice to her, but why? Instead of asking, she simply nodded, looking around the room. It wasn't much, but the bed looked soft, the furniture would hold her things, and the bathing chamber was private. It was much nicer than the quarters she was usually assigned. When she turned back to Shift, she realized she was smiling.

"It's perfect. Thank you."

"So you know, I'm two doors down in fourteen. Arctic is next door on the other side in eleven, and Zep is across the street in seventeen. The others are scattered on this row, but if you need us..." He let the words trail off, an open invitation.

Sal thanked him again, then shooed him out of her small but private space. The door barely closed behind him before she peeled out of her uniform. Folding it carefully, she set it beside the table and began to unpack, hanging her clothes to let the wrinkles fall out. Her mind wandered over the Lieutenant's words. Her chances were probably slim, but he hadn't told her to give up. Instead, he seemed pleased that she was willing to fight to earn her place.

Finally reaching the bottom of her bag, she pulled out a worn book on military basics. She cradled it to her chest as she flopped on the bed and opened the cover. Before she began studying, she dared to allow herself to hope.

"Please let me pass these trials. Please!" She whispered, then focused her mind on weapons regulations for mounted soldiers.

CHAPTER THREE

The first two days of the trials started with paperwork. Written tests on strategy and tactics, knowledge of weapons, poisons, and siege warfare were all covered. By the third day, the remaining applicants were excited to finally get the chance to show their combat proficiencies. When the Lieutenant approached, they sprang to their feet. Most stood at parade rest, others at attention, but they all hoped to make a good impression. That was how they'd get picked, after all.

LT looked them over. "Be at ease. Today, you get to prove your fighting skills. Report to your assigned officer where you will be assessed on various styles of combat from hand to hand through the basic weapons. Today is melee only, so no, you won't get to shoot any shit."

The recruits chuckled politely, and he continued, "The order of weapons is to be determined by the officer in charge. You will be given a score based on your proficiency with each type, as well as your innovation and decorum in combat. Questions?"

With none forthcoming, they split into their groups. Shift waited with another Black Blade – the dark-skinned human. Riblour,

Saong, and Kinetry - the recruits from her group - gathered around them. When she approached, Shift nodded in her direction but made no attempt to introduce the new elite, and Sal refused to ask. The Lieutenant made it sound like the Blades were all iliri, but this man was obviously human. It made her wonder how truthful her initial meeting had really been.

Keeping silent, she followed the group into a small pasture covered in lush winter grass where practice weapons waited on a canvas tarp spread across the grass. Each of the recruits retrieved a set, and Shift put them through the standard military warm-up. Today, his mind stayed silent, locked well away from hers. She hoped he was just trying to stay impartial.

The entire time, the human stood with a scowl on his face.

Shift demonstrated new moves with the sword, staff, spear, and knife, guiding each applicant through the proper execution with a patience Sal wouldn't have expected. Over and over, he made corrections, working them until the moves flowed easily. When the moons began to overtake the sun, he called a break in their training.

"Ok, so ya pretty much got it. Take five and catch your breath, then we'll see if any of you are as badass as you think."

Sal set her weapons down, the size of them too large for her small body, and swung her arms, keeping them limber. Taking the brief respite for what it was, she stretched and breathed deeply, forcing air to her tired muscles. When her male competitors began to mutter about the lack of refreshments, she rolled her eyes.

On the battlefield, there would be no organized breaks. There certainly wouldn't be refreshments. It wasn't even hot at this time of year! This trial wasn't supposed to be about making them comfortable, but rather about seeing if they had what it took to keep up with the Black Blades. They were supposed to be proving that they could make the cut.

Instead, these humans were the lucky entitled few from their units. They'd been taught that they would be pampered for the smallest effort. Promotions came too easily, resulting in pay raises that brought extra luxuries. To them, the military was nothing more than a way to live the easy life, but elite operations weren't supposed to be easy. They were supposed to turn the tide of battles and save lives.

This wasn't about fame or fortune. It was supposed to be about making a difference. For Sal, becoming an elite would mean safety. Ironic, since so many elites were killed, and yet she'd get extra training. Her assignments wouldn't be suicide missions. Her value to the country as a whole would give her more protection than anything else - and *that* was why she needed this.

Sooner than she expected, Shift called them back to their feet. "Ok, pair up. Riblour with Saong, Kinetry with Luxx," he said, "and Zep, if you can run through Luxx and Kinetry?"

The human nodded, one of his tiny, shoulder-length braids blowing across his eyes, but he ignored it.

Sal moved to where he gestured, away from the other pair. In the distance, another Black Blade watched their group, leaning against the base of a tree. Evidently, she'd become a spectacle.

"Here's the deal," Zep said sternly, demanding her attention. "You will fight. If I believe that one of you is about to be irreparably harmed, I will stop you with the command 'hold.' Full contact is expected. A blow that should kill you will be declared by myself. Otherwise, you will fight until one of you surrenders. The winner wins. The loser is the one dead or the quitter. Understood?"

Kinetry nodded, but Sal had to know, "Any weapon limitations, sir?"

Emotion finally found it's way to Zep's face. A glimmer in his eye told her she'd asked the right question. "None," he said. "Just like real combat."

She turned, removed her cap, and laid her weapons out for easy access, keeping an ear on her opponent. Kinetry, across from her, did the same, glancing up every few steps. When she approved of her spacing, Sal turned to Zep, waiting for a sign to begin the combat. His brown eyes studied her briefly before returning to watch Kinetry's broad back.

As the recruit turned, Zep said calmly, "Lay on."

Kinetry sprang into motion. Dropping to his knees, he grabbed a spear and thrust at her. He was slow – strong, but slow. Without reaching for her own weapons, Sal stepped to the side, watching how he placed his feet, smelling his nervousness, but holding her instincts in check. Kinetry circled to match her. His heels crushed the grass as he moved, his knees too tense. When she made no attempt to attack, he began poking at her with the wooden spear. Its head was round but solid, and would definitely hurt if it connected.

Sal watched how his face changed before the real strike came and shifted casually to the right, grabbing the spear with both hands. Growling, she pulled in the direction of his thrust. It sailed harmlessly past her hip and out of his grasp, surprising the man with how easily she'd just disarmed him.

Frantic, he hurried back to his stash of weapons for a wooden sword. Sal kept her attention on him as she returned to her own pile for something her size. She found a practice knife. Placing it in her belt, she just waited, still squatting.

Kinetry rushed her. Rolling, she snaked her hand out and grabbed the butt of her spear. Resting the point on the ground, the shaft served as a shield for the wild blows her opponent threw. With so little control, it didn't take long for his arms to tire. That was when she lifted the tip and yanked it sideways, knocking his feet out from under him.

He hit hard, but she had to gain control of the weapon before she could finish him. Moving up the shaft, she placed her body midway along the length of it. Just as she found the balance, the recruit flung himself to his feet.

Not daring to waste the chance, she shoved the point at his unprotected chest. The round, wooden tip struck hard, knocking him back into the dirt. A true spear would have impaled a man with that force, so Sal waited to hear her victory called.

"Light. A wound," Zep said instead.

Shocked, she missed her chance to point the tip at Kinetry again. He'd already found his feet, and with unexpected force, he swatted the spear from her hands. She retreated, dodging the rest of his blows with ease. Twisting out of his way, she found herself among his weapons. A staff lay at her feet, begging for her attention, so she took it and countered blow for blow. Each time he left an opening, she scored a hit: his thigh, a hand, his ribs. Bruised and winded, Kinetry powered on with sheer stubbornness.

She aimed at his shoulder, shocked when her weapon skipped off and connected with the side of his neck. Gasping, he staggered to his knees, disoriented, and Sal flicked an ear at Zep – who said nothing. Her fellow soldier couldn't take more of this, she decided. It was time to end it.

The staff fell from her hand as she pulled the practice knife from her belt. Darting in, she looped her left arm around Kinetry's neck, flowing with his movement as he tried to spin. Her right hand held the knife securely at the soldier's throat, the point to his jugular, and she squeezed slightly while he pulled at her arms. Zep just watched, showing no signs of calling the match.

"What more do you want?" she snarled at the Black Blade.

"Could you do it?" Zep countered. "Could you finish him, or just secure him for a stronger, harder soldier to come clean up your mess?"

She tightened her arm on Kinetry's neck and growled, locking her ears back. Humans always assumed her small size meant she was weak. Always! She would show him just how "weak" she was. Her lip curled slightly, the low, deep sound resonating in her throat. Eyes locked with Zep's, Sal held the pressure while Kinetry's struggles grew weaker, his hands frantic to pry her arm from his throat. With one leg shoved against his back, she waited for the weight of his sweet-smelling body to be completely in her control. Eventually, his eyes rolled in his head, and his mass sagged to the ground.

Zep finally called out, "Luxx wins!"

She eased the man down while his unconscious body gasped for breath, then stepped back. Shift, Riblour, and Saong stood just meters away, the scent of their surprise strong on the early spring breeze. Shift moved to Kinetry's side, placing his hand on the recruit's neck to check his vitals with a deep sigh. Slowly, Kinetry's breathing eased and his eyes fluttered open.

"Sorry, man, you lost," Shift told him.

"I knew I would," Kinetry croaked through his damaged throat. "I saw her get slapped to the ground and immediately jump back up on that first day, and no one taught me how to beat that type of agility."

At the respect in his ragged voice, Sal's anger subsided, leaving shame for her lack of control in its wake. Maybe the humans were right. She'd done it again, acting like little more than the beast they accused her of, and all because the human had taunted her.

"Zep," Shift said, never taking his attention from the man on the ground, "you're supposed to shake the hand of the victor."

Still glaring, Zep offered his hand, and Sal grasped it, expecting the rotten feel of human flesh. To her surprise, his mind crawled weakly into her consciousness, his touch warm and pleasurable. Standing so close to him, she smelled nothing but human sugar, but otherwise, he felt like the other Black Blades: pleasant.

I didn't think you had it in you, he admitted, *I was wrong. I just don't want fancy footwork to be all I have to back me up if things go bad.*

Dark eyes glared at her with seeming hatred, but his mental voice acknowledged that she'd impressed him. Slightly. She sent the equivalent of a mental nod, having nothing else to say, and held her lips closed. He was like no human she'd met before, and she didn't trust him.

At the same time, Kinetry was assisted to his feet. While he was taken to the infirmary, Shift escorted his group back to where the rest waited. The other recruits lounged around the fountain with

LT, relaxed and waiting. Their conversation hummed in excited tones.

Sal moved to a clear spot. Riblour and Saong chose to sit with a group of recruits across from her, keeping their distance. She could see them talking, their heads turned in her direction. No matter how hard she tried to ignore it, telling herself that soldiers loved to gossip and the rumors would only make them keep their distance, it didn't stop the resentment. Evidently, she'd never be anything but a freak.

CHAPTER FOUR

*A*round the courtyard, stablehands were lighting lanterns, easing the grip of coming night. It was the time of year when it got dark early, and that made the breeze feel chilly. The warm glow cast flickering shadows across the neat gravel, the forms of the recruits dancing in silhouette. Next to the fountain, a rack of practice weapons had been set up, and a clear area was marked on the ground.

"Ok, it's time," Arctic called out, moving to the center of the group. Soldiers pulled themselves to their feet, the grace of the morning long gone.

"Tuovo and Lennert, report to Razor," he said, pointing at the officer. "The rest of you aren't done yet." Arctic stepped aside as LT took his place.

"I have already heard complaints running among you," LT started. "You think certain applicants aren't qualified or others are getting it easier. Well, I want to put that out of your minds." His gaze touched each of them, some recruits nodding, others with confused looks on their faces.

"Of course, we also want to know the skills of those who may fight beside us." He gestured to the men in black fatigues behind him. "So tonight, each Blade gets to choose one recruit for a public spar." The recruits grinned, and LT waited for the excitement to abate. "Relax. Get cozy. I think this may take a while."

The First Officer, Arctic, gestured to a young man seated next to Sal. Barely more than a boy, only his age set him apart from being completely average. Tawny skin and brown hair on a frame of medium height and weight, the kid moved like a predator. Arctic handed him a pair of practice knives, then grabbed a two-handed sword for himself. When the Lieutenant called for them to "lay on," Sal's eyes were glued to the fight.

Arctic used his mass to deflect the whirling blades of the boy, forcing the kid to expend his energy to stay out of his reach. In a few short minutes, it became obvious that the First Officer was more than just a tactician. The moment the boy began to slow, Arctic moved in and dropped the sword, disarming him with a kick to one hand and a slap to the other, then manhandled him to the floor.

A murmur of appreciation swelled among the recruits for Arctic's skill. Few soldiers had been privileged enough to see elites at work, and the Black Blades held the reputation of the most ruthless fighters the CFC could boast. When the combatants left the ring, another man in black stepped up.

"Cyno," LT said. Sal recognized him as the man who'd assisted Kinetry off the field, the same one who'd checked her papers the first day.

Cyno gestured at a tall man, a cold smile on his face as he swept his arm back to indicate the rack of weapons behind him. The recruit appeared to be from a wealthy family from the jewel at his throat, immaculate hair, and fashionable but non-standard accessories to his uniform. In stark contrast, Cyno's simple black uniform was scuffed and well worn. His angular features cast shadows against his face, and he stood a head shorter.

While the pampered recruit made his selection, Cyno slowly

unbuttoned his shirt, peeled it off, and carefully hung it on the edge of the weapon rack. Tattoos covered his chest. Black designs swirled and wove their way across his body to disappear beneath the waistband of his pants, heavier on his left, leaving the far right side bare. They did nothing to hide the ripcord of muscles that covered his lean frame. Dark stubble shadowed his head and made the vivid blue of his eyes startling, yet his cold gaze seemed to look right through them all.

The recruit chose a pike, the only weapon on the rack close to his height. He tossed it gingerly, getting a feel for it, before casually walking to one side of the combat arena and glancing at the Lieutenant. Cyno nodded at LT. His hands were still empty.

At the call, the recruit struck. None of them lacked skill. If they had, they wouldn't have made it this far, but this one never stood a chance. At the first sign of motion, Cyno plucked the weapon from his opponent's grip, hooked the butt behind his calves, and knocked the man's legs out from under him. He tossed the pike away and met the soldier's body before it even hit the ground. A wooden dagger had appeared as if by magic. With one hand on the recruit's throat, the other held the tip millimeters from his eye.

"I yield," the guy whispered.

"Damn right ya do," Cyno snarled, "and do na ever look down yer nose at me again or I may actually put some effort inta it."

The Blade stood, nodded calmly at the Lieutenant, then retrieved his shirt. Dressing, he made his way to the far wall while keeping the applicants fully in his sight.

A shocked silence hung in the air. Sal believed it when Cyno implied he hadn't even tried yet had still taken the spoiled brat down in seconds. She wished she could move like that! Staring at him, she wondered how long it would take to acquire such skill. He looked like a man in his late twenties but moved with the kind of grace that took decades to perfect.

When her inspection reached his face, she realized his eyes were waiting, and she struggled to keep her expression neutral.

Their gazes danced for a few seconds before a smile crept to his lips, flaunting his sharp incisors and double canines – just like her own. He nodded at her before glancing at the First Officer.

Cyno wants me to tell you he'll teach you, Arctic's voice said in her head. *He assumes that's what your inspection meant at any rate.*

It is! Please let him know I've never seen anything like that, he moves like perfection, she thought back while another Black Blade walked into the center of the ring.

The lithe man grinned when he received the message. Inside her mind, she felt more than heard a click, and a harsh voice entered. *Thank ya fer the compliment.* His blue eyes sparkled at her across the courtyard, and Sal noticed his pupils were oblong instead of round. *Never been called perfection b'fore, an' Shift says ya move like a demon possessed yerself. Ya make it past this an' I'll show ya ever'thing I know.*

Thank you! she thought, meaning it.

Do na thank me yet, little one. First, ya gotta prove that ya can take what we're offerin'.

Sal nodded at him and the link dissolved. While they spoke, Shift had entered the ring and called up Riblour. He fought with a pike and short sword against the applicant's great sword. The wood rang against each other but Shift beat back the recruit step by step. Unlike the grace of the previous two fighters, Shift fought with power and determination, but when the recruit changed tactics, so did he. His now agile steps matched Riblour's, dragging the battle on. The recruit held up to the prowess of the Black Blade, but Sal thought Shift was toying with him. He danced and dodged, Riblour swung and jumped, slowly being pushed across the gravel. Eventually, Shift brought the game to an end with such finality they all knew he'd been tormenting the soldier. The men shook hands civilly and left the ring.

"Risk, our medic," LT introduced the next Blade.

A man with feline-like grace stepped into the ring. His silvered skin offset pale gold hair that emphasized amber eyes. *He is a crossbred*, Sal thought, remembering him from the first day. Risk's oblique features and unnatural coloring marked his iliri ancestry clearly. He reached for a staff from the rack before addressing the recruits before him.

"I have nothing to settle with any of you." Like Cyno, his voice was richly accented. "So, I'll take whoever wants to try me."

The recruits muttered to themselves, a hum of voices growing while they chattered. A few eyes looked her way before one man stepped up. "I'll try," he said.

This recruit was older, an obvious veteran of the wars. His face was streaked with scars, his shoulders well-muscled, but he waited for Risk's nod before making his way to the rack to select a pair of hand axes. At the call to lay on, Risk and the veteran casually moved toward each other, neither rushing to throw the first blow. With a feint, Risk scored a tap on the veteran's arm, and the combat began in earnest. More blocks and parries, but in the end, the veteran's claim to fame was a solid hit on Risk's shoulder before being knocked to the ground, defeated.

The same held for the next bout. Razor chose Saong, a large and well-muscled man. Their olive skins rippled and sweat gleamed under the lanterns in defiance of the cold evening. In moments, the Blade finished like the others, with his opponent yielding. Only one remained: Zep.

The large, dark man stalked to the center of the ring, his braids sweeping over the leather on his shoulders. Black bracers on each forearm were his only concession to sleeves, barely a shade darker than his skin, and they showed signs of true combat. Like this, he was everything she'd imagined a Black Blade to be, all shadows and danger. Then he locked eyes with her and nodded.

Sal stood, listening to the amused voices whispering behind her. They hoped to see her fail, and like everyone before her, she had no intention of that.

Waiting for her beside the weapon rack, Zep chose a pair of curved, light wooden swords. She looked over the options, hefting and discarding a few that failed to deliver on the promise of their appearance. Behind Zep, a matched set of sabers called to her. She glanced at him, and he stepped aside for her to reach the weapons. They felt right in her hands, light and balanced slightly toward the hilt. When she turned to make her way across the ring, Zep's hand shot out, pulling the cap from her head.

"Let's just leave this here, shall we?" he sneered. "See what we can do when that hair of yours is flung around, begging someone to pull it?"

The recruits laughed softly, but she wanted to growl. Her long, white ponytail swayed against her back, and she turned to face him without moving away for the advantage distance offered. Zep squared his stance, finding an easy balance, and looked down at her. Sal's head didn't even reach his shoulders. His chest was twice as wide as her body. They stood face to face, close enough to touch, Zep's jet black skin contrasting perfectly with Sal's alabaster.

"Maybe I should be petting your ears," he taunted so only she could hear. "Such cute things with the way they wiggle like that."

"I hear it's a human fetish," she remarked snidely. "Sir."

He glared until the call from the Lieutenant came to lay on.

Those words were like a flame to fuel. Action erupted instantly. Zep swept a foot out to knock Sal's legs out from under her. She hopped in place, drawing her knees close while striking out with one of the blades, brushing his arm as he leaned out of her reach. Instantly, his sword moved to take advantage of the opening, and Sal blocked it with her off-hand. Never retreating, they bent, danced, and leapt in perfect timing. The watching recruits gasped, but she blocked out everything except Zep's next move. The speed of his swings increased to match hers. No matter how hard she pushed, using all of her iliri-born agility, he interrupted her next attack, ready to push her defense.

The gravel crunched and scuffed under their moving feet. Both were soon covered in a fine sheen of sweat and dust, but they never took their eyes off each other. He poked and she prodded. For every sway she made, he'd lean, and for each step he took, Sal matched it. Minutes ticked past and neither sword touched skin. He grunted when he dodged and she growled as she attacked. The sweet human scent tried to distract her, but she refused to lose control again.

Zep's hits became harder as he tried to force her weapons out of his way, but she would not retreat. She could feel her strength fading and looked harder for an opening – or a way to make one – but the attacks kept coming. His dark eyes were as angry now as when the fight started, and his body showed no signs of fatigue. Having tried everything else, she thought of Cyno's quick ending. If she lost, she was no worse off than any other recruit. If she could just score a touch, she'd be far ahead of most of them. Sal tossed away the idea of winning this fight and settled on simply not embarrassing herself.

Zep struck at her neck with his right hand, but rather than dodging, she threw her back against his chest, moving inside his guard. As she spun, she passed her main sword into her left hand alongside the first, settling the tip against the inside of his thigh, the other pointing up to block her body. Without a pause, her empty hand snatched Zep's curved weapon, wrenched it free, and aimed his sword above her head. The wooden blade paused against his neck.

They both froze. Sal could feel Zep's heart pounding against her back. She could smell the sugar in his sweat, so close to her, but no other emotions. Silence hung in the air for a few seconds before Zep spoke up.

"I yield," he said, calmly.

The onlookers gasped, and Sal dared to look at his face. Gone was the smoldering anger, replaced with genuine respect. Pulling herself from the confines of his strong arms, all too aware of his hot body against her back, she wasn't sure what to do. Clumsily, she offered the wooden weapons to him. He took the swords and turned away, completely at ease.

The eyes of the recruits smothered her when she crossed the ring to ease her tired body against the fence post once more. The respect felt good, but the surprise in their eyes brought a whole new resentment. Before she could dwell on the faults of her human competition, the Lieutenant addressed them again.

"Now that you've seen my Blades in action, you know what is, and will be, expected of each of you. Few of you could match them in combat," he said with a nod to Sal and the veteran, "but you will have to be as good as any of them to pass these trials. If you cannot improve – and quickly – there is no shame in resigning your application. It will not be looked on poorly if you do and choose to apply again at a later date. Razor is bunked in cabin ten. He will arrange transportation for anyone who chooses to rethink his preparedness.

"Now, you get the rest of the night off. The pub is behind the barns, on the far side of the compound. We will meet again tomorrow at 1300, this time at the arena. Enjoy yourselves, and really think about why you are here." He strode out of the courtyard in the direction of their cabins.

CHAPTER FIVE

Sal staggered into her room and began peeling the form-fitting clothes from her body before realizing she wasn't alone. The smell of a human permeated the air. With her shirt unbuttoned, she folded her ears against her skull and pulled her arms from the sleeves. Tossing it to the floor, she turned to her bed, thankful for the standard-issue tank all female military personnel were expected to wear. Zep eyed her intently.

"Go ahead. Don't let me stop you," he said. "I won't complain about seeing a woman out of her clothes."

"What are you doing here?" she snapped, tired and aching to the core of her being.

"I owe you one. Whether you realized it or not, I made a bet with you that I could throw you off your game, and you won. I figured I'd pay up and buy you as many drinks as you can throw down at the pub. Besides, it won't hurt for you and me to be seen together... pleasantly."

"Mhm. A few drinks. Seriously, sir?" she asked. "I'm tired, I'm bumped and bruised, and all I want in this world is to pass these trials. Unless your drinks can miraculously make these aches leave in time for whatever we'll do tomorrow, then the only thing I'm interested in is a hot bath and a long sleep!"

"Well, I can offer two things to mollify you. First, all you'll need tomorrow is your brain. Second..." he trailed off, and she heard him yelling mentally, but couldn't make out the words since it wasn't directed at her. "I can get someone to help those bruises, too."

The link clicked in her head when Shift joined the conversation, *I can help with that, but Zep, you owe me one.* The image of a woman's cleavage flashed across her mind, and Zep laughed.

You don't like her anyway, man, Zep shot back. *So I think you're the one that owes me!* He dropped the link and looked to Sal. "Ok, you grab that bath you want so bad, and I'll make myself presentable enough to be seen with you. Oh, and wear the red one. It's in the closet." He walked confidently out of her room without waiting for a response.

When the door closed, she shook her head and pinned the lock, amused at Zep's arrogance. Then she stripped out of the last of her clothes. After scrubbing the worries of the day from her body, she returned to her wardrobe and pulled it open. A selection of new clothes hung beside her uniforms. Clothes she'd never seen before.

Not only had someone been in her room, but they'd gone shopping for her? Sal was pretty sure this was not a standard part of the trials, so why? What was going on? She also wasn't stubborn enough to protest, since the only clothes she owned were standard blue uniforms. Not exactly the kind of thing people wore to the pub.

Digging a little, she found the "red one" Zep had referred to. It was a fitted jacket and corset combo, complete with tails. Black and red brocade formed the corset; the jacket was made of a brilliant red velvet. The pants matched the ensemble, a delicate red pattern woven throughout.

The clothes were beautiful, and of a quality she'd never worn. They were the sort of things that human women had access to, not someone like her. Oddly, that made the outfit even more appealing. Sal had no intention of passing up the chance to wear something so beautiful - and in colors that worked so well with her milk-white skin.

She pulled on the skin-hugging outfit and was lacing the corset when she heard the knock. Crossing the room in her stockinged feet, Sal unpinned the lock and welcomed Shift in. He stopped in his tracks, looking her over.

"I'm glad I didn't miss this. Wow, Sal. You look amazing!" His words made her smile in a way she hadn't known was possible.

He walked all the way around her, making appreciative noises before pushing her to a chair. "Ok, business first. You're gonna want to be sitting for this."

Kneeling before her, he grabbed her hands and looked deep into her eyes. Sal felt like a player in a bad proposal until it hit her. The world jerked sideways and her vision split. The room doubled: two wardrobes, two walls, and more importantly, two Shifts. Suddenly, she realized how he earned his name. It felt like he'd shifted reality. When he released her hands, she swayed, waiting for the room to settle and her vision to return to normal. Sal tried to concentrate on her breathing and closed her eyes while the vertigo passed.

"That's the best I can do," he said, "but you're an easy patient. The bruises should be gone, and no, the aches won't return tomorrow."

"You just... fixed me?" she asked.

"Yep." He rubbed her knee gently. "Try not to think about it too hard."

"Thank you, Shift," she managed to say. "I do feel better." It was true. The dizziness passed and her aching muscles felt fit and ready to use. The bruises no longer screamed beneath the corset. "I guess that's your special trick, huh?"

"And there you go, already thinking about it too hard. Finish getting ready, Sal, and make Zep look like the big man he thinks he is. Oh, and use the riding boots, they'll go perfectly. Plus, you'll want to break them in."

Sal didn't even know what to make of all this. He'd just healed her aches but clearly didn't want to talk about it. Zep was picking her clothes. They all played it off like no big deal, but it was. She just wasn't quite brave enough to ask, not if her questions might end up getting her dismissed!

Still, how did the Blades have such intimate knowledge of her wardrobe? The one in her locked room! Why were they so interested in her, of all people? It was almost like they treated her as their latest toy, a doll for them to dress up or something. She wasn't sure if she should like it, and yet she still did. It was kinda nice to finally be noticed by anyone - especially them.

Not quite a doll, Shift assured her as he closed the door behind him. *In reality, it's because Razor will requisition a set of armor for you if you make it far enough. Risk looked up your stats in your file, and we all found a reason you needed something nice. Oh, and if you don't want us in your head, you're going to have to learn to stop sending. You always leak your feelings loud and clear.*

She sighed instead of responding, refusing to let the weirdness of this keep her from feeling beautiful for once in her life. Pulling on the riding boots like Shift suggested, she sent a thought across the street to Zep. Then, she took one last look in the mirror. The brilliant colors made her look washed out, but she had a few cosmetics. Her white iliri skin was smooth and – after Shift's efforts – blemish free. Grabbing kohl, she lined her lids, unsure if she approved of how it accented her white eyes and lashes, making them look so stark. A few swipes of dark mascara helped even out the look. Just as Zep entered her room, she found a tube of brilliant red lipstick. Sal stained her lips before turning to acknowledge him.

Dressed in a double-breasted and ornately piped jacket that hugged his broad chest, with pants of almost liquid leather, Zep stood one step inside her door with his mouth hanging open. After a few false attempts, he finally managed, "The red was a good choice."

She'd never been complimented like this before. These weren't empty words, because the smell of him matched. The Black Blades treated her like she was beautiful, attractive, and almost human. To most people, her iliri features were strange, alien even. No matter how she tried to deny it, Sal enjoyed it.

She'd always been aware of how beastly her features were. Her ears sat on the top of her head and swiveled like a rodent's. Her nose was convex rather than dished. Her eyes were too large, her teeth looked more like they belonged in the mouth of a dog than a person, and of course her milk-white skin and hair.

She wasn't beautiful. That had been drilled into her head since she was a child. In fact, about the only thing she had in common with humans was that they both walked on two feet, yet even Zep reacted as if he thought she was honestly attractive. The Black Blades weren't just being polite either; this man smelled like desire. She liked it, but she didn't know how to take it, and the feelings confused her, so she simply ignored them.

Zep gallantly offered his arm, and she took it with a shy smile instead of fumbling words. Together, they made their way to the pub. The music and laughter became audible before the building could be seen. Once inside, he escorted her to a quiet table at the back where the walls deflected the sound from the main room enough for a conversation to be held in levels other than screaming. Leaving her for a moment, Zep wound his way to the bar, returning with two drinks. He slid one to her and sipped at his own. The entire time, Sal openly watched the people roaming about.

Most were obviously soldiers. A few were civilians, their mannerisms and posture giving it away. The soldiers moved like warriors, some with the swaying gait from too many hours in the saddle, others with the catlike grace of infantry. And they were everywhere, packed in the building to find a good time. From where she sat, Sal could see a second story with even more people. The pub's decor in bold stripes and bright colors made the whole thing look like a wild party.

Zep leaned over, touching Sal lightly on her wrist, then pointed beside her. Following his finger, she saw the Lieutenant, a drink in hand, laughing with a group of women before pulling himself away and heading up the stairs.

Even LT takes some time to relax, Zep thought at her. *You need to learn how to enjoy yourself a bit.*

The direct contact made his words clear in her head rather than sounding like he screamed across a vast distance. She didn't break the touch. Instead, she sent him a scrap of her past.

She showed her life as an aide in an office, applying time after time for a promotion to the field, always being denied because her kind "would go feral." Another flash of working out on the pells. Her off-hours were the only time she could train for combat, and cadets amused themselves by throwing trash at her while she practiced. A scrap of her before the military, as a girl of twelve with knees raw and fingers bleeding from the caustic chemicals she scrubbed with, cleaning ground-in dirt from the expensive engravings on the entryway tiles.

I am enjoying myself, Zep, but I worked too hard to get here to take it for granted.

He patted her hand in understanding. *We've all been there, believe it or not. LT, too. But you kicked my ass today. All that work paid off. Everything from here on out is going to take your brains, not your training, to get through. Finish your drink, I'll get another.*

She swallowed what was left, clenching her teeth at the warmth when it slid down her throat. Zep stood, grabbed her wrist once more to judge her mind before smirking and heading to the bar. He returned quickly, this time empty-handed.

"I have a waitress bringing a selection over. I plan to get you drunk and make you admit how you managed to get inside my guard," he teased.

The waitress arrived a moment later with a tray full of shots and left them on the table. Zep tipped the girl and slid a tiny glass at Sal.

"Bottoms up," he said, matching action to words.

She tipped the glass to her lips, swallowing and blinking. Another took its place. By the third, Sal couldn't deny the effects. A comfortable warmth embraced her, and the smile refused to leave her lips, letting her edged teeth flash. When Zep invited her to dance, she couldn't find a reason not to. Gyrating to the hypnotic music, she whirled and tipped, not always intentionally.

Eventually, another black-clad man cut in, and Sal recognized Razor through the haze in her head. They, too, spun and writhed, Sal laughing at the seriousness of his efforts. At the break in each song, she found Zep's hand filled with another tiny glass. Each time, the man encouraged her to swallow the liquid inside.

A whisper of a thought alerted her to a third Blade joining their crowd on the dance floor. His pleasant scent drifted to her clearly, even in the packed room. The sharp edge of his mind cut through her haze when his calloused hand gently caressed the back of her neck. She turned to face him and found herself standing with Cyno. The man's thumb resting against the pulse in her throat.

Care ta dance, kitten? he asked.

She nodded, and he gently took her hand as a slower and more intimate song played. Cyno's shoulder was even with her eyes, and in her intoxicated state, she couldn't see a reason not to rest her head on it. He smelled like home should, and she inhaled deeply, trying to take it in.

He slipped one hand around her waist to the small of her back, gently pulling her closer. It was the sort of contact she craved, and together they wove patterns on the floor, their bodies touching completely. His heart beat against her body. The pace of it was a little too fast, and a strange look crossed his face each time he met her eyes. However, he couldn't hold her gaze. When she dared to look, the man's eyes dropped to the ground.

But once the music ended, he pulled himself away. Like a perfect gentleman, he offered to escort her from the dance floor. A shy smile tugged at the corner of his lips. She wanted to ask what he found so amusing, but didn't get the chance.

My turn, she heard, the thought interrupting the moment.

The pair paused when yet another dance partner stepped from

the crowd. This time it was Risk. Sal hadn't been formally introduced to the iliri crossbred, but she recognized the similarities he shared with her own features. That was enough to convince her lowered inhibitions to send a thought his way. *I hear you easily. I heard a few others easily, but some I have to touch before I can get in their mind. Why?*

It's the iliri in us, he replied as he led her back to the dance floor. *The more blood we share with you, the easier we can hear each other. That's why poor Zep is always screaming in our heads but still so very quiet.*

You too? I thought maybe it was just because I'd been so angry with him, or he was closing me out.

No, no. Nothing like that. It's an iliri trick. We need a catalyst, you see, and for us, that's Arctic. While the music played, Risk guided her with a sinuous grace she hadn't expected. Dancing languidly, he used his entire body to move with the sounds.

Arctic is the linker, and to share thoughts like this, we need a link, he explained. *Without him keeping a 'channel' open, we'd be as silent in your head as any human. Even Zep, who has no iliri blood as far as we can tell, can be heard with Arctic's help, but he has to work harder.*

Does Arctic have to concentrate to do it? I mean... Words failed her, so she sent a jumble of worry over Arctic meditating in a room so the Black Blades could use his mind for their own entertainment.

No, nothing like that, Risk assured her, his tone filled with amusement. *For him it's natural. He's here, and we get the benefits of it. Did your pack teach you none of this?*

I never knew my parents, Sal admitted, hoping that was what he meant, *besides a story told by my former owner. They bought me at a young age. I only managed to get myself conscripted when I refused to become entertainment for an officer visiting my master.* In her drunken state, Sal decided the obviously strange Risk would understand her better than the others. *When I said I'd rather die than become the plaything of some human, the officer agreed. He enlisted me right then and there, and it's the best thing that ever happened to me.*

Took me over three years, she continued, *but I got a promotion and managed to get permission to apply to the elite forces. The Black Blades are the only ones to ever consider me, though.*

Oh, I think we might do more than consider, Risk assured her, *but you're very drunk.* With that, he broke the physical contact and led her back to the table where the squad of Blades had gathered.

"Oh damn, Sal," Arctic said, seeing her for the first time out of uniform, "I think we owe Zep a drink for that outfit. Wow!"

They raised their glasses to Zep, who grinned and lifted his own before tossing back the shot.

CHAPTER SIX

On the balcony above, LT looked down with pride. The girl seemed to be working out. Since the loss of Circus, the Blades had been operating short-staffed. His men deserved nothing but the best, but the last trial had left them empty-handed. As their reputation increased, so did the applications, and weeding through the bland questions Command permitted was anything but easy.

And now, here, mingling as though already a part of the group, was a pure iliri woman. She had no idea what she was capable of. And it wasn't just her breeding that made her such an appealing applicant. She worked hard, just like he expected of his men. She fought like a "demon possessed," as Shift called it, comparing her rarity to ancient myths. She also begged to learn more. This iliri bitch was everything he could hope for, even if a part of him worried about adding a female into his delicately balanced group.

The men were already making it clear they found her attractive and weren't opposed to her alien features. They snuck trinkets into her room, stole dances, and stared at her with open admiration when she moved. Blaec didn't know how she felt about the attention, or if she even understood the implications. Each time he touched her mind, he only got a sense of her hatred for being so different – but most iliri despised their non-human traits.

She'd probably never been told how the iliri were created. Stories said their race had been bred to serve and protect humanity, but Sal seemed unaware of the power of her iliri nature. She hid her beastly desires behind a wall of human conditioning, and Blaec wondered what would happen when she finally embraced her instincts.

The scrape of a chair pulled his mind back to the present. General Sturmgren dropped his aging body into it with a sigh and a strained smile.

"Good evening, Lieutenant," the General said. "How are your tryouts going so far?"

Blaec nodded in greeting. "It looks promising, sir. I have two that might do, and one I seem to prefer."

"Good. Then how long will it take you to get back into fighting shape?"

"About three months, give or take. Depends upon which recruit makes it to the end."

"And then? Do you think you'll have the unit ready?" the General asked.

"Yes, sir. We should be able to remove at least three of those officials and probably four Warlords along the border, leaving the Empire weak enough for you to get the army across."

"Good, very good." Turning in his chair, the General signaled for a waitress.

Their conversation paused while the woman brought another round and pocketed the generous tip Ran Sturmgren handed her. Reaching for his drink, the old man watched the girl sashay away before resuming.

"They're pushing us hard, Blaec," he said. "We've lost a few hundred men just trying to halt their advance, and the Emperor just keeps sending more. He refuses to deal with us diplomatically, and we can't match him militarily."

"Which is why you need us," Blaec realized.

The General sighed. "I know the Black Blades prefer less restrictive jobs, but without this push, we'll be trading in our blue and gold for the black and purple of the Empire. If you get the army across the border, I'll find you an assignment to be proud of."

Blaec nodded. General Sturmgren was an honest man, and his word was as good as any contract. While Blaec hated to ask his Blades to do the military's dirty work, they could - with their eyes closed. This war had waged on for far too long. About twenty years ago, maybe more, the Empire had appeared from nowhere as scattered provinces came together under a new banner. Their leader, calling himself simply "the Emperor," had gathered his citizens into armies and began to take over the territories surrounding them. The Conglomerate hadn't paid attention until Unav fell. The peaceful nation had shared their border with Terric for centuries with little more than trade disagreements, and never a military conflict.

Intelligence now said the Emperor was intent on conquering the entire continent. His rhetoric centered around his hate for the iliri. An abomination, he called them, proclaiming he had the right to exterminate the species from the face of the planet. That was why he'd hit Unav so hard - because of the large numbers of iliri and iliri crossbreds living there - and he killed everyone with iliri ancestry he came across.

Blaec remembered those early days of the war well. He'd been a young boy, thinking he was a man, when he heard the news that Unav had fallen. His family was from there, his mother and kin presumed dead. He'd tried to join the CFC military that very day, but they'd turned him away due to his age. On his eighteenth birthday, he'd returned and worked his way up through the ranks. If a few assassinations would help the Conglomerate of Free Citizens break this siege, then he'd order his men to do them.

Unfortunately, the Conglomerate only cared about protecting their borders - nothing else. The fate of Unav or the other countries

Terric had targeted weren't the CFC's problem. The extermination of an entire species held little concern for the nation's politicians - since the iliri were despised by most humans - but the loss of their political districts compelled them to fight back. For now, it was enough.

"I just need a few more months, Ran," Blaec said. "With an eight-man unit, being down a soldier would be a death sentence. I won't send my men into that. I'm sorry, but I won't."

"And I wouldn't ask you to," the General assured him. "It'll take us a couple months or more to prepare. Pick the right recruit, Blaec, and train him up. An army of this size doesn't move quickly, and three months is just the blink of an eye for the military. Knowing you'll do it is all I needed. Means I can start working on tactics."

The General pushed his chair back and made to stand. Blaec climbed to his feet in a sign of respect. "Sir?" he asked before the General could leave. "I may need a favor."

General Sturmgren looked at the Lieutenant curiously. Blaec rarely asked for anything, and the man clearly knew it. "Go on."

"One of my potentials is pure iliri."

"Ah," the General said, understanding. "Document the trials well. If he obviously outperforms the others based on your recruitment needs, I'll back you on this. Is he really that good, or do you think you might be biased?"

"*She's* that good." Blaec smiled at the General's surprised reaction. "I'd take her if she was human, sir. She beat Zep in a fair spar."

General Sturmgren chuckled. "Ok, you win. Send me her file, and I'll start laying the groundwork. How'd you find a female iliri?"

Blaec shrugged. "She applied. She's a conscript."

The old man's eyes narrowed. "Private Luxx?"

"Yes, sir," Blaec replied, shocked he knew her name.

"Good. I already have her file. Seems the little bitch has applied for every elite opening in the last year."

With a nod, the General extended his hand and Blaec grasped it firmly, returning to his seat once the old man left. Glancing back at his Blades, a cluster of black in the sea of blue and gold, Blaec hoped that this time one of his recruits would pass the tests. He didn't dare choose a favorite, but a brilliant red flash among them let him know that his men already had.

She'd bested Zep in combat. Only Blaec could do that consistently, but she didn't need to know that. Zep was the weapons specialist of the unit. He had an affinity for fighting that no other human – and few iliri – possessed. Not only were her combat skills impressive, she presented herself professionally and kept her iliri instincts under control. Above all else, she'd stumbled into their minds, tapping into Arctic's ability naturally. She easily heard all of them, and his men preferred to speak to her mentally, feeling at ease with the touch of her thoughts. Having experienced it himself, Blaec knew why. Her mind was sharp but gentle, a pleasant caress he found himself wanting to embrace.

He pushed that thought away as quickly as it came.

Most novices shoved their thoughts around without any elegance. Sal never barged into his head, but glided in when invited, a rare talent. Plus, according to Arctic, some of his men intended to keep in contact with her even if she didn't pass the trials. Iliri men were drawn to dominant women, and Sal might pretend to be a quiet and willing servant, but as easily as she'd held his gaze, Blaec knew better. He knew what she really was and longed to submit to a woman like her. If only that wouldn't cause problems in the unit.

Blaec had been raised by his iliri mother and two fathers. It took him nearly a decade to learn to act like a human in Conglomerate society, but once he had, they'd accepted him without question. His mind still longed for the comforts of his mother's people, but he wasn't willing to give up all that his human position offered his men. They were the only family he had, and only as a human could he protect them.

Sal seemed to understand that. She hadn't made him spell it out in her interview, but she seemed to accept that they had to play by the military's rules. The only problem was that she still had to learn to ride. A Blade without a mount was like an arrow without a bow. The other possibility, a young man with experience on the street, could ride. He'd served a year with the light cavalry, but he couldn't fight any better than a common soldier, hadn't been invited into their minds, and Blaec had not seen him befriend a single Blade. The bond just wasn't there. No matter how hard he tried to stay impartial, the facts were clear.

Sal was his best bet, even if her presence would result in a few squabbles. Blaec told himself that his men had settled worse and come out stronger for it. They could handle a pretty girl in their midst. He refused to think about the effect a Kaisae had on her men. The girl had submitted to him, he reminded himself. If she passed the trials, she should work out, no matter how nice she smelled. He was only a half breed, so it wasn't like his instincts would take over. He wouldn't let them. His men needed him to be the barrier between them and the rest of the country, so he'd make sure not to give in.

Below him, the party was breaking up. The Black Blades left in a group, one shining red spot the only color in their cluster of black. Looking at them from above, Blaec saw nothing but smiles and true camaraderie. Sal took Zep's arm on one side, Cyno's on the other, with the rest closing ranks around them. The girl staggered, obviously drunk, and laughter reached his ears. She'd feel it in the morning, he thought, but if she could still pass the tests, it wouldn't matter.

He decided to send her medication, just to be sure.

CHAPTER SEVEN

The powder helped. Sal's head no longer throbbed. She had no idea who'd been thoughtful enough to send her the meds, but wished she could thank him. Now, if only her mouth would be as cooperative. She took another pull on the flask – nothing more than water for her dehydrated body – and stared up at the pair of moons in the too-blue sky, hoping to ease the nervous tension in her neck.

She was early, thinking the fresh air would wipe the last of the cobwebs from her mind. Last night, Zep told her their next trial would require her brain, so she certainly didn't need a hangover holding her back. She needed to be at her best. In reality, she simply watched stablehands catching horses. Once haltered, the animals were passed to a groom who cleaned, tacked, and tied them along the rail inside the arena.

Four warhorses stood quietly, heads bowed, dozing in the afternoon sun. Two more were being brushed, and a handler led in a third. Sal counted on her fingers, her head still not clear enough for calculations, and arrived at seven total.

What would the test be? Zep's hint tugged at the back of her mind. Riding wasn't exactly a mental skill, but it was Sal's weakness. She'd spent months tallying the inventory for the stable in her time with the military, but none in the saddle. Through necessity, she'd learned the basics of working around horses and the care each required, but few Privates were awarded the luxury of riding lessons unless their families had enough wealth to supply it. Sitting on the sidelines, she'd listened to the basics over and over: heels down, hands soft, eyes up, don't balance on the reins, but that was different from putting it into practice. Maybe this test would be to analyze the mechanics of riding?

Looking over her shoulder to see across the pastures, her eyes kept returning to a lone horse in the field. Covered in mud, contained in a small paddock away from the rest of the impressive stock, it kept calling into the wind, prancing around the perimeter of the paddock with its tail flagged. She wondered if the horse whinnied to a foal recently weaned, or if she was a new addition, quarantined to prevent spreading disease.

While she thought, Sal's dehydrated mouth begged for another drink. She sucked at her flask, wishing she hadn't gotten so drunk. Yes, getting to know the Blades had been nice, but drinking that much? Dumb idea. Not exactly the professional front she wanted to present. Behind her, the mare continued her protest against the confinement unabated.

Turning to the seven horses tied along the fence, Sal tried to focus on the differences in each and analyzed them. The ax-headed beast near the end had the traits to make a good battle steed, but only barely. The rest were more suited for parades. A high headed palomino spooked at recruits walking up, pulling hard against its tether and digging its heels into the soft arena sand until stablehands shooed it back onto its feet. The chestnut, a brilliant, deep red with high white socks and a near perfect blaze, showed signs of age in his joints and posture. From the animals before her, he suited her abilities the best. His age and attitude were that of a veteran. His experience could cover for what Sal's lacked.

Eventually, the Black Blades arrived, making a grand entrance on their own battle-ready steeds. LT sat his black like he was born there and addressed the six recruits before him from the saddle.

"A special operations unit is nothing without transportation. In our case, our mounts are a second arm, a tool we use more than even our weapons. The six of you are all that remains from the fifteen we started with, so I had seven animals pulled up. Choose the horse from this stable that seems suited to be your permanent mount. If you pass these trials, it will be assigned to you, purchased and paid for in full by the CFC.

"This horse will serve as your day to day transportation, it will be the mount you depend upon in the midst of combat, and it will be how you drag your broken body back to camp when a mission goes bad. You are looking for a smart animal, a willing partner, and one brave enough to do what is needed in the midst of war. These horses have only the basic training, which is why we have you choose now, so the staff can focus on the needs of each rider."

It was another test, but this time the Lieutenant didn't tell them what they would be scored on. The pressure to choose wisely weighed on each of them.

"Feel free to inspect the horses, but you may not ride them. The staff will be happy to have them move out for you to appraise. You have one hour."

Sal ducked between the rails of the arena fence and, like the other recruits, made her way to get a closer view. While the chestnut would be well suited to her, the thought of limiting herself with an aged and already weary partner left a bad taste in her mouth. The men clustered around the impressive black, the flashy pinto, or the hot-blooded palomino, none of which had the mind for the job the Blades would ask of it. Sal remembered stories of the Black Blades pushing their mounts to the limit, riding over mountains at breakneck speeds to gain a better angle from which to harry larger forces. The ax-headed roan could handle that, and possibly the fat bay.

She managed to find a handler and pointed out the ones that might be tolerable, asking to see them move like LT suggested. The black lost her interest immediately. Her initial assessment had been correct. He was better suited for a parade mount than a warhorse.

She turned away in disgust. None of these horses were anything like what the Blades were mounted on. They were culls. She turned to the fields, her mind still foggy from the hangover, and saw that the pastures were filled with horses – more than usual. She thought back over the Lieutenant's words and realized he hadn't limited them to these seven, merely said he'd had them pulled up. She looked harder, her catlike eyes allowing her to see farther than most humans. The quality horses were out there!

Sal stole a glance over her shoulder and saw Zep leaning over his own seal bay mare, eying her. Beside him, Arctic followed Zep's gaze, but before she could reach out, he smothered the link from her head. The Blades whipped around, the Lieutenant included, and Arctic gestured in her direction. Still astride his horse, LT laughed, the ringing tones carrying across the arena clearly. He held up a finger and wagged it at her, but the smile on his face showed only amusement.

Confused, Sal realized they were actually speaking to each other out loud, heads bent to keep their words private. Arctic must have shut down the link! She pushed a thought toward him and found nothing, his mind gone from her perception. That proved it to her. The horses before them were *not* the horses they were expected to choose!

Turning her attention to the fields, she narrowed her options. To her right, the mare's calling caused the horses near her to shift and drift. A well-muscled colt caught her eye with his sweeping walk and secured his place on her list with his easy transition into the canter. While she worked to narrow the choices, the Lieutenant's voice broke her line of thought.

"Ok, you've had enough time. Which of you wants to choose first?" he asked.

The veteran spoke up, "I know the one I'd take."

The Lieutenant leaned forward in his saddle, his expression asking for the soldier to continue.

"That roan. His head's as ugly as can be, but he's got talent, I think."

LT nodded and signaled a handler to remove the animal from the line. A few voices murmured. The roan had been the choice of many.

"Next?" LT asked.

"I'll take the black," a clean-cut man said. His horse was also led out of the arena.

"The bay for me," called another, followed by chuckles from the group.

"Which one?" Shift asked.

"The heavy one, not the one with the star," the soldier replied.

"The blonde," a man yelled, "I always did like the blondes!"

With three horses and only two recruits left to choose, Sal held her tongue. The Lieutenant looked from her to the nondescript boy, waiting for one to speak up.

"Luxx, Passel, you're the only ones left."

Sal's mind whirled. She still didn't know which she preferred. Glancing out at the pastures, she scanned them one more time. The mare screamed again, and the realization hit her. That animal was exhibiting the exact traits a good warhorse should have! After moving for over an hour, she'd barely broken a sweat. She had all the endurance Sal could ask for and more grace and ability than most seasoned battle mounts. Her choice was obvious.

"Sir?" she spoke up. When he acknowledged her, she continued, "The mare in the paddock. That's the horse I choose."

"Which?" he asked.

"The mud covered one making a fool of herself," she said, pointing.

The applicants laughed openly, seeing little more than a filthy animal that wasn't one of the choices, and Sal finally realized the point of this test. The others had taken only the clues offered and made assumptions about the rules that had never been said. She'd analyzed the orders and looked for options outside the arena. The Lieutenant had been testing them not just on their knowledge of horseflesh, but on their ability to find the boundaries of a problem before them. By looking at horses outside the arena, Sal had passed, and she knew it.

The Lieutenant directed a handler to retrieve the mare from her paddock. Once in hand, the horse bowed into the halter and pranced elegantly beside him. The recruits let their laughter trail off when they realized she'd seen something they missed. The stablehand presented the mare for LT's inspection, and he directed the staff to clean her off. Buckets of water and curries were applied, and the mud flowed away, leaving blobs of color in its wake. Not quite clean, but now merely dirty instead of mud-encrusted, her true color was as impressive as her form. The mare appeared to be white, covered from nose to toes in large dark dots the size of Sal's fist and bigger. On her face and legs, the spots clustered, giving the impression of dark points.

"I don't even know what her color is called," Sal whispered in awe.

"Pinzgauer," Arctic replied. "They're relatively rare."

"So, Passel," the Lieutenant said while Sal's horse headed to the barn, "you find one that will work?"

The boy shrugged, "I just thought the chestnut out there would be good enough, and he might blend in a bit more than that thing."

LT nodded, sent a handler to pull in the colt Sal had initially looked at, then said, "Your mounts will be cared for, and soon we should know if they will need their training finished – or started. I want to speak with my troops, and we will meet back at the fountain in an hour."

The Blades turned, not quite in unison with the blackout in their minds, and cantered off. The recruits also dispersed, leaving

Sal unsure of what to do with her time. She decided she wanted to see the mare again, so headed toward the barns.

The Stables at Stonewater were a haven for horses. The barns were large and expansive, unlike the cabins used for recruits. The smell of fresh straw and horse sweat greeted her nose when Sal walked in. She never knew why horses didn't set off her predatory instincts, but she'd always liked them.

Cross tied in the alley, a cob danced while the rider pulled his mane. Sal stepped around them carefully. A few stalls down, she saw the unmistakable head of the veteran's roan. Across the aisle, her mare and the chestnut colt were stabled, bedded in deep straw and contentedly munching on green hay. She peered over the half door and stared at the horse. It felt so unreal. Only a few days ago, Sal had been little more than nothing. Now, she stared at the possibility that she would soon not only ride, but own a horse of her own.

Holding a hand out, she clicked softly at the mare and giggled when velvet lips caressed her palm. Taking the opportunity, she stroked the long muscular neck, straining to feel a difference between the dark spots and the white base of the mare's coat. Her hand came back lined with grime.

"Hey!" a voice said behind her, causing Sal to tense. "That mare ain't for the likes of you." A calloused stablehand gripped his rake in one hand and a grimace contorted his face. He looked her over, his distaste obvious. "You scrubbers shouldn't go 'round touching things that don't belong to you. Good thing you can't swipe a horse or I'd be calling guards!"

"Actually," Sal replied, feigning a calm she didn't feel, "this mare *is* for the 'likes' of me. You're more than welcome to call my commanding officer. It's Lieutenant Blaec Doll. Maybe you've heard of him?" She couldn't keep the sneer out of her voice, but she did restrain her snarl.

The stablehand's eyes widened at the mention of the Lieutenant. His body stuttered in place until his mind finally caught up, then he scurried down the aisle, rake still in hand. At the door, he tossed a glance over his shoulder and, finding her still watching, hurried out.

Sal growled softly. She would never escape the hatred of humans. For each success she achieved, there was always some dark-skinned fool there waiting to laugh in her face. Every time she proved herself, some human went out of his way to find flaws in what she'd accomplished. The urge to throw a childish tantrum and run screaming from the barn welled up inside her, but she pushed it down, knowing it would only please the humans to see it.

"Don't mind him," a shy voice said. "He pretty much hates everyone on two legs."

She turned to see a willowy young man. His face was covered in muck, his clothing had been liberally stained, but the youth still smiled at her, and his brown eyes were kind.

"He's good with the horses, which is about the only reason he keeps his job here. So you got the spotted mare?" he asked, looking past her into the stall.

"Yeah," Sal said noncommittally.

"Good call. She goes back to Donner, through Aiden, by Tragedy," he recited. "I don't think there's a finer horse on the farm than her. She's working well in her schooling. Already started in upper-level work, too." His obvious pride in the animal impressed Sal.

"I didn't understand why that Blade asked me to turn her out in the slew bottom last night," the guy went on. "I told him she'd get herself coated in filth, but he said it was important. Said her pretty hide might not bring the kind of attention he wanted. So how'd ya get her anyways? Win a bet or something?"

"Something like that," she admitted. "It was one of our trials. We had to evaluate the horses."

"Ah, well you did a good job. That colt over there isn't too bad, but this girl... She's already got the training and the skill, and she's as sweet and loyal as a puppy. No need to spend half a year trying to play catch up. Of the lot we pulled out today, you got the nicest!"

"Thank you..." She paused, giving the kid time to fill in his name.

"Oh sorry, it's Ahn Tilso. I'd offer you my hand, but..." He held his palms out. Dirt stained them completely.

Her faith in humanity restored, Sal offered him hers, the grime from her mare visible against her white skin. "Salryc Luxx."

Without hesitating, the boy clasped it, "Well met, very well met. Maybe one day, I'll get to care for a horse like yours. But I'm always in here. If you ever need anything, you just ask for me, ok? Then you won't have to deal with grumpy old men thinking they know too much."

"I will," she promised.

"I gotta go, they'll be yelling at me in a minute if I don't get Barn Three cleaned. Well met again, Ms. Luxx. I hope you enjoy your mare!"

With a wave, the guy darted through the barn aisle in the same direction as the old man had, reminding her of the time. She turned her feet toward the courtyard and the fountain where the Blades always met, smiling. That mare might not be hers yet, but she'd figured out how the Black Blades thought. If this kept up, the horse and a place in the most respected elite outfit of the Conglomerate would be hers.

CHAPTER EIGHT

Smug recruits reclined where they could, mostly on the edge of the fountain or the fence behind it. They spoke among themselves about the horses they'd chosen, each one bragging more than the next. A festive mood consumed them, and it disgusted her. In only a few short days, the privilege of being an applicant to the Black Blades had started to change how they acted.

Sal found a quiet place, well removed from the rest, and settled herself to wait for the impending arrival of the Lieutenant. The boy, Passel, took a spot beside her. She turned to look at him, at first annoyed that her isolation had been breached, but it appeared he also wanted to avoid the mass of soldiers.

On closer inspection, Passel was older than he looked but still young, maybe in his early twenties, so about Sal's age. The way he leaned against the wall showed his feral grace, but his features were nothing more than shades of brown. If she had to describe him, she'd have trouble citing anything that set him apart.

"They think it's a game," he said, breaking the silence.

She nodded, wishing he'd stop talking to her.

"I don't think they realize yet that most of them failed. The

Lieutenant, he likes us to be thinkers." His gaze never looked away from the recruits on the wagon. "I didn't think you were going to get it, not when I saw you asking them to get horses to move out, but you did. That's why I wanted to go last, so I didn't give away the answer."

"It took me a bit," she admitted, aware that he wasn't going to go away, "but the horses they offered didn't make much sense. Granted, I don't have a lot of riding experience, but I listened when I worked here."

"Ah, that explains it. So, I'm better with horses than you, but you obviously fight better than me. Can't wait to see what's going to be the tiebreaker."

"Me either. I admit, I'm nervous about it, but I'm ready to know. I'd wish you luck, but it would be a lie." She shrugged. Maybe he'd write her off as a threat.

"Same here. Let's just wish each other a good recommendation, fair 'nough?" He held out his hand.

She took it, disliking the feel of his human flesh. "Fair 'nough."

Although, knowing she'd passed the test was different than being told, so when the Lieutenant sauntered toward them, her stomach tried to climb out of her throat. Beside her, Passel stiffened, but the other recruits seemed oblivious to the upcoming culling. Sal and Passel stood respectfully to face the Lieutenant, but the rest stayed seated, lowering their conversations until they were called to attention.

The Lieutenant didn't bother. "Some of you have guessed by now that the horses were a test. What you may not be aware of is that it was about more than just the horses. We wanted to determine your situational awareness and your ability to assess the environment. Only two of you met our expectations," LT said.

Those were the words that pulled the recruits to their feet. Shocked expressions took over their faces, and they muttered in confusion. Sal couldn't help but think of them as a group; so few of them showed any independence. It made her appreciate the trials more. In less than a week, the apparently routine tests had allowed the true character of the soldiers to creep to the surface. The easily overlooked Passel had become her strongest competition, while the decorated men across from her were barely worth her notice.

"Lance Corporal Arton Wheton," the Lieutenant went on, "your ability to recognize horseflesh and take the initiative has given you a score just high enough to continue with the trials. Specialist Doron Passel and Private Salryc Luxx, you both completed the task as we hoped, resulting in another passed test. The rest of you, speak with Arctic. He will sign your release papers and arrange transport back to your previous post. The horses you chose will be returned to the pastures, or you have the option of purchasing them at a discount as your bonus for the trials. Additional training is available at your own expense. You are dismissed.

"Wheton, Luxx, and Passel, come with me." the Lieutenant said, turning away.

They followed him through what passed for streets to his cabin. Little had changed since her last visit and, at a gesture from LT, Sal found a seat before the desk. This time, Wheton and Passel flanked her rather than the officers of the Black Blades.

"Your final trial won't be as easy, I'm afraid," LT began. "Each of you will have two days to prepare, then you will lead the Blades through a training mission. Orders will be given immediately before the start time, but you have your assignment now. I encourage you to use any means necessary to gain intelligence about the mission details."

"Espionage?" Passel asked.

"Expected," LT agreed.

"Rules of engagement?" Wheton wanted to know.

"Enemy territory."

Eyes turned to Sal. With a smirk, she reclined into the chair. "Can we treat off-duty personnel as resources? Is funding for bribes and equipment refundable? And finally, does our assignment brief list a location?"

"It does." LT chose to answer her questions in reverse. "The assignment lists Stonewater Creek. You will be given a stipend to draw from for preparations so those of you with less personal resources will not be unfairly penalized. And yes, until your start time for the mission, assume that all personnel are to be treated as enemy civilians.

"In addition, you are granted access to any military base within fifteen kilometers. You have two full days to use in preparation, after which time you will either start the trial or be confined to your rooms until your trial starts."

Passel spoke up, "So, what happens in the event of a tie? Say all of us pass this trial? What then?"

"You have scores and will be graded for each step of preparation and execution," LT said. "A tie is unlikely, but in the event that happens, we will assign an additional task. Keep in mind, the opinion of all Black Blades is considered in the scoring. Being the best is not enough; you must be approved and respected by the unit as a whole."

The recruits fell silent. With only three of them left, Sal had no idea where she stood in the rankings. She hoped she led the class, but her insecurities made her doubt it. They all probably harbored the same fears.

"Now, if you have no further questions, you have tonight to contemplate your course of action, celebrate your passing into the last phase, or do whatever it is you want. Your clocks start tomorrow, at dawn." The Lieutenant stood.

The recruits did the same. With a nod, they were dismissed, and the three made their way to the street outside. Tensions between them were already rising, each casting glances at the others out of the corners of their eyes.

"Ok," Sal said. "I'm heading to my rooms, and I suspect I won't see any of you until our results are announced."

With a sigh, Passel nodded. "You're right. Good

recommendation, Luxx. May it serve you well. And here's hoping for a good recommendation for you too, Lance Corporal Wheton."

"Same to you, Passel," she replied. "And to you, Wheton, I hope that you earn a good recommendation because I don't dare wish you good luck."

The veteran chuckled. "A good recommendation to both of you as well then."

With that, they turned their separate ways, none of them looking back to watch their competition.

CHAPTER NINE

The sun still trickled in through her window, but Sal lay on her bed trying to chase the thoughts racing through her mind. She had two days to prepare her plan, and if she wanted to win this, then she'd have to be perfect. She'd have to be twice as good as the humans to even stand a chance, but how?

The Lieutenant said they could use any means necessary, yet trying to devise a way to gain intelligence about the upcoming mission had her stumped. She also couldn't forget his warning. He couldn't make exceptions for her, and he couldn't judge her easier than the rest. If she pushed too hard, she'd likely be dismissed because of her species. Anti-iliri sentiment was strong in the military, after all. So *how?*

When the answer eluded her, she paced her room like a caged animal. If she looked like anything but an iliri bitch, then maybe she could get information from the staff, but so few people opened up to her kind. Iliri were despised, only tolerated when they were under a human's control, and she wasn't right now. Turning, she looked into her mirror, wondering if makeup might be enough for a disguise, but her vertically slit, white eyes stared back.

She wished, with all her might, that her eyes were a common deep brown, with round pupils and normal white sclera. If she'd been born human, she could just talk the staff out of the information she needed. A smile over a drink, a soft word of appreciation for the favor, a lie about a brother she didn't have... Sal knew how to deal with men. If she just could be one of them, she could get what she needed. She could hide her snow-white skin with makeup. Dye could change her hair. Her hair could cover her ears. If she didn't open her mouth when she smiled, no one would see her teeth. Sal had been pretending to act like a human for years. All she needed were eyes that looked like everyone else's.

Bemoaning her breeding, she glanced again at her freakishly white eyes and found herself meeting a reflection she didn't recognize. Brown eyes looked back from her face, the pupils round and dilated.

Letting out a gasp, she took a step away from the mirror. The brown eyes faded back to white, and the pupils stretched back to vertical slits. She'd seen it, though. Her own eyes, in her own face, had changed to those of someone else. Not just anyone else, but common *human* eyes! What had she done? How was this possible?

Sal looked around her room, her mind struggling to grasp what had happened. Had she seen someone else? Was it because of the medication from that morning? Hallucinations were common side effects, weren't they? Were the Blades playing a joke on her? She glanced again and saw only her own face glance back.

Flinging herself back on her bed, she tried to explain it. Sal thought of all she knew about her species, which sadly wasn't much. She'd witnessed things that made no sense during her trial, so she dared to hope. Arctic allowed people to talk in each other's heads and blamed it on his iliri ancestry. Shift could heal with a wish. Maybe she could do something like that?

Out of desperation, Sal tried to envision a beautiful woman, the type of person she longed to be. Long, coffee-colored hair, tawny skin, and eyes as brown as freshly turned soil. She'd be curvaceous and desirable. Her nose would be dished and delicate instead of rounded like a beast. Her eyes would fit her face, not overtake it. She would be dark – not too dark, she didn't want to appear well-bred – and have normal ears. The kind that stayed against the side of her head like they should.

Carefully, she built the image in her mind: seductively beautiful but not out of reach. Men's tongues wagged more to a pretty face, hence that was the type of face she wanted. She focused on the details of her imagined facade then pulled herself from the bed and glanced at the mirror. Looking back at her, she found her own reflection with darkened eyes. Frustrated, she tried harder. She wished her pale hair would curl and change, thinking about it morphing from her skull to the ends. Staring intently at her reflection, she strained her mind for just a bit more color, just a bit more curl – and then saw it happening, something deep in her brain struggling to comply. From her scalp, a tint of color washed down. Where it passed, the hair twisted, becoming shorter with each bend.

Hoping, but not really believing it possible, Sal's mouth fell open. She took in the transformation, looking out from her new brown eyes. She'd done it! Miraculously, she could alter her own appearance!

Then it stopped.

Once she lost the image in her mind, her body began to revert. Her hair lost color, the locks falling limp and straight once more. The eyes faded and her own alien ones returned. Frustrated, she snarled and flung her fist out, catching the nearby wall. Pain shot up her arm, chiding her for the insolence.

Sal threw her head back and growled at the ceiling. If she could do this, if she could master it, she would have all she needed to achieve her dream. To be valued as a soldier, respected as a fighter, and have the power of authority behind her to protect her from the hate of humans. It was all she'd ever wanted, and in order to get it, she needed to be able to blend in. If the partially-human Blades could find amazing powers within themselves, then Sal could do this. Being iliri had to have *some* advantage! She just needed to focus harder, build a better image, and have patience. Tilting her head back to the mirror, she concentrated.

In her mind, she pictured the woman she wanted to be. She thought about the way her face and body would change: pigment was needed here, curls there. When she focused, it happened. Slowly at first, the color creeping in so subtly that it would've been easy to miss, but she refused to give up. When the bones of her face shifted, her skin swelled and softened. It was awkward, but oddly, it didn't hurt. Her cheeks rounded, her lips plumped, and her overly large eyes slimmed to fit her new features. Her skin simply darkened until standing there was the woman she wanted. She'd become a human.

Before Sal shifted her position, she thought about how this new body would move. She'd be slower, less precise, and more languid in her actions. She'd move like a dancer, not a fighter. Holding that vision, she asked her body to do it, watching as her new reflection obeyed. The strange woman leaned away from the mirror and stepped back, turning while holding Sal's eyes. She walked across her small room, around the bed, and out of sight of the reflection. She sat, then lay on the bed, before climbing back to her feet and looking in the mirror again.

A beautiful, soft woman looked back wearing Sal's standard issue military fatigues. All her life, she'd wished to be darker skinned, taller, and less exotic. Like anyone, she longed to be beautiful, to have the power to draw eyes at her whim. Her mind wandered, thinking about the men from her past like the clerk from Fort Landing or that one officer. What would those men think now, seeing this new body? She envisioned the revenge she could have but realized her new form was fading. She quickly turned her mind back to her ideal and focused on staying in this amazing body. The fading stopped and color returned when her mind held the image.

It got easier the more she tried. It also seemed that she had to always keep a portion of her attention on how she should look. When her mind wandered, her body changed back to the form it knew best. Pondering that, she allowed the visage to slip, resuming her blanched features, and again threw herself on her bed. She stared at the ceiling, trying to wrap her mind around her new-found ability.

She could change her form. Were there limits? Would it wear off suddenly? Could she become a man? She tried to find ways this could set her ahead of her competition. The easiest would be to impersonate a Black Blade and ask for clarification from another, but their mental link made that problematic. Deciding it was worth knowing, Sal again made her way to the mirror.

She stripped out of her clothes and thought of the First Officer. Arctic's pale beauty, his strong features, and his piercing, icy gaze were easy to bring to mind. She focused on the way he moved, his mannerisms, and his amazing good looks. Slowly, the change began. Her entire body felt as though it turned to liquid, drifting under her skin before solidifying into something larger. To her own eyes, the appearance was disconcerting. Her petite features slid and distorted into that of someone else.

She changed into a man, but it was not the man she wanted. He could be Arctic's brother, but his shoulders were too broad, his nose too thin, and his eyes too large. She tried to adjust the features, concentrating on making Arctic stand before her, but her body didn't have a blueprint for him. It only achieved what she told it to.

Sal's mind just could not capture the nuances of a particular person. She could tell she wasn't Arctic, but couldn't figure out how to make the right changes. Evidently, she couldn't just take over the life of another to achieve her goals.

Curious, she looked down at the reflection of her masculine body. Her breasts were flat and between her legs hung flesh she was not accustomed to. Giggling, the sound of her masculine voice strange in her ears, she decided to continue the experiment. Sal moved into the washing room and wrapped her hand around the new appendage, then tried to release her bladder. A few drops preceded the stream, which arced out in a way she didn't expect. Urinating on the floor, she adjusted and managed to hit the basin. Empty, but laughing at herself, she grabbed a cloth and cleaned the mess – both on herself and in the room – while allowing her form to revert to the body she'd known all her life. Maybe being a man was harder than she expected.

But Sal had an advantage over her competitors now. Next, she needed to get a better understanding of how the Blades worked to assess their abilities. Knowing what was planned for the trial would do her little good if she didn't understand how to utilize the skills of the men. With that decided, she changed into clean clothing and headed to where she would find them: the pub.

CHAPTER TEN

*N*oise assaulted her ears as soon as she walked through the door. Sal wandered through the rooms, ordered a drink, then headed to the second floor. From here, she could see everything. She reached out mentally, hoping to find Shift, Arctic, or Zep, the Blades she felt closest to. The touch of an unfamiliar thought warned her to look around. Standing in the shadows behind her, Cyno leaned casually against the wall, his deep blue eyes watching her. She smiled warmly at him.

I needed to pick the brain of a Blade, she thought. *Wanna help me out, or would I be ruining your fun?*

Fun? Nah. But yeh, I can help ya.

Come sit? I'll buy you a drink, she cajoled.

Kitten, I think I should buy yer drink, na the other way around. Lemme do tha', an' it's a date... or should I say deal? His mental laugh at the halfhearted flirtation made her smile as he moved to the seat across from her and gestured for a waitress.

Ok, Sal started, *here's my problem. The last trial has us supposedly leading the Black Blades in a training mission.* Her mental tone conveyed her anxiety. *I want to do it right, but my combat experience is limited –*

I can na give ya advice on leading the mission, Sal. Ya know tha', he broke in.

I do, and that's not what I want. She thought about how to phrase her question, shards of images crossing the link to Cyno's mind. *What I want is just to know what each of you can do, and where you excel. Within the rules, of course.* She paused before adding, *It'd also be nice if I knew where the line was... like with this,* and she gestured at her head.

Hmm. Well, honestly, I dunno. We can ask the guys. Rather than say somethan I should na, an' get ya disqualified, I'd rather ask. Cyno met her eyes with as close to a friendly gaze as she'd ever seen from him. Just outside her reach, she heard the murmur of a conversation.

An', he continued after a pause, *we're supposed ta requisition a private room... fer eight. Follow me.* He offered her a hand, an odd look on his face when he wrapped her arm through his and led her down the stairs.

Escorting her across the noisy pub, Cyno made his way to the back. The music faded behind them, the halls grew narrower, and the decor more subdued. A large man dressed in navy stood up as they neared, his posture changing to respectful rather than intimidating once he saw Cyno.

"I need a room, 'nough to fit eight, if ya could?" Cyno asked.

"Yes, sir. Any additional accommodations?"

"Yeh, we'll need some food, I dunno, a bit of somethan fer each a us. An' a bottle of mead. Prepare Zep's usual, an' if ya see LT, could ya let him know where we are?" Cyno's demeanor suggested this was not uncommon for the Blades.

The guard nodded, "Yes, sir, I can do that. Since you're off, I assume you want the small room?"

"Yeh, perfect. Thanks, Jenner." He led Sal down the hall, her arm still linked with his, while his mind resumed their discussion.

We tend ta have a couple a rooms back here fer private meetings. It's a lot more comf'terble than what the military offers, and the service is better.

They made their way into a room with chairs around an oval table. Cyno closed the door, and the sounds of the pub faded to little more than a whisper.

"We fig're ya wanna talk, na dance t'nite," he said, his voice rough yet lyrical, "so's Arctic said ta grab a room. In here we can talk jus' fine, with nah ears trying ta listen in, an' ya will na hafta worry 'bout who's standing behind ya."

She nodded. "Thanks. You know I'm not trying to break the rules on this. I just wanted to ask you all in person rather than digging through records without your permission." She paused, thinking, before continuing. "It just seems wrong somehow. I mean, all of you have become what I would like to call friends, and to read your files without asking, it just seems like a breach of trust."

Cyno almost smiled at that. His perpetually hard face softened, offering a hint of the man he could have been with a different life. "Thanks, Sal. Yeh, our personnel files have a bit more inf'rmation in 'em than we'd like. I'd rather tell ya all my stories myself than have ya read somethan an' get the wrong idea. I'm thinking the others'd feel the same, ya know?"

Before she could answer, the door creaked open, and Arctic slipped in. "Party in here?" he joked as he pulled himself into a chair. Within seconds, four other black-clad men wandered in as a group. They made themselves comfortable, leaving the chair at the head of the table for Sal. When she opened her mouth to start speaking, Shift held up a hand.

"3, 2, 1..." he counted down before a rap sounded at the door. "Come!" he called.

The guard from the hall, Jenner, entered carrying a large tray of food with a bottle tucked under each arm. "Your meal, my good sirs... and um... lady?" he said, glancing at Arctic.

"It's alright, Jenner, she's supposed to be here," Arctic assured the man. "And she's a sir, too."

The guard nodded and put down the tray of sausage, cheese, and other finger foods. There wasn't a vegetable in sight, which made Sal happy. The Blades reached for food, mumbling their thanks as he left the room. Then the men pulled out glasses and filled them with the golden liquor.

"Sal had questions, and neither of us knew if I coulda answered 'em," Cyno started.

"What questions?" Arctic asked.

"Well," Sal said. "I'm supposed to lead the training mission. I assume that means the decisions will be mine, and that you'll look to me for orders?"

Arctic nodded.

"So," she said, "that means I need to have a better understanding of each of your skills. On the surface, the Black Blades are known to be skirmish fighters, overcoming amazing odds and enjoying outnumbered fights. Well, that's nice and all, but it also doesn't match what I have seen."

Around the table, eyebrows raised into hairlines. A few men cracked smiles while she struggled to explain, "I mean, I've already seen that you have skills you don't casually share with others. I also saw that each of you fights with a unique style. What I'm thinking is that you all have strengths and weaknesses..."

She paused when the door behind her opened one more time. The Lieutenant stepped in and made his way to the foot of the table.

"Go on, Sal," he said.

"Ok, so strengths and weaknesses. Since I haven't really trained with any of you, I have to ask what areas of combat you excel in. Cyno wasn't sure it was allowed," she explained to the Lieutenant.

"It's ok, guys." He looked at each before turning back to Sal. "I'm impressed you came directly to us instead of just trying to find it in their files."

"It doesn't seem right, sir," she repeated. "I know how much I would hate the idea, and snooping in the files without asking just seems backhanded. Besides, I'll get better information if I ask."

LT smiled. "It's true, you will."

"So," she persisted, "what can each of you tell me about your skills? Fighting first, if you would?"

The Lieutenant chuckled at that. "Go on, guys. Tell her what she needs. She's the first one to figure out that we do more than just swing swords. If she can figure out how to use what we can do, then great. If not... who would believe her?"

"Well, I guess we'll go around the table. As the highest ranking, I'll go first?" Arctic suggested. "I prefer to shoot rather than hit things. I excel with the jakentron, all bows, as well as thrown weapons. I do well enough in hand to hand combat and can beat most with a sword. Give me a shield and my sword work is even better. Is that the type of thing you want?"

"Yes! Exactly what I need to know. Arctic, I never would have guessed you for an archer," Sal said. "But I've only ever heard rumors of the jakentron."

"It's a pneumatic weapon, typically cast in resin, sometimes acrylics," he explained. "Once charged with pressurized air, it shoots a needle or dart and can reach over five hundred meters. And sniping works for me. Keeping my distance reduces the chances of getting taken out, blacking out the link. You already know about that, having been chatting us up with it."

"Ok, so... Is it an all or nothing thing, or can you close out someone if you need to?"

"No," he said sadly, "I can, and after dawn tomorrow, I plan to shut you out. It's not easy to do, but I can drop anyone that doesn't outrank me. We don't need to be listening to what you think, and I can't quite trust you to not stumble across a stray thought from one of these men. So far, we don't have any real mission details, so I figured it wouldn't hurt to keep you in for a while longer. With that said, I have to make tough calls sometimes, like blocking out someone wounded because we can't think with his cries across the link. It's always been a part of me, but like you probably guessed, only those with iliri ancestry can use it. Well... and Zep."

"Hey!" Zep said, "I keep telling you, my great-great-granny liked her iliri servants. And all of her kids coulda been blondes. I'm a part bred too... just not a big part!"

Arctic rolled his eyes so Zep could see. Jokingly, Zep tossed a sausage at Arctic's head.

"Guys," Razor said, "c'mon. Besides, Zep has to have some iliri... no other human has been able to link. But Sal, for combat, I tend to do well with polearms. Pikes, lances, halberds, you name it and I can use it. Figure they're all variations of the same. I don't do infiltration well. I tend to be too intense, too loud, and lack the discipline to not say what I think. I'm a slower fighter than the others, but I think I make up for it with strength."

Sal nodded, mentally making notes.

"As for my ability, well... I'm a compass." He shrugged, "I find things, and I don't really know how. If I focus on something, I can point you at it. Not really useful, unless someone tries to lose you in the woods."

The Blades laughed, obviously having experienced Razor's skill themselves.

"Ok, so I'm next," Shift spoke up. "Well, I do the infiltration work that Razor won't. I blend in, and people tend to just like me, so getting information is easy. I also work with most of the hand to hand weapons but can't hit the broad side of a barn with anything from a distance. I'm lucky if I can hit a table when I drop my dagger! I prefer sword and pike, like you saw at the sparring match. And let's see... my ability is that I can heal minor wounds or stabilize the serious ones."

Sal nodded and looked to Cyno.

"I'm easy," he said, meeting her eyes and holding them. "I kill people. I like close weapons: daggers, knives, even a short sword'll do. I can handle any of 'em, though. If ya want sum'un dead, then

I'm yer man. If ya wanna jus' hold the line, ya use one of the others. I do na fight pretty, I jus' kill."

"So," Sal asked delicately, "an assassin?"

"Yeh," he replied flatly. "I move fast, an' I do na care 'bout none of the posing crap some do. I fig're, get in, get it done, an' be over it."

"Do you have an ability too, then?" she asked.

"I touch things," he said. "I mean, usually it's people, but objects of affection can do it, too. I can tell ya if sum'un is lying or guilty, or stuff. I sometimes can get real strong stuff from an item, like if somethan bad happened when they held it, or if they were thinking 'bout it when using the item, but they hafta do that a lot."

"What, think about it a lot?" she asked.

"Yeh, like if a boy breaks a girl's heart, and she holds her pillow and cries about him ever' night, then I can get bits and pieces of what she was thinking happened. It's na as good as touchin' the person, though."

Sal nodded, trying to think of how that could be used. Besides reading a specific person for a specific reason, she couldn't come up with much.

"Ok, Risk, what about you?" she asked.

"Well, I'm a jack of all trades type of fighter," he said. "When I joined the Blades, they made sure I could hold my own, but mostly I'm just support. I do the healing, and while Shift's method is faster, mine is stronger. I can repair almost anything, so long as my patient is still breathing when I get to him. It isn't a comfortable feeling."

Around the room, the men shook their heads in agreement. Sal assumed most of them had endured Risk's healing and hoped to never do it again.

"Think of it like all the pain shoved into a few minutes," Zep said. "It ain't fun."

"Ok, so what about you, then, Zep? What do you do?"

"Well, I fight." He smirked. "I can beat just about any of these guys at any weapon. I tend not to lose." His eyes met hers knowingly.

Sal realized he was saying her victory in their spar meant more than she thought. If Zep could beat most of the Blades at their weapons of choice, why had they put him up against her?

"Before your pretty head gets tied in knots," he went on, "I've lost a few times. You aren't that special. And yeah, I decided to fight you because I planned to show the others that you weren't unstoppable."

"I never thought I was!" she snapped at him. "I just wanted to score a touch on you before you took me out."

"Oh."

The room had gone still, the others acting uncomfortable, looking away from Sal as she glared at Zep.

"And your ability?" she growled. "Is it as impressive as your ego?"

"Sadly, no." Zep sighed, meeting her eyes. "I don't have one, it seems, or if I do, I haven't found it yet." He sighed again. "Look, Sal, I'm sorry. I come off rude at times, and like a hard-ass, but I don't mean anything by it. I just figured you were mentally patting yourself on the back because that's what I would have done."

"I wasn't. Actually, I'm even more shocked, because I never thought I'd win against you to start with." Looking around the room, she decided to just get it out. "I don't know how any of you came into elite service, but I'm lucky they even let me apply. My kind isn't typically a candidate for elite operations like the Blades, and this is my dream, something I've wanted for as long as I can remember. I never thought I'd have a chance, let alone make it this far. I always assumed you'd find some reason to force me out of the running because I can't blend in and play human, and *now* I wonder if that's why you chose me to spar with, because you wanted to get rid of the scrubber."

The room erupted at that. While voices decried her accusations, she heard the click signifying Arctic had opened her to the link. Into her mind swelled images of disbelief, denial, and appall that she could feel so unworthy. Feelings of their enthusiasm for her chances hit her, mingled with visions of her excelling at one thing or another. Through the deafening haze in her head, she found no thoughts against her.

"Sal," LT said from across the room, gesturing for Arctic to close the link. "I let Zep fight you for two reasons. First, because you were the only one that stood any chance against him. Second, I had to see how combat with a human would affect you. The sparring only demonstrated how unprepared a few candidates were, nothing more. If you haven't noticed, your breeding is an asset to us, not a reason for us to be fearful or shun you. I can promise you that the only reason you will be excluded from the Black Blades at this point will be due to your own actions, not ours."

She nodded, ashamed she hadn't trusted them more, but she'd always been treated like the outsider. Time and time again, humans said nice things to her before stabbing her in the back. It might be a bad habit to expect the worst, but it had protected her more than once.

"Did you get what you need?" he asked kindly.

"You didn't tell me what role you play, sir."

"Ah, in this case, it won't matter. I won't be among your soldiers." His eyes lit up wickedly, and Sal realized it was a hint - if she could ascertain what he meant. "But for now, I think we're done. Dawn comes sooner than we'd like, and I, for one, have a meeting with people who think they're important. C'mon guys, let's get to bed and let Sal get some sleep before she tries to figure out what it is I have planned."

Tossing back drinks, the Blades got to their feet and began to make their way out. Each one stopped to give her a word of encouragement and Shift amused her with a bear hug.

"Going my way, or you have a better place to sleep tonight than your cabin?" he asked, waggling his eyebrows in a parody of flirtation.

"Nah, Shift, I thought I'd climb in bed with Cyno. He's closer to my size, you know," she teased back, once again feeling like this was where she belonged. Even after a disagreement, she still had no desire to be anywhere else. And while she didn't know these guys well, at least they were willing to try.

Across the room, Cyno's head snapped around. His dark blue eyes stared into hers for a second before Shift grabbed him, hauling him into the hall.

"Fight you for her!" Shift laughed, dragging the little man along, leaving Sal to make her own way to her bed.

CHAPTER ELEVEN

The ceiling still looked the same, she thought as she lay on her bed staring at it. The night before, Sal had locked the door securely behind her before shifting her skin into that of the dark woman she longed to be. She'd spent hours waiting and checking, only to realize that as long as she felt like the other woman, then likely she still looked like her. A small corner of her mind had to always be aware of her new appearance but, with practice, it had grown so easy that Sal had tried sleeping in the new form. Now awake, she lay staring at the ceiling, struggling to convince herself to climb out of bed.

A glance in the mirror showed her skin still dark and her hair still wavy, even if it was disheveled from sleep. After hours of inspecting the new features of her altered self, she'd made a few adjustments. She now stood just under two meters tall, an average size for a human woman, but much taller than what she was used to. Walking took practice, but it only made her hold on this body more secure when she had to accommodate the longer limbs. She also had a less than perfect line of teeth, not crooked, but just enough perfection removed to give her a feeling of reality. A birthmark on her hip and a few "childhood scars" had finished the body.

Now, realizing her new form would hold even through sleep, she needed to put her plan into action. First, she had to be herself again. While Sal straightened her room and prepared for a few days away from it, she allowed her body to revert to the form it knew best. She packed a few belongings and put on a clean uniform before making what she hoped seemed to be a typical exit.

As she closed the door, she caught movement beside her. Cyno leaned casually against the wall of the cabin next to hers. He glanced over at her from the corner of his eye, and his lip curled as he tried to pretend he didn't see her.

"Morning," Sal said as she reached for her bag.

"Yeh."

She looked at him for a long moment, wondering if the Blades planned to keep track of her movements. The Lieutenant said they would be scored on their planning for this mission, and who better for surveillance than an assassin?

Cyno chuckled softly and turned to face her. "Nah, I'm na stalkin' ya. I'm just na supposed ta be talkin' to ya neither."

She cocked her head slightly, confused. "I thought I was out of the link?"

"Yeh, but tha' does na mean I can na smell yer concern."

"So why are you waiting outside my room?"

He jerked his thumb at the door beside him. "My rooms. Ya did na know I'm next door?"

Sal shook her head.

"Yeh. Jus' glad ya do na talk in yer sleep." He grinned at her but turned as Zep staggered across the street. "Yer late, big brother," Cyno called to him.

"Shove it, little brother, and stop talking to the applicants," Zep called back, walking toward them. "Morning, Sal."

"Morning, Zep."

"Now, go on. We've got practice, and you're not supposed to be talking to us."

Sal smiled up at him innocently. "Whatcha practicing?"

Cyno chuckled. "Ya wish ya knew. Go on, kitten."

"Kitten?" Zep asked, raising an eyebrow.

"Fuck off," Cyno grumbled.

Zep looked from Cyno to Sal, an amused expression on his face. "Gotcha, bro. And Sal, we ain't giving ya shit, so ya might as well finish whatever you were starting."

She sighed, defeated. "Ok. See ya both in two days, then," she called as she walked away.

"I'm rooting for ya, kid," Zep whispered when she was well away. Sal wasn't sure if he knew she could still hear him.

Her first stop was the requisition office. Once there, she retrieved her stipend and invoked her access to any information pertaining to the next trial. She scoured page after page of documents, taking note of items that seemed abnormal but, overall, finding nothing that gave her an insight into the test. From there, she began asking for a wagon into Fort Landing. The ride would take an hour, but her plan required it. She needed supplies from a larger outpost and an alibi.

It didn't take long before she jounced and bounced in the back of a supply cart, the driver casting suspicious glances at her the whole way. Sal started to ignore him, then realized that the prejudice against her own kind would actually work in her favor. Over the course of the ride, she took note of the way he checked her actions, how his face showed traces of disgust, and the tension in his body while he tried to pretend she wasn't there. She thought about how that could apply to her new form, for the dark-skinned woman would naturally have been taught that she was better than any iliri. Her prejudice would have to be minimal at best. Sal would never be able to give an honest portrayal of hate for her own kind.

When they reached the gates of Fort Landing, the driver kicked her out. Grabbing her bags, she casually turned without a backwards glance, amused at the smell of fear emanating from the human, then strolled across the dusty cobbles of the oldest fort in the Conglomerate. Her destination was an inn on the lower side that would ask few questions and serve her kind. After securing a room, she changed into a billowy dress and tossed her belongings into a parcel that she mailed back to the stable. The delivery was set for the date of the first trial. Her room now barren of personal belongings, Sal returned to the street. Her casual attire allowed her to blend with the citizens, even if her skin didn't.

A quick stop at the main requisition desk required her to sign in, proof that she was no longer at Stonewater Stables. She checked their records for any hint of her next mission, but found the Black Blades ordered little out of the ordinary. Not surprised at the lack of information, she thanked the attending official and put her plan into action.

A few blocks down the street, she ducked into a public restroom. The stench of the toilets distracted her, but she focused on the woman she was about to become. Once her bones solidified and her form stabilized, she walked to the mirror. There, looking back at her, was a human woman in a loose but well-fitting dress. The same dress that billowed around Sal's shins now brushed her new knees, and the neckline that hung limply against Sal's chest strained before her ample breasts. She twisted the curls of her hair into a serviceable knot, then made her way back to the street.

The change in how people reacted was immediate. Men turned to look, and women turned their eyes away. Pale-skinned humans and iliri crossbreds shot jealous glances at her. Sal pretended not to see them as she made her way to a local clothing store in the residential district. She entered and noticed yet another difference. Attendants glanced up at the sound of the door, immediately making their way to assist rather than ignoring her presence.

"Ma'am, what can we do for you today?" a chipper girl asked.

"I need something a bit more formal, it seems," she replied. "I've been invited to a few events this weekend and heard the most fashionable clothes in this area could be found here?"

"Oh yes, ma'am," the clerk assured her. "We outfit officers, their spouses, and even enlisted soldiers. Our clothing is brought in from Prin rather than made by local clothiers. May I ask what events you'll be attending so we can find the proper style to suit you?"

"Oh, my husband has planned lunch with some officers, so I need something appropriate for that. Nothing too fancy, since it'll be outdoors. Tonight, I hope to spend some time in the local pubs while he's in meetings. They always last all night, and sitting around in some fancy room alone just doesn't sound very exciting." She leaned her head closer to the girl and whispered, "Besides, my friends back home said I needed to see what the soldiers look like!"

The clerk giggled like the girl she was, "Oh yes, ma'am. They train all day and have bodies like you wouldn't believe. Ok, so let's see what we have..." She flicked through racks, pulling out a few selections, and gestured for Sal to follow her toward the fitting rooms.

The feel of expensive clothing was exciting. Fashion had always been a weakness Sal could never afford, so she made the most of it. In the end, she selected four outfits for her new form to suit different occasions. The clerk wrapped them carefully and placed them in a bag, never suspecting a thing.

Sal left the store dressed in soft brown breeches, knee-high boots, and a billowy white shirt, the type of attire found fashionable for travel. She then made her way back to the front gate and booked a trip to the Stables at Stonewater under the name Siana Praxis.

CHAPTER TWELVE

The carriage rumbled into the Stables and pulled to the side. As the passengers were assisted out, footmen retrieved their luggage, placing it in neat rows for the owners to retrieve. The horses were unhitched from the shafts and walked away while fresh ones were brought in to replace them. It was very organized and precise. Sal watched wide-eyed, knowing that the persona of Siana should be impressed. She looked around, taking in the sights before she made her way to her bag – filled only with the clothing she'd recently bought – and sought out an employee of the stables.

"Excuse me, sir, but can you point me to an inn or place to find lodging for the night?" she asked an older gentleman directing the harnessing of the horses.

He took a long look at her before answering. "Yes, ma'am. It's just down that east road there, about a block. Did you need me to have a boy carry your bags Ms..."

"Praxis," she supplied. "No, I appreciate it, but there's no need. I just have a strange layover. It seems the next carriage doesn't leave out of Eastward back to Merriton for two days, and in Fort Landing, they said the accommodations here are much nicer than my other options."

"Yes, ma'am. Sadly there's no straight route from Fort Landing to Merriton," he explained, more than happy to leave the horses to his underlings.

She tilted her head slightly and offered him a shy smile. "So, tell me, is there anything to do here while I'm stranded?"

"Well... The Twin Traveler is a nice tavern I hear. Good food and a quiet ambiance. If you're looking for something more local, the Broken Soldier is the pub the military prefer. It tends to be loud and rowdy, but the number of officers there makes it a safe place for a lady like yourself. Besides those, no, there's not much to do here at the stables other than watch mounted drills."

"I see. Well, is it ok if I wander around a bit? I don't want to get in anyone's way."

"No, ma'am, that isn't a problem at all. Just stay out of the barns – the staff are rather picky about the horses, you understand – and you won't have any problems."

She thanked him wholeheartedly and made her way in the direction he indicated. It was the longer route around the stables but had fewer turns to navigate. Sal took in the sights of military stabling with a new eye, pretending to see it for the first time. She made sure to step carefully over manure and to pause to check her bearings before entering the lobby of a building with the simple sign that said only "Inn."

A matronly woman behind the counter smiled at her when she entered. "Looking for a room, miss?"

"Yes'm," she said. "I'll need today and tomorrow at least, and it's possible I'll be here tomorrow night as well, depending on if my carriage to Merriton is an overnight or early morning trip."

"Not a problem. I'll just reserve the room for both nights then. And how will you be paying for that?"

"Krits," Sal replied. "Using credit on a trip like this is just too bothersome for both of us."

"Thank you, miss," the woman said. Handing over forms to sign, she politely took Sal's money before handing her a key and directing her to the second floor.

When Sal entered her room, she was impressed. As an iliri, she'd always been offered the lower class options, but in her guise of a human, she stood in a luxurious suite. The sleeping area was separate from the lounge, and the private bathing chamber was tucked out of the way. She'd never been in rooms this nice before, let alone able to claim them as her own.

Turning her attention to preparing her wardrobe, Sal removed the wrinkles and dust from her new attire, then hung it carefully while she thought over the reactions of each person she'd met. Siana Praxis was a vague enough name that it caused no eyes to be raised, and her story seemed to be accepted by everyone she'd come across. She'd only lost a few hours setting up her alibi. Time well spent, since Siana seemed to be able to get information much easier than Sal could in her own body. It was almost like people sought out Siana, reminding her how much different life would be if she'd been human.

But she didn't have time to think about that. With the day ahead of her, Sal decided to put her new form into action. She needed information about her upcoming test, after all. The prejudiced old man from the stables would be her first target.

First, she checked herself in the mirror. Satisfied that she was still a beautiful human, she walked out of her room, down the back stairs, and made her way to the barns.

Walking casually, soaking up the sights of magnificent warhorses being handled around her, she did her best to act like a naive human. She even asked to pet one of the horses, but the handler politely refused, explaining that the animal might bite. He sent her into the barn, giving her directions to more behaved mounts that she might be able to touch. Once there, contrary to what the carriage master had said, the staff offered a tour of the horses.

She barely blinked at her own mare when she passed, but fawned over a golden palomino a few stalls down. The stablehands were more than happy to tell her anything she asked, even laying out the schedules of the horses in their answers to her "innocent" questions. Through her tour, she learned the next trial would have mounted soldiers in it and the "enemy" forces would be using them. The horses would be rouncies, not true warhorses, since those were too aggressive for a casual training exercise.

Excusing herself from the overly friendly help of four young men, Sal made her way to one of the training arenas. There, she leaned on the rail for half an hour before she saw her target walk past. The grumpy stablehand was probably in his mid-forties, his skin leathered, and a constant scowl distorted his face. Sal called out to him, seeking assistance, and his frown barely lifted.

"I got stuff to be doing, girl. What is it you want?"

"I heard you might be the man to help me," she replied dripping saccharine.

"Yeah? And why would you think that?"

"Because some iliri bitch thinks she can get my baby brother kicked out of the trials for the Black Blades?" She cocked her head and looked deep into his eyes, checking to see if she'd overstepped her bounds.

"Mm, and what do I have to do with that?" he asked, interest showing in his voice.

"We Passels have always kept to our own kind," she explained, "and my brother doesn't deserve to lose his place to some bleached scrubber. I just need to know if you've heard anything that might give him a bit of help in planning his mission." Another kind smile was forced to her lips. "He said his officer gave them permission to learn anything they could, any way they could. Since that scrubber bitch made a big enough fuss about you talking to her the other day, I thought maybe..."

"Yeh, well, your brother's the kid, right?"

"Yeah, Doron. He's worked hard to get where he is, not like those scrubbers that just have it handed to them."

"I dunno, miss."

"Sir, I don't want you to get in trouble or anything, I just hoped that maybe you'd heard something or could point him somewhere. You know, the kind of thing you're allowed to do."

"Ok. Lemme take you to lunch at the Twins, and I'll see what I can tell ya." His weathered face turned smug, sure that she'd refuse.

Sal-as-Siana clasped her hands together, "Ok then, it's a date! But..." She put on a thoughtful expression, hoping she was convincing. "I don't even know your name. What should I call you?"

"Petur Knash, ma'am. I'll meet you in an hour."

Sal wandered the stables awhile before her anxiety got the better of her and she made her way to the Twin Traveler Tavern. Entering the dimly lit building, she asked for a table on the far side and seated herself in the front chair. She'd let Petur have his back to the wall to make him feel more confident. Sal had no worries about being caught, not in this form.

She ordered a cocktail and sipped at it while waiting impatiently. It took an eternity before the grumpy man entered, scanning the room for her. Turning at the sound of the door, Sal smiled brightly and lifted her hand to him.

"Ms. Passel," he greeted as she gestured to a seat.

"Find anything, Mr. Knash?"

"Well, yes, I have some information that might help you out, but it could cost me my job." He leaned in for dramatic effect.

Sal tried hard not to laugh in his face over the melodramatic performance. "Well, I can't offer you much, but I do have a little I can part with." She sighed. "I really hope it'll be enough – that and knowing you kept some scrubber from making a fool of yet another human." She slid a ten krit note at him, enough to pay for a week in the inn, and raised her eyebrow.

"Thanks, miss." He quickly pocketed the money. "Look, here's how it is. Them Blades, they have a pretty nice thing worked out.

The recruits are going to lead them to rescue their captured Lieutenant. Guarding him will be the light cavalry cadets. They'll have sniper students holed up somewhere, ready to take out anyone that tries to barge in and use the fighting skill of the Blades to overcome the odds. Thing is, there's some twist in the test, there always is, but I don't know much about that. Does that help Doron any?"

"Sir, you have no idea how much help that is!" She leaned over and wrapped her arms around him, kissing his cheek fondly. "Doron can go snooping around the cavalry and snipers now, and know that's covered."

She sat through the meal with him, smiling and agreeing about the atrocities the iliri had brought to the human race. If she'd been better at infiltration, she could've turned the discussion to something more useful, but Sal was happy with what she'd managed to get. By the end of the meal, the man's hate made her feel nauseous, so she made her excuses to leave, saying she needed to get the information to her brother as soon as possible.

Outside, she turned her feet in the direction of the Blade's barracks, making sure Petur saw. A few buildings over, she found a bench and sat. Pulling off her boot to remove an imaginary stone let her check for anyone following her. Life in the stables seemed to continue on as normal, though, which meant she hadn't given herself away yet.

Thinking through her plan, Sal realized she needed to know more about how the past combat trials had gone. It seemed LT liked impressing the other soldiers and showing off the abilities of his Blades. Hopefully, someone heard stories of previous attempts or participated in them. If she knew what he'd done before, then she might be able to guess what he'd do next.

For the rest of the day, she tried to casually stumble upon someone who might have more information, or even a Black Blade. She stopped to watch the light cavalry practice and memorized their maneuvers, guessing how the drills might pertain to the training mission only two days away. Some, like the mounted ring used for defense, were obvious. Others made little sense to her. She tried to catch a soldier and ask, but no opportunities arose.

When the sun set, the soldiers were released from their duties. Many began to make their way to the pub. With no better options, Sal decided to change into something more provocative and try her luck there.

Back at the inn, she chose a copper and green dress, the skirt short in front to show off her legs, the bustle in back falling to just below her knees. Stockings were pulled up to her thighs and secured with garters, and delicate capped sleeves left her shoulders bare. She pulled on a pair of medium brown boots, the heel long and delicate, and added the finishing touches to her hair. Lifting it off her neck, Sal allowed a few strands to fall across her bare collar bones, where the green jewel in her necklace lay. For the finishing touch, she dabbed perfume against her throat, chest, and wrists: a fragrance that smelled metallic and would remind her that she was supposed to be a human.

Dressed, she made her way down to the lobby and stopped at the counter to get directions, making sure to stumble over the name. The matron smiled and complimented her clothing, then drew a simple map. Following it, Sal came at the pub from the opposite side of the outpost. The music hadn't reached the levels of their late-night performances, and Doron Passel sat in a quiet corner near the door, leafing through a stack of paperwork. Feeling devious, she walked over and cleared her throat politely. When the boring, brown boy looked up, he didn't even bother to cover what he was reading. She leaned in slightly, checking out the spines of the books stacked beside him and the heading of the page he viewed. It was all on standard military tactics.

"Sir, can you point me to the bar? I'm not sure which door to take, and I'm dying for a drink!" she flirted.

Passel refused to rise to the bait. "Center door, straight down the hall, although there's a smaller bar in almost every room." He turned his nose back to his papers, lines of stress creasing his forehead.

She thanked him, made her way to the indicated bar, and ordered. "Something local," she said, and now held in her hand a fruit ale. Finding a table, she tasted the drink, trying to decide if she liked it or not while watching the crowd. A few sips in, she saw the first man in black. Shift waltzed in with a woman on each arm, making a production of himself. Unfortunately, the women would make approaching him difficult.

When the pub began to fill, she decided to work the room. She didn't have much experience in flirting since men tended to avoid intimate relationships with her kind – except for those willing to dredge the bottom of the barrel so they wouldn't go home alone. Trying to mimic the civilian women around her, Sal wandered, placing herself carefully, eying the crowd for potential soldiers with information she could talk them out of. She kept a drink in her hand, hoping it would help her fit in, but soon realized that her nervous sips were making her inebriated.

A few men approached her. None of them knew anything she could use, but their antics were amusing. They thought bragging and obvious falsehoods should be impressive. She nearly laughed in the face of one Private who tried to convince her he was a Captain, unaware she could read the insignia on his shoulders. Needless to say, it wasn't hard to slip away.

Unfortunately, she couldn't find any Black Blades needing companionship. The crush of bodies and the smell of humans made her senses useless. The music smothered the sounds of nearby conversations, and her fixed, human ears meant she had to turn her head to catch snippets of the talk around her. The pub's lighting cast irregular shadows, but Sal tried to peer into each one, always expecting to see Cyno hiding there. The alcohol blurring her vision didn't help.

Maybe a cavalry officer would know something, she thought, seeing quite a few of those sitting alone. At this hour, the Black

Blades should be off duty, but it seemed she'd need quite a bit of luck to simply stumble into one. She needed to think, and her brain felt muddled.

Sighing, she turned to find a place to sit and caught her heel on a rough board. Her new body failed her. The floor began to rush up quickly. Unable to untangle her long limbs, she let the drink go and threw her hands out to catch herself.

Sal landed on her knees, one arm across a man's lap at the table beside her, and she cursed her awkwardness. Instinctually, her anger flared, and she gnashed her teeth together, wishing for something to take her frustrations out on.

"Watch that board. It's a doozy," a gentle voice said.

Looking up into his face, Sal saw the pale green eyes of the Lieutenant looking back at her. Her stomach dropped into her toes as panic consumed her. Seated across from him, a Captain had risen halfway from his chair, his arm still outstretched in his desire to help.

CHAPTER THIRTEEN

"Oh, how embarrassing!" Sal tried to extract herself from her commanding officer's lap.

"Here, let me help," LT said, putting words into action.

She made to stand, but her head began to spin when she reached her feet. LT moved to assist, his hands reaching for her skin. She managed to lock down her mind as tight as she could just as he grabbed her, one hand on her waist, the other on her bare upper arm.

"New here?" His smile was flirtatious.

"Yeah." She ducked her head. It would be nice to blame the alcohol, but being so close reinforced his good looks. He smelled like leather, freshly tilled soil after the rain, and a hint of the same pungent odor she now recognized as iliri. With his face only inches away, her heart beat faster. She blamed the fear of discovery, refusing to admit it might be anything more. "I'll just return to my table and try to save some of my pride now. That wasn't quite the way I hoped to meet someone."

"Please, feel free to pull up a chair," LT offered, and the Captain across from him nodded emphatically. "It might be safer, and I'd be honored if you'd let me replace the drink you lost."

"Ugh, my drink!"

Sal breathed a sigh of relief when she saw that it'd hit nothing more deadly than the floor. The Captain raised his hand and called over a waitress, ordering a round for each of them. The men included her in their conversation easily, so Sal tried to relax. She asked what they did, stumbling over their ranks, struggling to feign a lack of knowledge about military discipline. They were happy to fill her in, although LT only called himself a Lieutenant of a small outfit and didn't offer to clarify. With her smiles turned to the one man that had the knowledge of her trials - knowledge Sal desperately wanted - the Captain took the hint and excused himself.

Alone, LT reached out for her hand. "So, I didn't catch your name. I'm Blaec." His fingers lightly grazed her knuckles.

"Siana," Sal replied without hesitation. "I'm just laying over for a few days until my carriage comes in. Over in the last fort thing, they told me this was the most comfortable place to get a room. Less crowded, and safer, and oh my, I think I'm rambling!"

"You're fine, Siana," Blaec said, savoring her name. She smiled when he said it.

"I'm also not nearly drunk enough to explain my poor manners." She giggled, feeling strangely shy. "I guess I should be thankful I managed to fall in the lap of a nice looking man. A very pleasant way to break my fall, I must say."

"Well, I'm glad you liked it."

Glancing up, she found his eyes looking gently into hers. She fought the urge to look away.

"You remind me of someone," he said, taking a long, deep breath, "and I can't quite place it. But I'm rather glad you managed to trip on that board. I was trying to convince that Captain that my men wouldn't be any help to him, and he just wasn't taking no for an answer. It seems you have very good timing."

"I dunno," Sal replied. "I'd much rather make a more impressive entrance."

"And throwing yourself at me isn't impressive?"

The conversation continued on like that. Sal flirted with him for the next hour, slowly bringing the topic around to his position. When he refused to take the bait, she pushed the issue.

"So, what does a Lieutenant do anyway?"

"Ah, I just give other people orders."

"And they listen?"

"Well, mine do, but I have some really good men under me." He tried to let the subject die, but her look of excited curiosity convinced him to continue. "My guys are pretty self-sufficient and more like friends than underlings or anything like that. We do a lot of work out in the field with only the eight, er, well seven of us, now."

"Oh, did someone quit?"

"No, not exactly. My second in command died in combat almost a year ago. He served with us for a long time."

"Oh, I'm... I'm so sorry, Blaec, I didn't mean to bring up wounds. I'm sure he was a good man." She reached out for his hand, hearing the pain in his voice.

Sal hadn't thought about why they needed a new soldier in the Blades, and knowing made her feel guilty for trying to use the Lieutenant this way. She found herself wanting to comfort him. It was stupid and wouldn't help her mission, but she still felt it.

"I don't know what to say. Sheesh, I really stuck my foot in that," she went on. "I'm sorry. I just, I don't know much about the military, and the war hasn't really seemed close to us in Merriton."

"No, you're lucky for that," he said. "A lot of good men have been lost in the last year or so, now that Terric is pushing on us. But I'm sure you don't want to listen to me dwell on tactics and treaties."

"It's better than marriages and merchanting, like my mother does!" she replied, trying to lighten the tone.

"Marriages, huh? So I suppose that means you're a single lady traveling across the Conglomerate alone?" His tone was a little too casual.

"I'm supposed to be getting it out of my system. I spent a week in Prin – shopping, I'm embarrassed to say – and all I've learned from it is that I don't seem to like most of the people I've met." She shrugged. "I don't know what that says about me, but there you have it. I feel lost with myself right now, and spending a few days in a working military post sounded like the best offer I'd had all month."

"And has it been worth it?"

"Yeah, I managed to fall into the lap of the nicest man I've met so far." Sal was shocked to realize she meant it.

He'd always been friendly to her, but also impersonal. Now that she knew why they needed a replacement, that distance made more sense. Her mission grew less important while she learned more about Blaec Doll. The loss of his man weighed heavily, and he carried guilt for a fight they'd had. The second in command had disagreed with the Lieutenant's orders, and those orders had resulted in his death, thanks to the incompetence of another unit. Blaec thought that if he'd only listened, the man would still be alive.

"You can't know that," she pointed out. "Even I know how hard this war has been."

Blaec shrugged. "It's just that we've lost so few over the years, and most of those were green recruits." He waved that away. "I'm sorry, I don't mean to dwell on the past."

"It's human nature." Sal mentally cursed herself for the phrase. "We all think about what could have been."

"True. Some days I wish I could be more like the iliri, always looking to the future."

Sal giggled at that. "It's not often you hear someone speak well of them. I take it you're a sympathizer?"

"Very much so." Blaec was watching her face for a reaction.

Sal smiled, letting her relief show. "Good. I was starting to think that everyone in the military hated them."

So he told her about his dream of iliri emancipation, his struggles to bring equality into the military, and the loneliness that came with his position. With each hour that passed, their conversation became more personal. Sal listened, distracted by the needs of the man before her. The Lieutenant buried his own problems so deep that only a stranger could ease the pain.

She pointed out the good he'd done, just from his own stories, and how he truly cared for his men as well as the people of the Conglomerate. Their drinks sat on the table, completely forgotten as this man looked deep into her eyes. So many times, he touched her. Little things, like his fingertip on her knuckles, but she liked it. His skin didn't repulse her. In truth, it was nice. Relaxing almost. But when the pub began to empty, she realized she hadn't learned a thing about her mission but had grown fond of the man before her who tried to protect the world.

"I suppose they're closing," he said, looking around.

She pouted slightly. "I enjoyed being with you too much, it seems. Time has just flown, and I'm not even tired!"

"Well, let me walk you back to your room?" he offered, but the scent of anxiety hit her. Not fear, but something else. Something she rarely had experienced.

"I'd like that very much, Blaec," she decided.

He stood and offered his hand, assisting her to her feet. When she twined her arm in his, he smiled down at her fondly. "I really do feel like I know you, Siana. And you say you haven't been in Fort Landing or Stonewater Stables before?"

"Sorry. I grew up in Merriton." Which was true. She just hadn't grown up as the daughter of a merchant, but rather the slave of one.

"Well, then I'm glad you made it through this way now." He pulled her hand to his lips and kissed it. Warmth rose at his touch; the feeling was not one she was used to.

He escorted her across the outpost, and she flirted unabashedly.

Blaec responded, his touch changing from gentlemanly to familiar, but never impolite. When the lights of the inn lit their path, Sal hesitated. She needed to be learning more about her upcoming trials, but she was enjoying her time with him, even if it was nothing more than a pretense.

He made her feel respected, beautiful, and safe. That had only happened once before in her life, and she wanted it again. The conniving part of her mind said she could easily use this to her advantage. Seducing the Lieutenant would lead to intimacies that might get her the information she wanted.

She'd done this before, but this time it was different. His broad shoulders and muscled chest were alluring. His quick wit made for pleasant talk, and his smile made her heart skip. Her orders were to learn all she could, by any means necessary, so Sal convinced herself she was simply following those orders when she reached up to trace a finger down the line of his throat.

"Would you care to come up and have one last drink, my kind sir?"

He licked his lips, letting his eyes run across her body. For a moment, he said nothing, clearly trying to make up his mind. The scent of desire made her think she had a chance, but the way he shuffled his feet meant she might have to work for it.

Just as Sal was going to flirt a little more, Blaec's lips curled into a gentle smile. "I think I just might take you up on that drink."

Entering the lobby, the matron looked up from her ever-present position behind the counter. Her eyes widened when she saw the soldier Sal had returned with.

"Lieutenant!" she exclaimed. "Can I get you anything?"

"No, Mrs. Heckly, I'm just escorting a lady back to her rooms for the night, to be sure she gets here safely."

"Yes, sir. That's the gentlemanly thing to do, sir," she agreed, turning her face back to her books, but her attention was focused on the couple as they made their way up the stairs.

Keeping quiet until she reached her rooms, Sal opened the door and invited Blaec in. "I take it you have a reputation around here, from the way the woman downstairs reacted. Do you come back to women's rooms on a regular basis?" She laughed as she said it.

"No, quite the opposite, I assure you. Normally I would have one of my men escort a lady across the compound."

"Well, I'm glad you didn't. Can I get you something to drink?" she asked, sauntering across the room.

"I'll get it. You get those boots off your feet before I have to catch you again."

"I don't know, I might like that." She cast a flirtatious glance back at him and gestured toward the small bar, then made her way into her sleeping chamber. Once there, she pulled off her boots and removed the bustle from her skirt, leaving only a short under-skirt and stockings. Feeling almost comfortable, Sal returned to the main room, walked directly to Blaec, and turned her back to him, gesturing to the laces of her corset.

"Can I talk you into untying it?"

"Oh, Siana, um, I can't promise that I'll stop," he said meekly.

"I didn't say I wanted you to." She pulled the pins from her hair and let it fall to her bare shoulders. "I'm sure you know that a drink is rarely just a drink."

His hands trembling, Blaec untied the laces, loosening them carefully. Sal reached behind her back and helped him un-thread them, peeling her tiny waist from the hard leather. She tossed it into a nearby chair then turned to face him. He looked at her in silence for a long moment, before reaching up to her face and running his thumb across her lips. Stepping into the touch, she placed her hands on his chest and gently met his mouth with her own.

"It's ok, Blaec. I want this. I think you do, too." At his nod, she began to unbutton his shirt.

Locking her mind away, she traced the lines of his hairless chest. When her hands touched his skin, his inhibitions left. He wrapped one arm around her and pulled her close, his tongue diving through her teeth. When she returned the kiss with as much interest, he swept her off her feet, into his arms, and headed straight for the bed.

CHAPTER FOURTEEN

False dawn cast a weak glow at the edge of the curtains, the morning not far off. The pale light was the only illumination in the room. Sal lay awake and satisfied in the bed, Blaec beside her, tracing lines on her bronze stomach with one hand. His other twined with hers while they both caught their breath. She turned her head to look at him, smiling gently when his soft eyes met hers.

"Tell me a secret, Siana," he begged, his gaze refusing to drop.

She glanced away, thinking of something she could share and not make herself feel any more guilty. "I didn't tell you the complete truth about myself, but I didn't exactly lie to you either," she said. "I just made the facts sound a bit better to impress you."

"I think we all do that, so that's not a very good secret. Try again, my dear."

"Ok..." She paused to think before answering. "How about this? I won't be able to tell anyone about you because they wouldn't understand?"

"And why is that?"

"Because spending such a wonderful night with some soldier

isn't what girls like me are expected to do. I do plan to treasure this memory." The words were as true as she could make them, aware that he'd smell a lie. "What about you, Blaec? Tell me a secret?"

"Ah, my secret is that I have to be in a meeting in an hour, and I should have been sleeping all night instead of spending it with you."

"Now see, that isn't a very good secret!" She giggled and flung a pillow at his chest, causing him to laugh at her. "Try again."

"Ok, ok. Let's see, I'm the commanding officer of the Black Blades, have you heard of them?"

"Oh, yeah. I think everyone has. That's you?" She widened her eyes in false surprise.

"Yeah, that's my unit. We're in the middle of recruitment, and I was supposed to finalize the details of my last test tonight, but for the first time in a long time, I seem to be biased toward the soldier I want to pass."

"Is that a bad thing?"

He let out a deep sigh. "I don't know if it is or not, but I've been unable to sleep for days, hoping that I make the right decision and that my trial is fair. My men deserve this recruit, and they seem to have already accepted her as one of their own."

"Her?" she asked, surprised he meant her. "Are they just trying to have a cute girl around or something? Is that why you're so worried?"

"No, it's nothing like that. She's an iliri, and while she's exotic and, yes, they find her attractive, she also just fits in with us. I don't know, I think it's that she cares about what we do rather than how much a position with the Black Blades would impress others."

He was wrong, but had just turned the conversation toward the information she needed. She wanted to ask more about the men thinking she was attractive, but he was confiding in her and seeking her opinion. She couldn't let the chance slip by.

"So, is she better than the others that you have to, I dunno, choose, or whatever?"

"I think so. While the others have more experience in combat, the girl is more skilled, and she seems willing to stand up for what she believes in. That's really why we take the risks we do, because no one else will."

"So why don't you just pick her?" Sal tried to feign ignorance.

"Well, it's a trial. I have to make a test that's complicated enough for only one of them to pass, but I have three trying out. The first is a long shot, and I'm pretty sure he doesn't have the mind to lead my men. The other guy? Well, he's good, but he's all about what's in it for him and the respect he'll gain as an elite soldier – bragging rights, you know, that sort of thing. The girl? She wants to make a difference, I think. The respect sure won't hurt, but she has a heart about her the others don't. No matter how many people try to crush her, she still gives back more than is asked. Not many people are like that."

Maybe he wasn't wrong, and it sounded like her chances were better than she thought. Besides, having the Lieutenant on her side certainly wouldn't hurt. Sal knew that if she pushed, he'd break down and explain.

"Ok, so why can't you just pick her? You're the one in charge, aren't you?"

"I am." He lifted a hand to rub at his brow. "But I also have to make sure there's no way for Command to prevent her transfer to my unit. A fair trial does that. She's pure iliri, you see."

"Ok, so then just make the trial one where combat experience doesn't count but saving others does?" Sal was thinking about the information the stablehand had given her the day before.

"Siana," Blaec said, "that's not a bad idea!" He sat up in the bed, staring at the light sneaking in the edge of the curtains, his mind obviously working out the details.

She continued, "So, I don't know, create a situation where they can either 'win' the test, or save people that don't seem to be related? Let the winner be the one that gives up on the test in order to do what a soldier should really do?"

He glanced at her, smiling, then leaned over to kiss her. "That's it, exactly. I can make that change easily with the mission I had planned and just make the cavalry charge through an area that'll end up running across 'civilians' played by some cadets. The best soldier for the Blades will sacrifice me in order to save our people."

He pinned her to the bed, kissing her deeply before pulling himself to his feet. "Sadly, I have to go, my dear. I have a meeting with a few Captains to finish planning this. With your new idea, I also need to run it past my men, to make sure they'd be happy with that as a trial for their next partner. When are you leaving? I would love to be more of a gentleman and buy you lunch at least." He left the offer hanging, sadness creeping into his eyes.

"I honestly don't know, Blaec. I'm supposed to check with the carriages and get today's schedule. I have to make it to Eastward before the one to Merriton departs."

He looked torn. She could see his duty called him, yet he didn't want to leave. "Siana..." he started. "I never meant to go this far."

"I know, Blaec. I'm glad it did. I got this chance, and I'll treasure the memories of you. Who knows, maybe we'll run into each other again?"

"At least leave me a way to get in touch with you?"

"If I don't see you at lunch, I'll leave something for you at the desk here. I'd love to have more time with you. You're a good man – sexy, brilliant, and with a caring heart. Nothing about you is self-centered, and you're nothing like I expected from an officer in the military." She spoke the truth. Sal had always wished to meet a man like him, and here she was, with a taste of something impossible. "You and I both know this can't be something permanent, but that doesn't mean I didn't enjoy it. I refuse to be sad about this. If a memory of you is all I get, then that's what it is." She smiled up at him. "Now get out of here before you're late."

"I..." Blaec shoved one hand deep into his hair. "Siana, I don't want you to think this didn't mean anything to me."

Sal shook her head. "No, Blaec. I think tonight meant more to you than you're willing to admit." She grabbed his arm and pulled him to her. "You almost make me feel like I took advantage of you. I swear this meant more to me than you can ever know, ok? Now get to work, sir."

The Lieutenant kissed her once more, then walked out of the room without looking back. Sal refused to open her thoughts to him, treasuring what she had, knowing the Lieutenant needed to think of his night with her as a sweet memory, not a breach of military protocol. She sighed and slipped deeper into the bed, convincing her body that she needed sleep. While her mind drifted away, she couldn't help but wonder how she'd keep this secret from the men she planned to share the rest of her life with.

Blaec made his way toward the inn. All morning, his memories of the night before had flashed through his head, making it hard to concentrate. As soon as they smelled him, his men knew where he'd spent his night. Naturally, there was teasing, but gently, and not as much as he'd expected. Mostly, they encouraged him to see her again before she left.

They also liked the new plan – which he presented as his own – for finding the right soldier for their unit. The idea of sacrificing their officer in order to save civilians was brilliant, and he had Siana to thank for that. Her idea solved all the problems he'd been worried about, and neither of the two men would be willing to risk failing their trial, even if it meant saving the lives of innocent people. Sal, he thought, would understand what she had to do.

When he entered the lobby of the inn, the matron was there, like always. "Lieutenant," she said calmly, looking at him like a mother. "I have a package for you, sir."

He nodded and waited while she walked into the back room. When she returned, she carried a small box no bigger than her hand and passed it across the counter to him.

"I take it she's left." He looked down at the box, his world feeling like it had just fallen out from under him.

"Yes, sir. She asked me to give this to you. Her carriage left over an hour ago now."

Blaec's shoulders sagged. He'd been so sure he'd catch her. There had been so much he planned to say. With a heavy heart, he accepted the small box from Mrs. Heckly.

"I'm sure you'll meet someone better, sir." She patted his arm. "Women like her are like iliri, Lieutenant. Always looking for what interests them now. You deserve better."

"That's not how iliri are," he whispered to himself, stroking the lip of the box.

Looking up, he nodded and thanked her, then tucked the package safely in his pocket before heading back to his own cabin. It had taken him most of the day to realize why she felt so familiar, and only a stray comment from Cyno about Sal made him realize what it was. Both had an easy laugh, both had a quiet self-confidence that he respected. They even smelled similar. Blaec couldn't help but wonder if Siana knew she had iliri ancestry.

Granted, Blaec hadn't been involved with a woman for years. The few times he found one that interested him, work got in the way. The Blades were an integral part of who he was. He and his men fought for more than just a paycheck. Usually, the ladies he met were just too human. They couldn't understand that the war wouldn't stop because he took a day off. They couldn't wrap their minds around why he was dedicated to this lifestyle. None of them could fathom the bond he had with his men – Blaec thought of them as his family, not just a military unit.

Siana, though, had accepted that and never once hinted at him doing anything else to be with her. While it was only one night, he felt connected to her in a way that he couldn't describe. He'd secretly hoped she would decide to stay at the stables or travel to whatever base he was stationed at next. It was impossible, and he couldn't see a future where they were together, but deep in his heart, he'd hoped.

Treading slowly back to his rooms, he thought about how he'd planned to tell her that her idea had been the answer he needed, and how he would have thanked her. Blaec had hoped for a quiet dinner. Some place to speak openly with her, without his men interrupting, even if they were always in his head. A chance to see if the pair of them could become more.

Now, he would never get to know her better, and his chances of finding his way to Merriton were slim. He could write to her, or maybe send a gift, but why? He told himself that in time, he would forget her and everything would be back to normal, but he doubted it. She'd smelled like perfection.

When he reached his cabin, he pinned the lock and pulled the box from his coat. He expected to find a lengthy letter in it, possibly even one that told him she couldn't talk to him again and had only wanted a single night. To his surprise, the package had a small item wrapped in soft papers. Carefully withdrawing the layers, he found himself holding a necklace. Not the necklace she'd worn the night before, but a large opal set on a black resin chain. Searching through the papers, hoping for an explanation, he found a note scrawled on the innermost layer in an elegant hand.

No one can let you down if you haven't been leaning on them.
Maybe it's time to start leaning.

CHAPTER FIFTEEN

Two days later, six men stood before Sal in full black battle armor. Her own was dark blue and had been assembled from spare pieces and barely fit, since administrators rarely requisitioned armor. Blaec – LT, she reminded herself – said it wouldn't be worth having a custom suit made. Either she would get a black set or return to her duties behind a desk. Sal tugged at the oversized chest piece again and began giving orders to "her" men.

"We have information that the Lieutenant has been taken captive and is being held at the bend in Stonewater Creek. The enemies are thought to be mounted, but their other assets are not known," she announced. The Blades had already performed this mission twice before with the other candidates, so they knew this.

"Arctic, can you reach his mind?" she asked, breaking protocol from the start.

"I cannot." His smile showed the answer was a part of the ruse.

"Then we must assume that he is unconscious, correct?"

"Yes, that's the –" He smirked, and she knew the Lieutenant was talking in his head. "– feeling I get from him."

"Then, Razor, can you find him or his body?" She turned to the dark man.

"Yes, I have a direct bearing on him. It seems to point in the general area claimed."

She looked at the rest of her men and ran her mind over the orders one more time. "Do we have any weapons left or taken when they captured LT?" She was hoping for a long shot.

"If we did?" Arctic asked.

"Then I'd ask Cyno to see if he can get anything that would help us understand who took him and what their plan was."

Arctic paused for a moment, then nodded at Cyno.

"Yeh, let's say I had one, an' that I can get..." Cyno shrugged. "I'm na so good at this role-playing," he grumbled. "Yeh, I held a weapon, an' it gave me an impression of a force trying ta breach the border of the Conglomerate. I get a feel of 'bout twenty-five men. The one who dropped the weapon was mounted, but na all are."

"Good enough, Cyno. And you just told me what I needed. There are more of them than us. Ok, guys, let's mount up. I'm the weakest rider, so I'll follow the path picked by Razor. I want to come around them from the side and spiral in. Arctic, you and Risk at the back, keep a few paces between us to give you room for a clear shot in case an ambush catches us. Once we're close enough, communications will be silent, so Arctic, keep the link up."

The men nodded, and Shift led her over to the gentle palfrey assigned to her for this mission. With their newly picked horses awaiting training, the recruits had been issued the use of a standard transport mount while the Blades used their own horses. Shift gave her a leg into the saddle, and she checked to make sure her concept of the commands were correct. While the other men mounted, Sal moved her horse around the staging area, asking it to stop, back, and turn a few times until she was sure she wouldn't hinder their efforts with her riding. When she had control, she nodded to Razor.

Ok, let's go find him, she thought. As one, they moved toward the creek, Zep falling in behind her.

Their horses trudged through the underbrush, stepping down hills and over trees. The Blades moved in near silence, the sound of their mounts no more distracting than the wildlife in the area. A few minutes in, she could tell their path spiraled like she'd ordered. When the sound of water trickled through the brush, she reached out to their minds again.

Razor, can you find something vague? she asked, the thought leaping into her mind.

Depends how vague, I suppose.

Are there men hiding near us? Sentries, archers, anything like that?

He looked over his shoulder, meeting her eyes, and smiled. His expression gave the answer away while she felt him check with the Lieutenant. *I feel like there's men in the trees.* He pointed up casually, and Sal looked for the soldiers she knew would be waiting.

Arctic, Risk, peel off and check for archers and snipers. Take out any you can, as quietly as possible.

The men nodded and reined their horses to the side, both pulling padded training arrows from their saddles and stringing their bows. Sal, and the four men with her, continued on. A kilometer farther, she saw a break in the trees, and Razor called a halt.

LT's about two hundred meters ahead of us. He's stationary, he thought.

Shift, see what you can. Do not give us away. Cyno, Razor, Zep, hold here until we get a better idea of the weapons we'll be up against.

Shift slipped off his horse and passed through the brush silently. The wait seemed to be endless before they heard him in their heads again. *I have ten men here, heavy armor, swords and shields. There's a lot of hoof prints, and I think there's probably cavalry close enough that we need to be concerned by it.*

Sal pulled her mind close, locking the others out, and wondered where the civilians would be. Blaec wouldn't make it easy, or obvious. In theory, this would be a group of enemy soldiers that had breached their border and were hiding out. They would have patrols and be overly aggressive with any civilians who spotted them, knowing one set of eyes would lead to more.

Guys, what's in this area besides the stables? she asked.

Not much, Sal, Shift told her. *We have the pastures a few klicks over, and this area is often used for training the military, the medical units, and such. Why?*

Is there any place they could be holing up? If they're a military incursion force, then wouldn't they want something more defensible than a creek bed? If they breached the border like Cyno suggested, then they have bigger plans than just capturing our leader, right?

She felt, rather than heard, the approval of the men in her head.

Zep spoke up. *I think there's some caves up the way a bit, might be they dug in there?*

Where? She asked, and he responded with a gesture to the north of them, on the other side of where the Lieutenant was supposedly being held.

Ok. Razor, any change on LT?

None.

Then you, Zep, and Shift make your way across the creek here, she directed. *Come at the camp – quietly mind you – from the other side. Pick off as many men as you can without alerting them, but watch your back for those extras. Cyno and I will start the same from here. Mounted or on foot, your choice. We're outnumbered two to one, so make it count. I don't care who gets to LT first, just get him out. Arctic, Risk, how's it going with the archers?*

We took out four so far. Looks like there might be a couple more up your way, Risk thought back.

Ok. Guys, keep your eyes up. These are probably snipers, so don't give them anything to see. I need you, Risk and Arctic, to cover our escape. Once we're engaged with the enemy, take out as many as you can, as fast as you can. You guys know what to do. Let's go.

They sent their agreement and faded into the brush like whispers. Sal slipped off her horse, surprised to see Cyno do the same. Together, they crept closer to the enemy, breaking apart and circling in opposite directions. Her heart hammered in her chest, and she resisted the urge to mentally check on the men she was responsible for. Until now, the mission felt theoretical but hearing voices so close, the real test was upon her.

Too soon, a man in royal blue walked only feet from where she crouched in the dense brush. She quickly checked her surroundings and, finding no one else near, reached out an arm to pull the man's feet out from under him. Calling on her iliri-born speed, she slapped her hand over his mouth before he hit the ground and touched her practice blade to his throat, making a slashing motion. The cadet, eyes wide in shock, nodded, accepting his "death." She crawled a few paces further to the right and saw a path into the clearing. Watching, she could just make out shadows crossing at the end. That meant more soldiers.

She avoided the path, instead choosing to keep to the underbrush, her ears working overtime. At the edge of the clearing, she could see the Lieutenant "tied" to a chair in clear view. The situation was amazingly cliché.

Before moving, she reached out with her mind to check the locations of "her" Blades. She could feel Cyno across from her. Shift, Zep, and Razor had nearly reached the opposite side of the clearing.

What's the status of the snipers? she asked.

Gone, Arctic assured her.

I think there's one left, Risk added, *but can't be sure.* He sent her an image of odd leaves above them.

She looked up and understood what he meant. A grouping of leaves was just a bit too dense for their location in that tree. *Arctic, keep an eye on that. When we make our move, toss an arrow in it just to be sure, then grab our mounts,* she sent a mental image of where they'd been left, *and head in here. We'll want to make a quick exit. If they have heavy cavalry, there's no way we'll stand up to that. Our best chance will be to grab LT and get out.*

The men sent her their agreement and understanding. Sal had

been keeping an eye on the clearing and could only count four enemies. They were beginning to look restless, since their fellow soldiers weren't returning. She assumed they knew an attack was coming but not what would happen. Before she could call a rush, Zep broke into her mind.

I'm still mounted, Sal, he thought. *From where Cessa and I are, we can take out most of them before you could even get close.*

Do it, Zep. Then grab LT and get out of here.

This mission should have a catch to it, but so far it seemed simple and straightforward. Zep spurred his horse, and the dark beast announced her charge with crashing branches. The "enemy" soldiers turned to the new threat in unison. Sal took the chance and darted forward, "stabbing" one in the back. The woman's nod was all Sal needed before moving toward the Lieutenant, while Zep "killed" those remaining. Cyno reached LT first and began "untying" the ropes.

His mind still blank to them, LT said, "I'm unconscious," and nothing more.

"Cyno, hand him up to Zep. If he happens to help in his unconscious state, fine, if not, haul his ass over the saddle," she ordered.

Cyno grinned and threatened to do like he was told before LT accepted Zep's hand and swung into a seat behind him.

Your horse is carrying double, Zep. Head back, but keep your mind open. We'll be right behind you.

Gotcha, don't take too long, Zep thought back, as Sal heard more horses heading to them.

She expected Arctic and Risk to be bringing in their own mounts, but the sounds didn't match their mental locations. That was all the warning she needed. *INCOMING!* she screamed into their minds.

The Blades scurried in different directions for cover, and Sal shot a thought at Arctic to get the horses to Cyno. She ducked and dodged between branches, trying to become invisible. Her heart pounded in her throat. They'd pass nearly right on top of her.

Guys, get back, get safe. I'm in a bad spot, she thought. *Arctic, take lead and regroup.*

Sal, Arctic sent, *you only pass if you make it back.*

I'll make it back, don't worry, but I'm not losing any of you on my first mission. I still have some tricks to use.

His understanding filled her mind before he directed the men out of the clearing toward a meeting point. He sent the location, and it tasted of hope.

Her navy armor gave her the benefit of blending into the forest shadows, but her hair and skin would draw the eye as soon as any horseman got close. Sal quickly thought of herself with skin of bark and hair of leaves while she ducked into a cluster of bushes at the base of two large trees, unsure if her camouflage would work. Glancing up from her cover, the first horse darted past, the rider never looking in her direction. Behind him followed two full squads, mounted and dressed like heavy cavalry. She sent the images to Arctic, updating him on the next wave they faced.

With the horses behind her, Sal began to creep forward, careful to avoid making any noise that would alert them to her location. She tried to slow her breathing, but her heart pounded so hard they had to hear it. Behind her, the cavalry officer bellowed his orders.

"I need one scout in each direction. You have two minutes to find me a track and report back. I have fifteen krits riding on the outcome of this mission, boys. Don't let me down. There's a round at the pub for each of you if we win!"

She ducked behind another tree and checked her hands to be sure she'd reverted to her pale self. Listening closely, she could make out a horse off to her right, heading in the general direction of their meeting place.

We've got scouts coming in. Heads up, men.

I got him. Shift sent back with a vision of a pike against his knee.

I'm just behind him, she explained, *but we only have two minutes to get clear before the cav comes looking.*

She raced through the forest as fast as she could, checking to be sure she wouldn't be seen by either the scout or the cavalry behind her. The forest fled under her feet, and she tried to keep her ears open as she darted toward their assigned meeting place. Just before her, a flash of red glinted in the sunlight: Shift on his bay, charging the scout. She reached them just as Shift knocked the boy from his saddle. With a grunt, the kid hit hard, and Sal pounced on him.

With her dagger at his throat, she asked, "Are you hurt?"

"No, sir, not any more than usual, but I agree I am dead."

She nodded and glanced up at the sound of Shift dismounting.

"Sal, take Boo. I'll grab the kid's horse – don't worry, soldier, I'll get her back to you in one piece." From the ground, the soldier nodded, and Shift tossed Sal's small form into the saddle. "Just hang on. He'll follow the rest for the most part."

Boo was larger than the palfrey she'd started with. He also moved with a power that intimidated her, but Sal grabbed a handful of mane and squeezed him forward, following Shift. They cantered into the clearing as the Blades heard Zep's cry.

I have pursuit!

Go, go! Sal told her men. While they raced after Zep's retreat, she shot orders at them. They needed to flank the enemy, harrying them to pull attention from Zep and his laden mare. On their faster horses, the Blades quickly caught up to the heavily armored cavalry. The extra armor slowed their mounts, just like Zep's second rider slowed his. She could just see the brown mare, dark with sweat, running flat out.

Sal clung to the horse beneath her with all her might. Every other stride, she feared she'd lose a stirrup. Both of her hands were woven into the gelding's mane, and she hoped Boo would just follow his herd-mates without losing her.

That was when she finally saw the supposed civilians. To their left, a group of medical students was being herded back to the creek

area by a second unit of mounted troops. Most of them were women, but a few men were mixed in. Zep and the Lieutenant were headed back to the staging area, what the mission considered "safe territory," but it lay in the opposite direction of the civilians. This was her choice, the idea she'd given Blaec a few nights before.

Zep, you're on your own, she sent. *Can you make it without us?*

I don't think so. They're gaining, and Cessa is blowing hard.

Try, Zep. You have to try, she thought before sending to them all, *Civilians to the left. We have to get them free.*

Sal, Arctic sent, *your mission is to rescue LT.*

I know, but this has to be a part of it too! Doing the impossible, isn't that what you're famous for? She pulled up Boo and reined him toward the medics, her mind racing.

Any of you with pikes, I need you to break up their formation. Cyno, do whatever it is you do, and archers, pick them off before we get there. Do not hurt the medics.

She had no idea what *she* would do. Pushing Boo toward the mounted soldiers, she watched them circle the knot of medics. Sal had never fought on horseback, but she'd be damned if she'd claim her lack of experience as a reason to give orders from the sideline. Falling in just behind the Blades, she knew she could do more from the ground, so pulled the gelding up and looked back at Shift's pack of wooden training weapons. Grabbing a pair of swords, she slipped down Boo's side, barely staying on her feet when she hit the ground.

Then Sal rushed toward the mounted men. She kept the link in her mind open to feel the positions of the Blades, and moved in the opposite direction. Screaming loudly as she came up before a horse, she caused the high-spirited beast to spook, then yanked the rider from the saddle when he lost his balance. A sword point to his throat made him nod in surrender.

She moved toward the next, who waited for her, and parried a pike blow. The man wheeled his horse. Again, she tried to scream and flail, but this rider had more skill. His horse ducked, the rider flowing with its movement as though made of water. He pushed the animal back toward Sal, the intent to run her over clear in his scowl.

She snarled and smacked the horse across the cannon bone with the flat of her wooden blade, then tried to dodge when the beast reacted. It reared, the injured leg catching Sal in the shoulder and jaw, making her head spin. She dropped to her knees and kept rolling, struggling to find her feet. A flash of black caught her eye as Cyno dove from his saddle, pulling her attacker to the ground, defeating him. He lifted his head and smiled like a pleased animal.

Looking around, the heavy cavalry had been "slaughtered." The soldiers sat on the ground or held their swords out in an obvious symbol of having been incapacitated.

Zep? she sent, in her heart knowing that by calling off the Blades there was no way he could have outpaced the men chasing him. She needed to hear it, though.

Seems Cessa had a little more speed in her after all, girly. He laughed in her head. *But you're gonna have to help me walk her out when you get back here. Poor mare's nostrils are about the size of your eyes. You did it, Sal! You did it.*

She heard what he said, but it took a moment before the news sank in. Not only had she passed the most critical test, but she'd also succeeded at the mission! She looked around at the grinning faces of the Black Blades. A few medics wandered among them, checking the "casualties" for actual injuries while all around her, men stood tired and covered in sweat. Her weapons forgotten in her hands, she stared, dazed, realizing what this meant.

She had passed the trials. She *would* be a Black Blade.

CHAPTER SIXTEEN

All total, they'd "killed" thirty-one men: ten infantry at the creek bed, five snipers in the trees, four light cavalry, and the twelve heavy cavalry cadets with the medical students. No participants had been seriously injured, and the bruise to Sal's face was one of the worst of the training mission. The Blades made a fuss over her – Zep even let her out of her promise to help walk his horse out. In the end, the last trial of the Black Blades was considered to be a success by all, except those who hadn't passed it.

The veteran had led the Blades right into the snipers, counting on their combat abilities to overcome anything in their way, never thinking of distance weapons. He'd been politely dismissed with a recommendation to an infantry based outfit. Doron Passel had fared a bit better. He'd armed Shift and Risk with bows then became distraught when Shift's aim had been as poor as he claimed. Zep and Razor had been "taken out" by snipers before Passel adjusted and rescued the Lieutenant himself. When the Calvary gave chase, he ordered the Blades to cover him, leaving the medics behind without a second thought, losing the entire force before he got even halfway to the safe zone. Mounted on the slower palfrey, he never stood a chance of outrunning the fleet rouncies the cavalry used.

The Blades had shared their perspectives of the previous missions with her, and now, standing before the Lieutenant's door, she waited anxiously to be invited in. The latch finally clicked open, and Passel walked out, a blank expression on his face. Beyond him, she could see the entire outfit clustered around the Lieutenant's desk before the door closed.

"It's a good recommendation for me, Luxx," Passel said, pasting on something that resembled a smile. "I really thought this time would work out, but LT assures me I'll have elite forces seeking me out with the recommendation he's going to write."

"I'm sorry, Passel, but you'll make the next one. We both know it."

"I think so, too. I heard you did well. Congratulations." He tried to smile again, but Sal could hear his disappointment.

"Thank you. I appreciate it. Good luck to you, sir."

He nodded at her then made his way back toward his cabin, most likely to begin packing.

She took a deep breath and released it, unsure of what came next. Lifting her bruised chin, all she could do was walk in the door, giving her pale eyes a second to adjust to the dimly lit room. The Blades crowded the space, the Lieutenant seated behind his desk, all in their full black uniforms. He gestured for her to take a seat.

"Private Salryc Luxx," he began, "you not only completed the mission you were given, but you also adapted and passed the final trial. Perfectly, I might add. Your total score, out of a possible one thousand points, was nine hundred eighty-seven. To date, this is the best score ever given to a recruit for the Black Blades."

Sal's eyes widened. She thought she was doing well, but she'd had no idea of her score, until now.

The Lieutenant continued. "I would like to formally offer you a position with the Black Blades. Will you accept?"

"I would be honored, sir," she replied, her stomach in knots.

Beside her, Arctic stood and made his way to her side. She glanced up at him as he reached down for her collar. With one hand on the underside, he opened the other, showing her a pin in the shape of a pair of swords crossed into an X, made of some dark stone. With a quick glance into her eyes, he secured it and stepped back. Around her, the men grinned.

Shift winked at her. "You're one of us now, sister."

"Yeah, but I can't look at her and think 'sister,'" Zep joked.

Glancing over to the Lieutenant, Sal could see sadness in his eyes. Her position with the Blades replaced that of a man he'd been very close to. He smiled at her, letting the men offer her a drink and fill her with congratulations, but she noticed that his fingers played with the chain of her necklace. The large opal was the color of her own iliri eyes, and she wondered what would happen when he grasped the meaning. She didn't dare let her gaze linger too long.

Looking around the room, she saw Zep and Cyno leaning casually against the far wall. Zep smiled at her openly, but Cyno cocked his head slightly, glancing from the Lieutenant's hands back to Sal. When he realized she was watching him, Cyno met her gaze with no trace of emotion on his face. He took a long, deep breath, and Sal realized that he knew.

Pushing her concerns away, she tried to enjoy the moment. She'd achieved what she'd dedicated her life to. As a Black Blade, she was *someone*, not just another iliri to be pushed around. She was supposed to be thrilled, not nervous.

But the Lieutenant's mood cut the celebration short. After only a few drinks, Sal was directed to see Shift to have her bruised face healed then begin packing her old uniforms. Training started the next morning.

When she returned to her rooms, a new uniform in the style of the Black Blades was waiting on her bed. The black was stark against her skin, but she liked the look. Shift had come and gone, her bruises now faded to little more than a memory, and he warned that the next morning would be the start of her new life. Her old uniforms were now stored in the regulation bag all common soldiers were issued.

All that remained in her closets were the clothes the Blades had purchased for her and the outfits she had for Siana, almost as if her old life had never happened. It seemed like she'd been here forever, but counting back, only a little over a week had passed. Would she miss the blue she'd grown accustomed to over so many years or would black become like a second skin?

A soft tap at her door pulled her thoughts to the present. Without checking for a mental signature, she unpinned the latch, finding herself face to face with the Lieutenant.

"May I?" he asked politely.

After a stunned pause, she said, "Come in, sir," and moved aside for him.

"I have a few other things to go over with you, and I figured you wouldn't want it to be public knowledge."

She nodded, unsure of what to say.

"I was just looking through your file and saw that you're listed as a Private, First Class. Is that right?" His eyes glinted mischievously.

"Yes, sir, it is."

"Well, as your commanding officer, I'm authorized to raise your rank to that which I see more fitting. I believe we'll jump right up to Corporal if that suits you?"

"Uh," she stammered, "sir? That's three ranks! I'd hoped to be raised to Specialist, with Lance Corporal by the end of the year. Wow... why, though?"

"Well, you have what it takes. Not only did you figure out my little test, but you also put the right men in the right places for this mission rather than trying to get as many accolades as possible. To me, that says you have the ability to lead, and in our unit, we often end up giving orders to the regular military. A Corporal isn't someone that people choose to ignore. Basically, it just makes my life easier, and I think you honestly deserve it."

"Thank you, sir! I don't know what to say, but... yeah... thank you!" The words tumbled out of her mouth.

"And here's a form outlining your wage schedule." He passed her a folded piece of paper. "As an elite soldier you get hazard pay on top of your rank wages."

She opened the page and saw a number four times what she'd been earning. Scanning down, she realized that was before the hazard pay bonus. Due to her promotion and service in the elite forces, her weekly pay would now exceed what she'd previously made in a month. Sal stared at the numbers for a moment, unable to wrap her mind around them.

"I also noticed," LT said, "that your wages were on the lower end of your rank scale while at your last station. This is common with iliri and iliri crossbreds. Having suffered it myself, I decided to fix that for you."

She glanced up at him, and all she could do was share her feelings. A line of her amazement and gratitude swept over him, and the Lieutenant nodded to let her know he understood. "Look, Sal, I also have to address something with you. It's sensitive, so please tell me if I'm out of line."

"Yes, sir."

"I've never had a woman in my unit before. You know we work closely together and often spend quite a lot of time in the field, right?"

"Yes, sir, I do. That's why I wanted to join the Blades so badly."

"Well, I need to know your thoughts on relationships within the unit." He sat down in the one chair the room held, gesturing for Sal to take the bed next to him.

"I'm not sure I'm following you."

"I assume you are attracted to men? If not, that does make this easier."

"Sorry, LT." She tried out the more casual form of his name. "I do like men."

"Ok, so what happens when you end up in bed with one of them?" he asked. "I'm not really sure how to be polite about this, but you and I do need to know. I mean, they're men, and they have been trying to get your attention. I can't tell you not to take them up on it – and Sal, I *wouldn't* do that – I just need to know what happens when someone gets jealous or upset."

"Sir, I'm iliri. Casual sex is about the best I can hope to get. I'd like to say that it won't be a problem, but I hope to serve with you for a few years at least. They may see me as safer than another woman, and at times I may be. It's just how it is in a unit."

"I know. That's why I had to ask. Do you think you can keep it from causing a rift in the Blades?"

"I honestly do. A few minutes ago, I would have said that my rank made it unlikely to be a concern, but since you just granted me a commission with the promotion, the regulations against it are mostly gone. That doesn't change the fact that I'm still iliri. Men don't really look for long-term relationships with my kind."

He paused, cocking his head slightly. "You haven't realized yet that all of the Blades, except Zep, are iliri?"

"Crossbreds, yeah."

"The Black Blades excel *because* we're iliri, Sal."

That wasn't what she'd expected him to say. "I understand, sir."

"Sal," he tried, pausing. "I don't think you do. I'm saying this not as your commanding officer, but as an iliri. You need to understand that not all men think the same. We don't all want dark skins and dull teeth." He ducked his head and smiled at the ground. "I know you find it hard to believe, but quite a few of the Blades find you attractive. They prefer your white skin and iliri traits to those of humans because you're our own kind. It doesn't often work the other way around."

Sal looked away, embarrassed, but the words made her smile. "Sir, I've never had men interested in me. Not like that." She shrugged. "I guess you'll just have to trust me."

"I do trust you. That's why we accepted you. It's been a long time since I've been impressed by a recruit."

"I swear to you, sir, I'm more interested in being a good soldier than in finding a mate. I won't let my gender disrupt your unit."

"Our unit, Corporal. Just so long as we're on the same page. I'm sorry to have brought it up at all." The Lieutenant eased himself up, the awkward conversation over.

He turned to leave, but stopped suddenly. Following his gaze, she saw her wardrobe standing open, the copper and green dress she'd worn as Siana hanging in plain sight. He had to recognize it! Panic welled up as she tried to think of a way to explain it – a lie to stop what she knew was coming.

"Is that yours?" LT asked too carefully.

Too late. "It is." She stood, her ears dropping in shame.

He peered deep into her eyes for a moment, his body stiff, the scent of fear trickling off him. Looking down, he pulled his hand from his pocket and examined it. When his fingers opened, she saw the opal clenched in his fist.

"Where are you from, Sal?"

"Merriton. I was the slave of a merchant."

Before she could blink, he closed the space between them, his expression unreadable. She stepped back until she hit the wall, and he followed. The man had just become a predator, and she could feel the change. When his face was mere inches from her own, he stopped, but no trace of emotion was visible. Her heart hammered in her chest, and her stomach coiled.

This was not how it was supposed to happen! She wanted him to know, but he'd given her so much. Sal had assumed that one day she'd be able to tell him how she'd passed her trials, long after any of it mattered. Not now. Not when the emotions were still so raw. The last thing she wanted was to be the one to betray him.

"How?" he whispered, his lip lifting to show his teeth in an iliri snarl.

"The iliri have abilities, sir, and I found mine. I seem to be able to change. I can take on the form I need at the time."

"So you decided to infiltrate me?" he asked, neither amused nor angry. He simply asked.

"Not exactly. I tripped. That was honest. I'd been looking for the others and found myself face first in your lap. I tried to excuse myself a few times but never quite could." She kept her sentences short, just simple explanations. "I found myself losing sight of my mission a few times, and the hours slipped away from me."

"Me, too," he whispered, his eyes flicking to the ground while his mind replayed the memories.

"When I invited you to my room, I tried to convince myself that my orders made me do it, sir, but that's a lie. I invited you to my room because I hoped that you'd take longer to figure it out." She took a deep breath, then blurted, "I know I was out of line, and that as an iliri I had no right to do that, but," she paused, needing to force out the words, "I couldn't stop myself."

It was true. It was all true, and she knew he could smell it. Dangling between them was an unspoken question: was she the only one to feel something that night? His answer was to lean in and press his mouth softly into hers.

Just a gentle and sweet kiss, nothing more. She relaxed into his touch, feeling his skin, then it was over, teasing her. A muffled complaint came from the back of her throat as he pulled away. Looking up, she met pale green eyes. Then she felt it.

A line of thought entered her mind, determined. Rather than fighting him, she opened up, waiting for him to grab her memory of their night together.

"I can't find it," he said.

"Here." She guided him to the dark corner where she'd hidden it. His mind only tasted the surface before he broke off.

"It really was you?" he asked.

Timidly, she nodded.

Again, he pulled her against him. This time, Sal let her mouth submit to his, and she savored the taste of him. His tongue caressed hers, ignoring the danger of her teeth, and Blaec kissed her as deeply as he had that night when she was Siana. Sal wanted this. She tried to pull him closer, but he was too tense. When her hand found the side of his face, Blaec shied away, breaking the contact.

"This can't happen, you know." He made it a statement, but she still answered.

"I know, sir." Their eyes met for a long time before Sal realized it must be said. "Sir, if you want me to refuse the outfit, I still can. The paperwork hasn't been processed. I can find an excuse the men will believe."

"It wouldn't change anything between us, Sal."

"I know, but it might make life easier for you. I betrayed you, and you don't need to be reminded of that each time you turn around."

"No one can let you down if you haven't been leaning on them," he quoted. "You were right. And you did not betray me. Siana made it clear that she wouldn't be around long. She told me blatantly that our relationship couldn't continue. I accepted that when I agreed to come up to her – your – room. This has changed something between us, but I doubt it's what you'd expect."

She waited for him to continue, feeling his mood lighten as he came to his decision.

"Sal, I'm not used to people getting one over on me. You not only did that, but you also followed my orders to the letter *and* the spirit. You learned about our secret trial, then you encouraged me to change it in a way that made both of us happy. You kept this secret hidden, and you showed no sign of what we shared. All of this while you managed to complete the tasks I gave you, found an ability that is beyond priceless to our type of outfit, and on top of that, you eased the burden I refused to share with my men.

"No, Sal, the only thing this changes is how much I do respect you. You *will* stay with the Blades, on one condition." He smiled when he said it, the last of his tension gone.

"Sir?"

"You may find me taking you up on your suggestion. Siana made me realize that a long, lonely life is not what I want." He huffed as if that was supposed to be funny somehow. "If I need an ear, will you lend me one?"

"Of course!" Her mind spun. This was not the reaction she'd expected. Not at *all.*

"And please," he said, "wear this. You chose a good chain for it, and it should withstand what we put it through. I think it would be good to remind both of us why you gave it to me."

He handed her the necklace, but rather than accept it, she turned and lifted her long, pale locks above her neck. Blaec stepped closer, his breath on her ear as he clasped it around her neck. The opal fell just at the hollow of her throat. The large stone would be visible above her uniform but not loose enough to slap around in her combat training. She'd chosen it because it matched her natural eyes, convincing herself that it complemented a more formal outfit she'd anticipated using in her role as Siana.

"Can we tell the men?" LT asked when she released her hair and faced him.

She raised an eyebrow and found herself giggling. "That I seduced you?"

"No!" He laughed. "That you found your ability. I'd planned to make Risk work you through a few of the common ones, hoping to trigger something. Now that we know what it is, I can have him find ways to perfect your use of it."

Still giggling, she nodded. "Sure, *that* I think you can tell them."

He turned to leave, but she dared to grab him before he opened the door. "Blaec, I just..." she felt herself fumbling for words, "I want you to know it meant something to me. I know you can't, but... the offer will always be there."

He seemed to change the subject. "Did I tell you I went to meet Siana for lunch? She'd already left, as you know, but I wanted to tell her why she seemed so familiar. After thinking about her all day, I realized she reminded me of you. She smelled like you. In so many ways she was like you, but unlike you, she was safe and right there within my reach."

He turned back to the door, pausing with his hand on the knob, speaking with his back to her. "And Sal," he said, not looking back, "I can't. I don't want my men to think I'm using my rank for something like that. I want them to respect what you are. Maybe sometime later, in a few years, but not now, and not soon." She heard him swallow. "I want to, though. It wouldn't be fair to anyone, but I do. I have since I touched you that first day."

He finally turned, catching her eyes. "You should never be ashamed of being iliri. You are *amazing*. When you stop trying to hide from the humans, you're everything an iliri should be: proud, strong, and beautiful. Sal..." he smiled sadly and turned back to the door, "you're twice as beautiful as any human. You're the kind of woman that men die for."

Before she could say anything else, he walked out. As the door closed, she heard him call, "Training ground at 0800 sharp, Corporal!"

Inside, her heart couldn't decide if it was rejoicing or breaking.

CHAPTER SEVENTEEN

The next morning, Sal made her way to the Black Blades' practice arena through the barns. A group of men stood casually, leaning against the back of one building, watching her too closely. The sight of a new soldier in black drew attention. When it was one with skin as white as fresh snow, even more so. The stables had been abuzz with the news that the Blades had accepted a new recruit, and when she passed, the stablehands fell in behind her.

She counted four men. All appeared to work in the barns. She'd dealt with worse odds before, but it was a bad way to start her first day. A few steps further down the alley, she turned into one of the busiest barns, ducking inside the corner. Opening her mind, she felt Zep's presence as the closest to her.

Zep, I might be a bit late. I think I made some new friends. Before he could reply, she saw shadows darken the entrance and released the mental contact.

Hoping she was mistaken about their intent, Sal casually leaned just inside the door, easing her nerves. The first of them walked past, a few steps into the barn, and paused with his back to her while the others caught up. The third man noticed her.

"Hey, what are you doing in here?" he asked.

"Just killing time," she said blandly, watching as barn staff turned to look at the commotion.

The fourth joined them, and the first two turned to face her. Standing so close, their anxiety wafted to her nose. This was no accidental meeting.

"Can I help you?" she asked, prodding them.

"Yeah!" the first said, stepping closer, "You can get to work doing your job and scrub the aisle here."

"I'm sorry, that's your job. Not mine." She tried to stay polite but was failing.

"Like hell, it ain't!" he snapped. "Your kind doesn't deserve anything better. Walking around in those black fatigues like you're someone important and shit? I think you need a human to put you back in your place, bitch."

Anger flared. "Did you really just walk this far to tell me about your prejudices? I have places to be." She stood up to walk away, hoping it would be so easy.

Of course, it never was. The humans' hatred for her kind made them irrational. Her uniform, and all that it symbolized, didn't slow them at all. Before she could even turn to the door, the man reached out and pulled her to face him.

"You may have slept your way into the Blades, but that doesn't make you a real soldier," he sneered. "But you must be pretty damned good at it, and maybe I wanna see for myself what the fuss is about, fucking a scrubber. Maybe you should show me some of those special tricks."

"Yeah, you aren't my type," she snarled. "I like my men to smell like something other than shit, thanks."

"You think your smart mouth is helping you any? I'll show you where you can put it." He tried to push her to her knees.

Sal ducked out of his grip and stepped away, turning to the door and walking into the alley as if the men hadn't stopped her. The four of them raced after her, catching up quickly, but Sal refused to run, hoping to look professional in front of the dozens of eyes watching the scene. The first two men to reach her grabbed her on either side.

"Get your hands off of me," she said, calmly.

"Fuck you, whore," the one on her right said. The one on her left just giggled nervously.

Patiently, she waited until the last two men were before her, then acted. Yanking both of her arms away, she stepped back. The sudden force made the giggling man lose his grip, and she easily pulled the other off his feet. Seeing her break free, the other two rushed her. Sal kicked the first in the stomach and danced to the side, letting the second dart past. When he turned to come back like an enraged bull charging, she stepped into his path and grabbed his arm. Tossing him over her shoulder, she put him onto the ground as well. The first guy tried to stand, but the giggling one scurried out of the alley. Sal let him go.

With three men now facing her, it seemed that only true force would stop the assault. Pushing them off wasn't working. Proving she was faster hadn't discouraged them. So, before the one closest could get to his feet, she kicked him solidly in the diaphragm, knocking the wind from him, then turned to the man now standing.

"Do you really want more of this?" she asked, the warning clear in her voice.

His answer was another brutish charge. These men were not soldiers, just common idiots. Their movements had none of the grace training offered, and Sal could put them on the ground repeatedly. She stepped to the side and, this time, kicked out at his knee. The hit was hard enough to make it fail him, but not hard enough to cause permanent damage. She defended herself with nothing more than moves taught to every soldier in their initial training.

Movement caught her eye: another stablehand running into the fray. Sal turned to face him, expecting the worst, but he yanked one of her attackers off balance by the sleeve of his shirt, pulling the man against him. Looping his arms through the attacker's elbows, the stablehand secured him. As the assailant struggled, the young man looked at her and Sal recognized Tilso, the kind boy from her first trip into the barns. Dozens of people were now in the alley, all of them looking at her.

She checked the two men on the ground. Neither looked like he would be moving any time soon.

Trying to stand proudly, she asked, "Does anyone know these men?"

Eyes refused to meet hers and voices muttered quietly.

"Let me try that again," Sal said, reminding herself that she not only had the rank to make these demands, she also had to think of the reputation of her unit. Years of being conditioned that humans deserved respect warned her to simply let it go, but Blaec's words from the night before fueled her pride. "Who are you, and what makes you think you can assault a Black Blade?" Sal asked the men on the ground.

The sound of hooves made their way through the press of bodies. A dark horse pushed the spectators to the side as Zep arrived on his mare, Cessa. Across his saddle, the giggling man struggled. Behind him, LT and Arctic sat their mounts quietly. At their stirrups, a handful of darkly dressed soldiers glared.

Risk, Shift, Cyno, and Razor made their way into the space around Sal and her attackers. Razor walked over to her while the other three secured the defeated men. Cyno rested a hand on Tilso's arm, tensing for a second before taking the man from the stablehand. LT, with a scowl on his face, took in the staff around him before nodding for Razor to address the crowd.

"I believe my Blade asked if anyone knew these men," Razor said in his parade voice. His attitude made it clear that there would be repercussions if no one spoke up.

"Sir," Tilso said, "they work over in Barn Twelve." He gestured to the other side of the stable. "There's no reason they should've been over here, not even for a break."

"Thank you," Razor said to the young man. "Would you please have their superior meet me at the officer's hall?"

"Yes, sir!" Tilso immediately left through the barn in the direction he'd indicated.

LT edged his horse into the center of the crowd and turned him lazily, addressing everyone watching the commotion. "I would like to make it clear that Corporal Luxx is now a Black Blade. She enjoys all of the respect that title commands. While I understand that not all of you agree with our choice of recruit, the day you can best any of us in combat, including Luxx, is the day you can tell me how to run my outfit."

The crowd muttered, a few heads nodded in agreement, and a few eyes looked at the ground, refusing to meet the Lieutenant's piercing gaze.

"The Stables at Stonewater has been our base of operations for over two years now, but if I do not feel as though my soldiers are welcome here, we will gladly move. There are many places closer to the front lines that would be proud to host us and call us their own. I will not tolerate my soldiers being treated like second-class citizens, not even my newest recruit. Is that understood?"

A murmur of assent spread through the crowd. If the Black Blades pulled their operations from these stables, over half the staff would lose their jobs. The base of any elite outfit thrived due to the influx of soldiers, the tourists that were drawn, and the requisitions that naturally followed a specialist group. At a nod from LT, the Blades holding men directed them toward the officer's hall and Zep followed, the man still crushed across the pommel of his saddle like a sack of grain.

Razor patted her shoulder and thought, *Go with LT and Arctic,* as he turned to follow Zep.

Sal made her way to the officers, both mounted, and Arctic

reached down. *Grab my hand, place your foot on mine, and swing up behind me.*

When her fingers closed on his wrist, he pulled her up enough to allow her foot to reach. The momentum carried her up behind him.

"I will not have this conversation with the staff again," The Lieutenant warned before he cued his horse.

Hang on, Arctic thought as he squeezed his mare into a smooth canter.

The crowd parted easily before them. With LT in the lead on his black, the trio made their way through the barn alleys to an enclosed arena at the edge of the compound. LT slid off his horse and pushed the door open, allowing Arctic and Sal to enter before pulling it closed behind them.

Arctic twisted in the saddle to offer his arm. Clasping her palm around it, she again put her foot on his and slid off the side of the horse. The Black Blades had a fondness for large mounts, and while she waited to meet the ground, Sal realized how far down it really was. Arctic easily dropped behind her.

"You know this is going to keep happening, right, Sal?" LT asked, his horse standing hip-shot beside him.

"In all honesty, sir, I didn't think about it. That sort of thing is pretty common for me." She shrugged. "Between being female, short, and iliri, I seem to be a target for the type that hates my kind."

"Our kind," Arctic said beside her. "Or did you forget so quickly?"

"Well, yes and no, Arctic. Sir, while you get the benefits of your iliri ancestry, I get the prejudices. Your dark hair, Razor's dark skin, LT's green eyes... except for Risk, and maybe Cyno, most of you can blend into a crowd."

"She has a point," LT grumbled. "No matter how much we've been harassed in our lives for being too light, or told that our mothers must have slept with the staff – or whatever else people seem to think is insulting – we're still seen as human. Only Sal and Risk feel the full weight of discrimination."

"So how do we stop it?" Arctic asked.

"You can't," Sal answered before the Lieutenant could speak up. "Nothing you can do will make others like me. When they see my white skin and hair, these strange ears and slit eyes - or worst of all, my sharp teeth - they know I'm different, and people hate different. Just..." she paused and looked at LT. "Just forgive me when it happens, sir. I promise I will always act with respect for the unit, but there will be more situations like this."

Both officers nodded at her.

"I don't know how you do it, Sal," LT said. "If you hadn't been so calm, I would have ridden into that crowd swinging."

"But you can't do that," she reminded him. "They're already saying I slept my way into the outfit. If you start treating me like I'm some damsel in distress, they'll be sure of it, and that won't help the reputation the Blades have worked so hard to get."

"That's a load of crap!" Arctic hissed.

"You know we treat Risk the same, right, Sal?" LT asked as the others slipped in from their excursion with the thugs.

"No, sir, but I assumed you did. I don't think you're pampering me, but I also know that no one worried about Risk sleeping his way in." She tossed a too casual glance up at the Lieutenant and heard Risk chuckle behind her.

LT blushed subtly and laughed. "Fair point. I think we'll just let you deal with it for now, little demon, on the condition that you let us know when you need backup. Deal?"

"Thank you, sir."

"With that said, we have work to get through this morning," the Lieutenant said. "Sal, I have three months to get you ready and get us back into working shape. We have a mission."

CHAPTER EIGHTEEN

News of an upcoming mission caught the interest of the men. They turned expectantly, their complete focus locked on LT. Sal wasn't any better. For her, this would be her first official mission as an elite soldier.

"This is not going to be our usual, guys, and I'm sorry," LT said. "We have to cause a breach in the border so the main army can push into Escea. I have a handful of assassinations that need to be well timed and quick enough that word won't spread to give the next target the chance to seclude himself. Four politicians and at least three officers – more have been requested – need to be removed. Cyno, Shift, Arctic, and Sal, I will be relying upon you for the assassinations of the politicians."

"Think Sal's ready for it?" Zep asked.

LT looked at her. "I don't know. Are you, Sal?"

"Well, I have a few tricks up my sleeve," she said, "and if you're worried about me killing a man, don't be."

"Have ya killed a man b'fore?" Cyno asked quietly.

Sal turned and met his eyes. "It's not legal for a slave to act on her employers."

"So ya never had blood on yer hands, then." He nodded without judgment.

The men accepted that as nothing more than fact. None of them seemed to think less of her for it. She looked from one face to the other, trying to find the catch.

"So, Sal," LT said, bringing her attention to him, "tell them what you learned during your preparation for our last trial?"

"I seem to have discovered my own ability." She shrugged, feeling strangely self conscious about it. "And the Lieutenant thinks it will be very useful."

"Go on," Risk encouraged.

"If I concentrate, I can change my appearance."

"How much concentration and how big of a change?" Zep asked.

"A few minutes of focusing, and well," she smiled, "I learned that it's not as easy as I thought to piss while standing, if that's big enough for you?"

"Oh!" LT choked out. "You didn't tell me you could change genders too!"

"It didn't seem appropriate at the time, sir."

"Is it just me," Shift spoke up, "or does anyone else feel like there's something they know that we don't?"

The other men chuckled and agreed.

"I put the Lieutenant in an awkward situation, you see," Sal explained. "When practicing, I found that few of my disguises wear the same size I normally do. LT caught me with my clothes off. Once I explained about my ability, he understood, but," she couldn't stifle the giggle, "he does blush a very nice shade of red."

LT's thoughts shot into her mind, *Thank you for embarrassing me. Shift's right, you really are a demon!*

Remembering being told that Arctic could listen in on anything that passed through one of his mental links, Sal kept her reply as cryptic. *I never said I wouldn't poke fun at you, did I?*

The Blades were giving LT grief about his perverse ways and sneaking into a woman's room, so Sal decided she should step in and help. "Guys, it was just awkward timing. Don't be jealous, I'm sure all of you will get to see me undressed at some point."

"Ok," Cyno broke in, sounding unimpressed. "Sal, let's see this new trick of yers... without shedding yer clothes if possible? I do na how many of these boys could take it."

She concentrated, thinking about turning herself as black as her uniform. Without a mirror, all she could do was focus on the tingling feeling crawling across her skin, mentally tracing the progression from her head to her feet. When it stopped, she glanced at her hands, finding they were pure ebony, the skin a matte leather color.

The Blades stared in silent fascination. Cyno walked around her as though inspecting a new horse for flaws.

"Smile?" he asked, and she complied. "That's an impressive shift. Even yer insides look black." He appeared fascinated. "Can ya become me?"

"No. Sadly, it seems I can't make an exact copy." Sal released her hold on the mental image and felt the color fade. "I can look like a sibling or from the same family, but I can't quite master all the details of a person. Not enough to pass for him or her."

Cyno nodded. "LT, I get the first run with her. If yer sending her in for assassinations, I wanna make sure she can do more than just play a part."

"No." The Lieutenant shook his head. "I need her riding, first. You can have her for two hours each evening if you want, but more than anything else, we need her on a horse."

Cyno nodded, but he didn't like it.

"She rode Boo in the trials, you know," Shift said. "Maybe we should put her up on him? He's quiet enough when he wants to be, and I'm not sure how far along her mare is, yet."

"Speaking of horses," Razor broke in. "That kid that helped you out. Sal, how do you know him?"

"He works in the barns. Some stablehand accused me of being

in the wrong place a few days ago – sorry, LT, I threw your name around – and the kid stepped up to apologize. Why?"

Cyno glanced to the Lieutenant. "I touched him this morning. LT, he's in awe of the Blades. He's also a little bit in love with Sal, but only 'cause she's a Black Blade who spoke ta him. Razor and I talked 'bout it on our way back."

Razor added, "I want to put him on our horses and make him our head groom. It'd save a lot of problems and prevent anyone from harming the horses to show how much they hate iliri."

"Let Sal tell him," Zep suggested.

The Lieutenant nodded. "Agreed. The kid jumped into a fray to help her out, so the least she can do is tell him about his promotion. Ok, Zep, you check on Sal's mare's training. Razor, you get the kid assigned and see if you can get all of our horses moved into the same barn. The closer to this building, the better. Sal, you get your ass up on Boo. Shift, would you do me the favor of putting Scorch up?"

The men agreed and turned to their tasks. Before they left the arena, LT called out to them, "Guys, when you're done there, stop by my room and get the files from my desk. Start doing some intel on them, and we'll meet up at lunch. Sal's going to be barely able to stand by then, so grab our room if you would?"

"Can do, boss," Shift said, and the others mumbled their assent.

Once they were alone in the arena, the Lieutenant's demeanor softened. "Let's get you up on this gelding and show you how to ride. And no making me blush while we do this."

"I can't promise that!" She smirked at him as she walked over to the blood bay and tossed the reins over his neck.

"How much experience do you have with horses, Sal?" LT asked. "You move around them like a natural."

"I worked here for over a year," she explained. "I've only ridden a handful of times in my life and, except for Boo, never a real battle-trained horse, sir."

"It's just us, Sal. I'm Blaec to you. I hope that with us being alone, you can relax. I mean, I've seen you naked already, how much more embarrassing can it be, right?"

"Well, I've seen *you* naked but it's not quite true the other way around, you know."

"I have a good imagination. Now get on the horse."

She laughed, then tried to reach her foot into a stirrup that hung level with her throat. Her short leg could almost touch it, but she couldn't stretch high enough to bear her weight.

"So, now what?" she asked, annoyed. "I can't go growing longer legs each time I need on a horse!"

Smothering a laugh of his own, Blaec stepped in close behind her. "Put your left hand here." He moved her hand to the base of the horse's neck. "And grab the mane. Can you reach?"

"Yeah." She clasped a fistful of the horse's hair in her hand.

"Ok, now, what you need to do is swing your outside leg back, pull down on that hand, and use your foot like a pendulum to throw your body over the horse's back."

She looked at him with a confused expression. "What?"

"Let me show you." He guided her over a step and took her place. "Like this."

Blaec stepped toward the horse's rear with his left side for momentum, then swung his right leg hard. His body followed it up and into the saddle. "Think you can try that?"

"Trying is all I promise. Ok, move."

Blaec slid off and stood to the side. She grabbed a larger handful of mane this time while Boo stood quietly. With one huge step forward, she tried to throw her weight through her outside leg over the saddle - and felt her knee collide with the gelding's ribs. Laughing, she patted the horse on the shoulder and tried again. On the fifth attempt, she hooked her ankle over the saddle and wiggled her way onto the horse's back.

"Again," Blaec ordered. "You have to get all the way up. We'll do this every day until you can mount any horse without effort. And Sal? You realize your mare is taller, right?"

"Seriously? Why did I choose that horse?"

"Because she's the best animal this farm had to offer for a recruit?" Blaec smirked at her. "It just took me a bit to figure out how to hide her pretty color, because some idiot would have chosen her for that. So, stop talking and get on your horse, girl."

Again and again, she flung herself at the horse's side, until her muscles would barely lift her. Only then did Blaec let her rest. "There's water at the side rail. Get a drink and shake out your aches. I'm going to see how this guy goes, then we'll let you do more than jump at the horses."

The Lieutenant swung up, clicked at the gelding, and Boo moved out easily. He passed through walk, trot, and into a canter, then half passed, changed leads, and transitioned down into an extended trot. When LT exhaled, the gelding halted square, relaxed but ready to move with a shift in the rider's weight.

"There's no way I can learn all of that in a few months!" Sal yelled across the arena.

"You're not supposed to. I just need you to sit the gaits. We'll teach you the rest later."

"Why is it so important to be such a fancy rider? None of the other outfits stress it as much." She hated feeling so far behind in a skill she might need to support her brothers in arms.

"Well, tell me, can you see a use for this?" He drew his sword and squeezed the horse up. Boo half passed while Blaec pointed his weapon in the direction of travel. "Or this?" and he mocked a parry while asking the horse to rein back. "And of course there's this." With a look of concentration, he brought the horse into a collected canter and gave an imperceptible aid. Boo leapt from the ground, kicking out behind him.

"It's combat maneuvers, Sal," he said, riding up to her. "The more you can handle, the more you can, well... handle in the field. Don't worry, all you need for now are the basics."

He slid off the horse and gestured to her. Knowing this was more than just parlor tricks, Sal put more effort into it and concentrated as she swung herself into the saddle. This time she made it – although it still wasn't pretty.

"Not bad," he said, resting his hand on her thigh. "Ok, now I want you to just walk him around the wall of the arena. Keep yourself far enough off the rail that you don't catch your feet on the wall, and we'll start adjusting your seat."

She smiled down at him, her eyes moving to his familiar touch on her leg. "You'd better pay more attention to your mannerisms in public, Blaec." She squeezed the horse into a walk.

He blushed again. It seemed she had that effect on him.

As she steered the horse around the rail, he called out corrections, most of which revolved around relaxing her body and keeping her heels down. She finally began to get the feel for it, and Boo bent into the bridle.

A voice broke into both of their heads with a click. *LT, let the girl eat. We've been waiting for thirty minutes already. She's got to be about to fall apart. Sal, you're allowed to remind him about the time,* Arctic chided.

"Ok," Blaec laughed. "That means we're good for now. After lunch, we'll see how you do on your mare if Zep thinks she's ready. Come over here and dismount." *I'm calling the lesson now and giving her another hour of lunch. Are you happy, Arctic?*

Yep, now c'mon. We ordered some real food in here.

Sal rode up next to him, giggling from having heard it all. Blaec grabbed the gelding's reins while she slid off. Her exhausted legs hit the ground and buckled. Sal reached for the stirrup, but Blaec caught her, preventing her from falling. Braced against his body, she relaxed her head, letting it fall back on his chest. His heart was pounding against her.

"I feel like I'm made of water, but I can still hear that." Sighing deeply, she pulled herself onto her own feet and turned to face him. "Are you sure you're ok with this?"

"No," he admitted, "but I'm going to have to learn. Just treat me the same as the other love-sick puppies around here, and I'll get over it. I promise I will."

"I'm not so sure I want you to, but I do understand. I'll try." She pushed the stray hair away from her face. "Just remember, I haven't had a whole lot of men fawning over me. It's flattering and distracting to me as well."

"I'm trying, Sal. That's why I'm giving you the lessons. The more time I spend with you, the more comfortable I'll be with this, and the less the others will think of it. At least I have a good excuse for being your instructor."

"Because you're my commanding officer?"

"Well, that, yeah, and I'm the best rider we have. I grew up on horses, unlike most of these guys. I trained them all. Now let's tack down poor Boo and get some food in you before you waste away."

CHAPTER NINETEEN

Shift looked up from the file he was reading so he could refill his glass. LT should've been here by now. Around the table, he wasn't the only one getting anxious. With a grunt, Arctic dropped his eyes to the table, most likely reaching out to the Lieutenant. The rest of the men shared a glance. It wasn't like LT to be late.

Zep gave in and grabbed a plate, then he reached for the food on the table. "So, is he going to spend all day with her, or does he plan to let her eat? I'm not waiting for them anymore."

"I just asked, and you know how he gets," Arctic said. "She started doing well, and he just kept pushing."

"Yeah, and Sal won't stop. She'll try until she drops, if I'm reading that girl right," Shift added.

"Ya are," Cyno agreed around a mouthful of food. "She's got a spine on her, that'n. Does na know that she can na do somethan, an' would rather die than show any weakness."

"Oh? Did you read her?" Shift asked.

"Can na help but. When Zep got her drunk, she danced with

me, an' all her guards were down. She's the real deal, guys. Do na fuck with her."

"Even I can smell it," Risk piped in. "She also knows exactly nothing."

Arctic nodded. "But having her around is going to make things complicated." He sighed. "We can't rush this. Just treat her with respect and she'll learn everything soon enough."

"An' she's ours," Cyno muttered. "That's gonna change ever'thing."

The Blades nodded at that, but the more Shift thought about it, the more questions Cyno's cryptic remarks made. Most of the Blades found her iliri features attractive; she was one of their own. That also meant they'd show her nothing but respect. For the first time in years, they had a recruit they felt truly comfortable with. The last one to blend in so seamlessly had been Cyno, two years before.

Too often, new recruits worried about impressing the outfit, made a bad decision, and found themselves dead for it. Circus had been one of those stupid mistakes, even if he hadn't been a new recruit, and LT had taken it too personally. While Sal was nothing like the melancholy soldier, she had no idea how perfectly she filled the hole he left.

"What's her story, Cyno?" Shift asked.

"Na my story ta tell. Ask Sal."

"Ok, well, let me be blunt then," Shift said, "since the pair of them will be a while still. What's the deal with her and LT?" They'd all seen the looks the pair passed between them.

"I dunno nothin' 'bout that. Look, I jus' know she does na think as well of herself as we think of her, ok?"

"Guys, I can't be the only one that saw it. Or are all of you so interested in catching her eye first that you're trying to ignore it?" Shift refused to just let this go.

Across the table, the men looked at each other. Zep put his fork down, pushed his plate back, and took a long drink of mead before answering. "Yeah, we saw it. We also know LT doesn't tend to throw himself at women casually - not even when he can - and he sure as hell wouldn't force his attention on *her*. If something happens there, I say let it happen."

"She's diff'rent," Cyno said. "She's nice to look at, she smells amazing, and yeh, it's na gonna be easy to treat her like one of ya, but..." He let the thought trail off.

"Go on," Shift pushed, "You're the one that knows."

"Ok, look. That girl's had the shit kicked outta her in her life, ya get me?" Cyno looked at each of them. "Her heart's pretty tough, she's na made of glass or anything, but she does na need ta get the same crap from us. She's never had anyone she could rely on b'fore, and does na know shit 'bout our ways. If ya wanna impress her, then just do na fuck with her."

"Fair 'nough," Shift said, letting the talk die down for a moment.

"So, does it bother you, Shift?" Risk asked into the awkward silence.

"Huh?" Shift couldn't keep up with the way Risk's mind worked sometimes.

"Her and LT, a couple, does that bother you?"

"Nah. She smells like my sister, so I'm out of the running right there. I like to see her smile, but I'd prefer she's fully dressed when doing it." He raised an eyebrow, wondering where this was going.

"So, why do you care so much?" Risk asked.

"Well." Shift leaned back in his chair. "I kinda like the idea of LT having someone he can trust. We know how he's pulled away lately."

"Lately?" Zep asked. "Only if you consider over a year to be 'lately!'"

"Well, true. But isn't that more reason for that," and Shift gestured to the two empty seats, "to happen? Or like I asked before, do any of you have a problem with it?"

Unanimously, the men shook their heads.

"Then what will it take to make it happen?" Shift persisted. "Is it

Sal or is it LT that's throwing ice on things between them, you think?"

"Seriously, Shift," Arctic said. "You're worse than a human at times."

"Yeah, and you still know I'm right. If we don't push this, nothing will ever happen. I just want to make sure I'm pushing in the right place."

"LT," Cyno said.

"Ah ha!" Shift exclaimed. "You do know something!"

"Shove it, man. Ya know I do na say shit about what I catch off any of ya. But yeh, it's LT, na Sal. And it is na gonna be a bit of pushing, but more like moving a mountain, so just let it alone already."

"Damn, man," Shift said. "Sometimes you really kinda scare me, ya know that, Cyno?"

"And it's na cuz I could kill ya in yer sleep?" the assassin mocked.

"Nah, anyone here could do that. It's cuz you could kill me when I'm awake."

Arctic casually returned the conversation to the intelligence they'd been seeking all morning. As details came out about each target, it became clear that this mission would not be an easy one. One of them might not come back, and in their usual way, they refused to speak openly about it. Shift worried about Sal the most, since this looked to be one of the hardest in years and her inexperience would be a weakness that could get her killed. He tried to remind himself that she was nothing like their other recruits but kept finding himself thinking about the worst.

"Cyno?" Shift asked.

"Again?" The wiry man snarled at him.

"No teeth, man, damn," Shift said. "Just train her good. We can't lose her. Ok?"

"Shift." Cyno looked up at him with ice in his eyes. "She'll be better than me in less than a week. She will be fine. Now let it alone."

"So..." Arctic said, "About those reports, guys?" The mental echo of their companions proved the last two were close. By the time the door opened, the men were pointing at papers and barely looked up, but they all caught LT's hand on Sal's back as he guided her to a chair.

"How'd Boo do for ya?" Shift asked.

"He stands very nicely," Sal said, grimacing to show her distaste for the day's lesson.

LT chuckled. "I think she's got it. She made it up quite a few times, and I had her working on her seat when Arctic reminded me that I have no track of time around horses. I'm giving her an extra hour before she has to get back in the saddle to make up for it."

"Good," Razor said, "because after we eat, I need you to hire us a horseman. That Tilso kid. Seems his superior is more than happy to let him go. LT, what are you planning with him?"

"With Sal's recent fan club, I just think that it's a good idea to have our horses housed together with staff who do not care how pale the skin of the rider is. Why?"

"His old manager said the kid gets a bit above himself, wanting to change the horse's rations, tracking their training, and such. I did some poking into his background, and I'm thinking he'd make a better barn manager, so I got the paperwork filled out. Just need you to sign it. Get him to keep his eyes open for, say, two more stablehands, and you and Zep won't have to worry about all that. Sal's mare is one the kid had an interest in, and she's well ahead of her year mates in training and condition, plus she's still sane. Says a lot to me."

"Cyno?" LT asked. "Think he can handle it?"

"Yeh, I think he's made fer it, and ya might wanna think 'bout using him fer more than just the home base. Kid's got the knack, he's loyal to a fault, an' he sees the horses as an equal part of our outfit."

"They are," LT said.

"Yeah," Zep pointed out, "but we know most of the staff think we can get another and not bat an eye."

"I dug up some pretty interesting information on him," Razor added, passing a set of papers across the table. The Lieutenant read through it, a smile spreading across his face.

"Ok. Sal, would you like to make the offer?" LT asked.

"Actually, I'd love to," she said. "Do you care how public I make it?"

"Nope. Here." He reached over and grabbed her wrist, sending the thought right into her mind. "Look at that. That's what I'm thinking for a position."

"Did you seriously just light her mind on fire?" Shift asked. He had experienced the Lieutenant's fondness for sharing memory flames a few times more than he wanted. They burned brightly, making them impossible to ignore. "I hate it when you do that to me."

"It's the easiest way to send a concept, Shift," LT said.

Sal sat quietly, looking at the thought LT had given her. "You realize you just made him very happy, right?" she asked LT.

"I hope so," he said. "Loyalty deserves to be rewarded."

CHAPTER TWENTY

*D*ust clung to her black uniform, and her legs still felt weak, but the walk would do her good. Sal strode through Barn Three, looking for Tilso. No one was around, but she hoped to give him the bragging rights of being publicly offered a promotion. Finding nothing, she turned toward Barn Four. When she walked through the doors, she heard the jeers of teenagers.

A group of boys crowded around Tilso, who stood defiantly before a stall. Sal squared her shoulders and walked toward them, letting her footsteps ring out on the stone floor.

"Look, here's yer scrubber bitch now," one of them muttered, thinking she wouldn't be able to hear him.

"Shut it, or I'll put you in a coma, boy," she snarled at the teen, allowing her teeth to show. His mouth flapped open and closed while her white eyes bore into his. Seeing their leader speechless, the others backed away.

Sal turned to Tilso, who stood with his chin up, glaring at the group before him. "Tilso, I wanted to thank you for helping me earlier. It's nice to see a man willing to step up and do what he believes is right."

"It wasn't a big deal, Ms. Luxx. You got a good eye for horses is all. I can respect anyone that knows a good horse. That's all." The kid was rambling nervously.

"That's actually what I wanted to talk to you about," she said, ignoring his awkwardness. "LT sent me here to see if I could find you. He moved our horses over to Barn Twenty-one, next to our arena."

"Yes, sir. I was trying to take Arden over there just now." Tilso gestured at her horse. "I didn't mean to keep the Lieutenant waiting, sir."

"Actually, we're hoping that you'd be willing to transfer with our horses to the new barn." She smiled up at him.

The young man seemed to grow taller with pride. "Yes, sir! I'd be honored to tend to your horses. I've been keeping an eye on them –"

She held up her hand, stopping him mid-sentence, and shook her head. His face started to fall, but she kept hers stoic. "Well, we need a couple of stablehands, too, but that's not what LT was thinking for you."

"I see. Well, I'd still be willing to do what ya need, sir," he said hopefully.

"Good, because we're in desperate need of a barn manager." For a moment the words didn't seem to register.

Tilso had been working as a mere stall cleaner for the last six months, hoping to prove his skill in caring for the horses. Razor had also learned that before the war, the kid had grown up on a border farm, one known for quality horses. His father had been killed in a skirmish out there, leaving Tilso, his mother, and two sisters to move further into the Conglomerate, abandoning their farm and all of his ties to horses.

When he realized she meant the position of barn manager was for him, Tilso's face brightened, but he didn't dare believe it. "You want me to manage the Black Blades' barn, Ms. Luxx?"

"Yes, Mr. Tilso," she answered, giving him the honorific that such a position would deserve. "Your family produced some of the best horses around here, and if I'm not mistaken, most of ours can trace their lines back to those from your family farm?"

He nodded, his eyes wide but happy.

"LT didn't realize we had such quality horsemen here at Stonewater Stables until you stood up today. Since you understand how important they are to the Blades, we'd like to offer you the position first. He's been unable to find anyone more suited to the job than himself or Zep, but most elite units have someone assigned to handle their mounts. I understand if you choose to decline, but," she passed him a piece of paper, "here's the wages we can offer you."

She waited only long enough for him to take the paper. "Unfortunately, the position would require you to move into the loft – naturally, your family is welcome as well, if you have one – and you might be required to travel with us."

The young man nodded, so she kept going. "You would also be responsible for obtaining our pack animals, arranging the training of our mounts around our schedules, adjusting their feeding rations as needed, and caring for any injuries they sustain in battle. We would expect you to hire an assistant manager, with the Lieutenant's approval, who would watch the barn during such times as we're deployed, and we will need at least two stablehands that can be trusted to care for the horses in the manner they require. Are you interested?"

Tilso's eyes never left the paper. The figure was impressive for a barn manager and astronomical for a stablehand, but the Blades would make him earn every krit of it. "Ms. Luxx, am I required to hire an assistant from within the Stables already?"

"No," she said, wondering where his mind was heading. "But you'll need to speak to the Lieutenant before making the offer. He wanted me to relay that if you're interested, he would appreciate you making sure the horses are settled and then meeting with him in his office at the barn."

"Yes, sir," he said, turning to the boys across the aisle. "And if you don't want to get fired, step away from my horse."

"Tilso?" Sal asked when the boy turned for a halter to grab her mare from the stall. "Is that her name? Arden?"

"Yes, sir. Ardent Dawn. She's the last foal bred from my da's farm. We always called her Arden."

"It suits her, thank you. I'd been trying to find something that fits." She held out her hand, clean this time, to the horseman before her. He glanced at his own, covered in dirt, but reached up to clasp hers regardless. "I promise to treat her right, Mr. Tilso," she said, "and to listen when you tell me how to treat her better."

"Thank you, Ms. Luxx," he said smiling. "Thank you very much, sir."

CHAPTER TWENTY-ONE

Three months was not a lot of time to train a recruit, but the Lieutenant thought Sal had risen to the challenge. While Blaec worked her daily in her riding lessons, Cyno was as relentless each evening. Her free time had been a mess of intelligence meetings, extra riding practice with the new barn manager, and scuffles with humans who couldn't accept an iliri that outranked them. The girl had finally used her authority, firing two men on the spot and ordering a unit of infantry who'd been watching the spectacle to escort them off the stable grounds. After that, the displays against her subsided.

He was proud of her, but even after so much time, Blaec still couldn't be in the same room without noticing how she smelled or catching himself smiling like a fool. Most of his men seemed to ignore it when he acted like a teenager with a crush – except Shift. His Sergeant had always been straight to the point, and tonight was no different.

"She's as ready as she's going to be, LT," Shift said, sitting across from him. "Let her have a night off before we head out in the morning. Cyno says she's already surpassed anything he can show her, her pure breeding making her faster, more agile, and more intuitive than any of us could hope. Zep said she's his equal with any weapon, so long as she can find its balance, and she discards those she's too small for. Even Risk said she has more control of her ability than he would expect."

"I know, Shift, but this isn't exactly a good mission for her first one. It's too risky." He sighed. They'd already been around this argument twice, and Shift wasn't about to let him win. "I should scrap the assassination and have the Blades do a full-on assault of the Chancery -"

"Only if you want more of us to die and like telling the Empire that we're coming. There are too many guards stationed there for us to be sure we get them all. Our target is the Chancellor, and just the Chancellor. You know as well as I do that his appetite for women is the only way we're going to get in there, and Sal can slip in without a problem using her ability. You can't be that jealous. You know she's just there to kill him."

"I'm not jealous, Shift, I'm worried about her lack of experience."

"You've tested her yourself, you know she can take down a -"

"But she's never dealt with that many guards before," Blaec interrupted.

Shift continued without a pause. "She's gotten past all of us at some point this week, so stop acting like her mother."

"I'm not acting like her mother!"

"You are. If you trust her, then just let her do this and stop trying to convince her that she'll have a problem."

"But what if-"

"What if nothing!" Shift's voice grew louder.

"We can't replace her, damn it!" Blaec yelled back.

"We won't need to."

"It's an assassination, Shift. What if she gets caught up in it?"

Shift shrugged, looking devious. "What if she does? Cyno deals with it well enough."

"If you consider the hell he goes through as 'dealing with it'!"

"Then sleep with her!"

"I already have!"

The words hung in the air between them for a second before Shift leaned back in his chair and smirked. "So that's what this is about, then?"

"No, that's not what I meant."

"LT, did you sleep with her?" Shift's tone was light but demanded an answer. His deep breath proved he was expecting a lie.

"It's not like that." Blaec sighed, but when Shift just stared, he continued, "She infiltrated me for the trials. She's the woman I spent the night with. The one that gave me the idea about the civilians."

"I see... was she any good?" Shift asked wickedly.

"Shift!"

"Look, I can't even make a joke without you getting upset about it. You're not looking at her like her commanding officer but like a human. Stop it already and let us have the soldier she is. Let us all make use of her skills. Does she feel the same way about you as you do about her?"

"I don't know. If she does or not, it doesn't matter. I can't do anything about it. I'm her commanding officer."

Shift grunted at that. "So, what if one of us was in your position, what would you tell us?"

"You know what I'd say." Blaec tried to get out of answering the question.

"No, we've never had a woman in the outfit before, so it's never come up. What would you tell one of us, Blaec?"

Defeated, he answered, "That so long as it didn't cause any problems, you could accept it if things ended, and everything looked respectable on the outside, then do what you want. You're adults."

"So why are you different? Why doesn't that apply to you?"

"My position. How many times do I have to say it? I'm her

commanding officer, and yours, and all of theirs! It's against military regulations."

"And?" Shift persisted. "When did human rules apply to us?"

"What about Cyno?" Blaec tried. "He's gotten very close to Sal over the last few months. What if he's set his sights on her? The disruption in the ranks could cripple us."

"He thinks you're good for her." Shift brushed that off. "I asked. But that's not what you're worried about, is it?"

"Look, if she's like him, he's the only one that can handle her," Blaec grumbled.

"Then figure that out when it comes, but don't let it stop you now."

"Damn it, man! This isn't something I can just give an order and make happen."

"Blaec, we've known you're smitten with her since her first day in black. You suck at hiding it, and I'm pretty sure she knows, too. We can all smell it. Just sleep with her." Shift grinned at him. "Not sleeping with her doesn't seem to be working very well, so you'd best try something new before one of us kills you."

"It still doesn't answer how I'm supposed to make sure she gets out of this alive." Blaec tried to bring the conversation back around to the point he'd started it with.

"You're right. Nor does it tell you how you'll make sure Cyno, or Zep, or Risk, or Razor, or Arctic, or even I will. You just trust us. We trust her. So get your head out of your ass and deal with this problem before you *do* end up getting her killed by trying to be too protective." Shift stood and made to leave the room. "Give her the night off, let her know you're interested, and get your head back in the game, LT. She can probably kick your ass at anything besides mounted combat. Just keep her feet on the ground, and she'll come home fine."

"Thanks, Shift." Blaec sighed, knowing he'd lost this battle. "You sure the others are ok with this?"

"That's not the word they'd use. Most of them are ready to beat you with a pike if you don't stop fawning over her. Blaec, she's the real deal, and you're our leader. It works."

"Then do me one more favor?" Blaec begged.

"Depends."

"Take her to the pub tonight? Give me a chance to do more than order her around?"

"Now *that*, I think I can handle," Shift said while mentally calling out for Zep to meet him at Sal's.

---

*A*s Sal rinsed the lather from her body, she heard her door creak. Opening her mind, she felt Shift and Zep in her room. An unlikely pair, and one that never amounted to much good. She finished her bath, the dirt from her last lesson with Tilso and Blaec finally gone from her skin, and stepped out. Rubbing her long hair with the towel before wrapping it around her body, she walked into her sleeping chamber.

Shift had his head in her wardrobe, and Zep lay on her bed, casually looking up at the ceiling. Her feet barely made a sound as she moved to the side. Leaning against the wall, Sal watched them for a bit before either man noticed.

"Uh, nice outfit there, Sal," Zep said, his complexion growing darker as she stared at him.

"Mhm, I think we've done this before. Why are you here?"

"Same as before, actually. Pretty clothes and a good looking woman trying to get naked in front of me."

"Eww." Shift glanced around the wardrobe door at Sal. "Damn, girl, put some clothes on or something. You'll catch a cold like that." He stepped back and held up pieces from her wardrobe, all in black.

Zep nodded. "Yeah, that'll do. She'll look like a Blade and make the common men drool. Best way to keep up our reputation the night before we deploy. What do you think, demon?"

She just raised an eyebrow, saying nothing.

"Hm," Shift said, staring at her throat where the black and opal necklace lay. "You always wear that thing?"

"Yeah, I do. Why?"

"Where'd ya get it?" He side-stepped her question.

"It was a gift when I became a Blade. Why?" she asked again, looking directly into his eyes.

"Oh, no reason." He smiled at her knowingly as his focus returned to the clothing. "Oh yeah, and you've got the night off. We're escorting you to the pub if you hadn't figured that out."

"I'm scheduled to meet with Cyno for another run-through of the mission plans. What changed?"

"Well," Zep said, "we basically browbeat LT until he admitted that another night of training wouldn't do you any good and relaxing will. So he said to enjoy yourself in any way you desire. We desire you to accompany us to the pub, so thought we'd help you find something to wear that wouldn't embarrass us."

Sal finally smiled and gestured at the wardrobe. "Shift, put those pants back in there and find the black lace-up boots? Zep, in the drawer beside you, pick out the pair of stockings you like the best."

Both men complied. Zep raised his eyebrows when he opened Sal's lingerie drawer.

"Don't think I've ever been in one of these..." he mumbled.

"Stop pawing the silks and just pick a pair of stockings, Zep," she chided.

"Ok, these? Oh, those are soft." He held up a pair of sheer black hose in his hands.

"That works. Shift, on the far right, grab me the skirt? Yes, it's black too." She could hear him moving clothes about. "Really? It's all the way to the right."

"The belt?" he asked, pulling out a wide black piece of cloth.

"Yes, the belt." She snatched it from his hand, then stepped into it under the towel. "Now hand me that under-shirt."

Reaching behind him without looking, Shift passed across the top he'd picked out earlier. Sal dropped the towel and laughed when Zep shifted his eyes to the floor.

So she teased, "Figured you'd be taking it in, big guy. When did you suddenly get shy?"

He grumbled something under his breath, making Sal laugh. She straightened her skirt, tucked the under-shirt into it, grabbed the corset Shift had dropped on her bed, and then began lacing herself into it.

"Ok, Shift. Now, I need an overskirt for this. I have a few that are mostly black. Pick one."

He rummaged for a few moments before pulling out two skirts, one with navy threading, the other a black on black pattern. Holding them up in the light, he passed her the darker of the two and returned the other to the wardrobe. Sal sat on her bed, her back to Zep, and pulled up her stockings, clipping them on, she then buttoned the overskirt around her waist. Finished, she turned for their inspection.

"You can both look, I'm decent now. And you're going to have to get over this if LT plans to use my abilities. Dressing the part is half of it, you know. So, will I make you proud enough?"

"Except for the wet hair, yeah," Zep said.

"No, she needs makeup. Not the red lips tonight, though," Shift said, making his way to her mirror and the cosmetics arranged neatly before it. "What else do you have?"

"Pinks, purples, a few browns and golds... I don't tend to spend a lot of time painting my face before I'm going to end up sweating it off," she told him as she ran a brush through her hair.

Shift rummaged through her cosmetics like he had her clothes, placing a few items to the side. "Zep, bring me that chair. Sal, sit." He then began painting her face with an expertise she never expected, talking the entire time.

"I have sisters and figured out that their cosmetics could help me change my own look, too. A bit of stubble can be faked pretty easy, and they can add or take away years. It's a hazard of the elite forces, ya know," he explained while he worked. "Ok, look."

Sal did. Staring at her from the mirror was a seductively beautiful woman. He'd managed to make her eyes piercing, yet gentle, while accenting her smooth complexion and adding just a touch of color to her lips. The opal at her throat hung on its dark resin chain, blending with her skin and outfit. Sal adjusted her cleavage, pulling the edges of her under-shirt just enough to draw the eye.

Zep turned away, a noise in his throat that she couldn't identify. "Sal, you're killing me over here. C'mon, you're lovely. Let's go show you off now."

"One more thing," she said, heading to the wardrobe to reach inside. She grabbed something small and walked over to Zep. "Would you do me the honors, if showing me off is really all you want?" An evil smile played on her lips.

She handed him the crossed sword pin that she'd received with her commission. Zep ran his eyes over her outfit, trying to find enough material to attach it to, and settling on a strap at her shoulder. Sal giggled at his discomfort. Once the pin was secure, she grabbed her escorts and directed them from the room.

"I don't think I've ever seen either of you quite so tongue-tied," she teased while they walked to the pub. "So why the sudden shyness?"

"Sal," Zep said, "you've never just stripped in front of us before!"

"You'll get used to it," she promised. "And I'm willing to bet we won't get fancy cabins after tonight, so I figure it's time to start being one of the guys."

"Yeah," Shift muttered. "No. I don't think you can quite manage that. Trust me, we may accept you as one of our own, but you'll never be one of the guys. You're just going to have to get used to laughing at us, I think."

"Fair enough. So which of you is buying me the first drink?"

"I am," Arctic said behind her. "And that's a nice color, Sal. You fit right in." The others were with him. All of them wore clothing in nothing but shades of black. Only the Lieutenant was missing, but Sal shrugged that off. With the morning's deployment, he'd be going over their intelligence reports one more time. She wished she could pull him away from it, though.

The Blades made their entrance a spectacular one, with Sal leading them into the pub. Her alabaster skin shined under the lanterns, turning the men behind her into shadows trailing in her wake. The music died and all eyes turned to them as Arctic spoke up.

"Tomorrow, we head out to save the Conglomerate again. But tonight, we celebrate!"

Cheers went up around the pub, and the musicians resumed. A waitress made her way to their table, a full tray of drinks balanced before her, and whispered in Shift's ear. He nodded to her once and kissed her hand before sending to them all, *First round's on the house tonight, guys. Drink up!*

The mood of the men seemed somewhat desperate, like they wanted to savor everything they could before the night ended. Sal recognized the symptoms, having seen many soldiers act like this before battle. Men who might die always tried to live as much as possible the night before. Later, when her friends began to mingle in the crowd, she made her way up to the second floor, remembering the last time she'd been here.

It felt like years had passed since she'd played the part of Siana, yet the memories were so clear. She smiled to herself and took another sip, glancing around for the loose board only a few steps over.

"That last step is a doozy I hear."

Sal turned her head, a smile finding her lips when she saw LT. "It really is. I am glad you decided to come tonight."

"A friend told me I'd be a fool to miss this, and I have to say he was right. Sal, you look amazing. Black suits you." He smiled at her in a way she'd never seen, the joy going all the way into his eyes.

"Do that more, it looks good on you," she told him.

"What?"

"Smile like you mean it. It melts the ice a bit."

"I'll try. I can't promise I'll succeed, but I can promise to try."

"I'll take what I can get."

He nodded, suddenly smelling nervous. "I'd ask to buy you a drink, but you already have one."

"Yeah, the bartender bought the Blades a round," she explained. "The rest have pre-deployment nerves and are busy trying to live life to the fullest. Do they always do this?"

"Not always," he admitted. "Sometimes they prefer to spend their time together, away from others. It just depends on what the mission is. We've been holed up here for nearly four months now, and they know we have a few days together before the fighting will start." He looked over the rail at his men weaving through the crowd. "What about you, Sal? Why aren't you down there trying to find someone to entertain you for the evening or enough drinks to make you forget?"

"Honestly?" she asked, turning to meet his gaze.

"Yeah, honestly." His eyes never left hers, but it didn't feel challenging.

"Because I don't care. I spent my entire life wanting to do what I'm about to. I know I'll succeed, and yes, I know there's a chance I'll die doing it, but I'm ok with that." She smiled to take the edge off her words. "I've found people I can trust, I have friends closer than I ever knew I wanted, and I dunno – it doesn't make any sense to say it, but the truth is, Blaec, this feels right."

"I hope it is." He offered his arm. "Dance with me, Sal?"

"I'd be glad to, if it won't hurt your image." She glanced down for a moment to show her respect.

To prove her wrong, he took her arm, laced it into his, and escorted her down the main stairs. When they neared the dance floor, the music changed to a slower song intended for dancing close. Sal cocked an eyebrow at him, but Blaec kept going. One hand in his, the other properly on his shoulder, she let him lead her around the crowded dance floor.

I've never seen you dance before, she thought. *I wasn't sure you knew how.*

I managed to learn at some point in my life. I just haven't had a lot of reasons to want to.

And now?

That dress could convince any man to make a fool of himself. I see you still have the necklace, too.

You did tell me to keep it to remind you, she pointed out.

I did. Although it doesn't remind me of what it should. His hand settled lower on her back, and she stepped closer into his embrace.

So then how do we get you to let one of us in if you won't let me do it? she prodded.

You don't let me say no all the time, that's how.

Then stop telling me no, she countered. *I won't go against an order you give me, but I know as well as you that you're trying to keep yourself bottled up. You've been running us ragged for the past month at least. That's probably why the guys are blowing it off now.*

Sal, he thought, *I'm terrified I'm going to lose you. That we'll lose you. I'm not sure if I can take feeling another mind ripped out of my head. That's why I've been pushing you so hard. We have to keep you safe.*

She took the last step into his embrace and rested her head on his shoulder, giving him no option but to put both arms around her. She breathed in the non-human smell of him, savoring it.

Do you really think I can't handle myself out there? If that's the case, then why did you accept me? We both know I'm as good as any man you have, and you have some damned fine men here, Blaec. Stop thinking like some human and act like our commander. We trust you, and the men take their confidence from you.

I know, he thought, *and I try, but...*

No excuses. She paused, then asked, *Why me, Blaec? Any of us* can die out there. Arctic, Zep, even you. Why are you so worried about me?

Rather than answer, he ran his hand down the back of her neck and pulled her closer to him. He rested his lips against the top of her head as the music drifted to a finale. Sal politely stepped back from his embrace and looked up at him, trying to gauge his mind. His eyes looked deep into hers for a long moment, then dropped to her lips. When the next song started, Sal walked off the dance floor, knowing Blaec would follow. She found a quiet corner in the back of the pub and turned to him.

Blaec, I'm not Circus. I'm not going to throw away my life because I'm distracted by a fight with you. I don't always agree with you as it is; none of us do.

He sighed. *I know, but this is the biggest mission we've had since that one. It doesn't help me any that it's your first.*

And I don't want it to be your last, Lieutenant. We're as worried about you as you seem to be about me, she pointed out. *So, Blaec, why me? You can't keep on like this. Either sideline me or admit your real problem, but don't drag your men into it because of your pride.*

She expected him to answer, thinking that having him admit his feelings across a link that Arctic might be listening to would give her a way to explain that he'd done nothing improper. What he did, instead, was the last thing she expected in a crowded bar filled with soldiers.

He kissed her.

CHAPTER TWENTY-TWO

*H*is mouth touched hers in the most gentle and delicate kiss she'd ever experienced, but Sal stepped back. He stood quietly, waiting, his pale green eyes like those of a scared young man rather than the leader of the top special operations outfit in their nation. She reached up and touched his cheek.

Why now? What happened to your rank and it being improper? she asked. *What about the restrictions on commanding officers mingling with subordinates?*

The truth? he asked. *I got my ass chewed. The men know there's something... I dunno, that I have something for you.*

She nodded at him again, encouraging him to keep going.

It doesn't bother them, Sal. It doesn't bother you. It's been months, and the only one that's bothered by me worrying about how things look is, well... me. Shift made me realize I was being a fool, and that if I lose you in this mission, I'd never be able to forgive myself for worrying about something that matters so little, when it comes right down to it. Come home with me tonight, Sal?

She gently clasped his arm. *Meet me at the door. I need to take care of something, but it'll only take a second.*

When he nodded, she strode blatantly across the pub to the nearest man in black: Arctic. The moment she touched his shoulder, he grabbed her hand and looked up. His eyes widened when he realized she wasn't one of the many women courting him.

Standing, his mind reached for hers. *What's wrong?*

I need this out loud. LT just kissed me in front of every soldier in this place. We both know he'll regret that in the morning, she thought, while she said, "The Lieutenant's drunk and thinks I'm some woman he spent the night with a few weeks ago."

He may, but will you regret it in the morning? Arctic asked, as he played the doublespeak the Blades were good at. "Shit, need a hand?"

She shook her head in response to both the verbal and nonverbal conversation. "Nah, he's more than willing to follow me anywhere, and it's probably easiest if I handle this. Just make sure you check on him later?" *I would only regret it if I wasn't going home with him. Anyone going to have a problem with this? I ask because you're the second in command, and obviously, LT can't be unbiased.*

No, we've been hoping he'd get around to it. It's why none of us tried, in all honesty. "Yeah, I'll grab him some meds for the morning. Now, do you mind? You're not helping me here."

"Doesn't look like you're having a problem to me." *Thanks, Arctic,* she thought as she made her way to the door of the pub.

No problem, demon. I'm locking the two of you out of the main link. Send to me if you need anything. You won't be able to reach anyone else, and unless it's a direct poke, I sure as hell won't be snooping in either of your brains tonight. Just be gentle with him. He's fragile right now.

I know, she sent as she walked to the door. Eyes watched her pass. The rumors were already spreading. Her mind felt strangely quiet when she reached out to Blaec. *You've already started tongues wagging, you know.*

Yeah, I see that. He sounded embarrassed.

The story going around is that you've had a bit too much to drink and think I'm some woman you met a few weeks ago. Go with it, and I'll go home with you. Ruin your reputation, and I'm staying here, she threatened.

Ouch, you don't play fair.

No, I don't. You deserve a woman as devious as you. We have a deal?

"Siana!" he slurred at her in answer. "You keep running off when I least expect it. Damn, girl, you have some serious legs." *You really do have amazing legs, you know.*

"C'mon, LT, let's get you to bed, sir," she said loud enough for those closest to hear. "Your head is going to be killing you in the morning." Draping his arm over her shoulder, she walked him out of the pub, toward his cabin.

Once out of sight, he turned and kissed her again. *You would stop me if you weren't interested, wouldn't you?*

I'd probably put you on the floor, in all honesty, she admitted. *Blaec, I told you before that when you decided you were ready, I would still be here. I'm here. Still.*

I don't want this to be like last time, you know, he said sheepishly. *I want to romance you, sweep you off your feet, and impress you with how wonderful I can be. I don't seem to be doing so well at it.*

I dunno. I think risking a court-martial for a kiss is pretty romantic. She found herself smiling at him. *And I know you a bit better than I did last time. I trust you now; I didn't before.*

Their feet carried them to his door. He opened it and escorted her in, calmly making his way around the room in near darkness with ease, lighting the lamps around the room.

I didn't know you could see in the dark, she thought.

I got all of my mother's abilities, it seems, and my father's looks. Well, mostly. Some would say it's the perfect blend.

I'm one of them. Your father must have been a very sexy man if he's to blame for your looks.

He stopped before her and touched the opal at her throat. *Why me, Sal? Why not any of them? Why did you come back here with me tonight?*

Blaec... she caressed his name in her mind. *There's more to you than even you seem to know. You're brilliant, you're tactical, and you hold this motley crew of crossbreds together with nothing more than your charm. The more I learn about you, the more I respect you, and the more impressed I am by you. And –*

You could have all that without coming home with me. Why me, Sal? Why are you here? It was his turn to push the issue.

The truth is, I don't know. You don't scare me. I can't stop thinking about you. I find something about you tugs at me, at my instincts. You keep me calm, almost human. The truth is, I don't have a lot of experience with what to do after the first night. Most men don't want a relationship with an iliri.

And if I do?

Then I'm here, willing. And if you don't, then I'm still here, willing to serve. I don't expect something that will last forever, not in our line of work. I just want this, for now. I want to let it run its course, and enjoy each second of it while it does.

He nodded at her, standing so close she could feel his heart pounding in his chest and smell his excitement. Slowly, she reached up to his face and traced his lip with her thumb. Her eyes took in every nuance of his features, but he put his hand on hers, pulling it away.

Sal, before anything happens, I want to make this clear. I will never ask you to be faithful to me. Loyal, yes, as a soldier, but I know you can't be faithful – not if it means getting yourself out or completing a mission, or just being iliri. I don't ever want to make you feel guilty. If the worst happens, and you're ever captured...

I know, Blaec, she told him. *It's ok, I understand.* She opened her mind, to show him, and felt his arms pull her to him.

When she melted into his embrace, he turned her gently, walking her through a door in the back wall. She entered his sleeping chamber wrapped in his arms while he kissed her neck and slowly unlaced her corset. Slipping her out of it, he eased her onto the edge of the bed and knelt to unlace her boots.

Stay the night, Sal? he asked. *Let me wake up with you tomorrow?*

Her only answer was to reach up and pull him to her.

She woke with her head on Blaec's chest and a sound in the room. One ear flicked to the disturbance. Cracking her eyes open, Sal saw Arctic slipping in the door. His eyes met hers. The link to the Blades returned the moment she felt Arctic slide into her head.

My, don't you look comfortable there. Can you get him awake, Sal? he asked. *It's past time for him to be giving us directions. We've been doing our best to let you both sleep, but it's well after dawn and questions are being asked.*

She nodded at him, then leaned over to kiss Blaec's forehead, running her fingers along his face. *Blaec,* she whispered into his mind. His eyes opened and met hers, a smile coming easily to his lips when he reached an arm up to pull her to him.

She resisted and glanced over at Arctic. "Lieutenant, it seems you're late for work."

He followed her gaze, groaning when he saw his First Officer in the room. "Damn it, Arctic. You sure know how to ruin my morning."

"You'll get over it," Arctic teased, exposing sharp teeth with his grin. "It's almost an hour after dawn. The horses are being saddled, and Tilso needs to know how many pack animals you need or if you want wagons instead. The supply depot shorted us a pavilion, Raven threw a shoe – the farrier is adamant she won't be sound for travel – and someone had to bring Sal's riding clothes over because I'm pretty sure neither of you thought about that last night." He pointed at a pile of black clothing folded neatly on the desk next to him.

"Thanks," Sal said, pulling the covers to her chest as she sat up. "Did you get my boots, too?"

"Yep, just outside the door."

"Ok." Blaec shoved another pillow under his head. "Have Tilso look at Raven. Cyno won't go anywhere without her, and I'm sure Tilso either can take care of it or knows someone that can. Show him our route and let him decide on the supply wagons, too. What else was there?" He reached out to trace a line down Sal's arm.

She kissed his hand, then climbed out of bed, making no move to cover herself. "The pavilion." Grabbing one of LT's shirts from the floor, she spoke to the First Officer. "Arctic, if there's not a spare, it's fine. Do you really think Blaec will let me sleep in the ranks? Besides, he gets a nicer bed."

"Right," Arctic said, looking politely at the floor while she pulled on the too-large shirt. "I'll make sure it'll fit two. What about when we meet up with the regular army?"

"Don't I get a say in this?" Blaec asked.

"No," Sal and Arctic replied in unison.

She turned to Arctic. "Just toss another cot in the supplies. I can bunk with one of the guys on those nights."

"Perfect. Thanks, Sal. You just solved our biggest problem, I think." He smiled at her and turned to leave. *Don't mess this up,* he sent, closing the door behind him. *We missed the old Lieutenant, but I think he's back.*

Me, too, Blaec agreed, smiling at Sal while she rummaged through his drawers.

And I can get you another half hour, but not much more.

They made sure to use the time wisely.

CHAPTER TWENTY-THREE

The Black Blades traveled lightly. Most of their supplies were strapped on their horses. Tilso trimmed the rest down to only what four pack animals could carry. The mules were tethered to each other and would follow Risk's mare, Phoenix. The hours Sal had spent in training made her comfortable in the saddle, and Arden picked her way across the grass easily on a loose rein. At the front of the line, Arctic, Shift, and the Lieutenant rode abreast, making last minute changes to the plans, fretting about things it was too late to change.

"They allus do this," Cyno said, pulling his blue roan mare back next to her. "He's na snubbing ya, ya know."

She couldn't help but smile. "I know, Cyno. I just slept with the man, I didn't become his puppet."

His cold eyes looked at her. "If ya think that's all it is, then yer a fool."

"You think I'm his puppet?" she tossed back.

"Nah, but I also do na think ya *jus'* slept with him. It's na that casual – fer him a'least."

"That I know, but I'm still one of his men, same as you. I don't expect to be treated any differently than I was yesterday."

He nodded, satisfied with her answer, but he refused to look away even as his eyes warmed. "Do na let it distract ya, neither. Ok?"

"I'll try not to," she promised. "I'm being realistic. I really am."

"Ok." He sounded like he didn't believe her.

"Cyno, I'm pretty used to things ending after the first night. I'm iliri, remember?"

"Wha' does that hafta do with it?" he asked, clearly confused.

"You ever met a man who dreamed of a long-term relationship with an iliri?"

He tried not to, but couldn't stop himself from smiling. "Yeh. There's least seven here in the Blades."

"Who'd choose an iliri lover over anyone else?"

"Yeh. Ya sayin' ya'd prefer a human over one of our own kind?"

Sal thought about that for a moment. "I dunno. Doesn't it matter more how the person treats you than what species they are?"

"Does na their species kinda affect how they treat ya?" he asked back. "Sal, yer jus'... I dunno." The pause stretched on, and slowly, he lowered his eyes to hers again. "Yer a good friend."

She nudged her mare closer to his. Picking at the reins when Arden pinned her ears at Raven, Sal reached over to grab his hand. She smiled at him, but he glanced down for a moment before pulling his away.

"Ya prolly do na wanna make a habit a that." His eyes slipped closed as he spoke.

"Of what?"

"Touching me, kitten. Each time ya do, yer sharin' yer secrets." He once again looked at her with his midnight gaze.

"You just read me?"

He shrugged and nodded once. "I can na control it, Sal. Ya touch me, I get somethan. And na all a us men are like the ones ya knew b'fore. LT'd never treat ya like that. I've read him, too."

Sal felt her skin prickle. "How much have you gotten from me?"

His words hinted at secrets she'd never shared.

"Enough." He sighed. "Enough ta know ya do na believe it when he says yer beautiful. Ya are, though. Strong, magnificent, brilliant. Even the humans see it, Sal. But ya do na know what yer instincts are screaming 'bout, do ya?"

"No," she admitted. "I keep trying to ignore it. Cyno, I don't want to be a beast. I don't want to be the animal humans always say I am. I just want to be a damned good soldier!"

"Then maybe start listenin' ta what yer body's demanding. They call us beasts 'cause they're jealous. It is na cuz they're better than us; it's cuz they're scared of us, and they have damned good reason ta be."

"I'm sure growling, snarling, and biting don't help any. Not like any of that is exactly civilized."

"And lying, cheating, or backstabbing are? Being diff'rent does na make it better. There's more a them than us, and it's gotta be hard fer ya."

"What do you mean?"

"Being female," Cyno said, cocking his head. "Has na anyone told ya 'bout that?"

Sal shook her head. "No. I just keep hearing that we're rare."

"Only 'bout one female is born fer every four or five males. Of those, maybe one in ten is an alpha type. We call them kaisaes. Pack Leaders."

"How do you know all this?" Sal asked, amazed.

"I was raised iliri. Pretty rare ta find purebreds anymore, but that does na mean we do na still keep the traditions. That's why it makes so much sense for ya ta end up with LT. Ya both got the vis." He shrugged and glanced away. "Makes me a bit jealous, though. I'm na the type ta be ahnor, but does na mean I would na wanna be."

Sal just shook her head, confused. "Cyno, I think you just lost me. I don't know what half of those words mean."

"Damn," he whispered. "I can na believe I told ya that. Look, never mind, kay? Yer a good friend Sal. Ya jus' happen ta be the best smelling friend I ever had. LT's a lucky man."

With a last glance at her, he kneed Raven into a canter and moved forward in line. She looked up and saw Blaec glance over his shoulder at the sound of hooves. His brow creased when he saw Cyno.

He's embarrassed, she sent to Blaec. *He actually gave me a compliment and didn't know what to do next.*

Do I need to talk to him? Blaec asked.

No, that's the worst thing you can do, I think. He's good, he just wasn't sure how to tell me that he's ok with this.

Are you still ok with this?

I am, she told him. *Stop worrying, Blaec.*

I won't promise anything, he teased as he retreated from her mind.

"It will be hard for him, you know," a smooth voice said behind her.

Sal slowed her mare and fell in beside Risk. "For who?"

"Cyno. He trained you, he feels responsible for you, and he feels a connection with you." He stared at her with his amber eyes for a moment, then explained, "Where he comes from, iliri act nothing like humans and relationships are very different. He's trying to work that out. He trusts LT. He respects you. He's just not sure how to feel happy about something that goes against all his instincts."

"Where's he from?"

"Guttertown in Prin." Risk named the slum so notorious that everyone in the Conglomerate knew of it. "He got conscripted when he – let's say they caught him stealing food. LT saw him working on the walls of some outpost we passed and got his name. When we had the next round of applications, he sent for Cyno, even though he hadn't applied. Like you, he passed each test, except riding. Took us almost a year to get him in the saddle, which is why he'll only ride Raven, now."

"So how long has he been with the Blades?"

"He's the newest. I think he's been with us about two years. The others we got before him didn't live that long. Most of the guys in the Blades have been in the Blades a *very* long time."

Their conversation drifted into companionable silence for a few kilometers, and then a few kilometers more. Throughout the day, the Blades moved through the ranks, entertaining themselves as they could. Sal took in scenery she'd never seen. Open plains turned to rolling hills and trees made lines along the horizon. Each night they cared for their horses first then set up the pavilions, finding their way into their beds by the time darkness took over the sky. Each morning, she woke up next to Blaec and made it her duty to pack the communal items of the camp. On the ninth evening, when the sky began to show streaks of pinks, the glow of a military encampment signaled their destination in the shadow of a foothill.

Riding at the rear of the column, Sal smiled when the Lieutenant pulled his horse to the side, looking for her. She squeezed Arden into a smooth trot, and pulled ahead of Risk and the pack mules, into an opening in the line. Seeing her, LT nudged Scorch over, reaching across to grab her hand.

"We're bunking down with the main army for a few weeks," he told her.

"I see that." She nodded toward the campfires twinkling in the distance. "I guess this means I get a new roommate for the night?"

"No, stay with me." He flashed her a charming grin. "Let the men say what they will."

"How about a compromise? I'll visit you, but I'll bunk with Risk." She called over her shoulder, "If you're ok with it, that is?"

"Us scrubbers have to stick together, you know," Risk yelled at the couple.

"Keeps your reputation pristine and doesn't give any of those grunts the wrong idea about what *I* will do in my free time." Her pale eyes looked up at Blaec with a warning in them. "We both know there's going to be at least one scuffle. We don't need to add any fuel to that fire."

"Fair enough, but I plan to change your mind." He brought their entwined hands to his lips.

The moment his mouth touched the back of her hand, his eyes widened and his grip released. Scorch stopped in his tracks at an unseen command. Shocked, Sal reined Arden to a halt.

"Blaec?" she asked, seeing his eyes staring at nothing.

Hold up! Risk sent into the minds of the Black Blades. *LT's seen something.*

Confused, Sal looked at Risk. "Is this normal?" Blaec still sat his saddle like a statue.

"Not exactly," Risk told her, while the other men nosed their horses closer. "It's his ability. Happens often enough that we know what it is, but not so often that we ever get used to it."

With a gasp, Blaec became animated, blinking and looking around him to get his bearings. When his eyes met hers, he relaxed.

"Sal, whatever you do, don't take the dun," he said with a calm intensity. "That's an order, do you hear me?"

"Yes, sir?" She was confused. "What dun?"

"I don't know," he said, looking to the Blades, seeking answers he didn't have. "I just know it'll break a leg, and if you choose the dun, you'll be under it. The bay is fast. If you take the bay, it will be ok."

"Sal," Arctic said, pushing Bazya beside Arden. "It'll make sense when it needs to. It always seems to."

"What else did you get, boss?" Shift asked.

"Damn, I hate this." Blaec rubbed his head. "We need to hit all targets when the moons are only a sliver. If we do it then – "

"That's tomorrow night, LT," Razor interrupted.

"Ok, then we go tomorrow. We'll drop each target if we do it then. Otherwise, we'll miss two of them. I don't know why. Cyno?"

"Yeh?"

"Watch out for the son. He's going to make a late call on his father and may surprise you. Shift?"

"Yeah, boss?"

"The girl has to go. She'll seem like a working girl, but she's really his bodyguard. Take her out first, and you can walk out the front door without anyone stopping you."

Shift nodded, and the Lieutenant turned to Arctic.

"Don't try to go in. Just after the evening bells ring, he'll close the east windows. A good shot will take him down without you needing to be near."

"I can do that, sir," Arctic said.

"And Sal..." he broke off. "Guys, can I have a moment?" The Blades nodded and moved their horses, giving LT and Sal space to ride off the road, out of earshot. "Remember that promise I made you give me?" he asked. "About being faithful?"

"I do," she said nervously.

"Good. I meant it." He looked at her for a long moment, sadness in his eyes, until he came to a decision. "You're going to have to catch the Chancellor's eye tomorrow afternoon. He'll have his men secure you and bring you to his rooms. I'm sorry, love, but I don't know all the details, there's just too many options. I just know you'll be undressed, with golden hair and green eyes, kneeling over him in his bed. You'll be able to sneak through the halls – remember that the first room on the right has servant's clothes in it. Out the door, turn right, first door. Can you remember that?"

"I can."

"When you get to the stables, they'll raise the alarm. The boy will try to stop you. Don't let him. If you wait, they'll catch you. If you stop to incapacitate him, they'll catch you. If you try to change your appearance, they'll catch you. And don't take the dun. Please, Sal, swear to me you won't take the dun?"

"The bay, Blaec, I promise."

"I just saw the dun go down, pinning you beneath it. A guard cuts your throat..." He blinked and looked at the sky. "Sal, I can't let you do this."

"You already said it'd be fine so long as I don't take the dun. I swear to you, dearest, I will walk before I climb on any dun." She slid from her saddle, ducked under Scorch's neck, and moved to Blaec's stirrup.

The Lieutenant dropped beside her, wrapping his arms around her. "I saw you try to call my name while you bled out, and I saw myself kiss your hand when we found your body." He buried her head into his chest.

"But the bay is fast? You said the bay is fast," she insisted.

"Yeah, I saw you on the bay, racing for the top of a hill. Fuck, I know what hill that is, too." He sucked in a breath. "I need a map! If you can make the hill, Zep's there with a squad of infantry. They'll hold off the guards, and you can make it back. You'll have something... I don't know what, but you'll have something we need."

He bent and kissed her, then looked in her eyes for too long, something still worrying him, before turning back to his horse with the thought unspoken. Sal ducked back under her own mare and swung into the saddle easily. Blaec was already moving toward the men before she found her stirrups and nudged Arden forward. She caught the tail end of the conversation.

"Ok, I'll have someone meet you at the edge of the camp where we need to set up," Blaec said before he turned his horse and raced off toward the army encampment with Arctic on his heels.

Sal fell into line again while Shift and Razor led them at a sedate walk toward the camp.

They went to find a map, Shift told her. *LT said it's important. What's with the dun?*

If I take the dun, Blaec said I'll die. That's all, Sal sent back calmly.

Oh! Damn, girl, then don't take the dun.

I know. Swore to him I'll walk before I ride a dun, now.

Shift chuckled. "Risk, remember to tell Tilso no duns for Sal or LT will fire him."

The men laughed. It had a hint of nervousness to it, but even Sal felt the tension ease because of the lame joke.

CHAPTER TWENTY-FOUR

Sal pulled the clean, but well-worn, clothes onto her new form. "I need a name and a reason to be in the Chancery."

Blaec nodded. "That we have. You're Arisha Jocose, the daughter of the washerwoman. She took ill recently – the washerwoman that is – and we bribed her with medicines to get you in. Her husband served the Conglomerate but was lost in the first battle. She does have a daughter, but the real Arisha has been living in Prin with an aunt for a decade. She started telling people that her girl would come visit since she's ill, so it'll be no surprise when you show up."

"Can I meet this woman? Does she know why I'm here?" Sal asked.

"You will, and all she knows is that we need you to get inside the building any way possible. You sure you're ok with this, Sal?"

"Arisha, and yes. I'm sure."

"Ok." He turned to the door. "Let me introduce you to your mother, then." *I'm sorry, but I can't touch you like that. You might as well be any normal human the way you look now.*

That's a good thing, Blaec. If you don't recognize me, then no one else will either. Make it up to me later.

I will, I promise.

She followed him through the tent flap and into a small pavilion a few rows down. Ducking inside, she found herself next to an elderly woman.

"Pardon me," she said.

The old lady looked up, her rheumy eyes a pale shade of green that had been vibrant in its youth. "She'll do," the woman said to LT when he entered behind her. "She looks enough like me at her age, no-un'll doubt she's mine."

"Good," Sal said. "So what shall I call you?"

"Risha allus called me Mam. I'm Mrs. Jyor Jocose, though. Round here, they just call me Vina, if they call me anythin' atall."

"Ok, Mam. Tell me about myself. What do I like, what have I done?"

As the old woman told stories of her daughter, Sal couldn't help but feel a pang of sympathy. Most likely, the real Arisha was selling her body or dead by now. Prin was a hard place for a girl this age.

She sent a thought to Zep. *What's the going price for a whore in Prin?*

High class or Guttertown? he sent back.

Both. And where would a washerwoman's daughter, living with her aunt, end up?

She could go either way. Guttertown gets about twenty-five pents and is measured in two-hour sessions. High-class whores in Prin can get up to a krit a night. They also have courtesans, but they only serve the elite and start out at ten krits.

Ok, Zep, where would a girl like this one likely be? Blonde with green eyes, if that matters, but her mother - while pale - is pure human.

Hard to say. Humans can have blonde hair, but it's usually considered an iliri thing. Mostly depends on the shade, really. Tan or yellow?

Yellow, Sal replied.

So, an iliri mutt or a human who looks like one. That'd put her in Guttertown. If she doesn't have the accent, she might do a fair trade in the working class areas regardless of her coloring. If her teeth are dull? Yeah, she'd make plenty. Lot of well-bred men want to see what your kind can do. Why? You're thinking something, aren't ya?

Yep, she told him. *Don't tell Blaec, but I have a feeling a whore is much more interesting than a washerwoman's daughter. Considering the Chancellor is known to have a fondness for young blonde human girls? I just need to know how to play it.*

I can help you with that, Zep thought smugly. *Grab me when you're done. I'll give you a burning of some memories – and only of the good ones I've been with.*

Thanks, I think.

While she chatted with Zep, Blaec had been asking the old woman questions about her daily routine and explaining what they needed. Mrs. Jocose was adamant that no one could get into the Chancery. The only people allowed past the servants' area were those invited – or detained. From Blaec's questions, it was obvious he was trying to play it safe. Not that it mattered. The Chancellor was a paranoid and private man. Sal wasn't going to be able to just walk in. She had to be invited. That meant she needed to get the Chancellor's attention, and the Lieutenant wouldn't like it.

Excusing herself, Sal left Blaec to explain their plan to the woman. She headed straight to Zep. In less than fifty meters, a young soldier stepped into her path.

"How much, miss?" he asked.

Sal-as-Risha smiled at him coyly. "Forty pents for a ride, sixty for the night."

The youth reached into his pocket, checking his money by feel.

"Get lost, kid," Zep said, striding up behind him. Sal had to smother a laugh when the soldier blanched and nodded.

"Sorry, sir." He gulped. "I didn't know she was spoken for."

"Get yer ass over here, wench." Zep grabbed her by her arm and hauled her around the corner. *Nice,* he thought. *You're a natural at this. Did I mention I have sixty pents for a blonde?*

Keep dreaming, Zep.

Ok, figured I'd try before you see this. Hang on.

He pushed his memories to her. They burned brightly in her mind but gave off only light – no heat. Unlike the bright flames Blaec had shared with her, Zep's hit like a sledgehammer. When Sal focused on the glow, faces of girls passed across her mind. Each one was involved in a sexual act with "her," since the perspective seemed to be from Zep's eyes. Also, they were all iliri crossbreds.

The impact of the images made her stagger. Zep didn't have the mental skill to compartmentalize his memories like those with iliri ancestry. Instead of a stream of consciousness, the jumble of partial thoughts made her feel almost dizzy. As her knees went weak, he grabbed her and held her against his massive chest until she sighed.

Sorry, kid, he said. *I warned you it'd be rough.*

Just the packaging was, she replied, patting him to show she could stand on her own. *And by the way, nice tattoo.*

She'd caught a few glimpses of a tattoo on the inside of his hip, a place where few would see it. It was hard to make out but looked like an intricate swirl. The ink was silver. From the taste of his memories, she knew it signified something important.

Yeah, thanks. His black skin turned a deeper shade. *Just, get what you need from that and meet me on that hill, ok?*

Ok, big boy, she teased, leaving him standing between the tents, blushing.

CHAPTER TWENTY-FIVE

It was late afternoon before "Mam" turned the cart toward the Chancery. Sal had been collecting filthy clothing and piles of unwashed bedding then returning baskets of clean linens for hours. Her shoulders burned in a way that sword work never caused. The weight of the baskets made her soft hands red and raw, causing a new appreciation for the work civilians did each day. It had been years since she'd done this type of thing and sworn she would rise above it. When she got conscripted, she never thought she'd miss the calluses. She could just add a few to her body, but it wouldn't help her image any. Sighing, she leaned against the cart.

"Mam? How much more of this do we have?"

"Enough," the old woman told her.

"How much is enough?" She let a whine creep into her voice, surprised at how easy it was.

"We still gotta get them linens to the Chancery, then take alla this back ta the house. If we get done early 'nough, ya can spend a few hours in town. I know ya ain't use ta it, Rish. It'll come in no time, though."

A groan fell out when she pulled herself away from the cart. "Fine," was all she said.

She turned and leaned into its weight, the heavy burden rolling slowly forward. She'd already propositioned a few young men – one from the Chancery – for later that evening. The guy smelled interested, and Sal hoped word would get back to the Chancellor. When they rolled to the servant's entrance, she noticed the guards. If Blaec's vision was right, she should find herself the center of attention soon.

At Mam's direction, she carried in the first basket of clean linens, flashing a coquettish smile at the guard inside the door. After placing the basket in the storage room, she adjusted her bodice, showing more cleavage, and got a dirty look from one of the serving women. Sal sniffed at the prude and shoved her chest out as she retraced her steps.

The guard looked at her openly this time. Again, she smiled at him. He bobbed a nod, casting a glance at the women in the room before smiling back. Outside, she grabbed another basket from the wagon and rolled her eyes when "Mam" shooed her back toward the building. This time, two different guards waited next to the door. A glance over her shoulder placed the first across the room, directing women toward her.

"Ms. Jocose?" he asked, and she nodded. "Please leave that with these women and come with us."

"I need ta finish helpin' Mam." She put on her best accent as she glanced from one to the other.

"Your mam will be just fine. She's been doing this long enough to know her way around. The Chancellor wants a word with you."

"Ok, lemme just tell her?" She tried to play her part but was unwilling to miss the chance.

When she turned to the door, the nearest man grabbed her arm. "Look, ya lil' slut. Come with us nicely, or we'll drag you, got it?"

Sal nodded, keeping her eyes wide. She could take these men, but fought the instinct to pull free. Instead, she looked at a girl close to her.

"Tell my mam," she called, feigning panic. "Tell my mam the guards are taking me!"

The girl skittered out the door, and Sal could see her running to "Mam" and the washing cart. At least now the old woman would be able to get word back to the Blades that she was inside.

The guards pulled her along the halls, up two flights of stairs, and into an ornate room. The walls were carved with scenes of animals she'd never seen, walking through a forest of trees she didn't recognize. In the center of the room, they released her suddenly, causing her to collapse onto the floor. Pushing her golden curls back from her face, Sal saw a man in deep purple walk toward her from the dais.

She made to rise, and he spoke. "Uh uh, my little one. You'd do best to stay down there where you belong."

She looked to the stony faces of the guards while the man in purple made a lap around her. Stopping directly in front of her, he waited a long time before he asked, "Who are you, child?"

"Risha, I mean, Arisha Jocose, if it pleases you, sir," she stammered.

He smiled. "And do you know who I am?"

"No, sir."

"Good," he purred. "You've been trying to sell yourself in town all day. Sixty pents, I hear?" While she stared at him wide-eyed, he flicked two paper bills at her. "I'll pay you two Conglomerate krits for the night. You will not ask for names, and you will not scream, do you understand me, Ms. Jocose?"

She nodded.

"Go ahead, pick those up, child." He pointed at the money before gesturing to someone out of sight. A pair of women entered and curtsied to him. The man continued, "Clean her up and take her to the suite by sundown." Then he turned on his heel and strode out of the room.

When the carved door closed behind him, the older of the women said, "Come on, girl, we have to get you presentable. Up to yer feet now." Sal nodded and stood, noticing the guards still watched over them. The older woman just huffed under her breath. "Follow us, girl, and I'll only be havin' one of you come to help. The rest of you can get your kicks somewheres else."

The younger woman reached out and grabbed Sal's wrist, pulling her along. The first guard stepped in behind them, getting foul looks from the men who'd dragged her up the stairs.

Sal followed her new jailers out of the room and up another flight of stairs, mentally mapping her path through the large building. The elder woman paused at a plain door before opening it, then ushered them through. Inside was a large, stone bathing chamber. Kettles of hot water sat steaming beside the tub.

"Make yourself useful, Harn, and pour the hot water in. Kasa, get the soap," the woman ordered, and both the younger woman and the guard obeyed. "Now you – Risha did you say?"

"Yes'm."

"Risha, the Chancellor demands that his women are clean before he'll touch them, so start scrubbing. If you don't do it well enough, I'll make Harn hold you while *I* scrub."

"Was that the Chancellor?" Sal asked, stepping out of her rags without embarrassment.

"No, that's the Viceroy. You'll meet the Chancellor later. And scrub harder."

Sal put effort into cleaning herself, but when Kasa reached for her discarded clothing, she paused. "Hey! What are you doing?"

"I'm just putting your clothes up to be cleaned," the younger woman said, confused.

"My krits're in there!" Sal made to stand in the tub.

"Kasa, just leave it," the older woman ordered.

"Yes, Marna. I'll just set it here for you," the girl said, placing the pile of clothes in Sal's sight.

"Thank you. That's enough to get Mam's meds." Those words elicited the first sign of emotion from the older woman.

"Is that why you're doing this, girl?"

"Yes'm. If Mam don't get some meds, she won't make it through the winter. Her cough's gotten bad. I came back to try an' get her ta move, but Mam's staying. Said Da died here, and she plans to be buried next to him. I don't know how to make much money, but the men say I'm pretty enough, and they pay well enough." Her accent wasn't perfect, but the story was close enough to the truth, and Sal figured that a little sympathy might be all she needed to get someone to look the other way.

Marna patted her wet shoulder and gestured for her to continue scrubbing. Sal complied. After the third time, the women allowed her out of the bath, wrapping her in soft towels. Harn leaned against the wall, his eyes following her without embarrassment. For all of his youth, he was the only real soldier she'd seen so far. *Where there was one, there were usually others*, Sal reminded herself, quoting Cyno's wisdom.

The women dressed her in fine satins and brocades, clothing a girl like Arisha would never have experienced. Unlike the evening attire worn further inside the country, this was demure and covered most of her body, more like Escean fashion. The gown reached to the floor, hugging her hips too tightly. The bodice, called a karakou, was sewn into the dress. Rather than lacing, it had bone hooks.

Sal would be infiltrating the Chancellor without any weapons. Shift carried an arsenal with him tonight, Cyno only needed a single blade, and Arctic would be using the jakentron, firing small poison filled needles. Only Sal had the skills to get into the Chancery, and only if she entered without any obvious supplies. She'd planned her clothing wisely. The laces were made of strong fibers and would work as a garrote. A few pins tucked into the hem were typical for a washerwoman. Hers were long enough to pierce the brain through either an eye or the ear. Now, she stood dressed in clothing not her own.

She looked it over for lethality. The satin was strong enough, but too thick to be easily used. The lack of laces made her wonder if the dress had been planned to be useless as a weapon. While the women dried and styled her hair, Sal's heart sank. They were going to leave it loose, not even giving her hairpins for a potential advantage. At least Cyno had trained her extensively on making the most of what was around – or using her own body to kill if she had no other options. Silently, she thanked the hard man for the hours he'd spent forcing her to prove she could best him with nothing more than her bare hands and teeth.

When the women declared her suitable, she was allowed out of the chair. A nod from Harn, and she followed him from the bathing chamber, through yet more halls. Marna trailed them placidly. Pink and violet light trickled through the window, signaling the day was nearly over. Sal's heart beat faster. She took a deep breath to slow it, but the older woman heard.

"Nervous?" Marna asked.

"Yes'm. I'm terrified. I've never worn clothes like this before, and I don't know what a fancy gentleman will expect of me."

"You'll do fine, child, I'm sure of that." She gestured to a bedchamber. "The Chancellor will be with you shortly, Risha."

Sal stepped in and looked around the room, hearing the door close behind her. She couldn't decide if she was terrified or pleased to see the decor. Ancient torture devices adorned every surface. It was a veritable arsenal. Knowing Arisha would have been scared to tears, she tried to call a few to her now nearly-human eyes.

The walls were lined with manacles. Screws and masks were set along the counters like prized sculpture. The deep purples of the room only made the aged items seem that much more ominous. Touching one, Sal felt actual metal, an item so rare it made sense they had a place of pride in the room. Military Command would definitely want to know about this. When the door opened behind her, she jerked her hand away as though burned.

"Do you like what you see?" The man's voice sounded bored.

"I don't know, sir," she said weakly. "It looks like a jail or such."

"It does, doesn't it?" He proudly walked around the room, glancing at the items as if on stage. This man was everything humans wanted to be. "What's your name, girl?"

"Arisha, sir."

"Arisha, come here."

She resisted the urge to walk right up to him, knowing he wanted to make her afraid. An ordinary girl would be terrified of a wealthy man like this. Sal ducked her head as she slowly shuffled closer. When he touched her shoulder, she trembled and wiped away the tears that should have come to her eyes.

His aged hand turned her chin up to his face, and he looked at her for a long moment. His teeth were nearly perfect, and his skin was almost as dark as Zep's. Black eyes stared deep into hers. She darted her glance from one eye to the next, biting her lower lip while the inspection continued.

"You'll suffice. Have you ever been with a man before?"

Sal nodded, hoping that was the answer he wanted.

"Good. I want you to do exactly as I tell you. If you please me enough, I will double your pay for the night."

She nodded again. He wasn't a bad looking man, probably in his forties, maybe as old as fifty, but his body had never seen the hardships that were common among the poor.

Checking the window behind him, she found darkness and a few last traces of twilight beyond. Night had just fallen. In less than an hour, Zep and a squad of men would be waiting for her. She was right on schedule but needed the Chancellor to be off guard before she incapacitated him. Otherwise, he might call out and bring guards into the room. Sal stepped toward him, trying to find a balance between terrified and seductive.

The Chancellor put his hands on her slender waist and pulled her against him. He smelled sweet and metallic. Her instincts screamed that he was her prey. With one hand wrapped in the hair at the back of her neck, he tilted her head back gently and kissed her throat. The air she'd been holding slid out, a soft sigh escaping her lips. The man grazed his teeth against vulnerable skin, biting softly, and she reached up to grasp his forearms. Remembering her dull human teeth, she fought the urge to bite back. When his lips met hers, she returned the kiss.

The Chancellor fumbled with the hooks at her back. His breath came quickly against her cheek while he unlatched each one, his erection pushing into her abdomen. She leaned into him, encouraging it, and glanced again at the window. Below, the city lights were starting to glow.

Feeling the last hook release, she ran her hands up to his chest against his expensive shirt. Slowly, he guided the gown from her shoulders. Only her closed arms prevented it from falling to the floor. Then he reached up and grasped her delicate wrists in his strong hands, kissing her neck, working down her collarbones to the tops of her breasts.

"Do you like that?" he asked.

"Yes," she whispered, trying to make it sound like the truth.

Without warning, he shoved her away. "So you are a slut."

Sal staggered a step back, eyes wide, and looked at him with honest confusion on her face. He closed the distance between them, but his demeanor had changed. No longer the timid lover, he looked at her with savage eyes.

A quick backhand caught her across the temple, and Sal swayed on her feet, fighting to keep her mind clear. When he reached for her again, she cowered, reminding herself not to dodge the blows, anticipating the pain that would come. A strike to her cheek followed.

While she was reeling on her feet, his hands pulled the now loose gown to her waist. Instinctively she covered her breasts with her arms, looking through her golden curls at the madman before her. His black eyes focused on her face as he said, "Now you will respect me, whore. Come here."

She nodded, once more trying to push tears to her eyes, and

realized he wanted her to fear him. She intentionally took a trembling step forward, until her crossed arms brushed his velvet shirt.

"Undress."

She complied, pushing the satin and brocade to her feet, then stepped out of the slippers. When she stood back up, she refused to look at his face, making note of the distances across the room and the location of the bed. The bruises were rising on her face, the blood at her temple throbbed. The Chancellor stood quietly for a moment, gazing at her, then reached up and pulled her arms down to her sides.

Sal did not resist.

Slowly, he ran his hands along her soft flesh. First her hips, then her ribs, but he avoided her breasts. She could feel her nipples rising in response to the evening chill and let the pathetic man think he caused it. When his hands made their way up her throat one more time, she braced for the worst, surprised when he only kissed her. Then his teeth bit into her lower lip. She had to fight the urge to snarl.

With one hand clasped on each side of her face, he devoured her mouth, his fingers digging into her flesh. Frantically, she pulled at his grip on her jaw. The harder she fought, the more excited he became, until he shoved her hard toward the bed. She staggered, dropping to her knees, and looked back at him with fear forced onto her face.

Come on, you bastard, she thought. *Come get me.*

As if reading her mind, he stalked her. Sal pulled her knees up, a squeal forced past her lips. The Chancellor grabbed her and threw her onto the bed face first, twisting one arm behind her to pin her there. When he started ripping at his breeches with his free hand, she reminded herself to squirm, listening for the cloth to come free. She struggled, her bare rump brushing across him intentionally, feeling exposed flesh as she tried to pull against his grip just enough to keep him distracted. Over her shoulder, she saw the human reach for something. A singing noise warned her just before the curved blade arced toward her face.

Cold metal burned as it sliced across her cheek and lips. The blood welled quickly, the taste of it flooding her mouth. Was it the metal that made it so sweet? It tasted like humans smelled. Across her body, her skin tingled in response to the shock.

The Chancellor rested the blade against her neck and pushed his chest over her back, so his lips were close to her ear. "Have you ever seen metal before, slut?"

She shook her head, careful to avoid cutting herself.

"The Emperor gives it to us. It cuts like nothing else. If you scream, I'll slit your pretty little throat, do you understand?"

Sal nodded, her mind working furiously. The Emperor had access to metal. Enough that he was giving it away to secure the loyalty of his men. Metal could change the war and was probably how he'd been conquering nations so easily. She felt the man grind into her bare flesh, his erection throbbing against her buttocks, and decided she'd had enough of this game. Glancing up, she saw his gaze focused on her ass, trusting the weapon to keep her tame.

The fool.

Without warning, she twisted under him, rolling her body toward her pinned arm. The Chancellor, caught off guard, lost his grip on the dagger, and Sal watched it fall into the folds of the covers while he tried to grab her shoulders. With her back braced against the bed, her legs between his, she looked him in the eyes and smiled.

Her knee met his crotch.

Moving with iliri speed, she grabbed his shoulders and twisted, forcing him under her, onto the bed. She pinned each of his arms beneath her knees, her muscled thighs strong enough to hold him easily, and leaned back, reaching for the blade near her feet. Her instincts begged to take control. She let them. This man needed to pay for all he'd done. She couldn't be the first woman he'd paid to torture.

As her hand closed on the sharp metal blade, he bucked, trying to throw her off. Sal balanced across his shoulders easily after so many hours learning to ride, but the sudden movement caused the blade to bite into her fingers. A sharp pain surged over her hand, then her own blood, sticky against the metal. Shifting her grip on the weapon, she pressed it against his throat.

"Do you like it rough?" she purred, glaring at his black eyes. The point of the blade traced a line down his chest.

Her pupils had dilated, making his movement even more obvious. His pulse hammered against his throat and his eyes widened slightly in fear. The scent of it encouraged her. She wanted nothing more than to sink her teeth into his flesh. He was her prey – and still didn't realize he'd lost.

Confused at the sudden change, the Chancellor made no attempt to call out. He tried to decide if she was playing games with him or if she was truly a threat. When he opened his mouth to speak, she moved the blade back to his neck and shook her head, holding a bloody finger to her lips as she glanced once more at the window. The night sky called to her, the stars easily visible. Smiling down at him cruelly, she placed her hand over his mouth and pulled the blade across his throat.

CHAPTER TWENTY-SIX

His skin was so tender. The flesh parted easily beneath the steel blade. His lips were moist against her hand, and she'd sliced deeply, like Cyno taught her. Sal counted two breaths before the blood began to leak from the cut, the smell so sweet. Bubbles formed in it before it ran down his neck, across his chest, and under her thighs. When the Chancellor realized his life was leaving him, he began to struggle, only making the blood flow faster. Sal just held him, savoring the scent of her kill. His chest pushed against her naked body, his heart pounded beneath her thighs, and she couldn't pull her eyes from his. With her hand smothering his moans, she found herself breathing faster, excited, and her lips pulled away from her teeth in a pleased snarl.

The light faded from his eyes, but she held him until she could no longer feel his heartbeat.

Sucking in a deep breath, the unexpected rush frightened her. She had to fight the desire to taste his blood. The man beneath her was still warm, but dead, and he smelled *so* sweet. Releasing his slack mouth, she sat up, looked out the window, and listened to the building around her. Hearing nothing, she rolled off the corpse.

Thick blood covered her, dripping to her feet. Sal pulled at the corner of the bed, wiping as much from herself as she could. There were no vessels for water in the room, so she spit on her hands, inspecting the wound on her right, then rubbed them in the bedding again, ignoring the pain.

She was not clean, but she could walk down a dark hallway without calling too much attention to herself. Sal pulled on the expensive dress and shoved her feet into the shoes. She tried to fasten the hooks behind her, but they were too small to close by feel alone. Instead, she settled her long blonde hair over her back. Walking to the window, her reflection served as a mirror. Checking her appearance, she decided it would have to do.

One more time across the room, past the dead man, and the metal blade caught her eye. She wiped it on the sheets before shoving it into her gown, between the layers of the bodice. A few smaller metal objects went beside it as proof of the Emperor's gifts. Satisfied that she'd accomplished her mission, Sal walked softly to the door and waited, listening to the sounds in the hall before opening it carefully.

Only darkness lay beyond. She slipped out, pulling the door closed behind her. Her iliri eyes turned the night into shades of grey, and she turned to the right. A few steps further on, she saw the plain door and stepped through it without hesitation. Hampers lined the walls, overflowing with dirty clothes. Sal picked through the piles, finding a pair of trousers close enough to her size and a servant's dress to go over it. She rolled the legs of the pants high enough so they couldn't be seen underneath her skirt, then shoved the metal trinkets in the pockets, only keeping the blade out.

Mentally, she traced her route through the expansive building. Servants' halls were common, and Sal tried to remember irregularities in the floor plan that would conceal them. One possibility leapt to mind.

A handful of clothing in her arms, she carried herself like she had a purpose, the knife tucked inside her bundle. Past the bathing chamber – moving quickly when women's voices came from inside – she ducked into an alcove as a guardsman climbed the stairs. With every sense alert, she waited for him to pass, then walked back into the main hall and continued down the corridor, stepping through a plain door that seemed to lead to nothing.

Her guess was right. She stood in an unused servant's passage. Jogging down the stairs with her heart pounding, she listened at each door. When the stairs ended, her mental compass told her she was on the ground floor. Only silence waited on the other side, so she opened it, surprised to find herself in the courtyard beside the stables.

The Lieutenant's warning rang in her mind, so Sal looked around for a stablehand. Nothing. She slid along the wall quietly, hoping no one looked at her. While she'd managed to change clothes, her face was cut and her body was covered in a dead man's blood. Thankfully, there was no one around to see her. Lights burned brightly inside, but she couldn't hear the sounds of people. Lifting her chin, she walked in.

Horses stood tied along the left wall, quietly munching hay in their mangers. The first, a boldly marked dun, would have been easy enough to grab, but Sal remembered the look on Blaec's face when he recited his vision. Down the line was a chestnut, then a leggy bay with a loose fitting halter. Across from him, a rack of bridles hung along the wall. Sal judged the size of the gelding's head and chose one that would be a close fit. Her plan made, she walked toward the bay, grabbed the bridle as she passed, dropped her rags on the floor, and slipped the bridle over the halter. When she bent to retrieve the knife, she heard a gasp of surprise. One swing cut through the rope, freeing the horse, and she swung onto his back. Her weight settled on the gelding as the guards cried out from the building.

Without hesitation, Sal shoved her calves against the lean horse, sparing nothing more than a glance at the stablehand as she spun the gelding in his stall and urged him toward the exit.

"Hey!" the boy cried, finding his voice. "Stop!"

The bay raced through the courtyard, toward the gates. They'd be closing soon, with all the yelling from the Chancery, and she begged the horse to run faster. He complied gladly, stretching his long legs. The ground flew past, buildings becoming a blur. They charged through the gates just as the portcullis gears began to move. That was just the first hurdle.

Outside, she pulled the gelding to a calm canter, hoping to keep him from exhausting himself too soon. Through the city streets, their path was to the west and north. When she passed the last building, she looked for the tall hill capped with twin trees.

Her ears strained for signs of chase as Sal pushed the bay into the hills, keeping to the trees and shadows. Hopefully, the uneven ground would hide her from pursuit. At a trot, they crested a hill, but lights glinted behind her, torches flickering through the trees, gaining on her quickly.

She squeezed the gelding, feeling the burn in her thighs as she struggled to grip his sleek hide. The willing horse pushed forward, covering ground. Leaning low on his neck, she gave him his head and checked over her shoulder. Watching behind her, she almost missed the line of guards cresting the hill to her left; only a twitch of her horse's head alerted her in time. Yanking hard to the right, she wrapped her fingers in his mane. The gelding bounded down the steep terrain. A few brave men followed. One horse lost its footing and tumbled onto its rider.

They were too close! She pushed the bay hard, his legs racing under him, covering ground, but sweat slicked his hair. They ran until the Chancery was lost in the darkness, not even the glow of the town around it visible. She knew she was pushing her mount beyond his limits, but she had no other choice. Slowly, pace by pace, the guards were catching up while her horse began to falter.

Zep! she cried out in her mind, *I'm not going to make it!* She hoped he could hear her across the distance and made for the hilltop that her eyes could barely see.

Thundering hooves, loud in her ears, came close. Sal looked over her shoulder, finding a guard reaching for her, hoping to catch her trailing hair or clothing. She flailed at him with the blade still in her hand, and he yanked his arm back. She forced the poor gelding on. Unable to kick and keep her grip, she slapped him with the flat of the blade, driving him for more speed. The exhausted horse tried, but simply could not pull away. They were catching her. The enemy was too close!

Looking toward the hill, still so far away, she called out again in her mind. *Zep!*

We're coming, Sal. Straight up the middle, baby, we're coming. She could barely hear him, but he shouted the thought hard, and it came through.

I'm riding hard. I don't know if this horse can make it.

Damn it! Just keep riding, Sal, I'm coming for you.

In the grey darkness, her eyes could make out a lone rider charging at them. She recognized Cessa by the set of the mare's head, and Sal guided her gelding past, squeezing hard to prevent the tired horse from slowing. Zep, in full resin armor, little more than a shadow against the dark mare, held his pike low against his horse's shoulder.

Sal looked back in time to see the weapon pierce the soldier closest to her, lifting him out of the saddle when Cessa slid to a hard stop. Zep dropped the pike and spun his mare, pulling a resin sword from the sheath at his back. He tilted the horse's head just enough for her to see the last man, then dropped the reins. Cessa pinned her ears and dug in, unwilling to let her target out of her sight.

Sal could feel the gelding failing beneath her. She only needed to make it over one more hill before they'd meet the infantry sent to protect them. She begged him to canter on with her hips, pushing the horse into each step. Hearing hoofbeats closing on her again, she only saw Zep racing to catch up, and relief flooded her. Cessa pulled abreast of Sal's horse, and the gelding seemed to find his second wind. He stretched his legs enough to make a true gallop, his neck and shoulders lathered, his breathing hard. Sal looked over at Zep to find his dark eyes looking back. She would be safe now.

Side by side, they passed behind the line of infantry and Sal pulled her weary horse up, slipping from his back before the poor bay could stop. She pulled the reins over his head and began to walk, slowly, letting the exhausted animal gulp air, even though her own knees were weak.

Thank you, Zep, she thought. *Shit, I can't thank you enough.*

You don't need to say it, Sal. I know you'd do the same for me. Are you ok to keep that horse walking?

I think so.

Ok, he thought, *let me give these boys orders. Head back to camp. I'll be back with you before you get ten meters.*

She sent him an acknowledgment and turned her feet toward the campfires in the distance. Exhaustion clawed at her, both the gash in her face and the bruises throbbing painfully. The smell of blood drifted from beneath her clothes and the weapon she held, making her mind twist in strange ways, but her fingers were too painful to release the blade. True to his word, Zep wasn't gone long. She heard Cessa's hooves behind her before she walked out of sight of the infantry.

Give me your hand, Sal. We can pony the poor horse back, and you don't need to be walking.

She looked up to find Zep's arm reaching for her. Out of habit, she offered her right hand, the blade still clutched tightly in her fist. He grabbed it, prying her blood-encrusted fingers away, and she moaned at the exquisite rush of pain. He looked at her quickly, his expression shocked. Tucking the weapon into his belt, he wrapped his hand around her forearm and pulled her into his lap, instead of behind him on the saddle, while Cessa resumed walking.

"Sal, what happened to you? You can barely stand," he said softly, holding her against his chest.

"The Chancellor is dead, the Emperor is providing metal

weapons – like the one in your belt – to his supporters, I didn't take the dun, and next time, I'll remember to saddle the bay."

She wrapped her bloody hand in his leathers and pulled herself close to him, inhaling his human sweetness. She wanted to bite him, to taste the salt of his skin and the sugar of his blood. The desire made her feel disgusted with herself. She wasn't a beast; she was a damned soldier who'd just completed her first mission as an elite!

"I need to report, Zep," she whispered, fighting her feral urges with discipline.

"That's where I'm taking you, little one," he promised. "LT's worried sick. You're the last one back."

"I can't be alone with him. Not yet."

"I'll be with you, and I'll make sure he knows you aren't staying. Don't worry about it. Just report to your commander. Your lover will understand."

"Ok," she agreed numbly, trying to hide her shame.

CHAPTER TWENTY-SEVEN

She made a sight when they rode into camp: a bloody and crumpled blonde mess held against the chest of a Black Blade. The reins of her gelding were still twined in her hand and trailing across Zep's leg. She didn't care. Her mind kept returning to the soft feeling of the man's flesh under the knife. Thinking about it, she licked her lips, clutching harder at Zep's leathers. Sal had never used metal weapons before. Their edges were sharp, but jagged in a way the resin swords of the Conglomerate weren't. The feeling seemed trapped in her arm, and the smell of blood clung to her, making her heart beat faster.

"You!" Zep called to the first soldier he came across. "Grab this horse, walk him out until he's cool, then bring him to the Black Blades. Tell them it's the bay, and there'll be a reward in it for ya."

"Yes, sir!" the man replied, reaching up for the horse's reins.

"Sal," Zep whispered into her hair, "let him have the horse."

She forced her hand to open, and the soldier turned the gelding away. Walking the animal toward the edge of camp, the soldier's gentle hand patted the tired horse's damp neck. She could hear Zep thinking and knew he was sending to one of the Blades. Glancing up at his face, she caught him watching her.

"Arctic's going to meet us," he said. "Unless you want me to drop you in the grass, I figured he'd be ok to help you down?"

"I'm sorry, Zep. Thank you," she breathed, and he nodded knowingly.

The moment Cessa stopped, Zep shifted Sal's weight. A second later, Arctic's voice touched her mind. *Sal, slide on down here. I got you.*

His strong hands reached up to grab her waist, the feel brotherly and nothing more. She couldn't help but notice the smell of him, warm and pungent, so different from Zep's sweetness. Arctic lifted her from the saddle easily, letting her lean on him until she could get her legs under her properly. Over her shoulder, he glanced at Zep meaningfully, but before she could ask, Arctic turned and walked away.

She stood alone with Zep before the Lieutenant's pavilion, able to smell the sweet scent inside. She knew it was Blaec, but couldn't stop thinking about her teeth piercing his body. It made her heart pound in her chest. Over and over, she sucked clear air into her lungs, convincing herself she could do this. She wasn't an animal! After a polite scratch at the tent flap, she ducked inside. Zep followed on her heels.

Blaec sat at a desk in the center of the room, a large map spread across it. At the sound of their entry, he looked up with a pained expression on his face. His eyes met hers, and he rose halfway from the chair but halted when Zep shook his head. Sighing deeply, Blaec nodded at Zep as he straightened his shoulders and turned to her.

"Corporal Luxx, can you report?" he asked professionally.

"Sir, the Chancellor has been eliminated," she replied in the same tone. "He claimed the Emperor had been supplying him with metal weapons." She handed him the items she had, then gestured to Zep, who passed the steel blade to LT. "And his room was entirely filled with various ancient metal items. I was only able to secure these."

"Well done, Corporal," he said, his eyes darting to Zep, but Zep refused to look at anything but her. Nodding, Blaec continued, "All four targets have been eliminated tonight. We have a few weeks before we begin the next attack, so find yourself a bath, soldier, and take the rest of the night off."

Together, Sal and Zep saluted and turned to the exit, but before she could leave, she heard LT's voice behind her. "You're a good soldier, Sal. I'm glad you took the bay."

In the fresh air outside the pavilion, a hush covered their camp. The occasional crescendo of voices could be heard from the main army as soldiers distracted themselves, but the Black Blades were reserved, most of their conversations being in their minds. Sal kept hers locked tight, scared of what might leak. She took a deep breath of night air and licked at the blood on her lips, then turned to look for Zep.

He stood only feet from her, holding Cessa's reins, waiting. She started to walk to him, then saw the lean form of Cyno squatting against the side of the pavilion. His cold eyes stalked her.

"Sal," he said, his rough voice gentle. "C'mon. Ya need a bath, and Zep can na help ya." He stood, slowly, allowing her to predict his movement. With a tilt of his head, he urged her to follow him, and smiled when she nodded. "Go on, Zep, I got her."

"Thanks, little brother," Zep replied, his brown eyes soft when he looked at Sal.

They walked in silence, Cyno staying at her side. His movements were calculated, but he made no attempt to meet her eyes. He just led her to a brilliant blue tent, borrowed from the army, set up at the edge of their camp.

"I can either come in with ya or guard the door out here," he said. "Yer choice, but there's a nice hot bath waiting an' a pair of blacks in yer size."

She struggled to find her voice. "I – I'm not quite ready to be alone yet, Cyno."

"I know, kitten. Trust me, of all the men here, I know." He guided her into the tent, tying the door securely behind them. "Sal, ya gotta let the form go. That's first. Come back ta yerself, and ya'll feel better fer it."

She relaxed. As she peeled the soiled clothes over her head, she felt her skin tingle. Pushing the trousers to her ankles, she refused to look at Cyno, not caring if he saw her undressed. A part of her hoped he enjoyed it. By the time she stepped into the tub, her skin had bleached back to white, the blood stains a dried brown smear against her flesh. Her hair, now straight and nearly silver, hung to her waist without the curls.

Stepping into the tub, the water swirled around her, turning red from the blood dissolving off her body. Sal closed her eyes, forcing herself to breathe deeply before slipping her head below the water to rinse her face. Her cuts burned, and she gasped at the sharply erotic feel of them.

Cyno pulled a stool behind her and sat, his back against hers, the wall of the tub separating them. "Tell me 'bout it," he whispered.

"It was easy, Cyno. Too easy," she said. "He wanted to rape me. He paid that girl for the night, and then did his best to scare me enough to make it rape." She fell silent, her thoughts crashing into her head too quickly.

"And?" he pushed.

"And I got mad! I didn't just do it because it was an order. I *wanted* to." She swallowed hard when her throat threatened to close. "Damn it, Cyno, I wanted to make him suffer for what he tried to do. I couldn't control it. I acted like a damned beast."

"It feels good, though," he said, the honesty in his voice shocking her.

"It shouldn't."

"Maybe na, but it still does."

Sal nodded, knowing he couldn't see, then leaned her head

back, finding his shoulder there, waiting. "I know Blaec's been terrified, but I can't see him right now."

"Why na?" Cyno kept his questions simple, making her sort through her own feelings.

"I don't want him to see me like this." She tried to act like that was an answer.

"Like what, Sal?"

"Dirty."

"Ya've been covered in worse, and he's still wanted ya."

"Like a damned animal then," she snapped.

"Ya've always been iliri."

She sighed while the water lapped against her skin. "You won't let me out of this, will you?"

"No." He turned to look at her, his eyes never leaving hers, but not challenging. "I will na. I've been there, Sal. I know what yer thinkin' right now. I am thinkin' it myself, and no one ever understood 'nough ta make me face it."

She looked into his blue eyes, realizing they were the color of twilight. He waited, his gaze frozen, for her to answer the question that still hung between them.

"It excited me," she whispered, breaking the stalemate.

Grabbing a cloth, she began to scrub the stains from her skin, embarrassed that she felt so aroused by killing a man. The feelings were too intense. She knew Cyno was behind her, watching her. Even as she tried to ignore it, the last hint of his breath caught her damp skin.

"Tell me, kitten," he whispered.

She nodded without looking at him, thinking about where to begin. After a deep breath, she started where it made the most sense. "He pinned me down, my face in the bed, and cut me." She gestured to the gash across her lips, still staring at the swirls of blood in the water. "I knew I could break free any time I wanted. I toyed with him, waiting to get more information, playing the weak woman he wanted me to be."

Cyno reached out and tucked a damp wisp of her hair behind her ear. His gentle touch contrasted with the memory she sorted through.

"When he said the Emperor had given him the metal, I knew I had what I needed, so I turned on him." She was all too aware of the fingers lingering on the back of her neck. "Like you taught me, I used his mass to pin him. I was completely naked, straddling him..." she trailed off as her breathing began to quicken.

"How did ya feel, knowing ya had control like that?" he asked, pushing her hair back again, unable to prevent his fingers from tracing a line down her spine.

"It made me aroused," she whispered.

"Is that all?"

She let her eyes close. "Metal tastes sweet, did you know that? It tastes like they smell. I held him there, and I cut his throat, and I watched the life drain from his neck. I wanted to lick it. I watched his eyes fade. Cyno, I was covered in his blood, and all I could think about was how much I wanted it."

"Wanted what, Sal?" he pressed. "Tell me."

She looked up at him, finally. His serene face was so close to hers. She could smell him. So close, so perfect.

Sal surged from the tub, turning to press her mouth to his in answer. The feel of his lips ignited a passion she couldn't contain. Water spilled down her skin, soaking his black shirt, but neither noticed. His hands clung to her, one reaching for her ass, the other tight against her back, drawing her closer. She could taste her own blood when the cut across her lips broke open, enticing them both. He growled softly, but she heard it. She felt it.

Her teeth bit into his lip, fueling his excitement, and she made her way down his neck as her hands fumbled at his shirt. She struggled to reach his skin, but he buried his fingers in her hair, pulling her back, exposing her throat. His teeth pierced the skin above her pulse, intense pleasure coursing through her body, then he teased the line of her jaw and kissed the corner of her mouth, lingering on her salty blood. She opened her eyes to find him staring at her like a predator. His cold gaze burned with raw desire.

Cyno took a deep, shuddering breath and slid his hands up her wet body, to her arms, before leaning away from her.

"This, Sal. This is what it's like ever' time." He was panting.

With the water cooling around her, she watched him stand and slip his now wet shirt over his head. His tattoos seemed to swirl in the flickering light, drawing her eyes across his chest. She made to stand, but he took a step away from her.

"I jus' killed a man, Sal. I waited under his bed while he fought with his son, then slipped out and shoved my knife through his back, into his heart." He looked at her intently. "It felt like sliding into a willing woman. I can na refuse ya right now, kitten, even though I know I should. LT knows, too. Why do ya think he let ya leave without an answer?"

"I don't know," she whispered.

"He knows. He knows 'bout the need within us. He's just so happy ta have ya back, he's willing ta let ya do what ya need."

Sal felt the guilt returning so she pulled herself from the tub, stepping out on the opposite side from Cyno. He smiled at her weakly, his shirt still clutched in his hands, held before him like a talisman.

As she wrapped herself in a towel, she thought about her feelings. Blaec was like a rock, the stability she could turn to when she needed it. He was patient, kind, and always supportive. Cyno burned like a flame, too hot for the eye to see. His feral nature pulled at her, calling her with some power she couldn't refuse. He smelled like a drug she needed more of.

"Is it always like this?" she asked.

"Yeh, it is."

"Is it the same for everyone?"

"Nah." He shook his head. "Some of us get the bloodlust, others do na."

"Blaec?"

He shook his head. "I dunno, Sal. Go ask him. He knows, an' he'll tell ya honestly. It's a part a who we are, an' it's jus' how we cope with being so close ta death."

"How long will I feel like this?"

"I dunno," he said, again. "Fer most of us, sleeping eases it. That does na mean it'll be easy ta find sleep, though."

She nodded and pulled herself into her clean blacks. With her hair still wet and her boots in her hand, she walked past Cyno, feeling the electricity when she neared him. He made her skin tingle. When she looked, his eyes were still burning, his knuckles white around the shirt in his hands.

He stepped back, his muscles standing out in ripcords on his shoulders. She took a long, slow breath as she ducked through the door. Cyno's scent had none of the sweetness of a human, but she owed it to Blaec to see him, to tell him. She didn't feel so beastly now that Cyno explained it, but she couldn't stop thinking about the tattooed man and how tempting he smelled.

CHAPTER TWENTY-EIGHT

Silently, Sal slipped into the pavilion. Blaec sat at his desk, his maps before him, but his eyes stared blankly at the wall, lost in his own thoughts. She dropped her boots by the door. The sound made him turn.

"Sal?"

"I'm sorry, Blaec. I just needed..."

He stood and walked to her, his green eyes soft, trying to keep his face stoic. "You get it too, don't you?"

"Cyno calls it the bloodlust. I thought I just couldn't control the iliri in me. I don't want to be a monster."

He placed his hands gently on her shoulders and shook his head. She sighed deeply. Blaec watched her, trying to smell what she was thinking. It was bitter, and the tension nearly made her muscles tremble.

"Sweetness," he said softly, "it's ok. You're not a monster. Remember when I told you to take the bay?"

She nodded. He had to tell her the truth.

"I knew if you took the bay, you'd make it back. But that's not all

I saw." He paused, trying to memorize every detail of her face. "I also saw you in another man's arms."

Her eyes widened, but he kept his touch kind and gentle. He also kept his distance, refusing to let her see anything but acceptance. He knew this moment was important, even if he hated it.

"I know it happens, but it doesn't to me. I'm not pure enough. I also don't own you. I don't possess you like a trophy, Sal. You made me a promise, and I'm ok with it." He caressed her upper arm with his thumb. "All I want is for you to come back to me in the morning. Go. Burn yourself out. Find Cyno, or any man that can handle you right now, and burn it out."

She didn't move. He could smell desire and fear on her, but there was something else. If he had to name it, he'd say determination, but it was so much more. It was purely iliri. The scent was strength of will and pride as she fought against her own instincts. Sal shook her head.

Blaec smiled and stepped close enough to kiss her forehead. "I never asked you to be faithful, sweetness, I only asked you to be loyal. There's nothing wrong with being iliri. There's nothing wrong with this. Breathe, you can smell it." He gently turned her toward the door and gave her a soft push. "I'll be here tomorrow. I'm just glad to have all of my Blades home."

Sal cast one glance back at him. He nodded, proving he meant it. Without a word, she left the tent as silently as she entered, her boots the only sign of her visit, laying discarded by the door. He sighed, letting the tension go with the air that slid from his lungs.

"You're a better man than I," Risk said from the corner. "I couldn't have done that, I don't think."

"Trust me, I don't like it."

"Like or not, you still did it," Risk reminded him.

"I did it because it matters. It wasn't a choice I wanted to make, but I have to live with it."

Risk dragged a hand over his mouth. "I won't ask. At least you know she'll be more yours because of it, right?"

"No. I can hope, but I also know this won't be the last time."

"Probably not. How do you think he'll take it?"

"Cyno?" Blaec asked. "Willingly, I would think."

Risk laughed. "That's not what I meant, and you know it. I mean tomorrow, when he wakes up beside her, knowing the line he crossed."

"Damn," Blaec growled under his breath. "I hadn't thought of that. Should I talk to him?"

"You know that won't help." Risk shook his head. "Just thank him privately once she's gone and leave it at that. She'll be back in the morning, and I'm betting tensions will be high. Acknowledging it – and not making anything of it – will be the best for Cyno."

"She needs this," Blaec said. "She needs to know she can make her own decisions."

"And they'll both be better for it. It's their nature, even if it's not yours. Might melt some of Cyno's ice. He's kept to himself for far too long already, and she's about the only thing that can crack his shell."

"That's what I hope. Hers, too."

"Hers will be more complicated," Risk said. "But she's making us all less human. Even you."

Blaec sighed. "I know, and I don't know what to do about that."

"Nothing," Risk assured him, moving to rest his hand on the Lieutenant's shoulder.

Blaec chuckled but shook his head. "And letting the world find out what we are is a good idea?"

"Who knows? But you need to warn Arctic, and I need to find my own bed. I have a feeling I'll be patching up a few Blades come dawn, since Shift is headed out."

With one last look at the Lieutenant, Risk made his way through the door. Blaec sat down and leaned back in his chair. Sleep would elude him. Each time he closed his eyes, the image of Sal wrapped in tattooed arms flashed in his mind. He sighed again and stared at the canvas of the wall. She'd made it home, and he saw that she'd come back. He just needed to make it through tonight and stop thinking about it. This would be ok. They were on the right path.

He turned back to the map. The next mission was as good of a distraction as anything else.

Sal tried not to feel guilty as she crept through camp. Her heart beat fast, pounding in excitement when she stepped through the door of his tent. Her iliri sight allowed nothing to hide in the dark.

Cyno, eyes closed, reclined on a folding wooden chair. His head was tilted back, his pants hung open, legs spread, and his hand gripped hard, pale flesh. Slowly, he stroked himself. At the sight, she felt her body sing like a finely tuned string.

His eyes opened, looking at her. The shadows clearly hid her no better from him. Without a word, she pulled her shirt over her head and dropped it on the ground. His soft sigh crossed the room with the scent of his arousal. Unlacing her breeches, she made her way closer. Only his hand moved, slowly toying with his dick as he watched her. She worked the soft leather over her hips and stepped out of her pants, standing before him naked.

Cyno smiled gently and reached out for her. His calluses brushed against her skin as she leaned into him, the sensations more clear than anything she'd felt before. His mouth kissed the lines of her stomach as soon as she was close enough. Then his hands reached higher, both thumbs trailing just under her breasts in the most seductive tease she could imagine.

"Why did ya come back?" he asked, his voice rough.

"I need you."

"Sal." He paused. "I can na do this to him." His hands made lies of his words, his thumbs still caressing, moving higher with each pass, making her skin shiver in response.

"He knows, Cyno," she whispered as she leaned in. "He saw it, in his vision, and he sent me to you. He knows." She moved onto his lap, straddling his knees to push her body closer to his.

He groaned deeply and let desire take over. That was all the acceptance she got. There were no words, not even a nod to show he wanted this. All she had was the feel of his touch and the way he shifted to give her complete access. She sank lower.

His hands moved to her hips and guided her onto his length. Hard and throbbing, he was ready for her and she let her eyes close as he filled her body. His touch calmed the storm raging inside her mind, and she clung to his bare arms, her nails digging into the black lines on his skin as her body stretched around him.

Then he slammed into her, thrusting his pelvis up, holding her to him. Her body jerked with the forcefulness of it, but she just wanted more. Sal sought his mouth to hold in her moan. Their tongues clashed, fighting for control. Her teeth sank into his lip and he moaned again, his own nails tearing the flesh across her ass.

Ripping his mouth from hers, he sought out her neck, alternating kisses and bites on her milky white skin. She felt his teeth break through, the pain so sweet, but she stopped her cries in her throat, a high moan the only hint of her ecstasy. She could feel a line of blood trickling down her neck, and Cyno ran his tongue through it, nipping at her while she thrust herself onto him.

It was carnal. There was no emotion, just pure sensation. Their touches were hard and violent to pierce through the haze in their minds. She growled, fighting the urge to shove her teeth deep into the muscles of his shoulder, clenching her jaw against the instinct. His snarls were just as intense, making it clear she wasn't the only one who needed this.

Cyno impaled her repeatedly, his hands bruising her skin as he pulled harder and shoved deeper. He gave her no escape from the pleasure until it began to build, swelling into a feeling she couldn't ignore, taking control of her body. Then, something inside her burst, her body tensing as she lost control. A feral sound escaped as she threw her head back. She'd never felt pleasure so intense and gave herself to it. Below her, he thrust again and again, her whimpers encouraging him until he found his own release.

Breathing heavily, drunk on the scent of their crazed need, Sal collapsed against him. Cyno sighed, relaxing as well and wrapped his arms around her protectively. As fast as it had come, the ferocity of their need faded and his touches turned gentle.

With their chests pressed together, their hearts pounded in unison. Both fought to catch their breath, feeling the unnatural desire release its hold. Gently, Cyno leaned forward, sliding Sal off him as he stood. Her knees buckled, still weak from the passion they'd shared, and he steadied her against his body. Pressed against his chest, standing, she realized just how small he truly was. Only centimeters taller than her, she didn't need to contort her neck to reach his lips. The thought crossed her mind, and she found herself doing just that.

His mouth was soft, and now gentle, against her own. His callused hand reached up, caressing the side of her face. When the kiss broke, she opened her eyes to find him looking at her, his deep blue eyes filled with a warmth she'd never seen. He smiled softly then bent and picked her up, her weight like nothing in his arms. Never looking away from her face, he placed her on his bed, the mattress sinking beneath her. She turned toward him, and he lowered his body – his breeches still hanging open – to sit at the edge, looking down at her. Her fingers traced his bare arm, the one closest to her, devoid of tattoos.

"I'm so sorry, Sal." He caressed her face again.

"Why?"

"I should na have done that." He glanced away, embarrassed, only to look back at her.

"Cyno, I think I did that." She chuckled. "And I think I needed that."

"Ah, maast," he whispered. "I tried na to, kitten. I sent ya back to LT. Why'd ya come here?"

"I told you," she said, reaching out for his mind, offering him the memory of her talk with Blaec.

He pulled away from the flame, but she sent a tendril of thought to guide him back. "Cyno," she begged, "just look."

She watched his eyes focus on something outside the room, his face flushing while the memory played in his head. "He told ya ta come ta me?"

"Yeah. He made me promise him before. Cyno – " she paused, thinking for a second. "Cyno, I don't even know your real name."

He laughed, her change in conversation catching him off guard. "It's Jassant. Jassant Cynortas."

"Jase?" she asked.

"Sal, fer you, I'll answer ta anything." He smiled, and she saw the light in his eyes that had always been missing.

"Jase, I don't know where I'll be tomorrow. It might be a meter under for all any of us know. I don't know where you'll be either, and I sure don't want to wonder what I might have missed."

"Sal... oh, Sal. Ya really do na understand what's pushing ya, do ya?"

"No, not really. What do you mean?"

"My amma was nearly pure iliri. My dava? She said he looked like Risk." He paused. "Of all the Blades, we think I carry the most blood. I cut my hair cuz it grows out ta silver, darker than yers but still silver. Sal, ya call ta me in a way I can na even put inta words. Amma allus said it's the way of our kind."

She nodded, encouraging him to continue.

"Growing up, we knew, we jus' *knew* that there were two kinds. Some iliri kill, they called em berserkers in the early days. Others could seduce or captivate. My amma, she seduced. She convinced our people ta hold onto traditions with little more than her charm. But me? I kill, kitten. When I do it, it drives me. It's the only release I can find most days. Human women, they just do na tempt me, no more than..." he struggled to find a comparison. "Than they tempt you, I guess. Amma allus told me that I would na be able ta resist a seducer, though. Since I first saw ya, I caught myself daydreaming 'bout ya. When ya chose LT, I figur'd ya made it pretty clear, since ya do na follow the old ways and all."

He paused, and she let him, still caressing his arm, waiting. "I figur'd ya was the seducing type, Sal. I think LT is too, which is why he pulls at ya. We call it vis. Tonight, though, when I saw Zep carrying ya in, I saw the ice in yer eyes. Kitten, I think yer a bit of both. That's why I was there. I knew ya'd need someone ta tell ya it was ok. Yer love of death calls ta mine, and yer, I dunno, yer love of life I guess, it makes me unable ta resist ya. I never met a full iliri b'fore, so I dunno if this is jus' how ya are.

"Sal." He swallowed hard before continuing. "Kitten, ya'll be killin' again. LT can na ignore yer ability, and he'll use it, even if he hates it. Ever'time ya do, it'll feel like this. Ever'time. Ya can na keep running inta my bed, leaving LT's cold. He's too human fer that."

She nodded, thinking about what he said, remembering what Blaec had asked her about being a woman in a group of men. "What if I do though, Jase? Would you let me?"

"Ayati, Sal. I could na refuse ya, if that's what ya mean. Hell, look at me." He gestured to the gouges on his arms. "I did na say no tonight, kitten, I can na. I prolly never will."

"Then we'll have to see what happens when it happens," she whispered, pulling him to her.

He resisted, leaning closer, but refused to fall into the bed beside her. "Will ya go back ta LT tomorrow?"

"Probably."

"If we do this..." He leaned down and kissed her lips gently before continuing. "If *I* do this, will ya be here when I wake up?"

"Yes," she promised.

"Ayame. Sae sussa il." His words sounded perfect even if she didn't understand them. "Then I'll take what I can get. I'm already gonna suffer fer this; I might as well enjoy it." He finally succumbed to the pressure of her hands.

Looking deep into her pale eyes, he rolled above her. She kissed him and his inhibitions fled. This time, he gave himself to her completely, his kisses filled with an emotion he never showed, and his mind reached deeply into hers.

CHAPTER TWENTY-NINE

Cyno's lean muscles pillowed her head, and Sal heard Risk outside the tent. Her ears followed the movement, so she didn't need to open her eyes. His feet barely made a sound when he slipped into the tent. *This is becoming a habit,* she thought, starting to doze off again.

She came awake quickly when Cyno reacted to the presence in his home. He slid out from under her, reaching for a weapon before his eyes opened. Seeing his outfit-mate standing calmly before him, Cyno sighed.

"Damn it, Risk. Do na do that."

"You have to move faster than that to worry me, brother. Sal, LT sent your boots, and I'm supposed to make sure the two of you are presentable outside of this tent. Nice to see you didn't tear each other up too badly." Risk chuckled at them. "We need to fix your face up, but I didn't see any point in doing this twice."

Cyno groaned. "Maast, where's Shift? And does ever'one know?"

"They do, and LT has him tending the front line. Some skirmish started up near dawn: guards from Sal's escapade last night demanding the assassin be turned over to them." Risk smiled. "Oddly, no one has seen a busty blonde around here."

"Jus' do na set me off again, ok?" Cyno moved to find his pants in the mess of black clothing on the floor. Sal couldn't help but notice that his tattoos spiraled not only down his left arm but across his hip, caressing the top of his left thigh.

"You, I won't set off. It's her I'm worried about, actually." Risk kept his eyes on Sal while Cyno pulled his breeches on. "So you go first, and get me out of here if she starts up."

"Deal," Cyno replied, lowering himself into his chair and reaching out both hands.

The golden man took a deep breath and closed his fingers around Cyno's. When he exhaled, Sal watched Cyno clench his jaw, the muscles across his shoulders standing tense. Miraculously, the lines through his tattoos closed, the skin healed, and the ink returned, leaving no trace of the night before. The bruises and bites across his body faded like they'd never existed. It took only seconds, but when Risk released him, Cyno looked completely healed.

"Damn, man, I think LT's trying ta make me pay fer this," he growled.

Risk chuckled. "Probably. But was it worth it?"

Cyno looked at her, his blue eyes warm and content. "Yeh. Ayati, it really was."

"Sal," Risk said, moving toward her. "You aren't my type." The corner of his mouth lifted, his smirk lopsided. "That's why I need Cyno here for this. It's going to hurt. There's a chance it will set you off again."

"Kitten." Cyno moved next to her. "Ya know how I said we can na resist ya?"

"Yeah?"

"Yeh, well, I mean that literally," he explained. "Sometimes pain sets us off, sometimes it's blood. Death always does it. There's somethan about ya though..."

"Pheromones," Risk said.

"Well, it turns us inta dogs sniffing at a bitch in heat. We can na refuse it, even if we wanna. Even if ya are na our type."

"Ok."

"So, if you feel it coming, I'm here. Ok?"

"Is this really that bad?" she asked.

"It is," Risk answered, guiding her back on the bed. Then he knelt beside her. "Close your eyes, little demon, and relax."

She tried. Without warning, the pain hit her. Sal felt the side of her face peeling away from her skull as the bruises healed in seconds. The gash on her lip seared a line of white fire through her mouth, and she found herself straining to breathe. The bites across her body felt like coals pushed into her skin and every muscle struggled to escape the pain. When it receded, she lay still, gasping for air. A groan slipped out. She opened her eyes to stare at the canvas ceiling of Cyno's tent.

"Kitten?" he whispered.

"I'm ok," she gasped, "but damn, that hurts."

She heard Risk sigh and turned to look at him. His gold eyes watched her warily. "You both have an hour, then the Lieutenant's called a meeting. The strategy's changed since you brought back that metal, Sal."

They nodded, and Risk excused himself from the room. Sal forced herself out of the bed, shocked to find no trace of sore muscles. Cyno had placed clothes beside her, within reach, and when she stood to dress, she saw him distracting himself with anything his hands could find.

"Jase?"

"Yeh?" He answered without looking at her.

She tied her breeches and slipped the shirt over her head, then crossed the room to him. He tensed just before she touched his shoulder.

"What is it?" she asked.

"The morning after." He chuckled. "I do na know quite how ta act. Maast, most women do na wanna stay long enough fer there ta be a morning after."

"Maast?" she asked, trying to get her tongue around the strange word.

"It's jus' old iliri. It's the word for last night. Ya know, with the passion on us."

"Jase," she said again, turning him to face her. Cyno's blue eyes refused to meet hers. His face looked calm, but the smell of concern clung to him. She ran her hand across his cheek until he looked up. When their eyes met, she smiled. "Thank you for last night."

Her words made him glance away, a small smile on his lips. "This is gonna suck. Ya know that, right? I do na know how I'm gonna look LT in the eyes."

"He doesn't own me any more than you do," she reminded him. "Now shut up and kiss me one last time before this meeting."

Cyno complied willingly. "It was worth it. It was so worth it, kitten," he whispered.

Sal tried to convince Jase to escort her to the Lieutenant's pavilion, but he refused. He hoped she'd take the chance to return to LT alone – knowing they both needed it – and convinced himself that his own embarrassment had nothing to do with it. After she left his room, he tried to remove the traces of her, but her scent lingered, teasing him. He looked at his bed, the coverings straightened and clean, and felt his heart beat faster at the memory.

He'd never known a woman like her. She understood him like the rest of his brothers in arms. He trusted her, unlike any other woman in his life, yet he found himself so strongly attracted to her. He'd never felt the pull before, the desire to be owned, to be consumed by someone. It all started when he checked her recruitment papers that first day.

Iliri women chose their mates, not the other way around, and it wasn't uncommon for a woman to keep her own harem. But those were stories from centuries ago, passed from mother to child. Most tried to live like humans now. The Lieutenant had made it clear that he expected the Black Blades to blend into normal society and hide their iliri desires.

Besides, LT was a better match for her. Cyno knew death, and for most of his life, death had been his only love. These men accepted him and even embraced his strange passions, giving him an outlet for his needs. When he'd confessed to LT his desire to kill, the Lieutenant made him an assassin, training him carefully and completely. Cyno's natural speed and agility were assets that couldn't be overlooked. When Zep caught him in the midst of his bloodlust, he'd reacted with understanding, sending for a whore and warning the men away from his room for the night. The next morning they'd greeted him without reserve, treating him no different than before.

This was how he repaid all that. He took advantage of his commander's mate, and the entire outfit knew about it. He tried to remind himself that he couldn't have resisted her and that it was her choice who to spend her affection on, but it didn't help. Blaec was in charge. Sal had submitted to him. Their pack order was just fucked up, but he had to obey it.

Sighing, Cyno pulled his boots on, tucked his shirt into his pants, and decided to face it head-on. He strode out of his tent with his head up and walked directly to the Lieutenant's pavilion, knowing he was early. Still, he had to fight the urge to walk past the door but, taking a deep breath, he scratched at the tent flap.

"Come," LT called from the other side.

When Cyno ducked inside, he found LT alone with Risk, and Sal nowhere to be seen.

"She's not with you?" LT asked.

"Nah. I told her ta come here, ta talk with ya."

"She hasn't made it yet, but that's ok," LT assured him.

Glancing over his shoulder at Risk made the gold man smile and excuse himself from the room. When he passed Cyno, Risk patted him on the shoulder then stepped outside without a word.

"Cyno -" LT started.

"LT, I feel like shit, man. I did na mean – " Cyno tried to interrupt him, but a wave from the Lieutenant cut him off.

"Let me go first," LT said. "I wanted to say thank you."

"Why?"

"For taking care of her. For being there when I couldn't. For giving her what she needed." LT shrugged. "She's not my toy, and I don't know why everyone thinks she is. I'm lucky enough to spend time with her, and that's all there is to it."

"Yeh, I know what ya mean."

"Do you remember the first time it hit you?" LT asked.

"Yeh," Cyno said. "I also remember how ya made it easy fer me. I did na expect it. They allus said I was a beast."

"But you spent the night with a whore. Damn it, Cyno. Think about it. She pulls at all of us. Would you rather she spent last night with a whore?"

He could only shake his head, shame and understanding warring in his mind.

"Did you enjoy her any less knowing that she'd been with me?" LT asked.

"Yeh. Well, yeh and nah," Cyno said, thinking about it.

LT smiled. "Yes after, but not during, I bet."

Cyno fought the smile creeping to the corner of his mouth. "Yeh, pretty much."

"Will you hate me if I say I feel the same? If she comes back to me, I'll enjoy her and only think about how you might feel later?"

Cyno looked up, meeting LT's calm green eyes, trying to read something in them. When the silence stretched on, LT continued, "She'll go to you again, there's no way around that. I can't be upset about it. I know I don't have whatever it is you both need. I hope you'll do me the courtesy of not resenting it if I don't refuse her."

"LT..." Cyno started, unsure of his words. "I dunno. I know it is na right, but being second is na so bad fer me. It's just iliri."

"And I'm ok with that. I just don't want hard feelings between us. Any of the three of us, or however many more she decides to indulge herself with," LT said.

Cyno nodded. "I'll do it again, ya know." He dared to look into LT's eyes, a hint of challenge there.

"I know. In a few weeks actually. I'm sending the two of you out together."

Sal walked calmly to the Lieutenant's tent. She'd found every excuse to postpone this, but she wanted to speak with Blaec before the others arrived. Her heart beat inside her chest, but she ducked through the door like she'd only just returned. In the diffused light under the canvas, she saw Blaec standing with Jase, the two men talking, at ease with each other. At the sound of her steps, they turned to face her.

Seeing both men, Sal's stomach tied in knots. Green eyes beside blue, Blaec stood a head taller than Jase, and both of them smiled at her calmly with warmth in their eyes. She looked from one to the other before reminding herself that Cyno knew she'd go back to Blaec. She'd already told him that. Letting the tension drain from her shoulders, she turned to the Lieutenant.

"It's still morning," she said.

"It is."

Sal glanced to Jase, not sure what she expected.

"It's ok," Jase assured her. "I'll be back when the rest come. I think ya both need some time alone."

"Thanks, Cyno," LT said as the lithe man slipped out of the tent.

Sal closed her eyes, taking a deep breath. When she opened them, Blaec hadn't moved. He watched her with a worried look, smelling as if nothing at all was wrong.

She stepped into his arms. *It's still morning,* she thought at him. *I'm back, and I'm sorry, Blaec.*

Don't be, love. You have nothing to be sorry about.

I should have been with you. I told you I didn't want anyone else, and yet... She let the thought trail off.

Yeah, you told me that before you knew. I knew, Sal. I knew, and I'm ok with this. I was just worried that you wouldn't want to come back.

Maast, Blaec, she thought, borrowing the expression from Jase, *you make me feel safe. You confuse me, but you remind me how lucky I am – in so many ways.*

Good. He kissed her head. *Just keep coming back to me, and I won't care about what happens in between. Deal?*

A shy smile touched her lips. *I think I can agree to that.*

You'd better, because I'm going to ask you to do it again.

It? A flash of Jase's face crossed the link in her confusion.

And him, Blaec admitted. *I need the two of you to work together. It's the best chance we have.*

How can you do this? How can you send me out, knowing how I'll respond to it, putting me so close to him?

Sal, I'm the commander first. I made a promise to my men, and I have to put that over everything else, even my own desires. We need this done, and the pair of you are the best I have. It's convenient that you'll turn to him, and I trust him. It's convenient that he'll turn to you, and I trust you.

She nodded.

I was also raised by an iliri mother. I may look human, but my habits are those she gave me. I have no interest in possessing you like a pet. I'm a little old fashioned, I guess, and I want a woman who chooses me each time, not just the first.

Humans raised me, Blaec. I've been bought and sold, and I'm used to being possessed. These instincts, and your acceptance of them? It confuses me. It's going to take me a while to get used to this.

We've got time, Sal, he promised. *I'll be here every time you come back to me.*

CHAPTER THIRTY

Over the next few weeks, Cyno grew comfortable in Sal's presence, and the men even commented on how often he smiled. Now, Arden matched Raven stride for stride as they raced across the meadow. The speckled mare flicked her ears forward, making Sal scan the far tree line. She breathed a sigh of relief when a pair of deer was all she could see. Beside her, Cyno had also gone on high alert.

Terric can't know we're anywhere close, she thought to him.

Nah, but they can allus get lucky. I do na wanna risk it. Do ya?

No.

As one, they pushed their mares faster, the massive warhorses reaching with each stride, making the trees surge closer. Hidden in their shadow, both assassins slipped from their mounts and wound the reins around the horses' necks. Sal glanced at her partner. The silence was deafening, the wildlife frightened by their mad rush.

Cyno's mind whispered in hers, *Let's get away from the horses. If there's anyone here, they'll have seen where we came in.*

She nodded at him and stepped lightly, watching for detritus that would give her position away. Finding a bush huddled next to a tree, she tucked her small body among its branches. From here, she had a clear view of the horses, and anyone who saw them would surely find the animals hard to resist. A flash of light caught her eye when Cyno pressed himself against a branch high in the trees.

Watch your blades, she sent, *they're shiny.*

Maast, he thought back, *I jus' found a new one and forgot ta scuff it. The ceramic these things're cast from's sharp, but way too pretty.*

So, she said, trying to distract herself, *while we wait, why don't you tell me why you keep calling me kitten.*

Ha! Na, I do na think that'd do me any favors. I'd rather keep ya wondering.

You're a tease, you know that?

I can live with that, he thought.

Fine, then tell me about the tattoos. I always seem too busy to ask.

Since I think we'll be lying here a bit, I can do that. Whatcha wanna know?

What made you pick those? she asked.

Ya do na read Iliran do ya? Nah, never mind. I shoulda known better than ta ask that. It's a story, kinda, but na the good kind.

Go on, she begged. *I got a twig poking me in the ass. Help me keep my mind off it.*

Well, each time I killed a man, I allus thought a them by their deaths. Yeh, the ladies too. Like, there was the one whose neck I broke, or that bitch who screamed when she saw me. Each name is scrawled here, in the writing my amma taught me. They started in a book, but eventually, Risk agreed ta put 'em on me.

Ok, so why on the left? she pressed.

Ya did na know I'm left-handed?

No, actually, Sal replied. *I didn't. You fight as well with either, and I can't say I see you doing a whole lot of writing.*

Yeh, fair 'nough. I think we're being a bit twitchy, though, since the birds're singing and na a thing's moved yet, cept the mares.

Yeah, and the stick is still poking my ass.

Oh, kitten. Yer a tease, ya know that?

She didn't indulge him with a response. Instead, she made her way to Arden, listening to each sound while she moved. Reaching her mare, she checked Cyno's position and swung into the saddle, clicking for Raven to follow. If any attack came, she'd look like a lone rider trailing an extra horse. As she led the animals to Cyno's tree, the woods around them remained peaceful.

It's clear down here, she said.

Up here too. Comin' down.

She heard the rustle of bark when he descended, then he suddenly appeared at Raven's side. Together, they moved on, their horses carefully picking their way through the underbrush. Keeping their conversation in their minds, they chatted about anything that caught their attention while the pair meandered the two kilometers to the edge of the forest. Just inside the tree line, they looked down on the outpost below.

That's a lot more military than LT expected, Cyno thought.

You still up for this? Sal asked.

Yeh, but I'm na as eager as I'd be alone, I gotta say. I think that's why he stuck us t'gether.

Probably. Blaec does things like that. Look, if we make it down that ridge, Sal thought, pointing, *we can keep to the trees until the wall. Park the mares in there – doesn't look like there's a lot of traffic – and scale the wall after dark.*

Na bad. Yeh, that looks like it'll work, Cyno said, following the path she laid out. *It'll put us farther from the gates, but Raven'll come when I call her, and Arden should follow. If na, my girl can carry two until we catch yer spotted mule.*

Leave her spots out of this. Sal tossed a smile at him, teasing. *It means some backtracking, but I think it's safer than showing pale skin or our blacks.*

Cyno agreed, and together they began the long trip back through the woods. The sun hung a finger-length above the horizon when they reached the pocket of trees Sal had chosen. They secured their horses, checked their weapons, and Sal reminded Cyno to dull his new blade. With time left before darkness gave them the cover they needed, they sat in an awkward silence.

Ok, you're killing me, Jase, she told him. *Are you as nervous about this as I am?*

Nah, we'll be in and out of there with a few more notches on our belts. It will na be hard.

I didn't mean the job.

Yeh, the after? He kept his eyes on the ground.

She nodded.

It's a bit 'a both. Part of me wants it ta hit. It's so intense, and there's na a thing else like it. Part of me is worried about ya.

Me?

Yeh. It's nothing. Ferget I said anything.

You still have time, so you might as well get it out there, she pointed out.

Ok. It's like this. I know one of us will get the lust tonight. Prolly, both. Can na see how we both will na get a kill in there. I'm pretty sure we can make it out b'fore we start tearing at each other, but then what? What happens the next morning?

You mean Blaec? she asked.

Nah, I'm good with him. It's ya. Will ya still respect me in the morning? That kinda thing.

Jase? she asked, her mental voice conveying her amusement. *Are you saying you're worried you won't be good enough?*

Somethan like that. Yeh.

Your only concern, minutes before we're supposed to sneak into a fully manned military outpost, is if you'll be good in bed?

I knew ya would na understand.

Trying to keep from laughing, with guards possibly meters away from them on the other side of the wall, she kissed him. Jase leaned into it, his hand reaching up to her face. When their lips separated, he looked into her icy eyes.

It's time, kitten.

Together, they made their way to the three-meter high wall.

Cyno found a handhold and began scaling it like a spider. When he reached the top, he paused, his black leathers nearly invisible in the deep twilight. Sal pulled her hood over her hair and followed, moving slower and more cautiously. She reached the top and crouched beside him. Together, they mentally mapped their path to the Broch. From the wall to the roofs, Cyno's natural agility made Sal feel awkward. She focused on each step and was able to keep pace with him - barely.

Crouched on a rooftop, he pointed out the rough spot in their path. A gap longer than her own body lay before them. *Can ya make it?* he asked.

I can make it, but I can't promise to do it silently, she admitted.

Just follow me, kitten. When ya hit the other side, roll with it. Spread yer weight out and it will na be as loud.

I can do that. Just be ready to move if we need to, she warned.

Cyno waited for a moment, listening to the natural sounds around him, and leapt when a wagon passed a few streets over. He landed on the far roof, rolling gently, and Sal barely heard anything out of the ordinary. He turned to her and nodded.

She listened, and luck smiled on her. A group of mounted soldiers passed on the other side of her building, their horses' shoes ringing against the stones in the street. She rushed forward, leaping at the last second, and sailed across the gap. As she landed, she tucked her shoulder, felt the jarring impact, and allowed herself to roll. She made her way to her toes, squatting with her hands against the thatch roof, and glanced at Cyno. He smiled at her proudly, allowing his sharp teeth to show.

'Bout as good as I coulda asked fer. I think I'll keep ya.

As the streets grew quiet again, the couple crept over the roof, skipped across another, and found themselves standing in the shadow of the Broch wall.

Not too smart, letting the buildings stand so close like this, Sal thought.

Yeh, but who'd be dumb enough ta scale a Broch? he asked.

C'mon. We gotta get ta the third floor. Keep yer hair covered, or change it, but do na let it catch the light.

Yes, sir, she replied.

Ya got me confused with yer other man, I think. I am na yer 'sir.'

Shut up and climb. It's the only time I get to appreciate your ass without you noticing, she snapped back.

Grinning, he started up the wall. Sal made sure to place her hands and feet in the same places Cyno chose. When they reached the base of the third story window, they waited, listening for any voices or the sounds of movement before sliding through the opening. Cyno went in first. Sal counted to three before following. Finding themselves in a dark and dusty room, they took the chance to rub out tired muscles and catch their breath.

Ya feeling it yet? Cyno asked.

Nah. This isn't anything more than a training exercise, she told him. *Takes a little more to get me going. Sorry.*

Jus' checkin', since we have a nice room all ta ourselves. There was a wicked glint in his eyes. *Ready?*

She nodded and followed him into the hall. They slid along the walls, keeping to the shadows between lanterns, and made their way to the balcony over the great room. Below, a group of men sat at a table, the tone of their voices suggesting they argued about something. Carefully, Cyno slipped over the balcony wall, onto a cross beam that spanned the room. Sal moved to the other side, making one last check of her weapons before doing the same. They crept over the heads of the men below and paused, listening to the conversation.

"The Emperor swears he can supply us with enough for over one hundred swords each," a large man said, slamming his fist on the table. "That's a hundred metal swords. Not ceramic, not resin, but *metal* swords. I can't pass that up."

"Damn it, Dejan," another said, "What are you willing to give up for that? What does that bastard want for that much true steel?"

"He wants to take the Conglomerate," Dejan answered. "Swears there's more under one of their military bases.

A third man added his voice to the debate. "I'm with Dejan. Metal is worth more than some ancient covenant our ancestors created."

"Vilko's with me. Who else?" Dejan demanded. "The Emperor is bringing in Anglia next. If they take the steel he's sending, he won't need any of us. This isn't something we can wait to decide!"

"If he's after Anglia, why did he even make us the offer?" one man demanded.

"It takes a while to get across the continent," Vilko said. "The shipment's just now headed to the Escean pass. Means six months, maybe more before Anglia can help. The Emperor doesn't like to wait."

"Ok, I'm with ya."

"I figured ya would be, Rok. Jurij, you can't be scared of the Westerners, are ya?" Dejan taunted.

The second man answered violently. "I'm the only one of us on the border! It's pretty easy for you to make agreements, get paid in steel, and leave me to defend your territory. I want no part in this!" Jurij shoved away from the table, his wine spilling, and stormed from the room. "Keep your damned steel. It won't do me any good if I don't have a province left."

Which province does Jurij lord over? Sal asked.

Jurica, actually. They've been suing fer peace fer months now. I think, after this, they jus' might get it.

I count six left. Sal said.

That's what I got.

How do you want to play this, Jase?

That's three each, but each is a damned Warlord. Let's go safe. I'll take this side, ya take that. Lemme in yer head, Sal, jus' in case.

She opened her mind, his anticipation mingling across to meet with hers. Glancing up, she found him watching her with a feral smile. As the excitement began to build, she made her way to the far side of her beam, looking down a few paces behind where the men sat. Balancing carefully, she stood and saw Cyno do the same across from her. One last check of her weapons, the primary blades sheathed at her waist, then she looked across the distance, finding her partner still watching her. The first rush of her frenzy hit. Cyno's lips curled, his eyes glinting in the shadows.

Together, yet so far apart, they stepped into nothingness and dropped.

CHAPTER THIRTY-ONE

Both black-clad figures plummeted from the ceiling, landing softly. Crouched on one knee, their offhands a point of balance, they moved like one. Their main hands slid a blade from their sheaths when they stood. The man across the table from Sal gasped, pointing at her, and the man before her called out, seeing Cyno. Calmly, too calmly, she stepped behind him, her eyes on her partner, and wrapped her fingers in the old warrior's hair. Pulling his head back, she slid her blade – the steel one she earned in her first assassination – across his throat. On the other side of the room, Cyno mirrored her actions, their minds dancing harmoniously.

She felt the blood on her hand. Warm. Sticky. Her heart beat faster, and her lips parted. The room smelled so sweet. The frenzied panic of the Warlords drove her higher. The smell of fear and excitement were like a drug.

It had begun.

The four remaining warlords realized they were under attack and panicked. To her right, a large man reached for his sword. Her bloodlust slowed the world around her, making the giant move as though mired in time. He swung the heavy weapon over his head, intending to cleave her in two. Sal ducked beneath his hands, stepping as close to him as a lover, and buried her dagger in his chest once, twice, and finally a third time. Each plunge of the blade reminded her of a man thrusting into her body, a subtle revenge.

The warrior collapsed, his hands pulling the hood from her head, letting her pale hair gleam in the lantern light. There were only two left – and four bodies on the floor. Both Esceans were focused on her, thinking her the weaker target. She moved to the table, using a now-empty chair for a step, and leapt over a slash from Dejan. To her left, Vilko scrambled for the sword laying on the ground. Cyno rushed to help, and she turned, feeling a glass shatter beneath her boot. Bending, she ducked another wild swing from Dejan, and a flick of her wrist sent the steel dagger singing through the air. She watched the blade spin before it buried itself in Vilko's chest.

Sal grabbed another knife from her belt and calmly stepped toward Dejan, the veteran's eyes wide in fear. His mouth moved, but her mind refused to accept the sound of his voice. She just wanted him to die.

Beside her, Cyno also stalked him. Blood splattered across his face, his left hand red to the elbow, and the smile still played at his lips. She could feel his arousal. It matched her own.

Dejan made a wild swing at Cyno, but the little assassin dodged the slash with ease, grabbing the human's arm and pinning it to the wall behind him. She stepped in, her ceramic blade held at her waist. With all her might, she thrust upwards. The knife pierced Dejan's leathers and slid easily through his skin. She watched his face as the pain hit, feeling his heartbeat reverberate through the blade.

Cyno's hand covered hers, and together, they pulled the weapon up, feeling the flesh part beneath its edge. The Warlord's blood spilled out, rushing over their joined fingers. When the blade stopped against bone, Cyno guided her hand out, the knife still held between them, and she turned to him. Meeting his eyes, she thrust again. Together, they plunged the weapon deep, feeling the stone of the wall snap the tip on the other side. Dejan gasped one last time and sagged.

Sal looked to the last man, Vilko, with blood pooling from the steel in his chest, then back to her partner. She could feel Cyno's heart pounding in her mind, his need so intense he had to release it. He grabbed the back of her neck and pulled her to him. His lips crushed hers, and there was a soft growl in his throat. Her skin felt like it burned. The taste on his lips made her want more. Somehow, she forced herself away from him, grabbing his wrist to haul him toward the last man. Cyno moaned in ecstasy.

He's yers, kitten, he thought. *Yer kill.*

She pulled her eyes from his and leaned over the body, placing a foot beside her knife before she pulled her steel blade from his chest. Vilko looked up at her, his eyes pleading, and tried to struggle. Dropping a knee on one arm, she let him thrash, smiling as she pushed his jaw up, exposing his throat. She knew what Cyno wanted to see.

Vilko's free hand pulled at her arm, trying to pry her away, but he was too weak from blood loss. Sal licked her lips again and pulled the steel across his neck. His body arched off the floor, violently, making his last thrashes in vain. As the man died before them, Sal pulled Cyno to her, claiming his mouth with her own.

I want you so bad, she thought.

Soon, he promised. *We need ta leave. Now.*

She nodded and looked at her blade. For a moment, all she could think about was licking it clean. As she raised it to her mouth, Cyno caught her wrist.

Do na do that, he thought. *Do na taste them. It makes it harder ta stop.*

Shocked, she slid her blade into its sheath and climbed to her feet. She wanted to ask what he meant, but there wasn't time. Glancing above, she took a step over, placing herself under one of the beams. Cyno cupped his hands, and she leapt into them, feeling him propel her higher. The wood rushed at her, and she grabbed it, throwing her chest over the beam before sliding astride as though mounting a horse. With one leg on either side, she lay against the heavy timber, reaching her hand out for her partner.

He stepped back, then jogged toward the wall, jumping at the last minute to use the impact to bounce him higher. His wrist slapped into her hand, and she swung him up behind her. In unison, they stood. Rushing across the beam, the pair hopped over the balcony wall and retreated to the dusty room they'd started in.

The door was barely closed before Cyno was against her, their feral desire more than either could control. She bit his lip, drawing blood, and smiled when she heard him suck in a breath.

Back the way we came? she asked, pulling herself away.

Yeh, but when we hit the roof, we need ta make it ta the ground.

Got it.

She moved to the window, holding her breath to listen for sounds below. Hearing only silence, she slipped over the edge. Her feet found the gaps in the stones, and her hands closed securely on the rocks, leaving bloody prints behind. Careful to test each foot placement before she committed to it, Sal found herself stepping onto the thatch roof faster than she expected. She looked up and saw Cyno only a body length above her.

At the side of the smaller building, she crouched against the roofline and listened again. Before Cyno could reach her, she hopped over the edge, landing on her toes, her offhand securing her balance like she'd been taught. He dropped beside her, and they raced through the streets of the outpost side by side, sticking close to the walls so they could use the shadows for their cover.

How long do we have? she asked.

Dunno, but would rather we are na here ta find out, he replied, ducking around a corner ahead of her.

They judged their path by the trees outside the outpost wall and aimed for a spot close to the cluster their mares hid behind.

When they reached it, the Broch behind them was still silent. Sharing a look, the pair scaled the wall together, each trying to reach the top first. Cyno's hand grabbed a stone on the lip, but when he pulled himself up, it broke free. He struggled to retain his grip, and both assassins listened as the rock clattered loudly beneath them.

Move, he thought. *Now!*

Sal swung over the top of the wall and rushed the three steps to the far side, then slipped over without checking. Beside her, Cyno matched her for each step and hold. She hopped the last meter to the ground and hurried into the trees.

Her night vision allowed her to see the mares easily, both munching on the leaves around them, their reins still tight about their necks. Thankfully, the Broch was still quiet.

Coming up behind her, Cyno grabbed her around the waist, biting hard into her neck. She turned to find his mouth, their kiss both passionate and rushed before they had to go. Glancing over her horse once, she swung up into the saddle, working to find her stirrups while Cyno pushed his mare further into cover. Each rustle in the underbrush screamed in their ears, but they didn't dare slow their mounts to make less noise.

When they were away from the outpost wall, Cyno smiled over his shoulder at her and thought, *I can na take much more of this. Let's get outta here.*

Sal agreed, so they nudged their horses into an easy canter, letting the mares pick their paths in the darkness while keeping them beneath the trees. They set a quick pace, slowing the horses to a walk only enough to catch their breath and stay fresh before pushing on. Well over three kilometers from the Broch, they came to the meadow that marked the border to the Conglomerate.

Grinning at each other, knowing they would be safe on the other side, they kicked the mares into a run, the darkness of night hiding their flight across the open ground. Their iliri sight assured them they would see an enemy before they were seen. When they burst back under trees, they pulled the horses in, sitting deep in the saddle to stay astride.

Follow me, kitten, he thought, turning Raven into the woods.

No more than a hundred paces in, she saw a small building. Closer, she realized it was a well-aged cottage with a small paddock attached to the back where their horses would be free to relax.

Without warning, Cyno slid from Raven's back and made his way to Sal's stirrup, dragging her into his arms. The touch of his hands made her want him even more, but their mares couldn't wait.

She pried herself free to lead Arden into the enclosure and asked, *How did you know this was here?*

I did na, he admitted sheepishly, pulling the saddle from Raven, *but when we crossed the border, I told LT we'd made it back safe. He pointed me here.*

You can reach him from this far away? she asked, impressed.

Yeh, ya could too, if ya tried, but we both figur'd ya were na really in the mood fer that.

She chuckled, the sound mingling with the nature around them. *And he sent you here. Seems you two have gotten rather comfortable with this arrangement.*

It's an easy truce, I s'pose. He threw his saddle on top of hers and lifted them both. *Toss the bridles up here, then pump the water.*

He carried their tack inside while she worked the antique hand pump for the horse's trough. Cold, clear water spurted forth. When their mounts were taken care of, she felt her partner slip in behind her.

I like that, kitten. Do it again, he said, pulling her hips against him.

Sal leaned back, needing to feel him. The bloodlust still lingered, and she needed more. As if he could tell, Cyno slid his hands higher up her body, while his mouth teased the tendon along the side of her neck. She could still smell the blood on them both and turned to taste it on his lips, but he held her fast.

Go ahead, he thought, *struggle.*

She tried to break free, but he was stronger than her. It was alluring in a way she couldn't describe. His hands bruised her skin, and Sal found herself wanting him more for it. He bit her neck, alternating between gently caressing her with his teeth and nearly drawing blood. While he teased her into excitement, she felt his own response pressed hard against her ass. Again, she pulled, wanting more than his mouth, and he groaned softly as he held her still.

Please, Jase, she begged. *Please.*

Her pleading was what he'd been waiting for. He released her, allowing her to turn in his arms. Sal's eyes searched his face, finding only passion there, and she pressed into him greedily. Cyno lifted her around his hips, his hands holding her tight, and carried her inside the cottage, kissing the thin skin at her jaw. She barely noticed that the bed had been covered in blankets from their own packs, the floor cleared, and their saddles stacked carefully. All she wanted was more of the man in her arms.

Easing her back to the ground, her partner's desire crossed the connection between them. She could feel every need screaming in his mind. They were echoed in her own.

Cyno tugged her shirt from her waistband, pulled it over her head, and tossed it carelessly away. Then he leaned toward her and pulled the tie from her hair, flicking it in the direction of her shirt. His eyes drank in her body, and he knelt. While he fumbled to untie her breeches, his mouth drew a line of soft, teasing kisses above the waist of her pants, broken by nips from his serrated teeth.

Sal dragged her nails across his scalp, the soft stubble of his hair tickling her fingers. When the laces came loose, she slid her thumbs into her pants and slipped them over her hips, letting Cyno slide them down her thighs. She stepped out of both her pants and boots in one smooth motion.

Naked before him, her body begged for his touch. He teased her with gentle caresses, trailing his fingers across her skin as he stood to remove his own clothes. Together, naked in the dim light of the moons, she couldn't resist the desire any longer.

She pulled his face to hers, and he followed willingly. Their lips touched, his passion flared, and he devoured her, pushing her step by step toward the bed. Shoving one arm around her back, he pulled her to his chest as he slowly lowered them both onto the mattress.

She felt her lids close, but he made her look at him. A touch on her cheek begged her to open her eyes, the request little more than a feeling in her mind. She saw the anger, the desire, and the death lurking just beneath the deep blue surface. Staring at her like a predator, he thrust himself inside her.

Sal cried out, and he pressed his hand over her mouth, then thrust again and again. His teeth were bared, snarling the whole time. Her eyes stayed locked to his as she lost control of her body in the pleasure he created. That was how she saw the smile caressing his lips when he brought her to climax. Sal gave herself to the animalistic need, no longer trying to fight what she was.

Over and over, throughout the night, he had his way with her body, and she let him. When the passion eventually faded, they both fell exhausted into the covers, Cyno pulling Sal onto his chest and wrapping his arms tightly around her like he never planned to let her go. Their minds were still entwined.

CHAPTER THIRTY-TWO

Sal woke with a smile on her face, feeling Cyno's hands stroking her hair across her naked back. Enjoying the moment, she snuggled closer to his chest, murmuring softly, and he chuckled in response.

"Awake, kitten?" His voice was harsh against the morning silence. Sal shook her head and tried to push closer to him. He tightened his hold on her and gently caressed the side of her face. "Just tell me I did na hurt ya."

"Jase, you know I wanted it as badly as you. It's ok. I'm fine, I promise." She cracked open her eyes, but only barely.

"Ok. Then yer gonna have ta get outta this bed eventually," he whispered.

"I know, but I like it here."

"I like ya here too, kitten, but we do hafta report. LT covered fer us last night, but we got intel ta give. The war will na wait while I seduce ya."

Sal sighed and pulled herself out of the bed. While she moved about the room, Jase watched her. His eyes tracked her like a predator, but a smile played across his lips. It felt good, almost natural, like the thing she'd been missing her entire life.

But duty still called. She sorted through the black leathers on the floor, dropping some in disgust, and moved to the stacked saddles. Rummaging in her packs, she pulled out a fresh shirt. Stretching before she turned back to him, Sal carried her clothes to the bed. While his eyes still watched her, she slipped her arms into the sleeves and slowly began buttoning the shirt over her naked body.

"You can't stay there all day either, killer," she teased, standing just out of his reach.

"Nah, I know it, but I wanna enjoy the view while it lasts."

"What happened to morning after nerves?" She bent to step into her breeches, glancing at him through the fall of her tangled hair.

"I figur'd from the way ya were screaming last night, I got nothing ta be worried about." He laughed, then turned serious. "Nah, Sal, it's jus' that I really like this. For the first time, I do na feel embarrassed 'bout what happens ta me. Ya make me na regret it, ya know?" He paused. "I allus felt like I was different. Bad somehow, and that's why I like it so much, but seeing ya, I can na think a it as a bad thing." He shrugged. "I can na think of ya as wrong in any way."

"Stop talking like that, Jase, or we'll never get the horses saddled."

Cyno pulled himself from the bed, moving behind her to kiss the wounds on her neck as he slid his arms up the leather at her thighs. Sal tilted her head and kissed him, twining her fingers into his. When their lips parted, they both sighed.

"Ayati, Sal. One night, I wanna have ya without the need ta kill somethan first."

"When things aren't so crazy, and I'm not making Blaec feel so ignored," she told him, "you might get your wish. But from the sounds of it, might be a couple of weeks before either of us goes more than a few days without blood on our hands."

"I never loved my job so much." He laughed, stepping away from her. "Ok, kitten, let's get ya back ta yer other man and make sure the army knows 'bout the Empire's plans."

Cyno grabbed both saddles and pushed through the dilapidated door, shooting her a sheepish look for his show of chivalry. Outside, they made quick work of checking their horses and fitting the tack. When he pulled the reins over Raven's neck and moved to her side, Sal put a hand on his shoulder. He turned to look at her, and she reached up, caressing his face, noting there was no hint of stubble on his smooth cheek. When she stepped into him, he wrapped his arms around her for one last lingering, gentle kiss.

"C'mon, kitten," he whispered. "There'll be more next time. Do na tempt me. I am na that strong."

"Me either, Jase. Damn." She sighed and turned, slipping under Arden's neck. Grabbing a fistful of mane, she swung herself into the saddle, slipped her feet into the stirrups, and picked up her reins before looking at him again. Side by side, they guided the horses into a walk, the military camp only a few kilometers away.

Much of their ride was spent in companionable silence. Neither felt uncomfortable with their arrangement, the embarrassment of the first night long past. Blood still clung to them, streaked across their faces, and their bodies showed signs of more wounds than they'd acquired in battle, but the assassins were at peace with their strange desires. When the camp began to peek through the trees, Sal remembered that she hadn't spoken to her commanding officer since before she left.

Blaec? she sent, searching for the touch of his mind.

Sal, he replied, the feeling of a caress accompanying her name.

We're almost back to camp. Just leaving the woods now. Jase said he updated you last night?

He did, Blaec assured her, *and don't you dare worry about not sending to me yourself.*

I won't – much, she thought. *But we overheard some interesting stuff. You might want to get some officers in when we report.*

That serious? Shit. Ok, Sal, I can do that. Story from the Blades is that my assassins feared they were being tailed last night, so holed up in the woods. The Generals here accepted that. They still don't know how you get messages to me, so stay vague if you're asked.

Got it, sir, she responded, acknowledging both the Lieutenant and her lover in her tone.

Closing the link with Blaec, she reached for Cyno's mind and explained the situation. They worked out a plausible backstory that would prevent any questions about their battered state and the night in the woods. By the time they reached the sentries at the gate, both iliri were in good spirits, sitting easy in their saddles.

"Name, rank, and unit!" the guard on duty demanded.

"Salryc Luxx, Corporal, Black Blades."

"Jassant Cynortas, Corporal, Black Blades."

The young man's eyes widened, realizing he stood before legends in the military. "Sirs! Welcome back, sirs," he stammered.

Sal checked the rank on his shoulder and said, "At ease, Private. Where are we to report?"

"The General's pavilion," the soldier answered, gesturing across the camp. "Your Lieutenant should meet you there. I'll send a runner to inform them you're on your way."

"Thanks, kid," Cyno replied, his cold eyes doing little to set the boy at ease.

Once inside the gate, the couple slid from their mares, leading the horses by a single rein, and stretched their legs as they walked toward the General's large tent. With their heads bent together, they mentally discussed the implications of what they were about to tell the officers, ignoring the glares of the humans around them.

While most infantrymen were in awe of the elite soldiers, a few sneered at their pale skin and obvious iliri breeding. One man dared to spit at Sal when they passed, ducking back into the crowd at the murder in Cyno's stare. Sal rested a hand on his shoulder, calming him, and kept walking. Arden followed patiently.

They passed two more columns of tents, moving from the common infantry squads, through the pikemen, and into the housing for the cavalry. Less than twenty-five meters ahead, they could make out the General's pavilion and Scorch standing outside, a sign the Lieutenant was waiting. A sound to her right caught her attention, and she saw a group of men riding their way. Their black armor identified the rest of her unit before she could even make out the details of their features.

"Looks like we're all here," she said.

"Least there's that," Cyno agreed. "Allus hated reporting ta humans."

Sal glanced up at him, her ears flicking forward in confusion. "I'll take lead on it then, but why?"

He looked away, his jaw set to hide his embarrassment. "I do na speak Glish as well as ya. Soon as they hear my accent..." He shrugged.

Sal reached up and gently rubbed his arm reassuringly. "Guess that means I need to get out more. I didn't know there was anything else to speak. Besides, your accent is kinda cute."

"Oh, kitten," Cyno said, laughing. "The only real iliri I know of, an' ya do na speak Iliran. Yeh, there's more than jus' Glish. When we get time, I'll teach ya. Now let's get this over with."

They reached the front of the pavilion, their unit lingering before the doors. The assassins tied their mounts beside the rest and rejoined the only family they knew.

"Get something good?" Arctic asked when they walked up.

"Yeh," Cyno said. "Quite a bit."

"Ok. LT's already inside briefing General Albin on your mission. I know you hate this, Cyno, but – "

Sal interrupted, "I got it."

The Blades snapped their heads to her. Those simple words contradicted the orders of her superior officer, no matter how casually he'd given them. Sal met Arctic's eyes easily, and held them. Slowly, a smile began to pull at his mouth.

"Ok, Kaisae. You think you can take this, I'll let you." He refused to look away, but there was no malice in Arctic's gaze.

Sal quickly dropped her eyes, the realization of what she'd just done hitting her. "Sir..."

He waved it off. "You're right. We both know it. Now, let's get this done. You two smell like you were playing in your food, and I'm starving."

She nodded and entered the pavilion, moving to one side to stand at attention. The rest of the Black Blades followed behind her, forming up properly. Cyno took the place at her left. LT glanced at Arctic and nodded subtly, then turned to Sal.

"Corporal Luxx, report?"

"Sir, the Escean Warlords have been eliminated. Their sentries are lax, but there are about twice as many soldiers as we were told to expect. We entered through the third floor, made our way above the great hall, and overheard seven Warlords, each from a different province in Escea, discussing an offer the Emperor had recently made. One claimed that he'd been offered one hundred steel swords to join forces with the Empire of Terric, and a second confirmed the claim. Jurica refused. It appears his offers of peace are genuine. Corporal Cynortas and I allowed him to leave the meeting, before we," Sal couldn't help but smile, "introduced ourselves. Dejan, Rok, and Vilko were positively identified before they were eliminated, along with three other Warlords."

"Casualties?" the General asked.

Her eyes flicked toward him, a moment of confusion making her pause. "Six Warlords, sir. Corporal Cynortas and myself were unharmed."

"Lieutenant Doll, you only sent two soldiers for this mission?"

"Yes, sir. They are elite assassins. I felt that two was overkill, but I wanted to be sure of the mission's success."

"I see. Continue, Corporal."

"Yes, sir," Sal said. "Dejan believed the Emperor had enough steel to offer each of the seven men present one hundred swords.

Steel swords, sir. He also indicated that the Emperor's interest in the Conglomerate of Free Citizens is at least partially due to a cache of steel under one of our bases. Dejan made it sound as if the steel was to be payment for an organized attack on that base."

The General nodded, processing the information. "Did they mention where the metal was located, or which direction they planned to attack?"

"Not that I heard, sir. He also said that a shipment of steel is currently headed to the Escean Pass on its way to Anglia. The Emperor hopes to convince that nation to ally with him."

"How much steel, Sal?" LT asked.

"I do not know, sir, but from the conversation, I would guess a lot. They referred to a caravan of it."

"Shit," the General breathed. "If Anglia joins the Empire, there's nothing we can do to stand against them. It'd be at least five to one, and Myrosica will go whichever way Anglia does. How sure are you of this intel, girl?"

"I can only report what I heard, sir," Sal replied.

General Albin nodded. "Unfortunately, it corresponds to intelligence I'm getting from the north. There's a Terran convoy, well-laden, making its way into the Escean Pass." He turned to the Lieutenant, and added, "It seems the Black Widow Company has also been spotted in the area."

LT turned to his men, and Arctic met his eyes. They stared in silence for a moment, then LT spoke. "General, let me send an infiltrator to organize with the scouts while I prepare the Blades for an assault. We can secure the shipment and bring the metal back for the CFC."

"With just eight men?" General Albin asked. "No, send your infiltrator and get more intelligence. I'll organize two units of heavy cavalry, and your Black Blades can assist Llyr's men with the assault." The General called to someone outside the tent, "Private, get Llyr in here!"

Blaec scowled. He didn't like the orders, but he had to accept them. "Ok, Blades," he said, "that means you're dismissed. Cynortas, Luxx, get cleaned up. All of you meet in my pavilion in an hour for orders."

"Yes, sir!" The Black Blades said as one, saluting and making their way out of the door.

The officers waited until they were alone in the room, then LT asked, "Llyr will be directing the assault?"

"You have a problem with that?" General Albin sounded annoyed.

"It's not standard protocol for the regular military to direct the elites," Blaec pointed out. "I'm just surprised at your choice, sir."

"Lieutenant, Captain Llyr outranks you."

Blaec just smiled. He was rarely treated as merely a Lieutenant. Most of the military knew he could easily be wearing clusters instead of bars by now. "Yes, sir. I'm aware of my choice."

"And that choice has consequences, Lieutenant. The military isn't a place for your political protests and showing off. We're here to get a job done, damn it, and I didn't ask for your opinion."

"Yes, sir." Blaec set his jaw to wait in silence.

Eventually, Captain Dalton Llyr pushed through the door and into the General's pavilion with a smile on his face. He saluted the General, then waited.

Albin gestured to LT. "Lieutenant Doll's troops report that we may have a bribe passing through the Escean Pass, on its way to Anglia."

"Fuck," Llyr grumbled. "That's bad."

"Real bad. Sounds like it's a caravan filled with metal," LT said.

"What are the orders, sir?" Llyr asked, his question clearly for the General.

Albin sighed, sounding weary. "We'll send scouts up to get some intel. I figure you'll need two units of heavy, maybe three. The Black Blades are at your command as well. Secure the metal, bring it back. Should be pretty cut and dry, just make sure you get the damned metal."

Llyr looked over to LT. "The Black Blades are under my command?"

Blaec smiled up at him cruelly. "As much as we ever are, Captain."

The men stared at each other, tensions rising.

"General," Llyr said finally, turning his head. "Pretty sure the Heavy Cav can handle this without the elites."

"Sorry, Captain," Albin told him. "The Blades got the intelligence. They get to assist on this one."

"Understood, sir."

"Now get your initial preparations underway. When we get more, I'll pass it to you. Make sure you keep the Blades updated. Dismissed."

The Lieutenant and Llyr both saluted and turned for the door. Blaec waited, allowing Llyr to exit first, then walked through. Once outside, Llyr turned to him.

"You know this means I'm the one giving commands this time?"

Blaec chuckled wryly. "Yeah, I got that. Maybe that means you won't fuck it up."

"Kiss my ass, Doll. You still blaming me for that shit in Unav?"

"Your unit didn't hold the line. I lost a good man because of it, so yeah, I still blame you. Learn how to win this time, and I'll listen."

"You're this pissed about losing some damned scrubber?" Llyr sneered. "Fuck. That beast didn't know when to retreat. You can't blame me because your unit's more animal than man!"

"He saved your ass, so don't give me that shit. And we still have a better combat rating than you." Blaec turned to leave, aware that his control was slipping.

"Heard ya got a new one," Llyr called after him. "Little bitch this time. I know how much you like your iliri. Does that mean you're fucking her?"

Blaec paused. "Jealous?"

"Shit." Llyr laughed. "Wouldn't surprise me if you were. I know

Valcor Zepyr has a fondness for 'em. He's not even ashamed of it. Maybe it's starting to rub off?"

"If you're so interested, maybe you should give her a try," Blaec said. "I should warn you, though, Cyno said she bites."

"Maybe I will," Llyr taunted. "And then we'll see how you feel with her sneaking into my tent each night."

Blaec grinned at Llyr and raised an eyebrow. "You hear what her specialty is?"

"Fucking?"

"Nah, she's my best assassin."

Llyr looked at Blaec for a long moment. "What happened to Cyno? He's the best in the CFC."

"Not anymore. She also doesn't really like humans. Try it, Llyr. I'd love to see what happens when you attempt to tame that beast."

"You're starting to act like them, Doll. You need to keep the leash a bit shorter on your pets or the CFC might take them away."

Blaec shrugged. "Not if we keep winning. Just try to keep up, ok? If your damned cavalry is so impressive, *try* to keep up with the Black Blades. Think you can manage that for once?"

CHAPTER THIRTY-THREE

Sal stepped into Blaec's tent, clean. She tossed her towel on the ground and grabbed his shirt from the back of his chair, slipping her arms into the sleeves. Moving across the room, she rummaged in her pack for a pair of pants. At least Blaec was finally back. Since she'd returned, he'd been called to at least three meetings.

Standing by the opening to his sleeping area, the Lieutenant paused to watch her dress. "You going to be ready for a room full of Blades any time soon?"

"Am I not ready now?"

"I just wanted to check," he said before opening up his mind and sending a thought to his men. *Meeting in my pavilion. We got orders.*

She saw Blaec's face go distant while he listened to the replies. Quickly enough, he raised his eyes back to hers, "You got about five minutes, and you're in my shirt."

"Find another, I'm keeping this one."

He laughed and went to do just that, calling to her through the canvas walls of the other room. "You realize that means you're out of uniform, right soldier?"

"It's ok," she called back. "My commander loves me."

She heard his shuffling pause, then he walked back into the room, his face serious, a clean shirt in his hand. "You know that's true, right, Sal?" He looked into her eyes. "I do love you."

Unexpectedly, she felt her throat close, tight with emotion, and nodded. "I know," she whispered, reaching for him. "I do know. And I don't know why."

"I don't need a reason, little one," he said before kissing her. "I know it hasn't been long, and things have been crazy, but I can't help it."

"And I do love you, Blaec. I do. It's why I keep coming back." She watched the corners of his lips slide up into a soft smile.

"I'm glad you can say it, Sal." He kissed her deeply, lifting her off her feet.

Behind them, a man cleared his throat. They broke their embrace, looking over sheepishly. Risk stood inside the door with a smirk on his face.

"I'd say get a room, but we're about to converge on it."

One by one, the Blades slipped into the tent, all present except Shift. When they settled themselves and got comfortable, LT addressed them as a group.

"Ok, Blades, our orders came in. Shift's being embedded with a group of specialists, assisting them with infiltration. They found a supply train headed out of the capital of Escea. It's surrounded by guards in black and purple, so the General assumes it's the bribe from the Emperor. We're hoping this is the metal we've been warned about by Sal and Cyno. If it is, we will not be securing it."

Around the room, the men grumbled but knew the reason would become clear.

"Our job is to support the heavy cav. We'll be playing skirmishers this time. Once the enemy is cleared, the cavalry will secure the train and redirect it here. This is a simple smash and grab, boys – and Sal. Nothing fancy, nothing special, the General just needs some men that can handle skirmishing on uneven terrain."

"And Sal," Razor mumbled, causing the Blades to chuckle at LT.

"Yes, I'm well aware she's not one of the boys," Blaec told him.

"It was her little feet that tipped me off. How'd you figure it out, LT?" Arctic asked, grinning.

The Lieutenant threw his shirt at the First Officer. "I'll teach you about the difference between boys and girls when you grow up."

Sal found herself laughing with the rest, even as the butt of the jokes. The meeting descended into chaos and laughter, but she gave as good as she got. A few more questions were asked about their role, and answered, before LT released them, giving them thirty-six hours of free time before they were expected in the saddle. One by one, the Blades slipped out of the tent, Arctic waiting until the others were gone.

"We report to Llyr?" he asked, standing by the door.

"Yeah," Blaec said softly. "In theory."

"So long as it's theory only," Arctic told him. "I trust you, LT. I got your back no matter how this plays out."

"Thanks, man," he said as Arctic left.

Then Blaec sighed deeply and threw himself into the chair behind his desk. He rubbed at his head then began to shuffle through the papers before him, pulling a map to the front. Chewing on the end of his pen, he stared at it for a long moment, his finger tracing a line across its surface. Suddenly he threw the pen to the desk and buried his head in his hands.

"Blaec?" Sal asked.

"Circ died because of that man, Sal. He couldn't follow orders, and Circ *died*. Now I'm supposed to follow *his* orders?"

"In theory," Sal reminded him.

"He threw it in my face, today, that all of you are iliri."

"And you."

Blaec seemed to ignore that. "He doesn't understand why I'm upset that an iliri died. He said I'm acting like an iliri, and he asked if I was fucking you."

Sal sank into a chair across the room and curled her feet under her. "You are."

Blaec grumbled under his breath. "This is going to cause problems."

"Ignore it, Blaec," she soothed. "What can he do?"

He huffed something near a laugh and glared at her. "You don't understand, do you? If rumors get out about us, I'll be court-martialed. A *human* will be put in charge of the Blades. A man who thinks the lives of my soldiers don't matter. Someone who will throw all of you into the worst situations because iliri are so 'easy' to replace!"

"And I'm sleeping with Cyno," Sal countered. "I'm your trusted assassin. Where's the proof of anything unprofessional, sir?"

Blaec nodded. She knew she was right. It might be easier to change so the humans were happy, but it wouldn't do their unit any good. It wouldn't really keep them safer, even if he thought it might. Most of all, it wouldn't help him, and Blaec was still fragile in his own way.

"You don't smell human, Blaec," Sal added. "I know you need to play the human to them, but I wish you'd start thinking of yourself as one of us."

"Sal." He sighed, pausing for the right words. "You know as well as I do what iliri are treated like. You know that only if they think of us as humans can we achieve what we hope."

"And if we aren't trying to prove we're as good as them, what *exactly* is it we're hoping for?" she pressed.

He caught her eyes, his gaze challenging. "We're trying to win the damned war. What do you think we're doing?"

"I thought we were trying to prove we're as good, if not better than them." She tilted her head to the side, refusing to break the gaze.

"You don't even know your own history," he scoffed. "What does it matter to you? You're more human than half the men here."

"No," Sal said, "I'm not. I may not speak Iliran, I may not

understand why I have the instincts I do, but until I became a Black Blade, I also didn't understand what pride was either. Just because I didn't grow up in the culture doesn't mean I'm a human, Blaec. I'm *nothing* like them, and I no longer want to be. I'll put on a show in public if that's what you want, but that doesn't mean I'm human."

"Then why are you with me, Sal?"

"Because you're not human either," she said. "You taught me to be proud of who I am. For the last four months, you've told me there was nothing wrong with being iliri, and now you're ashamed that we're all iliri?"

"It's not like that." Their eyes were still locked. Blaec was reacting to the dominance in her gaze.

"Then what is it like?" she demanded.

"We have to bend with the rules of the world, Sal! We can't just stand up and say we're better so they should like us. It doesn't work like that!"

"How does it work, then? Do we stand up and say we're worse? Should we apologize for our mere existence? Humans hate us. They call us beasts and kill us off like livestock. The only reason we're valuable to them at all is because they'd rather we die than they do. Blaec, if we can't make them accept us because we're good as soldiers, then why are we so willing to die for them? Why are we even trying so hard?"

Blaec growled softly and leaned over his desk. "You regret joining the Blades now, Corporal?"

"You regret taking me, Lieutenant?" she snapped back, pulling her ears tight against her head. "Don't make this about me, Blaec. I'd be just as iliri sitting behind a desk in an office. I don't get the option of lying about what I am."

"So what do you want me to do? Tell the world I'm half iliri?"

She smiled, her sharp teeth peeking above her lip. "That would be a good start. You're the most decorated officer I know. The Black Blades are the most respected unit in the Conglomerate. Not even General Sturmgren has as much name recognition as you now! If you're not willing to use that for your own people, then what good is it?"

His growl faded to silence, but neither looked away.

She went on. "I applied to the Black Blades because I wanted to matter. A part of me also hoped I'd die young." She blinked and looked away, giving him back his dominance. "When I started to get to know the men, I felt so at home, like I'd found something I'd been missing all my life. Less than an hour ago, you told me you love me. Blaec?" Sal looked up at him, the question in her eyes. "How can you love me and be so ashamed of who we are?"

"I'm not, sweetness." He ran his hands through his short hair, walking to her side. "Sal, I'm not *ashamed* of you or the iliri. I'm not. I'm worried for us. I'm trying to protect us the only way I know how. I'm still half human, though. That half makes me a little bit like them. I'm caught in the middle in a world that doesn't understand us." He caressed her face, his anger fading. "I don't want to see any of my men treated like you were. If that means we need to keep a few Conglomerate habits, then that's what we'll do. I won't let them think of you as less than anyone else just because you're pale, ok?"

She nodded and caught his eyes again. "So why are we doing this? Why are you only accepting iliri into the Blades?" Her gaze demanded an answer and she knew Blaec's instincts wouldn't let him avoid it.

"Because we're better than them. We are," he said, "but don't ever challenge me, Sal. You'll lose."

She grinned and looked away. "I know," she said proudly. "And I'd never lose to a human."

CHAPTER THIRTY-FOUR

*T*hey sat on their horses quietly. The black resin of their matched armor soaked up the light around them. The breath from the horses steamed in the dawn light. The heavy cavalry kept their distance from the Black Blades, made uncomfortable by the silence they worked in and their synchronized movements. Even now, with the supply train rolling slowly into the valley, the messenger approached them fearfully, unable to determine the leader behind their matching resin helms.

"Sir?" he asked timidly.

"Report, soldier." The man on the black horse spoke, never turning his head away from the train below.

"Sir, you're to cover our flank and pick off anyone that tries to escape to get word back."

"Boy, tell Llyr he can shove his orders up his ass. My men will be where they're needed, and we'll make sure this shit gets done." The Lieutenant stared at what would become the battleground. "He wanted my damned Blades out here. He's got 'em. Now he has to deal with what that means."

The trembling soldier nodded, too intimidated to speak to the Black Blades again.

"And, boy?" LT growled, turning to the messenger. His pale eyes glared through the slit in his helm, pausing the kid before he could even turn his mount. "Tell the cav to stay the fuck out of our way."

"Yes, sir," the young man said, spurring his horse to retreat as fast as he could.

Sal sat to Blaec's left, Cyno flanking her other side. Two crossbows were strapped across her mare's flanks. She had a pair of sabers strapped to her back, her knives in sheaths at her waist, and a halberd in her hand. She was not the most heavily armed soldier in the group, either. They were ready.

Open us up, Arctic, LT ordered, and the Blades felt their minds spread apart, their thoughts combining with those of each man in the link.

Arctic's tactical reason, Razor's strength, Shift's adaptability and Zep's physical control flowed to enhance Cyno's speed, Sal's agility, Risk's calm logic, and the Lieutenant's rage. Every man could feel the others. All of them became a part of the whole until the Black Blades were one: a single organism with a single purpose. The anger simmered from them, the anticipation and intensity coursing through all of them. Each one ready. Each one a killer.

The heavy cavalry milled in the trees, their discipline failing in the close quarters. The Empire's supply train creaked through the narrow path, surrounded by pikemen and heavily armored soldiers. There were six wagons total, each pulled by four oxen struggling against their yokes. The weight of the load was enough to be steel or iron. The wagons had been traveling for hundreds of kilometers. The soldiers guarding it should be fatigued and travel weary, the weeks of inactivity lulling them into a false sense of security. The Blades knew better.

A horn sounded, and the Conglomerate Calvary spilled out of the trees in waves.

Wait for it.

Ceramic rang against resin below them and horses screamed when they ran onto the waiting pikes.

Wait for it.

Blood splattered the grass and rocks. Sal's heart began to beat faster, and she could feel Cyno's matching it. Men in purple were slaughtered by the dozens, outnumbered and unprepared for the cerulean soldiers cutting them down so easily.

Wait for it.

The sight of destruction called to her, and Sal felt seven hearts fall into rhythm with her own, each one feeding on the frenzy she and Cyno poured into the link. Each one straining for the desire she controlled.

Wait for it.

Below them, a sea of purple poured from the other side of the mountain. The Imperial cavalry surged forward, slicing into the unprotected back of the Conglomerate army, splitting the line and pushing toward the train.

Kill them all.

The Lieutenant released them, and the Black Blades shot forward, their horses lunging over the precipice, hips tucked under them, sliding and pulling toward the targets their riders chose. Ears pinned, teeth bared, they raced. Sal held her weight back, freeing Arden's shoulders while giving the mare her head, and her eyes locked on a pikeman who had spotted them.

As her horse's feet found the base of the hill, Sal lowered her weapon, the resin hook and spike aimed for the man's heart. He grounded his pike, pointed at Arden's chest, and she pushed her heel into the mare's side, feeling her horse bend and shift. With a twist, Sal snagged the enemy weapon with hers and wrenched the pole from the soldier's grip before directing her mare to swing around. Arden obeyed like an extension of Sal's own body. The pair surged forward and the halberd pierced through the man, his eyes widening in pain as he died. Her excitement peaked, and she turned for the next target.

Across the link, she felt Cyno cut down a soldier, slicing his head clean from his body, and the Blades drank in their need for more blood. When Shift drove his lance through a Terran horseman's breastplate, the bloodlust crossed the mental bridge. Each Blade drew it into himself, each Blade added to the pull for more death. Splitting in separate directions, they slaughtered easily, the mingling of their iliri minds giving speed and hyper-awareness to each of them. Behind them, they left a sea of purple and black corpses, nothing more than obstacles to steer their mounts around.

Sal spun Arden, seeking another life to destroy, and saw Cessa's dark hide shining in the morning sun. Zep engaged an enemy horseman, their blades swinging, their horses turning. Another Terran charged them, his pike lowered with the Blade in his sights. Calmly, she reached behind her, grabbed a crossbow, and loosed it in one smooth motion. The bolt sailed across the distance and lodged itself securely in the opening of his helm. The man slumped in his saddle even as his horse charged on. A surge of appreciation flowed like water into her mind, and Zep's blade sliced through the arm of the man before him.

The crossbow still in her hand, now nearly useless as a weapon, she pushed Arden forward. Riding past Razor and his opponent, she swung it like a club, catching a teamster in the head. His body left the ground before falling in a crumpled heap, broken. She responded to the need in her mind, a second swordsman here, an archer there. Each of the Black Blades knew the threats the others faced, and they cut them down one by one.

She could feel Blaec, a sword in each hand, Scorch responding to only his legs. The Lieutenant buried his weapon in the neck of a horse, the beast dropping to its knees, spilling its rider to die beneath his black stallion's hooves. Blaec turned to face the next threat, a group of four horsemen locked shoulder to shoulder, their lances aimed at the Lieutenant. He urged Scorch to run, pushing him around the line before spinning and falling in behind them. The young stallion surged, his ears pinned, reaching to bite the neck of the enemy horse when he pulled alongside. That horse shied, pushing into the mount on its other side, pinning the men's legs. Blaec swung, finding the gap at the man's neck. Blood poured down his blade. He urged Scorch closer and sliced along the loin of the second horse. It crumpled as its back legs became useless.

Another imperial charged at him. Only a thought from Risk warned the Lieutenant in time. Blaec threw up his armored arms, catching the full blow of the oncoming sword against the hardened resin, and slid off Scorch's hip, the horse running too hard to stop. Blaec rolled when he hit the ground, pulling another sword, and crouched, waiting for the rider to circle back.

"Scorch!" he yelled. His horse broke off the headlong charge to return to his master as he'd been trained.

The Imperial came for another pass, and Blaec waited. The rider bore down on him. At the last moment, Blaec surged forward, screaming his defiance, and sliced at the horse's legs while simultaneously ducking the blade swinging toward his head. The poor beast tried to continue another pace, his destroyed limbs failing him, but the Terran dove from the animal's back. Rolling when he hit the ground, the enemy turned to face his opponent. Behind Blaec, the two remaining lancers pivoted, ready to make another pass at the Lieutenant.

Blaec rushed the man before him, and a streak of black charged the lancers, Raven sliding to a stop at the last moment. Cyno used her inertia to throw him across the mounted men, pulling them from their horses. As they fell, he pushed the first below him, his knee at the Terran's throat, and twisted to sling the second away. The impact resulted in a sickening crack when the first man's neck broke, then Cyno leapt on the other, pinning him to the ground and sliding a dagger between the edges of his eye slit. Neither moved again.

Cyno turned to the Lieutenant only to see the swordsman dead at Blaec's feet. The two Blades nodded at each other in understanding before running to their horses. They swung into their saddles and sought out more enemies to kill.

As a unit, they destroyed anything in their way until there was nothing left but themselves and the soldiers in blue. The clearing stank of blood and shit as the dead emptied themselves. Looking around, finding nothing more to ravage, the desire ripped through them, demanding to be satiated. Sal could feel Cyno thinking of her pale skin, and she tried to bury her own need to hurt something else, to hear his cries of ecstasy.

Cyno, Sal, Go! Arctic, shut it down before they pull us in, Blaec ordered.

I'm good, LT. Sal can hold it too, jus' get us outta the damned link, Jase thought as the connection faded around them.

Are you ok, love? Blaec sent to her, his touch gentle in her mind.

No, but I can control it for a bit. We got this.

She desired nothing more than to feel Jase's hands on her, to claw at his skin, but she could hold off for a while longer. Her unit needed her. Even with her frenzy pulling at her, she had the strength to resist it.

The Blades reined their horses toward their commander. Falling into ranks, LT led them toward the wagons. Corpses littered the ground, and Sal guided her mare carefully to prevent a bad step. The air inside her helm felt close and confining, the view through the visor limited. She wrenched at the clasps along her neck, feeling them loosen, and pulled it off, sucking in the cool morning air. Glancing at the sky, she begged her body to give her control before securing the helm to her saddle. Around her, the others did the same, their faces flushed. When her eyes found Cyno, he stared, the need apparent on his face as if she were his prey.

Soon, she told him. *We're Blades first.*

I'm good. Jus' do na come near me yet, he warned, his mental voice a growl.

Sal nodded and pushed Arden away, moving to put Blaec

between them. He glanced at her once before turning to the captain of the Heavy Cavalry. Llyr strode toward them on foot.

"Where's your horse, sir?" LT asked snidely, the corner of his lip raised ever so slightly.

"Went down to a pike, Doll. Don't get all smart-ass on me," the Captain replied. "What took you so long to get in there? I lost men because of you."

"No," LT said, coldly. "You lost men because you refused to listen to me. I told you there was cavalry. My man was embedded with the scouts tracking them. You just refused to believe it."

"There was no sign of those bastards, damn it!"

"They were still there, Llyr. Fuck. If I hadn't held, my Blades would have been in the middle of that shit, too, not peeling your ass out of it. Now get your shit together and let's see if this is the steel we're here for."

"Lieutenant, you will not speak to me in that tone!" Llyr snapped, trying to intimidate the leader of the Black Blades.

"Sir," Arctic said, leaning forward, his forearm resting on his pommel. "I highly recommend you don't pull rank here. You know as well as everyone in the CFC that the only reason LT's not a damned General is because he won't take it, not because they haven't tried to give it to him. So take your sore ass and shove it, or I'll order these men to shove it for you. Check the damned *train!*"

Llyr turned his angry gaze to Arctic, but when his mouth opened, LT cut him off.

"And if you don't like my First Officer's tone, you take it up with me. Understood?"

Llyr's mouth clamped closed. The presence of eight heavily-armored soldiers, shoulder to shoulder, horse to horse, glaring at him, changed his attitude. "Yes, sir," he said. Storming off, he screamed orders at his men to open the wagons and secure the load.

"Thanks, men," LT said to the Blades around him. "Once we get this load moving, I want four of you to stay with it. I think you can all guess which. Cyno and Sal will need to get themselves under control. Shift, see if there's anyone you can help." He shot a warning look at Shift, before the Sergeant could make a sarcastic comment, and turned to Cyno. "So far, you both are doing well. If you aren't, get out of here. Her, too."

Cyno nodded.

They sat in silence for a few moments, Blaec watching the army fumbling in the back of the carts. Time passed, and still no cries of excitement came. The Blades started to trade glances.

"Ok, enough of this shit, let's see what the hell they're doing now." LT gestured for his Blades to follow him, nudging Scorch toward the train.

From their height on the horses, they could see into the wagon beds. Crates were stacked side by side, their tops cracked open, but the contents refused to make sense to Sal's eyes. These were not steel swords. It was not piles of ore. Packed in each box, like fruit headed to market, were what appeared to be heads – iliri heads – their white eyes staring sightlessly at the sky above them.

Cyno and Sal gasped as one, the unexpected death more than they could take in their heightened state. Sal tried to control her sudden urge to tear and rip. Her lips raised in a rabid snarl, and she willed herself to breathe, telling her muscles to relax. On the other side of LT, Cyno did the same, his knuckles white on his pommel, his breathing fast. Sal forced her eyes closed.

"Blades?" LT asked them both.

"I'm good, man," Cyno insisted. "I'm good."

Sal just nodded, reining Arden back. The smell of death was tantalizing and all around her. She heard Arctic push Bazya between her and the wagon, his hand on her reins, turning her mare.

"Breathe, Sal," he whispered.

"It's the smell that's doing it," she growled. "Arctic, just fucking give me something to kill!" She snarled as she opened her eyes.

"Easy, Corporal," he told her, his pale eyes boring into hers. "That's a fucking order, soldier."

She nodded and tried to smile, letting him know it was working. "I'm ok. Just give me a second. I'm ok," she whispered.

LT looked back, his concern obvious. At a nod from Arctic, he relaxed and turned back to the wagon. "What is this?" he asked the nearest soldier.

"Dunno, sir. Looks like a bunch of scrubber heads to me."

"Are they all like this?" LT persisted.

"Nah, most are, but a few in the last cart are filled with papers, or something like that, sir."

"Show me."

The Lieutenant followed the man down the line of carts while the Blades pulled back, forming a knot around Sal and Cyno. The two berserkers did their best to not look at each other until Zep pushed Cessa into the middle, putting a barrier between their instinctual desires. They waited tensely for the Lieutenant to return, but when he did, his face was solemn.

"There's no metal in this shipment," he told them, "but there are three crates of what appear to be iliri writing. The cav think its scribbles and want to dump it."

"Shit," Shift breathed.

"Yeah. I volunteered us to take it back, and I want to have a few of you look it over." LT sighed deeply before turning to Cyno. "I'm sorry, but I can only give you an hour, maybe an hour and a half. You're the most fluent among us, and I need you to look through the crates before we get back to the main camp."

"We can hold out, Blaec," Sal assured him.

"No, love, you can't. I can see it from here." He smiled up at her and rested his hand on Arden's neck, careful not to touch Sal. The gesture was obvious. "If you don't tear something – mainly Cyno – apart soon, one of you will tear apart a human. It's not pretty over there. They think the crates of heads are funny. The first bad joke, and one of you will rip a man to shreds. I can't risk that."

She nodded at him, knowing it was true.

"Cyno, I'm sorry, but make it fast. The rest of you, start moving those crates together."

Cyno turned his horse, pointing Raven into the woods, and glanced at her. *Come with me, kitten,* he thought, and she nodded, pushing Arden to follow.

Behind them, the rest of the Blades dismounted and moved toward the train. Zep cast a glance back at his friends, realizing he might be lucky that he didn't have to suffer the strains of being iliri.

One of the men in the carts pointed to the Blades riding away. "Hey, looks like the scrubber bitch didn't like seeing her own kind." The men around him laughed.

"You think that's funny, don't you, you stupid fuck," Zep growled.

"You talking to me?" the smart-mouthed soldier asked, puffing up.

"Yeah, I am. Don't fuck with my unit-mates. Don't talk shit about my mates. Fuck, don't even look at my mates. Get it?"

"What, you a scrubber lover?"

"Yeah. I am. Got a problem with that?" Zep asked, stepping into the man's face.

Behind him, another soldier whispered, "Granz, that's a Black Blade!"

"I am," Zep said. "They are, too."

"They're just fuckin' scrubbers. Can't believe that bitch couldn't take seeing a few dead ones. Or do you only like killing humans?" Granz didn't know when to quit.

Without warning, Zep reached up and grabbed the man's collar, dragging him from the bed of the wagon with one hand to slam him into the ground at his feet, then dropping one knee into his chest. Around him, the sound of blades sliding from their sheaths sang in the air.

"I wouldn't do that," Razor said, walking up. "Zep could take you all without drawing a sword. There's six more of us here, too. Do you really want to chance it?"

"You couldn't!" a man said, his sword point dropping.

"We could," Zep promised.

"And who is to say how many of you died to the Empire? Be a shame if the only ones to make it back were the Blades, hmm?" Razor smiled smugly. "Now, put away those weapons or shit is going to get really ugly."

The men around them returned their blades to their sheaths.

"Zep, let him up," Razor insisted.

Zep complied, taking his hands off the man, but his eyes held him in place. "Let me explain something to you all, real clear-like," he said, still watching the man on the ground. "Some of my friends like killing a bit too much. If you say the wrong thing to them, you might not live long enough to apologize, ya get me?"

Granz nodded.

"Eight of us pulled your asses out of that shit. How many men did you have?" Zep asked.

"Brought fifty," a man in the back admitted.

"And it just took *eight* of us to clean up your mess. Think about that before you pick on the little iliri bitch. She scares the shit outta me. Get it?"

CHAPTER THIRTY-FIVE

Sitting in the wagon, Cyno looked through page after page of iliri writing on a strange paper that none of them had seen before. It was smooth, like resin, but flexible. The writing was formed into the page itself. The strange arcs, curves, and colors of the Iliran words turned each one into a work of art. At the bottom of the second crate was a separate bundle. These were in Glish, the language used by humans.

"LT!" Cyno yelled. "Something ya need ta see."

"What did you find?" he asked, riding up.

"This is important." Cyno handed the papers over.

LT dropped his reins and flipped through the pages in his lap, reading in silence. Riding behind them, Sal watched him turn back and read the page again before flipping forward.

"Stop the damned cart," he ordered.

Razor pulled the oxen to a halt, looking back. The tone in the Lieutenant's voice pulled the Blades in around him. None of them spoke. The apparent importance of the documents in his hands caused them to tense, their horses fidgeting nervously beneath them.

"This cart was headed for Prin," LT told them.

Shift muttered, "Why send a train of iliri heads and a box of iliri... whatever they are, from Terric to Prin?"

"Because the Emperor thinks it's proof." LT met each of their eyes before continuing. "He thinks this is proof that they deserve to control us. He wants to convince Parliament to help him wipe iliri from the planet."

Around him, the Blades muttered their disbelief, each one trying to explain why the idea of removing an entire species from the planet was ludicrous.

"What are the documents, Jase?" Sal asked.

"They are old, Sal," Cyno said, shaking his head, his glance flicking to LT before turning back to the pages before him.

"Jase?" she insisted. "What are those documents?"

"It's our history," he whispered.

"You mean, like the Conglomerate's?" Shift asked.

Cyno shook his head, his eyes fixed on Sal.

"He means the history of the iliri," Zep said. "Their history. All of your history."

"Yeh. I mean, it's tha' too, but's more than that." Cyno reached for a page. "They talk 'bout the Landing like it's an event." He pointed at the sheet in his hand before flipping to another. "Here they talk 'bout invaders with brown skin and peace treaties." He looked up. "They talk 'bout gifts of metal – I mean, they do na call it that, but I'm pretty sure that's what it is. Maast, these documents are the iliri version of the Landing!"

The Black Blades fell silent. It was hard to comprehend documents as old as time itself sitting in their lap. Such things had only been stories until now. Myths and legends of a time before humans. For centuries, their histories only went back as far as the Landing, a time when humans had begun to settle the continent and form their own primitive countries. Here before them were records of an age before that. Answers to questions they'd never even thought to ask. The documents had to be more than three thousand years old.

"What do they say about us?" Risk asked quietly. "Why are they all in Iliran? They have to say something about *us*, not the humans."

Cyno nodded. "Yeh. I would na believe it if I had na read it. Ayati, I still can na believe it." He took a deep breath and reached for another page, scanning it quickly before he spoke. "Ok. I'm making this the short version, but yeh. When they landed – I do na know much 'bout that part, yet – the land was savage. White beasts struck in the night, coming from the north, killing and eating the humans. It upset them pretty bad. So, they did somethan, I do na quite get what yet, and they killed and captured us. They bred us, domesticating us, and used us ta protect themselves. They made two types, forcing us ta breed against our wills in some cases, and made slaves of us all. The quiet ones, they used in the houses. The savage ones? Them they used like hounds, setting us ta guard and shit. This," he gestured to the pile of documents around him, "was written by the pet of a human. She recorded the history of our people. Wrote it down, saying that we'd be lost in time and that the invaders would exterminate us, one way or another. Says she used his means ta write it out, ta preserve it."

They sat in silence, trying to understand what Cyno had just told them.

Looking around, Zep spoke up. "You were here first. We – the humans – we came and..." he broke off, shaking his head. "We forced you to become like us?"

"Yeah," Risk said. "It makes sense. The old stories – most of us heard them growing up – they say we're the playthings of the humans. That we were stronger, smarter, and better until the humans ruined us."

"My amma allus said," Cyno added, "that's why we're so different. The more iliri we are, the more we're like..."

"Like beasts," Sal whispered.

"Predators," Zep corrected.

Razor waved at the crates. "The Emperor thinks he can use this as proof that we need to be put down!"

"Yeh, but tha's na quite what it proves," Cyno said. "What this is saying is that we were designed ta be perfect fer what we do. We were made ta be soldiers – "

"And the Black Blades prove that," Arctic pointed out.

"Yeh," Cyno agreed, "an' that the more generations we're bred, the more tame we are." He shot a proud look at Sal, then turned back to the men. "These papers say that we exist cuz they made us, that we're smarter, stronger, an' faster than them cuz they *made* us ta be."

"Would they use it to control us?" Shift asked.

"They already do," Sal said. "How many of you weren't conscripted?"

They glanced at Zep, and he looked down, embarrassed. "I may have the right to quit, unlike the rest of you, but I sure as hell don't have the heart to."

"I know, big brother," Cyno said, patting his arm. "Is na yer fault, man."

"I enlisted, too," LT said. "They didn't ask; I didn't tell."

Sal looked over to Razor, the second darkest of the Black Blades. He shook his head.

"Nope. Got caught in Lewes." He grinned, showing sharp teeth. "Seems growling is a very distinctive trait. Worst way to lose a fight."

The men chuckled, understanding what he meant.

"So none of us own our lives as it is. One way or another, they control us." Sal gestured at the crates. "Then what do we have to lose? Worst that happens is nothing changes. The best? Maybe they understand us better?"

"It's worth it," Cyno said. "The risk is outweighed by the reward."

"So what now?" Zep asked. "We're sitting on the most important find I've heard of in centuries. What the fuck do we do with it?"

"We get it to the professors," Blaec decided. "Quietly. Once it's in their hands, there will be enough copies and enough documentation of its existence that they can't make it go away."

"And Jase," Sal said, holding his eyes when he looked up at her. "Keep reading," she told him. "Read as much as you can. Remember it."

Blaec turned at the tone of her voice, making her realize what she'd just done. Sal hadn't asked, she'd simply given an order as if it was her right. It wasn't the first time. She had a tendency to just take control, and the men instinctually did what she asked. They couldn't stop themselves – because it was in their nature to obey dominance – and half the time she didn't notice until it was done.

She saw his eyes on her and shot him an apologetic look, flicking her ears up. He smiled just as their horses reacted. Arden threw her head up, staring into the trees. Scorch and a few others spooked. The men quickly gained control of their mounts, heads looking in all directions for the cause, their mental voices battering each other's minds.

Quiet! Sal screamed at them.

Immediately, they fell silent, and she could hear beyond her head. She breathed in deeply, seeing a few of the others doing the same, but she couldn't find a scent. Her ears swiveled. She could hear something, but just barely. It was getting louder.

They're downwind, Arctic said.

I hear them, she thought. *A lot of them, and they aren't ours.*

CHAPTER THIRTY-SIX

"We need to move!" LT ordered.

Cyno shoved the documents back into the crates, securing the lids tightly. The Blades spun their horses in place, hands on their weapons, eyes scanning the trees around them. Sal's ears flicked behind her, and she heard it again. The sound may have been the step of a horse, or it could have just been a branch blowing in the gentle breeze. She breathed in but could only smell the anxiety of her brothers in arms.

The oxen will be too slow, she thought to Jase. Reaching behind her, she grabbed the horse's picket line from her pack and moved her mare up beside the wagon. "Jase," she called, throwing the rope at him when he looked up. *Tie them together, we'll throw it on Arden.*

What about you? he asked.

Raven can carry double.

He nodded and untied Raven from the back of the wagon, tossing her the reins, then turned his attention to tying knots. Sal moved to Raven's back and pulled Arden to her side, moving as close to the wagon as possible.

"We need ta get the packs on a horse. We'll move too slow otherwise," Cyno said to Razor.

He nodded, but Cyno had already started lifting the crates onto Arden. He balanced them as evenly as he could, securing the ropes to the rings on the saddle. Razor moved to his gelding's side and began tightening his girth, keeping one eye on the assassins. The Blades closed in around them, unwilling to leave any of their unit behind, but anxious to be on the move.

"Zep?" Cyno called.

"Yeah?"

"Take Arden, I'll get Sal."

Zep pushed Cessa close enough to grab the spotted mare's reins. Sal shifted back on Raven's hip, and Cyno leapt in front of her, awkwardly making his way into the saddle. He nodded for Sal to get comfortable.

When they were astride, LT said, "Good call, Cyno."

He shrugged and turned Raven into the trees. "Was Sal's idea."

The whole time, she kept her ears mobile, twisting and turning them for a sign of their pursuit while the Black Blades made their way into the wilderness. Sucking in deep breaths, she tasted the scent carefully as she clung to Cyno's waist. Whoever was after them was good. She only caught a hint of something, but not enough for her to feel any wiser.

Ravens? she asked the Blades.

Shit, Arctic thought, squeezing Bazya into a trot.

Terrans, Blaec replied tensely, matching the pace. *They fletch their arrows with raven feathers. What else? Anything you get... what else, Sal?*

She inhaled deeply and flicked her ears around again. The sound of the horses' hooves muffled anything she may have heard, but a strange scent teased the edge of her senses.

I smell something, but I don't know what it is.

Describe it, Zep suggested, yanking Arden between a pair of trees.

She searched her mind for the right words, but couldn't find anything. The concern flowing from the men made her feel rushed. *Fuck it. Blaec, here.* She threw the memory of the scent at him.

Shit, Shift thought, looking back wide-eyed while he wove Boo between the trees. *You shouldn't be able to do that! How did you do that? None of us can pass memories without touching!*

She just did it, Cyno said, gesturing to Blaec staring blankly at Scorch's shoulder.

She smelled oranges, Blaec told them.

Fuck, Zep thought, and the others agreed.

It's Black Widows, Arctic told Sal. *Their resin smells like citrus. How close are they?*

I don't know.

Sal, he demanded, his concern tinting his mental voice. *How close?*

She inhaled again. *They're gaining.*

I'd rather lose the horses than any of you, LT snapped in their heads, thinking of their destination. *So move! Two klicks. Go!*

They put their heels to their mounts. A full-speed retreat through the woods was very different from a leisurely canter. Trees seemed to appear under the horse's hooves as they ran. Leaves hid traps that could break their legs. The Escean foothills did not have the most predictable footing. Each stride became a nightmare.

Bazya stumbled, throwing Arctic against her neck, but they recovered. Arden followed on the wrong side of a tree, pulling her rein from Zep's hand, forcing him to circle around to catch her. Raven jumped a downed tree, and only Sal's grip on Cyno's waist kept her on the horse's back.

The noise of their mount's crashing hooves almost covered the sound. Almost. Sal heard the snort of a horse well behind her and snapped her head around. Sunlight flicked off a pale red hide then vanished into the undergrowth. She sent a warning to the men as she reached for the crossbow poking her leg from the back of the saddle. Jase's quiver was strapped to his back, pressing into her chest. She grabbed a bolt and loaded the weapon. It wasn't easy to do while the horse bounced her around.

In only a few strides, she saw it again. Leaning low on his mount's neck, the soldier was clad in black leather. His head was bare, and she could see his grimace, white teeth etched against his dark skin.

They're on us! she warned.

Blaec glanced over his shoulder. *Do what you can. We need to get to the creek bed!*

Sal shifted her grip on Cyno then leaned back. Watching between trees, she waited. When a man appeared, she lifted her arm and loosed. The bolt buried itself in his neck, his cry causing the Blades to look back.

One down, she said, *but there's more.*

Good, Arctic thought. *Pick 'em off, Sal. Lame the horses, kill the riders, I don't care, just make an opening!*

She pushed her thighs closer to Cyno and wedged the crossbow against her chest, sending an acknowledgment across the link while she grabbed another bolt. *Keep us at the back,* she thought.

Can do, kitten, he said, lifting the reins.

Raven collected, falling behind the other horses, then surged forward. Sal swayed on the slick hair, but Jase grabbed her leg until she was steady. This time, the Black Widows came at them in a group. Sal spotted the first horse and loosed, the bolt sinking deep into the flesh behind its jaw. It reared in its tracks, and she thought it was going to throw itself over, but trees obscured her view. She reloaded as fast as she could, pointing across her body.

Intent on the man before him, the Terran didn't notice Sal's weapon. She aimed for his throat, just as Raven jumped a cluster of brush. The shot went wild, hitting his horse's foreleg instead. The poor animal staggered, taking only two steps before carrying the leg and losing speed.

She grabbed another bolt. *Three,* she counted, pleased.

Her neck and back were starting to ache from contorting while trying to balance. She turned again and saw a soldier grin as he raised his own crossbow. Panic flared in her head and time slowed to a crawl. Her body wanted to dodge, but Cyno's unprotected back would take the hit if she did. While she watched the man's finger close on the trigger, Sal aimed. Their eyes met, and she smiled as she shifted to cover her partner and squeezed the release.

Searing pain lanced through her back, making Sal gasp. Her fingers dug into Jase's side as her shoulder went strangely numb. Her bolt, however, had lodged deep in the man's skull. When she looked again, he tumbled from his horse, dead.

Sal?! Jase asked, tilting his head over his shoulder.

Don't fucking stop! she screamed at his mind.

An intense warmth spread down her back. Her pupils dilated, and her senses sharpened, but her left arm grew weaker by the second. She struggled to load the crossbow yet again, her fingers not obeying the commands. Growling, she forced the bolt into the rail, unwilling to let the arrow in her back slow her.

Sal looked for another target. Shooting pain lanced down her spine and up into her jaw. She leaned into it and took aim. They were keeping back, now, but the terrain grew more difficult, making the shots even harder. She squeezed off another and heard a horse scream as her world seemed to drop out from under her. Raven staggered and caught herself, but Sal was thrown into Jase's back. Instinctually, she grabbed at him. When her left arm failed her, the right took over. The crossbow tumbled to the ground and Sal tilted precariously on the horse's back.

Go, Jase, just go. I lost the bow.

Ya hit? he asked.

Yeah. Just go, killer.

He went. Raven dug deep into the ground, each step like fire up Sal's spine. She shoved her head into his shoulder and groaned, but clung tightly. The Black Blades pulled closer, following Arctic as they hit a path then slid down into the creek bed.

We've been here before, Zep said, looking around.

Yeah, LT agreed. *There should be a set of caves close by.*

The Rokish assassins? Risk asked.

Yeah.

I remember, Risk said. *This way.* He turned Phoenix upstream.

The water splashed noisily but hid their tracks. Sal tried to find any hint of the Black Widow Company, but got nothing. It wasn't long before the water in the creek sloshed against their feet, well over the horses' knees. Soaked, they moved onto the far bank, into a stand of evergreens. A small opening brought smiles to the faces of the Black Blades. All except Zep.

Guys, I'm useless, he warned them as he slid from Cessa's back.

We've done this before, Arctic reminded him. *You just have to trust us.*

With my life, Zep agreed. There was no hint of joking in his voice.

The rest followed suit, dismounting and moving their horses into the small cave. Cyno hopped down from Raven then reached up, pulling Sal into his arms. LT saw and rushed to her side.

You're hit? Blaec asked.

Yeah.

Get in there, Blaec ordered. *Risk, Sal needs you.*

Once inside, the ground sloped down steeply, and the walls opened up. Arctic moved to Zep's side, resting his hand on his shoulder, and Sal staggered in behind them. Well inside the cave, she stopped and struggled to reach the bolt in her back, panting at the pain.

I need one of you to pull this, she snapped. *I can't reach it.*

Jase turned and forcefully shoved her against the wall, holding her face against the stone with his forearm, his hip pressing into her back. Sal sucked in a breath and tried to relax, knowing what came next. He leaned close, his breath against her neck, and paused.

Ya in the 'lust? he asked, his thoughts for her mind alone.

Yes. Sal looked at him over her shoulder.

Good, he purred, *tha' makes this easier.*

He bit her neck. His teeth sank into her flesh and Sal moaned softly, her eyes closing in pleasure when he shoved her against the rock even harder. She began to melt into the strength of him, then screamed as pure pain tore at her body. The sudden shock of it gave her the power to push Jase off, and she spun to face him, her teeth bared and her ears pinned close to her head.

He smiled at her and held the bloody bolt between them for explanation. *It hurts less if ya do na struggle.*

He tossed it on the ground and Risk moved cautiously to her side. She nodded and offered him her hand, but he looked quickly to Cyno and LT before taking it. When they made no move to stop him, he wrapped his fingers around hers, closed his eyes, and exhaled.

Sal clenched her teeth, expecting the pain this time. Cold fire traced up her back, and she reached for the wall behind her to keep from losing her balance. Just as her hand met the damp rock, the pain receded, and Sal pulled in a long slow breath, staggering. Stretching her arm, it moved like she expected.

You good, love? Blaec asked.

Sal nodded. *Yeah, and we've wasted enough time already.*

Then let's go. Deeper into the cave, Blaec ordered, yet Sal lingered at the entrance for a moment while the men moved further in. *Sal?* he asked.

Give me a second, she begged.

In the trees beyond, she'd heard something. Pressing her body against the rock, she waited. In moments, a shadow moved and her eyes focused on it. A dark man in black leathers huddled against the base of a tree, staring at the creek bed. Instinctively, she wished for skin the color of the rocks around her and felt the tingle. She bent slowly, distorting her silhouette.

They know we're here, she told the men.

Zep broke in. *Sal, we know they're coming. C'mon. There's too many twists and turns in here. You'll get lost.*

She chuckled to herself. *I won't. I can smell you, Zep. I could track you through here even if –* She stopped mid-sentence. Across the creek, more men moved into sight.

Sal? Zep asked.

I see them.

One man moved to the edge of the creek. His skin was as dark as Zep's, nearly the color of his uniform. When he leaned forward to look at the hoof prints in the sand, she saw a red mark on his shoulder. She looked harder and thought it looked like a spider. He peered after the trail, then pointed at the tree concealing the entrance. The tree whose branches Sal looked through.

"Pretty sure they didn't just walk into the damned cliff," he said.

"Fucking Blades," another man chuckled. "Who knows what they can do."

"Nothing we can't. There are caves back there, dumb-ass."

"You sure?"

"No, but they didn't just walk into the cliff."

Sal waited long enough to see the men begin to move her way. She counted quickly, making note of their armor and weapons before she moved silently into the shadows.

There's twenty-three, she thought. *They're in leathers, not resin, but most have short swords.*

Good work, LT sent. *Now catch up.*

I am, Sal thought, sharing her amusement. *And who decided to mark the trail?* The distinct scent of urine hung in the air before each turn.

Mine, Cyno said. *We got lost the last time we ended up in here. I do na wanna spend three days working our way out again.*

Pungent, Sal thought as she rounded the last corner, nearly jogging into Razor's back.

Zep and Shift clung to the men in front of them, unable to see anything in the dim light. LT and Razor dragged their hands against the walls, their night vision being better than that of humans but not as good as the rest. Arctic led the group, Risk had taken a place in the center of the line, and Cyno was nowhere to be seen. The horses walked slowly beside their riders, some pausing, unsure of their next step. Slowly, patiently, the men encouraged them forward.

One more turn, Jase assured them.

Before they even rounded the corner, Sal noticed the light. The halls began to change from shades of blacks to lighter greys. When she followed the men around the next bend, her eyes constricted at the sudden glare. Sunlight streamed through a small vent in the ceiling of the cavern.

It's not much, but at least I'm not completely blind, Zep thought thankfully.

Sal rubbed at her eyes. While the beam of light might not be much to Zep, it was too much for her night-adjusted vision to tolerate.

We hiding, or we fighting? she asked. *'Cause if we're fighting, this will ruin my ability to see anything.*

We're fighting, Blaec told her.

What's the plan? Shift asked.

We hold the room, Blaec said. *Two men can guard the corridor. We'll take turns. Medics at the back, keeping us repaired. Zep, you'll handle everything else, from water to supplies for the healers. With over twenty of them, they'll be doing the same, but they can't repair their wounds as fast as we can.*

That's stupid, Sal thought.

Blaec's head whipped around to her. *What?!*

We have the advantage, Blaec. We need to use it.

And I wasn't? Anger suffused his tone.

No, you weren't. Risk and Arctic, head back the way we came. Keep to the shadows. You can see them, but they can't see you any better than Zep can. Jase and I will move between them, picking them off as we can. Blaec, you and Razor need to hold the corridor just up from here. Shift, Zep, I need you to keep count and take care of any wounded. There's twenty-three of them. We'll need to make sure we get them all.

Blaec turned to her, the scent of anger and fear emanating from him. *You taking over?*

Sal faced him, staring right into his eyes, unblinking. *I'm helping you. I lived my life in the shadows, Blaec. I know how this works.*

Countermanding my orders?

Who the fuck cares? Arctic said, stepping between them. *She's right, LT. We can see in this shit; they can't. Fighting at the corridor like humans is stupid, so suck up your pride and approve her changes.*

Defeated, Blaec gave his assent. *Fine. This had better work, Sal.*

She smiled deviously. *Ever been scared of the dark?*

Without waiting for his answer, she turned to Jase, and together they moved into the darkness. Arctic patted LT on the shoulder, waiting for the Lieutenant to nod at him before he moved out with Risk.

She's right, Zep told LT.

She's challenging my command, Blaec grumbled.

Nah. She's just trying to save our lives. She's good enough that the men trust her.

You don't understand, Zep, Blaec grumbled.

Zep shrugged. *You're right. I don't. But this time she's right; you're not. What more is there to it? Never bothered you when one of us had a better idea.*

None of you challenged me, Blaec pointed out. *She's pulling at us. She'll end up taking over. Cyno's the worst, but she's changing us.*

Zep thought about it. *Ok, fair enough. But I still don't see what's wrong with it.*

You want to be a damned beast? You want to have the Conglomerate treat you like a second-class citizen?

Zep turned and walked into Blaec's face. Their chests only inches apart, he glared down at his commander. *You're a fucking idiot, LT. I'd give everything I have for a hint of what even Shift gets from being a little bit iliri. I'd give my soul to have as much as you do. I can't even imagine what Sal gets from it. I don't care if some damned Ace laughs at me. If I was an iliri, I'd know it was nothing more than jealousy. So, yeah. I'd gladly be treated like a second-class citizen to have half of what you take for granted.*

You don't know what you're talking about, Blaec told him. *We're not animals. We may be iliri, but we're not fucking beasts.*

Maybe we should be, Zep thought.

CHAPTER THIRTY-SEVEN

Silently, they moved through the stone passages, the sand softening their footsteps. Sal slipped her steel dagger from its sheath and glanced at her partner. He nodded, and they moved apart.

They're coming, he whispered in her mind. *Two of em.*

Then that's their mistake, she nearly purred.

The narrow passages were dark. Human eyes would see nothing but blackness, but the iliri could see enough to make out the irregular formations that would give them cover. Cyno stepped behind a stalagmite and Sal pressed her body into an alcove along the wall. Her ears twitched at the echoes bouncing off the rock around them. She could hear the footsteps moving closer.

They're almost here, Cyno warned, confirming what she thought.

A pair of shadows darkened the passage, and Sal gripped her blade tighter. She let them pass before moving silently behind them. In only a few steps, they were beside Jase. Together, the assassins pounced.

Sal grabbed the man on the left, slapping her hand over his

mouth and dragging him off his feet, her knife at his throat. Jase slashed at the unprotected neck of the man on the right. The smell of blood, so sweet, made her heart pound in her chest as the second man crumpled.

"Your friend is dead," Sal whispered. "Talk, or you're dead, too."

"Lance Corporal Torin Smain," was all he said.

"How many of you are there?" Sal asked.

"Lance Corporal – " he started again, but Sal dragged the edge of the blade across his body.

"Let me make this real clear," she snarled, the tip of the knife moving down his chest. "I only want to know two things." The blade bounced across the belt at his waist and moved lower. "How many of you are there, and how did you know where we were?"

"Lance Cor – "

Sal shoved her hand over his mouth and pushed the blade. The tip punctured the leather at his crotch, and his body flinched away from the pain. "Last time," she growled.

"Twenty-three of us," he said when she lifted her hand.

She pushed the blade again, feeling resistance. "And? I'll castrate you and leave you alive," she warned.

"We set the trap," he whispered into her palm.

"What trap?" Sal lifted her hand slightly.

"The heads. It was a win either way. We either caught the Black Blades, or we showed the CFC what the fuck the scrubbers are. You took the bait."

"And you're losing," Sal said.

"What are you going to do?" he sneered. "Hide in here until your supplies run out? We've got the door covered. Surrender and you might make it through this. Release me, and they might let you live."

"Yer trying ta draw us out?" Jase asked, amused. "That works both ways, boy."

He moved his knife to the man's throat, and Sal smiled. "Scream loud," she told him, and shoved her dagger up.

He did.

What are you doing? Blaec demanded. *They'll know exactly where we are!*

They already do, Sal thought, *and they're trying to lure us out. We're just going to convince them they really should come in.*

With torture? Blaec demanded.

Yeh, Cyno growled. *Just like Circ.*

He cut at the man again, resulting in another scream. The Terran's voice bounced through the stone passages, becoming even more disturbing with each echo.

"Good boy," Sal purred.

He thrashed, pulling his arm free, and took a swing at her. His fist collided with the side of her neck, and Sal snarled. Instinctually, she darted in, grabbing his throat in her teeth.

"Try it," Cyno whispered, a warning coursing through his voice as he caught the man's hand again. "I *will* let her eat ya."

The soldier began screaming again, this time from fear, not pain.

Take him further back, Sal thought, releasing him. *I'm going to see what they're doing up there.*

Jase smiled at her, his sharp teeth catching what little light existed. *I'll give him to Zep. We owe these fucks a bit.*

She nodded, torn between her desire to kill and her desire for her partner. Their eyes met and held for a moment before they moved in their separate directions. She heard the man's body being dragged against the soft floor.

Don't leave tracks, she warned.

I am, just na the right way.

Turn after turn, Sal crept forward. Alone, the sound of dripping water rang loudly into the silence. Another scream echoed through the tunnels, and she glanced back, shocked at how close it sounded. One more turn and she stood in the first cavern, daylight pouring in from the opening. She darkened her skin, feeling it tingle when the color took effect.

A group of men huddled in the bright light, forcing Sal to squint to see them. Their silhouettes shifted and moved as they communicated in only hand signals. She waited. One more scream was all it took.

Their decision made, the enemy soldiers drew weapons and converged on the caverns. Shoulder to shoulder, swords at the ready, twenty-one men pushed inside. Torches were held at intervals, spreading the light around them. Sal began to move back.

They're coming as a group, she told the Blades. *Split up, pick 'em off. Stay out of the light.*

They aren't even sure it's us, Cyno added, appearing beside her once more, *an' they're scared shitless. They reek of it.*

Arctic's voice joined theirs, *Then we keep 'em confused. If you get the chance, maul the bodies. Teeth, claw marks, whatever you can. Keep them on their toes.*

Blaec said nothing.

Arctic, she suddenly remembered, *can you open us up?*

Always, he agreed.

Sal felt her brothers join her mind. Cyno's lust hit her hard, the hair on the back of her neck rising in response. She stifled her desire to scream a snarl into the darkness. Razor's restraint retreated before the primal fury of the berserkers, and Blaec's anger only fueled it. Zep's delight stood in stark contrast.

I can see, he thought, surprised.

We can all see, Shift said. *Welcome to Sal's world.*

Jase and Sal slunk away from the men as they pushed into the tunnels. At the first turn, they took the wrong path, leaving clear footprints for their prey to follow. When the room opened into a spacious cavern, the assassins split, each taking a side, easily finding places in the rock formations. They could hear the Terrans following their trail, the feel of both Risk's and Arctic's minds behind them.

Anticipation flared when Risk made a kill in the shadows. Blaec's rage grew in response to Sal's desire for more death, and it fueled Risk's hate. He slashed at the body, leaving deep gouges in the flesh, then retreated just as the first men entered the cavern.

Sal swiveled her ears around the room, listening for the difference between the sound of their steps and the echoes. In the back of her mind, she felt Zep's awe and paused, gaining a new appreciation for something she'd simply accepted all her life.

We're down to twenty, she thought. *And stop distracting me, Zep.*

He sent a wave of amusement in response.

The Black Widows passed close to Jase's side of the room. He kept pace, stalking them. His body slid between the walls and the liquid-looking formations like little more than a shadow from their torchlight. One of them paused to look around, and Jase struck. His hands snaked out, gripped the man's head and jaw, and twisted. The snap of his neck carried in the stone room. The Terrans spun. Their companion lay dead in his tracks with nothing more than shadows watching.

"What the fuck?" whined a man holding a torch, the fear evident in his voice.

"Stay close," their leader commanded. "Fucking Blades! You can't hide in here forever!"

Scream, Sal, Arctic thought. *They've never heard an enraged iliri before, I bet.*

She watched them, perched high above their heads, her skin as dark as her leathers. The Black Widow Company closed ranks and shoved their torches deep into the rocks, looking for Cyno. Slowly, carefully, he moved out of the light, but Sal could see he'd soon be cornered. It was all the excuse she needed.

She roared. With her teeth bared to their fullest, she screamed years of frustration into the darkness of the cave, letting her rage have a voice. The sound was that of a predator, nothing human about it.

"What the -" a Terran gasped, backing closer to his shieldmate.

Their eyes darted around the room, looking for her. She growled and made her way higher, clinging to the rocks. The deep rumble echoed from all around them, hiding her position as it bounced through the room. The Terrans turned, nearly blind in the dim light. The echoing sound obscured the iliri's position. She jumped to the next rock, pebbles scattering under her feet, moving closer to the door.

Time to go, she thought to Jase.

Ahead of ya. When ya hit the ground, move. They'll be on yer tail.

We got the hall, Arctic assured her. *Take 'em straight to Razor.*

Yes, sir, Sal agreed, eying the landing. *They're about to have a real bad day.*

She dropped from the rock and hit with a thud, digging her hands into the sand to propel her forward, leaving claw marks in her wake. Behind her, the Black Widows gave chase. Running through grey tunnels, ducking easily under ragged rocky outcroppings, she slid into a crevasse and paused, sucking in two deep breaths and releasing them slowly. Around her, the world erupted with the screams of humans.

Eighteen, Risk thought, and Sal felt him sink his teeth into the shoulder of a man while he severed his spine with his dagger.

Seventeen! Arctic called just before he shoved one onto a sharp spear of rock. *Sixteen,* he added. The soldier's friend turned at the sound of the last man's death, and Arctic met him with two blades sunk deep in his chest.

Fifteen, Cyno purred before he pounced on the last man in line.

He slapped his hand across the soldier's mouth and yanked him into the next passage, ripping his throat out with his teeth. With their minds entangled, the sudden rush of warm blood carried to every member of the Black Blades. The sweet taste of human flooded her senses and pushed Sal even further into the bloodlust, dragging the rest with her.

CHAPTER THIRTY-EIGHT

They attacked like the beasts they were so often called. One by one, the men of the Black Widow Company fell before them, ripped away from their unit to die alone in the dark. Sal and Cyno fed their desires into the minds of every man in their link, calling forth their iliri natures. Zep, looking through Razor's eyes, met the men head on. The Lieutenant stormed through their formation, his blades slicing through flesh and tendons, his growl as feral as any of the others. Shift used his teeth, relying on his other senses more than sight.

When the iliri hit them, the Black Widows fell apart. Men scattered and screamed, some not even fighting back. They died like prey in the dark stone passages.

A group tried to retreat. Six men shoved through the demons that ravaged them, swinging their swords blindly as they hacked their way to freedom. Zep took a deep cut across his body but lashed out as he fell. Shift was grazed, the man's dagger leaving a long slice along his hand and arm. A shield hit Sal in the face, knocking her to the ground, but she recovered quickly and launched herself at the idiot who dared hit her. Her teeth met his throat, and she growled as she ripped at his body. He was dead before he hit the ground.

The rest of the group ran for the entrance. The Blades had no way to stop them.

Five, Zep said weakly in their minds. *Five left, and we should do that more often.*

Sal looked over at her brother in arms, leaning weakly against a boulder. He tried to hide it, but the pain was almost more than he could take. Through the link, she could feel how different he was from her. Her bruises taunted her, screaming a desire that she worked to hide. In his mind, the feeling was much more intense. The cut along his waist cried to her like a memory, clear, sharp, but far away. She moved toward him. For the first time, humans began to make sense.

Risk knelt at Zep's side, checking the wound in the darkness. *It's gonna scar, man,* he warned.

Fucking worth it, Zep said. *Hit me.*

You're linked, jackass, Risk replied, gesturing to Arctic. *I can't heal you if you're sending it back at me.*

Arctic? Sal asked.

He saw where she was looking – at Zep – and understood. *I'll leave you in,* he assured her, then told the rest, *Let me close this down.*

She watched the men's bodies relax when they returned to their own minds. Zep's wound still called to her, the smell of him so intense. He was sweet but like incense, not dessert. Slowly, she moved toward him, and his eyes met hers.

I still feel you, he whispered in her mind.

"Sorry, brother," Risk said, touching Zep's skin gently. "Sal, hold him."

"Don't let her bite him," Blaec grumbled under his breath.

She grabbed Zep's hand and placed her other on his shoulder, blocking out Blaec's snide remark. Risk took a long, deep breath. When he exhaled, Zep writhed. She clenched her teeth and held him still. The pain of Zep's healing flowed along her own nerves like ecstasy before returning to him. Risk breathed again, and Zep lurched, but linked with Sal, the pain's edge was no longer as sharp.

It teased through both of their skins like a lover, hinting at passions yet to be discovered. Zep writhed, but the moan in his throat didn't sound like pain. Then it was over, and Zep leaned forward before he could stop himself.

Sighing, Risk leaned back, out of the way. He glanced once at Sal and barely nodded before looking back to Zep. "Good as new, man."

"Just a little scratch," Zep joked, patting Sal's hand and sitting up. *Is that how it always is?*

Yeah.

Thanks, babe. I owe you. Both for my pride, and that.

Sal shrugged and glanced at Arctic. *That's the bloodlust,* she told Zep, as Arctic pulled her mind away.

Alone in her head, there was nothing to distract her from her desires. She could smell the human blood all around, and bodies lay scattered between the Black Blades. Cyno leaned against a rock, six men carefully placed between him and Sal.

"LT," Zep said, "You have a berserker problem to deal with."

"There's five left," Cyno growled softly, "and they need ta die."

"No." Blaec's voice left no room for argument, but he looked at Sal pointedly. "We just decimated this branch of the Black Widow Company. They'll be retreating. I don't care what any of you think, we're not animals. We will *not* commit war crimes. And this time my orders *will* be followed."

Sal looked at the ground, wiping the blood from her face, aware that his anger was directed at her. The Black Blades fell silent.

"Nothing, Sal?" Blaec asked.

"No, sir," she said, pulling her ears close to her skull.

"Good. Then get the horses. All of you. We need to get those damned crates back and report. Razor, see if you can identify any of the dead." The smell of his anger was unmistakable.

Sal felt shame as she moved to obey. Cyno's movements screamed at her like pure electricity to her senses, but she refused to even look at him. The power of Blaec's fury overruled her desire.

The Black Blades made their way to the horses, carefully releasing hobbles in the darkness. Arden stood quietly, the crates still slung across her back. Sal looked at her mare then glanced over at Raven, all too aware that being so close to Jase would be more than her instincts could tolerate. With a snarl, she threw her back against the wall, running her hands through her hair. Her body wanted more death. That, or Jase's teeth on her.

"Ya good, kid?" Zep asked, walking up to grab Cessa.

"Yeah." She sighed deeply.

"Sal?" Arctic moved beside her. He tilted his head, gesturing for Zep to check on Cyno. "Looks like you're gonna need a ride?"

Zep patted her shoulder, then led his mare toward the little man. Even across the distance, she could hear them.

"LT's pissed," Zep said softly.

"Yeh. I touch her, an' he'll lose it."

"Looks like she's riding with Arctic. You good, little brother?"

Cyno yanked his stirrup down. The crack of the leather was loud in the hollow cavern. "I've done it b'fore, Zep. It's her I'm worried 'bout."

Arctic grabbed her chin and turned her head back to face him. *Sal, this isn't right. He's punishing you by keeping you away from Cyno.*

He's pissed because he thinks I'm nothing but a damned animal, Arctic. We both know it. She glared at him, but the set of her ears showed there was no challenge, only anger in her thoughts.

He leaned closer. *So what are you going to do about it?*

Learn to be tame, she sneered. *Those papers say they made us. They didn't say they made us human.* Sal smashed her fist against the wall behind her, the rock slicing the side of her hand. With a soft growl in her throat, she brought it to her lips and sucked at the blood. *I was out of line, and we all know it, but I was fucking right.*

Yeah, you were.

Sal shook her head, unable to vent her anger on him. *Blaec wants us to be human, so I'd better learn quickly.*

You're not human, Arctic thought, reaching up for her face. *None of us are.*

Don't. She pressed her hand against his chest. *Don't touch me, Arctic. I won't be able to stop if you touch me.*

You're screaming at my mind, Kaisae. We know what happens when you two end up in the lust. Cyno's on his own, but let me help you with this? I can take it, and LT won't stop me.

When she said nothing, he pressed against her, resin pinning her against the rocks, and his fingers tangled in the hair at the back of her head. Then he kissed her. Those near-perfect lips were so soft, like velvet against her own. She desired more. She *needed* more. Her body begged her to feel, to live, but in the back of her mind, a flare of anger bloomed, and she realized it was her own.

She bit. Hard.

Her sharp teeth sliced through Arctic's lip and Sal wrenched her face free. "I said don't touch me," she snarled, pushing him back.

Blaec stormed toward them with his jaw set. Without a word, he grabbed Arctic's shoulder and shoved him into the ground, sand and rocks spraying at the impact. The Black Blades turned, tensed for an attack, but they froze with their hands on their hilts. Blaec stood over Arctic, anger clear on his face. The First Officer lay at his feet calmly, daring to look up into his commander's eyes, but the edge of his mouth fought a smile.

"You have her marks on your face!" Blaec snarled. "You bastard." Blaec grabbed Arctic by his pauldron, lifting him just to throw him down again.

Arctic made no move to resist, but his voice was cold. "You think this is what she deserves for saving our asses?"

Sal moved between them, her anger rising. "Stop," she growled, her ears pressing against her head.

"This is not your fight," Blaec snapped at her.

"Well, it sure as hell isn't his!"

"What, are you saying he didn't like that?" Blaec gestured to Arctic who still lay in the dirt behind her. "I told you to get the horses, not make out with my First Officer. I expect my orders to be *obeyed!*"

"When your orders make sense," she yelled, "they are!"

His face snapped to hers, and their eyes met. "No, Sal. They aren't. You blatantly challenged me."

"I did no such thing. You don't have to like what I am, but you damned sure better not take it out on my men." Her lips were pulled back in a snarl. Her teeth, with her second set of canines, ground together loud enough for the men behind them to hear.

"Your men? Just when did they become *your* men?" he demanded.

"When *you* put me in black. When you made this my family."

He paused, still angry, but he had nothing to say. Realizing she still held his gaze, Sal glanced away, looking to his hands instead before she continued.

"Your problem is with me. Deal with me and leave them out of it, Blaec."

She saw him nod and glanced up at his face once more before stepping to the side. Arctic knelt on the ground behind her, his lip bloody and swollen from her teeth. Calmly, he stood, placing himself before LT, saying nothing.

"Send them out, Arctic. I need to speak with her. We'll catch up," Blaec ordered.

"Yes, sir," the First Officer answered, glancing once at Sal before he walked away.

She heard the men move, giving them the privacy they needed, and felt eyes on her. Turning, she expected to see Jase, but was shocked to find the deep brown eyes of Zep instead. He nodded once and turned to Arden, shifting the packs. Working quickly, he re-secured the crates and spread them between Raven and Cessa, leaving her mare standing beside Scorch.

Neither Sal nor Blaec spoke while they waited for the men to leave.

They stared at each other, resentment smoldering between them. When the cave was quiet, and the last signs of their unit faded, he still said nothing. Sal refused to break the silence first.

"Why did you do that to me?" he finally asked.

"I'm not really sure what you mean," she admitted.

He met her eyes like a human, not an iliri. "You challenged me. In front of all of them, you challenged my orders. Why?"

"I was right, Blaec. We had the advantage, and we needed to use it."

"And then I find you kissing Arctic!" he howled.

She looked at him, confused, her mind racing to the kiss. "Blaec?" she asked softly.

"Don't lie to me, Sal."

"Blaec, he was worried about me, that's all."

"That's all? Damn it!" he yelled. "You marked him."

"The bloodlust. Did you forget about that? This is what happens when you let me kill. Maast, Blaec, you know that's how I react. You throw me at Cyno every time it happens so you don't have to deal with it."

"Damn it, Sal!" he said again. "I've only ever asked you to be loyal!"

"And I've been nothing but. I even refused him. Blaec, stop acting like a damned human!" She walked away, moving to her horse.

"I am a human, Sal. You'd better get used to it."

His words stopped her in her tracks. She looked back at him, her voice cold. "No. You aren't. You only wish you were. You wish we *all* were."

Blaec closed the distance between them, his jaw clenched, his eyes flaring. When he reached her, he grabbed her, yanking her around to face him. "This is who I am, Sal. I can't be your iliri pet. If that's what you want, you should have chosen Cyno. He's the closest thing we have. Maybe *he* wants a feral lover."

The flat of her pale hand struck his cheek just under the bone with an audible crack, and his head snapped back. He turned back to her, and she saw tears in his eyes.

"I won't fight you, Sal," he said. "I'm tired of fighting. I'm tired of trying to tame you. You're a damned good soldier and one of the best assassins I've seen, but I don't know if I can do this anymore. I just don't know if it's worth it."

"How dare you try to give me away," she hissed.

"You're not an animal. It doesn't always have to be about who is dominant and who submits, about who is stronger or who wins. Sometimes, I just need you to be mine, to be a little bit human, a little gentle." He sighed and wiped at his eyes. "Sal, I just want it to mean something when I'm with you. I don't want to own you. I don't want to fight you."

He stared at her for a long time, and she found herself unsure of what to say. "I'm not human," she whispered.

"You used to be. The woman I fell in love with could smile, she laughed, and she loved me." He glanced at the sky, blinking away more tears, "Sal, I don't want an animal. I understand you get the bloodlust. I can accept that. I can accept Cyno. What I can't accept is how casually you can throw away any semblance of civility. It's nothing more than hunting for you, and I don't want to be your prey. I'm not just another step for you to climb over."

"Blaec -"

"No." His hand cut off her words like a knife through the air. "Figure it out, Sal, or don't. It's your call, but I can't be with you like this."

He walked past her to Scorch and grabbed the horse's reins. Without looking back, he led the stallion into the dark passage to catch up with his men.

CHAPTER THIRTY-NINE

Arden walked slowly, feeling her rider was in no mood to hurry about anything. Sal swayed in the saddle, wishing for tears to ease the ache in her heart but unable to make her alien eyes cry. It looked so easy when the humans did it, but hers always failed her. Instead, she gasped at the air, her body sobbing even if the tears refused to fall. She knew the route back. They all did. She didn't need the Black Blades to make it home, and the way she felt, being around others was the last thing she wanted. Step after step, Arden walked on.

She couldn't imagine life without Blaec. She tried to convince herself that things would go back to normal and that he'd apologize to her, but it sounded like nothing but a young human's fantasy. No, he was truly done with her unless she could become the one thing she wasn't: a human.

Sal resigned herself to her misery until she saw a dark horse in the road. The rider, his skin too dark to be Blaec, waited patiently. When she reached him, Zep turned his mare in beside hers without a word. They walked in silence for an hour before Sal finally felt the need to speak.

"Did he ever apologize to Arctic?"

"Yeah." Zep nodded. "They're good."

"At least there's that."

"Arctic won't let Shift heal his face."

She nodded but said nothing more. They walked on for a while longer before Zep decided to push the issue.

"He told Cyno he could have you, Sal."

"Yeah. He told me the same."

Without warning, Zep reached over and grabbed Arden's reins, stopping the mare in her tracks and forcing Sal to look at him. "Enough of this. It's not his place! You're not a damned rug to be walked on like this."

"You don't understand," she said. "Just leave it alone."

"No." He looked into her eyes and shook his head. "Sal, you're my friend. I won't let you ride kilometers wallowing in your own pity. Do something. Anything! Just do *something*."

She sighed. "Zep, he wants me to be more human. I can't do that. I don't know how to do that!"

"Talk to me, demon," he begged.

She told him, reliving every detail of their fight. She admitted how she hit him in anger, and how ashamed she felt about it. In their time together they'd wrestled, pinned, held, and more, but neither had ever hit the other in anger.

"Why'd you do that, Sal?" Zep asked.

"Because he tried to act like he had the right to choose who I could be with? I don't know. He told me he didn't want me if I was just going to keep acting like a beast, though. Zep?"

"Yeah?"

"Am I that bad? Am I that different?" She sucked a quick breath of air. "Have I changed that much?"

Zep moved their horses forward again, his brow furrowed. "Yes and no. When you came to us, you were trying so hard. You knew nothing about who you were. Hell, your first response to the lust was to be ashamed! You resisted your urges, and you tried so hard to be human."

"And now?"

"Now," he sighed. "I think Cyno brings something out in you. Your minds in the link don't feel the same as the rest of ours, and we all know it. The more you're with him, the stronger it feels. At least to me. When we were up in Escean Pass, with the heavy cav?"

"Yeah?"

"I've linked with Cyno before, in combat. Hell, we ran a few ops together before you came. I could feel it across the link, but it wasn't the same. That was the first time I'd linked in with *you*, though. When you're there, it takes all of us. We hunt, we don't just fight." He paused, looking at her. "Sal, with you in the link, Cyno's more. I'm not sure what exactly, but he's more, and you. Yeah. You flood through us. I know each time you kill. I can feel these emotions – I don't even have words for them. You make us better than we've ever been, but I don't feel human when we do it."

"I'm sorry, Zep."

"Don't be. For me, it's the closest I can get. But the better you get, the *more* you get. Like Cyno. Yes, you've been changing. It's not bad. You're just accepting who you are. Least that's how I see it."

"How do I stop?" she whispered.

He asked her softly, "Do you really want to?"

"If it means Blaec, then yeah. I do."

"Are you really ready to spend the rest of your life fighting who you are to make a man happy? Is he really worth that much to you? I won't let you do that to yourself, demon."

She said nothing.

Together, they rode on. By nightfall, they caught up with the rest of the Black Blades. Tensions were high, but the men were quiet and subdued. Arctic kept himself on the far side of the camp, well away from her. They bedded down, weary from nearly thirty-five hours of combat, and Sal volunteered to take the first watch. Blaec barely spared her a glance. His body told her she would not be welcome with him now.

Letting out a sigh, she moved away from the glare of their fire. Then, resting her back against a tree, she lowered herself to the ground and sighed again. Around her, the men fell asleep quickly, their soft noises comforting to her ears. She found herself watching Blaec, his back to her as he slept. Hours passed, but Sal couldn't bring herself to wake the next man. They needed the rest, she thought, but the truth was she wouldn't sleep anyway, not with the ache in the back of her mind.

Hours later, a scuff of leaves alerted her. She stood and moved around her tree, steel blade in hand, only to meet the attacker's eyes with her knife against his throat. Brown eyes, nearly black, looked at her calmly.

It's well past your watch, little demon, Zep's mind whispered to her, and she lowered the blade. *I'm not foolish enough to tell you to sleep, but I will offer you a shoulder to lean on while you think.*

Thanks, Zep.

You in the mood to talk about it? he asked gently.

Not really. Yet again, she sighed. It seemed to be all she could do. *I dunno. I mean, that's the problem: I don't know.*

About why he's upset?

That, what to do about it, or what is going to happen. She looked into Zep's eyes, her pupils nearly round in the darkness. *I just don't understand.*

Oh, Sal, he thought and wrapped his arms around her, pulling her against his chest. His touch was comforting.

With her face pressed against him, she nodded, pulling herself closer. *What did I do so wrong?*

You made a decision, little one. Who knows, you may have saved the mission, you may have wasted your time, but you made a decision.

Am I going to lose him because of it? she asked.

He'll always be your commander.

She looked up at Zep's face, her pale eyes meeting his. *You know that's not what I mean. And what happens the next time? Or the time after that? Maast, Zep, am I supposed to just stay quiet when there's a better way to win? I didn't ask Arctic to try to kiss me!*

He smiled, just the barest corner of his lips raising as he ducked his head. *Do you really think that's why LT's so upset? Has he had a problem with you and Cyno? Is it what you did, or how you did it that's the issue?*

What do you mean?

It may be too human for you to understand, he told her.

I'm trying, Zep.

Look, this thing between you, he asked, *why do you care? Why do you keep going back to him? Why don't you just bed Cyno and follow the orders you're given?*

Because I love him, Sal replied, confused.

Why? Zep pressed.

She tensed against him, then pulled away to search his face while her mind whirled. For a long moment, she said nothing. Finally, glancing at Blaec's sleeping back, she answered. *I trust him.*

That can't be all there is to it, Zep told her. *I'd like to think you trust me?*

Yeah. I do.

But you aren't exactly in love with me.

She said nothing. With the night air growing colder, Zep wrapped an edge of his blanket around her shoulders.

So what else is it? he asked. *Is it just because he's in charge?*

No.

Then what?

She leaned her head onto his shoulder. Zep made her feel safe, like she could tell him anything. He'd never judge her, no matter how she answered his questions, so she honestly thought about how she felt about Blaec. It was different somehow. She trusted Blaec, but it was different. He was the first man who treated her like she was beautiful. He was the first man who hadn't demanded to own her. His authority pulled at her instincts, but she loved him because he made her feel important. Without him, who would she be?

It's because he takes care of us, I think. He keeps us safe and protects us from ourselves, even if it means he doesn't do the same for himself. He gives so much for all of us, and more for me. How can I not love him, Zep?

Sal? Zep asked, turning her face to his. *What do your instincts say? That part of you that isn't human. Why does it love him?*

Because he's stronger than me. He can protect me. He keeps me safe.

And you didn't let him do that, Zep pointed out. *You protected us. You took over, you challenged him, and you made him feel weak.*

She nodded, seeing what he meant.

And you encouraged them to embrace their natures. I felt it, Sal. We all felt it. You made a human feel like an iliri - what do you think that did to him? He's more proud than you think. You showed him that he's caught between two worlds, and you threatened his place in our unit. The one place where he can be just himself.

So what do I do now? she asked.

I wish I knew. Talking about it would be a good start, but what do I know? I'm human, Sal. I'll never see things the way you both do. I also know Cyno is taking this thing between you pretty hard. He doesn't want to comfort you for fear that he'll upset LT and make things worse. He doesn't want to leave you alone, either.

I wish I knew what to do, she said.

I know, Zep assured her. *First thing you need to do, though, is sleep. You won't be any good to us if you don't.*

She nodded, but made no move to leave.

My stuff's by the fire, he told her. *Go crawl in it and just try. Dawn will be here soon.*

What about you?

I've got the last watch. He hugged her, his embrace comforting, and kissed her on the forehead. Then he nudged her forward. *Sleep, demon.*

CHAPTER FORTY

Sal kept to the back of the group as they returned, the entire unit separating her from Blaec. They rode in near silence, the men subdued. Halfway through the journey, Cyno dropped back to her side, saying nothing. Blaec glared at the little assassin, but Cyno refused to acknowledge it. When they stopped to give the horses a break, he looked up at her, his eyes gentle, before reining Raven away.

Sal buried herself in her thoughts for the rest of the trip. She was losing Blaec, and she could feel it with each step they took closer to the Conglomerate. She was losing him because she was nothing more than a beast. Beasts couldn't feel love, and she couldn't explain her feelings. She could only wonder if that meant what she felt wasn't really love. It wasn't like she had a lot of experience with such things, so how would she know? Around and around, the thoughts went in her mind, throwing her deeper into despair.

When they returned to the encampment, she was emotionally battered and mentally fatigued. The cavalry had returned the day before, and the entire base was anxiously awaiting the Black Blades.

Having moved the crates to Razor's gelding, the men led their horses calmly through the throng of soldiers clustering around the narrow path between tents. Blaec walked at the front, proudly, with Arctic barely a step behind him. Sal trailed at the back, lagging well behind the rest, lost in her thoughts. Arden, head down and half asleep, followed lazily. The horses knew they were home and that a reprieve from the hours on the road waited for them.

A soldier stepped into her path, halting her. He looked vaguely familiar, but the scowl on his face warned her that his intentions were not kind.

"Remember me, bitch?" he asked.

She looked at him in confusion, his features not registering in her mind. She shook her head, "No, should I?"

"Well, you're wearing my blacks, scrubber."

She saw the blade too late, its oiled surface held close against his hip. The man stepped toward her, and Sal tried to dodge but Arden was too close. She slammed into the mare's shoulder. The sweet pain of the blade slipped between her ribs, and she gasped because it was all she *could* do. The bloodlust immediately exploded in her mind.

The movement caught Cyno's attention. He turned to Sal, but she was pressed between her mare and the man, slowly sliding down her horse toward the ground.

"*Sal!*" he screamed in her ears and mind at once.

She tried to react, but her body refused to move like she wanted. Her right hand pulled a knife, hours of training reminding her muscles of their job even as her mind failed her. The blade sliced at her attacker when her body collapsed, cutting into the man's thigh toward the inside of his knee. His flesh parted easily, but his leathers wrenched the weapon from her weak grasp. The human yanked his dagger from her body and liquid bubbled in her throat. It was her own blood.

Things were moving so slow. She felt Arden shy to the side and watched Cyno rush toward her like an enraged beast. He launched himself at the soldier, hitting him like a predator. His eyes were as cold as ice, his favorite resin blade catching the light when it aimed for the man's heart. His hand closed around the man's throat.

No. She stopped Cyno's blade with a whisper of a thought. *Don't.*

If Cyno killed the man in front of so many witnesses, not even Blaec would be able to prevent the military's punishment. While time crawled in her consciousness, she watched Cyno throw the man to the ground, the edge of his blade denting his skin without cutting.

Beautiful, she thought, and rested her head against the ground.

The searing pain in her side called to her, making her want to pull herself to her feet and tear Cyno's leathers from him, but her body couldn't do it. Moaning, she writhed on the ground, a spasm of coughing spewing blood from her lips as time caught back up.

Men from the crowd jumped on the attacker, pinning him to the dirt. Cyno released him and spun to her side. Feet thundered on the ground. The Blades were coming, they had to be. They wouldn't leave her alone. The cries of the men around her calling for aid blurred into a jumble, and only Cyno's eyes held her attention. She reached up, wanting him, but he ignored his desire and restrained her. He was breathing too fast, his muscles too tense. He wasn't giving in to the passion that enveloped them both. Blaec called into her mind, but she couldn't manage to answer him, her thoughts too weak to send.

"I want that man!" Blaec yelled above the commotion, wrath spilling from every syllable. "Secure him, damn it." Walking quickly, he made it to her side, gesturing for someone to hurry.

"Sal," he begged. "Hang on, love. Fuck, just hang on."

She coughed again, the spasms pulling her body from the ground, and realized that someone was pressing hard against her side. The pain of the assistance and the blood in her mouth caused her passions to flare. Her pale eyes met Blaec's, and she tried to let him know she was trying, while she gasped for breath through the blood thickening in her lungs. She needed to sit up but couldn't make either man understand. Both of her lovers whispered to her, begging her for something, refusing to comprehend that she was drowning.

Dark hooves sprayed sand across her, coming so close that Sal tried to move. Blaec slid his arms under her and pulled her from the ground, pain making her cry out. The sound was like a woman in ecstasy. She felt a second set of hands wrenching her apart before pressing her close against his chest. Her head up, Sal managed to find the air that had been eluding her. Sucking great gasps, she looked at the strong jaw of Zep, set hard in anger.

The rocking of Cessa beneath her was somehow soothing. They were moving. In this position, she could see over Zep's shoulder and watched her lovers fade into the dust of their wake. Blaec's green eyes were filled with longing. Cyno's pale face was streaked with tears. Those were her men, and she was going the wrong way. Letting out a sigh, her head met Zep's shoulder just as blackness took her.

Both men watched Zep's retreat for only a moment before turning to the attacker held by two men in blue. Blaec recognized his face, and his anger flared.

"Bardus," he spat. "You didn't figure out that I won't tolerate this when I kicked you out of the trials?"

"I just took yer iliri cunt from ya. How's it feel, Lieutenant?" the would-be assassin sneered.

Cyno lunged, but Blaec grabbed him across the chest, holding the powerful assassin back with every ounce of strength he had. "That's my cunt, ya piece of shit," Cyno growled. "She's *MINE!*"

Stop! Blaec ordered, the power of his voice in Cyno's mind the only thing able to pierce the haze the assassin was under. "Cyno," he said aloud this time, calmly. "Enough."

"Yes, sir." Cyno let out a breath, relaxing, but only barely.

The crowd parted as the General moved toward them. "Lieutenant, what's going on?" he asked, taking in the scene. Sal's blood still darkened the ground by their feet.

"General Albin, your soldier," Blaec said, "just tried to kill one of mine."

"That fuckin' scrubber cunt ain't a damned soldier!" Bardus said as he struggled to pull free of the men holding him, blood streaming down his leg. "It's his play toy. Ain't a scrubber able to make 'leet ops, everyone knows that."

Cyno lunged again, and this time Blaec let him get even closer. His deathly blue stare marked every feature of the man before him. Bardus shrank away from the vengeance in the assassin's eyes.

"Have you ever seen a berserker before, Lance Corporal Bardus?" Blaec asked, keeping his tone calm. "The sight of blood sends them into a frenzy. Only years of training can teach them how to control their urges. Only discipline can keep them in check."

Bardus gulped, transfixed by Cyno's stare while Blaec spoke. "I have two in the Blades. Each one is loyal to me, but loyalty can only restrain them so much. That girl you just knifed is one." He paused, watching Bardus try to peel his eyes from Cyno's. "This is the other, and you just spilled his lover's blood all over him."

"Fuck," Bardus whispered, realizing that his life was in real danger.

"I'm going ta skin ya, ya bastard, and make ya eat yer own flesh," Cyno breathed. "Ya will pay fer this."

"Cyno," the Lieutenant said again, sternly this time. *Not here.*

The lithe man forced himself to relax and turned away from the attacker. "I can na be here, LT," he said.

"We need your report, Cyno," Blaec told him, adding in his mind, *She's with Risk. Zep's there, too. We'll know as soon as they do, and you'd only hurt her more right now.*

"Yes, sir."

"I want the prisoner in the stocks!" the General commanded.

"Lieutenant, I need your report, and then I'll deal with that man. Was it your iliri he attacked?"

Cyno tensed at the tone of the General's voice, struggling to act professionally. Blaec assured him, again, that Risk would bring Sal through this as he answered. "Yes sir, it was. She was with us, heading in to report from our last mission. He seems to think she is the reason he failed out of the Black Blades."

"Ah, I see. Well, come tell me what you found." He expected their obedience.

The General walked into his tent and threw himself into a chair behind an elaborate desk, offering the simple chair across from it to the Lieutenant. Cyno stood beside his commander, his body at parade rest. Arctic, Shift, and Razor moved beside them, standing quietly.

"All right, tell me what you learned," the General said, a casual gesture encouraging them to get on with it.

"Sir," Blaec started, "I'm sure Llyr has already briefed you on the mission in the Escean Pass. The supply train was not hauling metal like we'd been led to believe, but iliri heads."

"Yes, yes," the General muttered. "I know that. And the Black Blades took some crates. Llyr said you seemed pretty impressed with them?"

"Yes, sir. The crates include documents from the Landing. They are written in Iliran, by an iliri."

"Not much use to us then."

"I had Cyno translate them," Blaec said, holding his face stoic.

The General looked at the small man, noticing just how pale his skin was. "Ah, you're iliri as well. Well, that makes more sense. What did the papers say, boy?"

"Says we, the iliri, were specific'lly designed and bred ta be the ideal soldiers, sir." He took a deep breath, and continued, working to control his accent. "They have detailed descriptions of human colonization of the continent as well."

"Good to know," the General said. "So what took you so long to get back?"

Blaec answered, "The oxen used to pull the wagon were slow. Just above Skyline Creek, we encountered the Black Widow Company. It appears the reports of their presence were correct."

"And you trailed them?"

"No, sir." A smile pulled at the corner of Blaec's lip. "The Black Widow Company set up the caravan through the Escean Pass as an ambush. They hoped to draw the Black Blades into combat, but it seems we cleaned that up too fast." He paused. "With the heavy cav's help, of course."

"Lieutenant, I don't care what's between you and Llyr. What I want to know is where the Black Widow Company is, and what we can do to stop them."

"About twenty a them are in a cave, rotting," Cyno growled softly.

The General glared at him, but Blaec nodded. "Corporal Cynortas is correct. We were ambushed by the Black Widows and took refuge in a set of caves along Skyline Creek – "

"There are caves up there?"

"Yes, sir. About a year ago, when Rok sent those assassins over the pass, that's where they were hiding. We flushed them out of the same caves, so had a bit of experience with them."

"And this time you hid from the Black Widows in there?"

"Lured, sir," Arctic clarified. "We used the caverns to even the odds."

"Give this to me straight, Doll. Tell me what I need to know without all the bullshit."

"Sir," Blaec said with a sigh. "We killed about twenty of the twenty-five men with this section of the Black Widow Company. Five were able to get away, and two others may have been only wounded on the way in instead of killed. It was somewhat hard to be sure at a full gallop."

"Casualties?"

"None, sir."

"Injuries?" the General pressed.

Shift held up his hand, the red line of his healing wound visible. "I stepped into a man's blade in the dark, sir."

The General nodded, processing the information. He reached for a pen, scrawled a few notes. "Do we have any idea of where the real bribe is?"

"Not yet, sir," Arctic answered.

"Thank you, soldier." He turned to Blaec, changing the subject. "Don't you think it's improper for your officers to fraternize so openly?"

Blaec felt the growl in Cyno's mind and shot his soldier a warning glance. "Sir, since there is no rule against officers of equal rank co-mingling, I refuse to make my men remain chaste any more than you do yours. Cynortas and Luxx are the best assassins I have, and I've heard no complaints from you about their efficacy. The Black Blades are an elite unit. My men are required to have skills that often carry baggage. If one of your soldiers hadn't spilled blood in the middle of camp, their relationship wouldn't have become public knowledge outside of our own ranks."

"Agreed. I can't say that I understand your urges, soldier," the General told Cyno, "but so long as you can maintain proper protocols, I won't make an issue of this."

"Sir?" Blaec asked. "What will Bardus's punishment be, and will I have a say in it?"

"Most likely he'll be digging latrines for a month." The General shrugged it off. "That should make him think next time."

"That's unacceptable, General," Blaec said too calmly. "That man just tried to murder a superior officer and has removed one-eighth of my operational forces."

"What do you want me to do, Lieutenant? Court-martial him?"

"That's exactly what I expect you to do, General."

"Shit, man!" the General gasped. "I can't go hanging a soldier for damaging a conscript. There are five more where she came from."

"Cyno!" Blaec snapped. "Wait for me outside. That's an order. The rest of you as well."

"Yes sir," Cyno said, his jaw clenched tightly. When he stormed from the tent, Blaec whispered thanks into his mind, conveying reassurance. The others followed him quietly.

"General," Blaec began, "I know this is hard for you to understand, but each of my soldiers is a unique unit. Regardless of the color of their skin, my men have passed extensive trials. Each one is worth five of your common soldiers on a bad day. The Conglomerate has invested hundreds of krits into their training, and they should be viewed as an asset to the nation, if nothing else."

"Damn it, Lieutenant, are you a scrubber sympathizer?"

"I value my troops, sir. That iliri woman your man just put in the infirmary could take me down on her worst day. How many humans do you think could say the same?"

"Fine. What do you want me to do? If I hang the man, we'll have a riot in the ranks."

"Treat her like an asset? Court-martial him for damaging the property of the Conglomerate. The punishment for destroying that many krits worth of inventory is death, isn't it?" Blaec raised an eyebrow smugly at the General, knowing he had no option but to agree.

"Fine. The jury will be made of his peers, though, and I'll have witnesses both from the ranks as well as your Black Blades. If the jury finds him guilty, we'll let them set the sentence, within the laws."

"Agreed." Blaec nodded once. "Now if you need nothing further, I have a soldier who may be dying. I'd like to check on her status."

"Fine. Just answer me one thing," the General said.

Blaec paused. "Sir?"

"Did just eight of you take out the Black Widow Company?"

"Yes sir, we did." Blaec smiled.

Maybe Sal had been right after all. Maybe proving they were better than humans really was the only way to win, but he knew it wouldn't be an easy fight. He just had to decide what he was willing to give up: her, his position, or the security they'd enjoyed for so long by pretending to be human. There were just too many options right now to know which was the right one. The problem was that something had to give, and he knew that no matter what, he'd be the one to pay for it.

"Thank you, Lieutenant," the General mumbled, "you're dismissed."

Blaec saluted and left the tent.

CHAPTER FORTY-ONE

She burned. Every nerve ending in her body cried out, first in pain, then desire. Her back arched, her nipples pressed against the rough black linen of her open shirt, and she screamed, begging for more, wishing for it to end. Strong hands pinned her shoulders to the bed, and she pulled at them. Her pale skin was stark against his black, the blood on her hands clung to him, and her thoughts whispered how much she wanted him closer. The whole time, her mind teased the edges of his thoughts, pulling Zep in with her.

Another wave of pain and another scream slipped from her. Sal's ears turned to the deep voice soothing her, but all she could manage to do was beg.

"Please," she whispered. "Please!"

"How much more, Risk?" Zep asked, her cries cutting through him. "I can't hold her forever, and she's clawing at my mind."

The golden iliri nodded, never taking his eyes from Sal. Her shirt was unbuttoned, exposing the wound. As Sal writhed, the fabric slipped, exposing her pale breast - only inches from Risk's hand. The deep red gash refused to close. He nodded again, filling his lungs, and when he exhaled, he focused so hard his brow wrinkled.

Sal screamed. Her pale eyes saw nothing as they flicked across the room, her body trying its best to preserve her sanity. When the convulsion passed, she began to relax, breathing deeply, excitedly, then screamed again at the next wave. Zep felt her mind begging for his as he watched the wound close until an angry pink line was the only sign that it had been there.

"Please," she whispered, grabbing at his arms.

"Risk?" Zep asked.

"She's good, as good as I can get her. The damned blade was poisoned. I got her fixed up, but it's going to leave the mark."

"She can deal with that. Damn it. Risk, I think it's time for you to go. It's got her hard."

Risk nodded and struggled to his feet. He swayed, grabbing Zep's shoulder for support before making his way out of the tent.

Seeing her laying in the street, Zep had thought she was already dead. When Blaec handed her up to him, he'd seen the look on Cyno's face, every protective instinct screaming at the assassin to guard what was his. Holding her now, Zep walked a fine line, but he hoped his history with the deadly little man would save him from Cyno's wrath. He released his hold on the girl, her body writhing, and glanced around the tent – Cyno's tent.

"Ah, shit," he breathed when Sal's eyes found his. The lust was truly on her, the taste of her own blood and the pain of the healing throwing her beyond any hope of control. "I'm here, Sal," he told her, brushing her hair from her face, hoping Cyno wasn't too far behind.

Her mind hit him hard, smothering him with feral sexual need.

She moaned softly and leaned toward him, grabbing his neck as she pulled him to her. The feel of her skin made his heart beat faster, calling to something inside him, and he wrapped one arm around her back, hauling her closer. Her breath caressed his lips just before her mouth hit his. Struggling for control, Zep crushed her against him, groaning when her hand slid up his thigh and her tongue down his throat.

He kissed the length of her neck, the bitter taste of her skin flavored by the salt of old blood, and he felt his need rising to meet hers. Sal struggled with his shirt, fumbling with the buttons in her haze. He pulled away only long enough to lift it over his head. Still, her small hands forced him up against her as if she couldn't tolerate that tiny separation. Then their lips met again, her fingers sliding below his waistband, smooth against the soft hair below his navel. He grabbed her wrists.

She was strong, he thought, damned strong, and his own desires were trying to convince him to let her have her way. He could feel his heart beating, pounding in his chest, and he heard his own breath, ragged in his ears.

Cyno! he called, begging the little man to hurry.

Her tongue traced lines against his shoulder and she drew a row of kisses, broken by rough bites, across his chest. Zep moaned softly. She heard his desire and bit harder, his flesh tearing beneath the pleasure of her teeth. When he gasped in pain, she pulled back before her teeth returned – gently this time. Bleeding, but caught inside Sal's mind, he felt his resistance slipping away.

Zep pulled her face to him, biting her lip and licking at the taste of her mouth. His hand slipped across her hip, cupping her rounded ass, and he shoved her against his erection, grinding against her soft body. He felt her reach for it, and again, grabbed her wrist, pinning her arm between them. He kissed her harder, until she bit him back. Deep in his throat, a groan slipped out. His need for her was more than he could control. Lifting her onto his lap, only their clothes prevented them from being one.

Her weight settled against his hips, and he slipped his hands beneath her open shirt, sliding up her body slowly, feeling her back arch as she accepted his touch. The feel of her new scar was tantalizing, but it made him pause. Watching her from his dark, human eyes, her exotic features called to him, so different from his own. He tried to stop, but she needed him – and he couldn't resist what she begged for. Holding her ribs, refusing to allow his hands higher, he was helpless against the demon writhing against his lap, the leather of his pants achingly soft against him. Zep closed his eyes and tried to resist, his breath coming fast, his blood throbbing beneath her.

Cold ceramic on his neck made his eyes jerk open, at odds with the sultry warmth of the woman seducing him so completely.

"Enough," a rough voice snarled in his ear.

The sharp edge just sliced the top layer of skin across his jugular. Sweat stung as it trickled down his neck. Zep nodded, all too aware of the real threat he faced.

"Cyno, let me up, and she's yours. You know I had to keep her off Risk. You *know* that, little brother."

The blade vanished, and Zep pushed Sal away even as she tried to cling to him in her animalistic desire. Cyno stepped behind her, wrapping his arms across her chest, holding her to him. His cold blue eyes never left Zep's face. His look screamed his claim on her as he kissed her neck too gently.

"She's mine," Cyno snarled possessively.

"I know, brother," Zep said, moving slowly to his feet. "You call her kitten. I know, man."

"I can na stop it." Cyno closed his eyes when Sal began to nip at his throat. He sounded apologetic. "I'm meant fer her. I need her."

"I know," Zep said again as he backed away from the couple. "I couldn't take her from you if I tried. She's yours, Jassant." He sighed and grabbed his shirt from the floor, whispering to himself, "Even if the rest of them haven't figured it out yet."

Outside the tent, he came face to face with the Lieutenant. LT glanced at him once, his eyes dropping to the wound across Zep's chest.

"You too?" he asked.

"It's not like that, LT," Zep answered. "Just had to stall her long enough to get Risk out."

LT nodded, glancing back to the tent. Carnal screams and moans passed through the canvas. "I don't know how I can match that, you know?"

"You can't if you keep shoving her away." Zep raised his eyebrow pointedly.

"I can't control her," LT said. "If she doesn't get control of herself..." he let the thought trail off.

"You're full of shit. I'm a damned human, and I know better than that. You're pissed because she's as good as you. You're scared because you want it." Zep's jaw was set, and he shook his head, trying to will his anger away.

"She'll go feral!"

Zep laughed ironically. "She's fucking feral right now!" He pointed at his chest. "She's as far in the lust as I've ever seen. She bit me, LT. Once. She bit me one fucking time, and stopped as soon as she realized it hurt."

"I can't control her," he said again.

"Then stop trying."

LT growled softly and leaned into Zep, their faces inches apart. "My berserkers just lost it in the middle of the fucking CFC army. The secret's out, Zep. Command will pull us apart for this mess. Cyno just lost his shit, and Sal? She's like something the rest of you can't get enough of."

"Or you."

"*Or* me! I can't let the Black Blades fall apart because of one damned girl!"

Zep huffed ironically. "You think we're falling apart? Are you fucking serious, LT? We haven't been this tight since Circus died." He leaned further down, his eyes meeting the Lieutenant's. "I'm a fucking *human*, and I know what's going on. She's a Kaisae – the real kind – and you're scared she'll figure out what that means. Let me tell ya something, man. Get over it real fucking quick."

"Zep," LT warned.

"We've been friends a long-ass time, sir. In those years, we've been through a hell of a lot together, so trust me when I tell you this. That little bitch is the best damned thing that ever happened to this unit." He held LT's eyes a second longer, then leaned back and patted his commander on the shoulder. "Figure it out, Blaec, but stop blaming her for being better than us."

"I can't take the risk," LT said, turning away.

"Of what?!" Zep demanded of his retreating officer.

"Of Parliament disbanding us," Blaec said, not looking back. "It would destroy everything."

CHAPTER FORTY-TWO

Seven days later, Sal was officially recovered. In just that short time, her life had turned upside down. She sighed, thinking about it. She'd been attacked, healed, had mauled her best friend, and been basically ostracized from the only family she'd ever known.

Then, General Albin had ordered the Blades to return to Stonewater Stables. The trip took only nine days, but those were nine days of isolation for Sal. Last winter, she'd been used to being alone, but now? It was amazing how quickly the companionship of friends became something a person needed. She threw her packs onto her own bed in the cabin she'd been assigned so long ago. Her cabin. Her room. Her punishment.

Memories taunted her in each corner. Shift had rummaged in her wardrobe over there. Zep had laid across her bed, here. Blaec had kissed her against that wall. Her rooms. They'd become their own kind of torture, all because she was iliri.

"Kitten?" a rough voice asked softly from the door.

"Leave me alone, Jase," Sal warned. "You know Blaec will take it out on you if you don't."

"It does na work like tha', Sal."

She turned to him, seeing concern on his face. "Then how does it work, Cyno?"

He shook his head. "Ya know nothing of what's happenin'. I know that, so I can na blame ya. We fucked up though, kitten. Ya and I. We both did, ok?"

She breathed out an ironic laugh and shook her head. "And what did *you* do, Jase?"

"I threatened ta kill the man that jacked ya." He smiled cruelly. "Kinda in front of the entire army."

"Thanks," she said, meaning it. "I didn't know that, Jase. That's really sweet."

He glanced down at his feet and grinned. "Ayati, Sal. Only ya would think that's sweet."

She shrugged. "It is, though. You're the best partner I could have asked for, you know that?"

He nodded. "Yer pretty good, yerself. I'll keep ya." He added, almost too soft for her to hear, "If ya'd let me."

"I bit Zep." She was changing the subject but felt it had to be said.

"Yeh."

"I remember it, Jase. I bit him, and it hurt."

"He told me."

She let her anguish show in her voice. "I don't know if I can control it anymore. I'm a fucking beast now! I bit one of the few friends I've ever had!"

He smiled at her wryly. "He un'erstands, Sal. Maast, he gets it more than LT does."

"I went feral on him, though!"

"It happens." He pushed himself away from the door and moved to her, grabbing her shoulders. "Sal, it's our nature, ok? Zep gets it. Stop avoiding him, and ya'll see that."

She shook her head, eyes wide, ears pulled close. "I don't know if I can." Sucking in a deep breath, she pulled away, his touch too familiar. "I used to be civilized, Jase. I could laugh back then. I don't know what happened, but I lost it somewhere. I just need more discipline and I can get it back. I'm sure of it."

He nodded, understanding. "Do na let them break ya, ok? I knew ya wanted ta be alone, but that does na mean I have na been watchin'. I'll keep outta yer way, but only cause ya want it, na cause of anythan else."

"I don't want to be alone, Jase. I want Blaec back."

Her words hit him hard and he looked away. "I know, kitten. He'll come around."

She sucked in a quick breath. Jase reached up and pushed her alabaster hair beneath her delicate ear, then cupped her jaw and made her look up at him. His eyes held hers, and he stepped closer.

"Arctic an' I are being deployed. There's a line on the Anglian bribe, and we need ta get intel. I'm gonna be gone fer a few."

She nodded sadly. "Be safe, ok?"

"Yeh. I'd rather have ya at my back, but I'll be safe. Promise me somethan?"

"Anything."

"Promise me ya'll stop backin' down because ya think ya should." His thumb caressed her pale cheek, and his blue eyes looked at her, filled with nothing but concern. "Ya can na help but challenge him. We all know it, an' it's the way of things, ok? So stop backing down. Either win or lose, but stop sittin' on the fence. Is na anything wrong with losing, ok?"

"That's not what I'm worried about, and you know it."

A smile crept to his lips, and Sal glanced at the sharp points of his teeth, so like her own. "I know. Is na a thing wrong with winnin' either, kitten. He'll still be the Lieutenant, and we'll work it out. That's how it is in a pack, ok? Ya will na break us, but ya need ta fig're this out. Promise?"

She leaned into his hand and closed her eyes, thinking over his words. "I can't do it without you, Jase."

"I will na leave ya, Sal. I can na. It's only a few days and Zep'll be here. Wait if ya wanna, but promise me ya'll stop avoiding it."

"I swear."

He nodded, accepting that. "Sal?" he asked, suddenly shy.

She waited for him to continue, but he glanced away instead, releasing her. "What, Jase?"

"Can..." His eyes flicked up. "I know yer na in the lust, and all, but..." He paused again, his eyes looking around her room for the words he wanted. "Can I kiss ya b'fore I go? Just once without havin' ta kill somethan first?"

"You're leaving now?"

He nodded.

Her heart stopped. *Now?* He was leaving now, not tomorrow, not in a couple of days, but now. Without Jase, she would be alone! Sal gasped and wrapped her arms around him, burying her face in his neck. He held her close and pressed his cheek against the top of her head.

"Come back safe, killer," she said, pulling back enough to look at his face. Then, she reached up and traced the sharp line of his jaw. "Kiss me, and come back."

He bent his head and touched his lips to hers gently. She pressed into him, begging for more, and he gave it. His teeth dragged along her lip and their tongues caressed, a low moan in the back of his throat. Sal clung to his shoulders, wanting to never let him go. With one last brush of his mouth against hers, he pulled back.

"LT's a fucking idiot," he said softly, caressing her cheek. With a sad smile, he stepped back. "Now be good while I'm gone, ok?"

"I'll try," Sal promised, smiling back.

Jase gave her one last glance and walked from her room. Across the street, Zep leaned against the wall of his cabin, looking at her through the open door.

CHAPTER FORTY-THREE

*B*e good. That was what Jase told her. Be more human. That was what Blaec expected of her. She was trying, Sal thought as she made her way through the mess hall. She watched the man next to her and tried to mimic his choices. Vegetables, well-cooked fish, and tubers went onto her plate. The smell of it turned her stomach, but she took it. It was what they ate, and if she wanted to be more human, she needed to do things that humans did.

She found a place in the corner, away from the traffic from the doors, and sat. Maybe her stomach would learn to deal with it if she kept eating this stuff long enough. Her fork speared something green, and she shoved it in her mouth. Chewing and chewing, her sharp teeth lacerated the vegetables into shreds but did little to make it swallowable. She forced it down with the juice of some fruit and tried something else.

Again, Sal needed the glass, closing her eyes while she made herself drink. Pulling in a long, deep breath, she willed her stomach to be silent while she looked across her plate. Ravenous, she chose the fish. That at least worked in her mouth. She chased the last bite with the juice and shoved the plate away. Leaning against the wall behind her, she controlled her stomach with nothing more than willpower.

"Glad I finally caught you." Zep dropped his plate onto the table and sat beside her.

The aroma of rare meat, cheese, and bread wafted up to her. Sal glanced away.

"Look," he said, mistaking her reaction, "I don't really care if you want to see me or not. You've been avoiding me since you got jacked."

"Zep?" said softly, "I – " She paused, overly aware that she hadn't spoken to him since her healing. "I didn't think you'd want to be near me. I mean, since you can't trust me and all."

"Why can't I trust you?" He slid a tall glass of milk toward her. "And drink that. I know you can't manage juices."

She pushed the glass away. "I went feral on you. I'm so sorry, Zep. I really am!"

He pushed it back. "I was serious when I told you to drink that." His deep brown eyes stared at her, his jaw set. "Drink that, and we'll talk."

She nodded and took a long drink then set the glass back on the table. He bit into his bread and gestured with it for her to finish. She did, her stomach quieting for the moment. "Happy?"

"Ok. Now, first things first. I accept your apology. You don't need to give it, and there's nothing to apologize for, but I know it matters to you, so I accept it. I'll even forgive you if you want, but hear me out first, ok?"

She nodded, confused.

"I owed ya one, from the cave. I think you forgot that little bit. You have no idea what it's like to undergo what Risk does, not as a human. There's a reason he told you to hold me, and it's because we've done that before. Second, I don't know anyone that can take a poisoned knife to the lungs and not lose it. When Cyno had to shove my guts back in me, I lost it. What you did pales in comparison, ok? When LT got that scar on his hip? Yeah, that's how Risk got the scar on his shoulder. When I carried you back, I knew you'd go berserk. I knew what I was doing, Sal. I didn't care. I just wanted to make sure my friend lived, ok?"

"Ok," she said weakly, staring at the table.

"One last thing we need to get clear between us." Zep reached out and tilted her chin up until she looked at him. "You stopped."

Sal waited for him to say more, but nothing followed. Zep merely smiled and watched her.

"But I hurt you."

"Yeah, kinda. Thing is, as deep in as you were, you still knew it, and you stopped. Cyno can't do that." He smiled and grabbed her hand. "I trust you, Sal. Yeah, you bit me, and yeah, it left one hell of a scar, but – "

A man passed by with a plate of something. The smell hit Sal. Her stomach rolled, and she climbed to her feet, halting Zep in the middle of his sentence. She looked at him before rushing from the mess tent, trying to maintain her composure.

"Sal!" Zep called after her.

"Piss off your scrubber?" a man at the next table sneered.

Zep said nothing, just grabbed the back of his head and shoved it hard into the table as he passed. There was a distinctive snap, most likely the man's nose breaking, but Zep didn't stop.

Outside the mess hall, Sal hopped a fence and darted into the pastures. The smell of horses was comforting, but her stomach refused to settle. She hurried out of sight and dropped to her knees, spilling her guts into the grass. Again and again, she heaved. Footsteps crunched behind her, but she could do nothing about it, her body focused on purging itself of the meals from the last few days.

A large hand grabbed her hair and pulled it away from her face. "Oh, demon, what are you doing to yourself?" Zep whispered, kneeling beside her.

Sal tried to wipe her chin before heaving yet again, until she had nothing left. When she could finally sit up, she felt too weak to do it. Zep helped her lean back.

"You good for a bit, kid?"

"Yeah."

"Can you stand?"

Sal thought about it, and her head tried to spin. "Not yet."

"Well, if you want to be human, I'll treat you like one." He lifted her into his arms. "Put your head on my shoulder, babe, and just close your eyes, ok? Let's get you in a bed."

He took the long way around, avoiding the traffic areas of the stables, and crossed through the pastures so no eyes would witness her weakness. She knew it would matter to her later, but right now, she just wanted to close her eyes. He carried her into her cabin and gently laid her on the bed, then poured a tall glass of water and set it on the table before easing himself into the chair beside her.

"I'm not leaving until you're good enough to eat something, and I don't mean any green shit, ok?"

"Ok," she agreed. "Thanks, Zep. I owe you one."

"Shit." He sighed. "Sal, we need to talk. There's shit you need to know."

"Ok." Her mind felt numb. "I'm not going anywhere soon."

"Look." Zep cleared his throat. "I owe you a bit of an apology."

"I thought I owed you one."

"Well, ya already tried that. Look. I know how it takes you mutts sometimes," he said. "Yeah, you're not a mutt, whatever. But there's something about all of you that sets me on edge, ya know?"

"No," Sal said, gently, smelling his embarrassment. "I don't."

"Yeah. You're right. Look." He took a deep breath. "Some of this shit I haven't talked to anyone about before, ya get me?" She nodded. "It never really came up until you got here. I mean, we were just a bunch of hormone-ridden men, trying to one-up each other all the time. Now, well, there's a new sensitivity or something going around."

"Zep, I'm sorry. I didn't mean to screw up a good thing."

"Nah, ya didn't screw it up. It just changed. It does each time we get a new one, which is why we're so picky about it." She nodded, listening, so Zep went on. "Ya got LT back to us. I mean, he was like the old LT – before that whole shit in the caverns. I owe ya one for that if nothing else. I've been serving with him for almost twelve years now, even before the Black Blades was the Black Blades, ya know?"

"And Cyno's always been a strange one," he continued. "He's damned good, don't get me wrong, but he needed to be handled a bit gentler than the others. He's kinda like a feral dog. Ya never quite knew if he'd turn on ya or not. But, for the most part, you being around has him straightened out, too."

She watched him talk, his face looking back in time, and quietly followed what he was saying, storing the bits of information he handed out so casually.

Zep smiled weakly. "Well, my point is, it seems like everyone in the Blades is a damned iliri mongrel. All of ya have something I can't quite touch, but it's like I almost can. Ya know?"

"Because you're human?"

"Yeah. I was basically raised by an iliri servant, and I've never much liked how you all get treated. That's why I stayed on when I saw what LT was building. Arctic managed to get me in the link. It took some time, but he did it, and I've been with 'em since. I've been a Blade for nine years, Sal. I've seen a lot of blood and lost a lot of friends in that time."

"Yeah," she whispered, understanding.

"The other day was the first time I've ever worried that I'd die. Cyno would have killed me if I hadn't pulled my hands off of you. And you pulled me in so deep, I didn't even care, hun."

"Zep. I'm so sorry -"

"It's not you I'm gettin' at, Sal. Well, yes and no. It's not your fault, though. Look. When it hit you, I tried to resist. I've never had a problem before. Usually a nice hack and slash, a few cracked skulls and all that; it just gets me ready to go. I find a whore, I bury myself in her, and I pay her when I'm done. That's all there is to it, no different than most of the men in this army." He gestured to the rooms around them. "That's why I had those memories ready for ya, 'member? Back for your first assassination."

"What's the tattoo, Zep?" She suddenly felt like it mattered.

"I'm getting there. So, back when Cyno was new to us, I stumbled upon him right after he did a job. Don't know if he ever told ya about that."

"We haven't really talked about it."

"Well, he was like a damned wild animal. I was scared shitless of him. I knew what he needed – you could see it all over his face, and from the damned tent in his pants – but shit. I hired him a whore, the kind that takes it rough, and kept the Blades from disturbing him the entire night. The next morning, the poor girl looked like she'd been mauled by a fucking wolf, so I tipped her extra for the time it'd take her to heal up, ya know?"

She nodded again.

"So, yeah. I knew it hit you all something fierce, but I really had no idea. I saw the miraculous things your kind can do: the speed, the power, the mental stuff. Risk heals with just the force of his will. I mean, that's pretty damned impressive. I was so jealous. I wanted to be iliri so much, to fit in. I guess so I wouldn't let LT down. That's when I got the tattoo."

He looked at her, blushing slightly. "It's supposed to be an iliri spell. I know there's no such shit and all, but it's written in your language, and basically says something like 'I'd give my life to be iliri.' I got it after I sent Cyno that whore."

Sal reached over and put her hand on his forearm, still listening.

"So yeah. I had no idea what being iliri really meant, not till I saw you after you got jacked. We thought you were going to die for a bit there, Sal. That bastard poisoned the blade he got you with. It took Risk a lot of work, and by the time you were good again, he barely had the strength to walk out of the room. That dumb-ass General had Cyno held up in his office, taking his sweet time, thinking nothing of one of our mates bleeding out. So yeah. It was me or Risk, and I figured, being human and all, I'd be able to hold you off, right? Especially since Risk doesn't really go for women, ya know?"

"I actually didn't know," she said, calmly. "But it didn't go so well for you."

"Shit, Sal, you have no idea. I felt it. I mean," he pulled his shirt back, showing her the scar on his chest, and Sal cringed at the memories. "You bit the shit outta me, and I liked it." He shook his head. "That's not quite right. More like I needed more of it. Don't get me wrong, you're one hell of a woman, and I could kiss your lips all night, but I don't usually go for the hard shit, ya know? But when you kissed me, I felt like I couldn't stop. It took everything I had, every ounce of will, to keep from just ripping your clothes off and having my way with you. Is that what it's like for you?"

"Yeah," she said. "That's pretty close. Your skin's on fire, your blood is pumping, and you need something. Only another's touch will do, but it always feels too soft, like you need more, harder."

"Yeah. And it's..." He looked over to the window. "It's exhilarating. It's amazing."

"It also is really inconvenient, Zep."

"Oh, I can see that, too." He laughed awkwardly. "But Sal, what I'm saying is that you're different. I think it's because you're pure. When I'm with you, I'm in the link. Not reaching for the link, but in it, easily. When that bloodlust shit took hold of you, you passed it to me. For a split second, I even thought about fighting Cyno for you like a damned bunch of dogs."

"That's how Jase explains it, too. Like a dog sniffing at a bitch in heat."

"Pretty much," he agreed. "What I wanted to say, though, and took a real long way around, is that I'm sorry. I've been jealous of you. You just settled right in and fell into the routine, and things have been changing around you. I wasn't sure I liked it so much.

You're a good girl, Sal. I like having you with us, but I don't want to sleep with you. Not really. But don't tell the guys that, ok?"

"Fair enough." She had to look away, struggling not to accidentally laugh at him because now was not the time. Not with what she needed to tell him. "Zep, I tried so hard not to bite you, but I couldn't stop. I'm so sorry. You taste like... like my blade – sweet, and kinda crisp."

"Probably because I'm about as human as the Blades will ever see." He shrugged and waved that away. "Thing is, Sal, I'm jealous. Before you came, I wished I was anything but human. But, I had no idea what I was wishing for. When you stayed linked with me, back in the cave, I got a taste of it. When you got jacked..." He sighed. "Sal, I didn't want to like it. I didn't, but I did. I can't stop thinking about it now. You made me iliri for just a little bit." He leaned back and rubbed at his eye, trying to make it look casual.

"I'm sorry, Zep." She squeezed his arm.

"You don't get it." He pressed his hand over hers. "You give me what I've always wanted. That's not something to be sorry for. I don't get what LT's on about with the whole too-iliri thing, and I don't think you should listen to him. If he's too fucking stupid to figure it out on his own, it's not like you can't find someone better."

"I can't. That's what you don't seem to understand."

"You can, Sal. Cyno, Arctic, Razor, hell, even Shift, but he'd never admit it. Why are you torturing yourself to make LT happy?"

She thought for a long time, trying to put her feelings into words. "Jase knows," was all she said.

"Yeah, that may be, but he sure won't say shit. You don't have to tell me, kid, but you need to figure it out for yourself, ok?"

Sal nodded and closed her eyes, leaning back into the bed. A small gasp slipped past her lips.

"Ah, Sal, don't cry on me." Zep moved to her side, pulling her to him.

"Don't worry." She buried her head against his shoulder. "I can't."

"Can't?"

"Can't." She lifted her eyes to his. "Doesn't make it easier, but I can't."

"Sal?" His voice was gentle. "How can you make yourself human if you can't cry?"

"I don't know, Zep. I keep trying, but it's not working. I thought that maybe if I changed my diet, it'd take away some of the aggression. I mean, not all women cry, right?"

Zep ignored that and pushed at the real question. "Why is Blaec that special?"

She pushed her head further into his chest. "He's my first, Zep. The first man who ever cared about me."

"Ah fuck." He looked up at the ceiling. "I didn't know you were a damned virgin. Ah, Sal, babe. I'm gonna fuckin' beat his ass."

"No," she cut him off. "I was a slave, Zep. I wasn't a virgin."

He pulled her closer. "I'm not sure that makes it better."

She shrugged. "No one knows that, ok?"

"Cept Cyno."

"Yeah. Cept Jase," she agreed.

"Ok, kid. Then if this is what you want, I'll help you make it happen," he conceded. "I'll stop trying to talk you out of it, and I'll help ya. I mean, I'm pretty sure I know what it's like to be a human."

She looked up at him, confused. "Why? Two minutes ago, you were telling me I could do better."

"I didn't say I was wrong. Look, you're a good friend, Sal. You and Cyno, you're the closest I have." He shrugged. "I'd rather see ya with Cyno, just cuz of that, but you're my friend, and if this is what you want, then this is what you're going to get, ok?"

"I don't understand you, Zep. I bit you, and you thank me. And now this? I can't keep up."

"You're kinda like the little sister I never had. Any time you need anything, I'm here, little one. I promise I'll keep my clothes on this time."

"Don't make a promise you can't keep," she warned him. "Blaec already taught me that."

"Ok, well, let's just say that I'll try to keep my clothes on, unless that happens again."

She glanced over to see if he was joking and realized he wasn't.

"If Cyno isn't around and you need someone, I'm here. I'll probably hate myself in the morning, but I think I can take it. Hell," he chuckled, "I'll probably even like it. But I don't want it. I just know it happens. I've seen what you two go through when there's no release."

Sal looked at him for a long moment, then did something so human it surprised even her. She hugged him, like a sister would her brother. "Thank you, Zep. It doesn't make any sense, but that means so much to me. I'm still getting used to all of this."

"I know."

"I try to put on a brave face for it all, but half the time I don't know what my own body is doing. All of you are the closest thing I have to family. You're the only people I can even call real friends. I don't want to fuck this up, Zep. I feel like I'm stepping in it really good and I'm scared to death it's going to bite me in the ass. I just don't want to screw up a good thing."

"I got yer back, kid. I'm here anytime you need me. I swear."

CHAPTER FORTY-FOUR

Zep stayed with her, making sure she ate something her body would tolerate and talking to her until her eyes were too heavy to stay open. She woke in the middle of the night and found him watching her while the moonlight streamed through the small window. He smiled and whispered her back to sleep.

When the sun rose, Sal was alone. She went through her usual morning routine, then decided to go for a ride to help clear her head. She needed something to take her mind off the heavy feeling of loneliness that kept trying to consume her. When she passed by cabin thirteen, she paused, but Jase's rooms were still silent. She missed him more than she'd expected – and she'd expected to miss him a lot. He was the only one who always seemed to understand her. Zep tried, but it wasn't quite the same. Realizing that only made her mood more bleak, so she lifted her chin and turned her feet to the barn.

Arden nickered when Sal stepped onto the packed alley. She grabbed a handful of hay and offered it to the mare, scratching her long neck over the stall door. It wasn't much, but Arden didn't ask for a lot in return for her affection.

None of the staff was around, but Sal had been in the field long enough that she felt uncomfortable asking someone else to tack up her horse. She'd learned her way around the barn during training, so grabbed a halter from the rack and a box of brushes from the shelf. Setting those beside the cross ties, she went to grab her saddle and bridle. Pulling open the door to the tack room, she paused. Risk and Tilso looked up guiltily, jerking their hands back to their sides. Suddenly, all the hints the guys had been dropping fell into place. She wasn't his type, but it appeared the Stablemaster, Tilso, was.

"Sal," Risk said, standing.

She smiled at him. "I just need my tack, guys."

"It's not what you think," Risk said, while Tilso tried to look anywhere but at her.

"What it looks like is a couple of guys trying to get off their feet and away from the craziness of the barns." She shrugged. "If that's not what it is, then you shouldn't be hiding it from people who don't care."

"Wise words," Risk pointed out, meeting her eyes. "I wish you'd learn to follow them."

"Fair enough," Sal agreed, knowing he was right.

"You're not going to say anything, are you, Miss Luxx?" Tilso asked.

"No, Mr. Tilso. I'm not going to say anything. Not if you don't want me to. Why would I go out of my way to mention the barn manager talking to one of the Black Blades in the tack room?" She stepped closer and patted the young man's arm. "Our tack did take quite a beating recently. Isn't any of my business if you're just checking stirrup leathers and girths, right? And I do wish you'd call me Sal."

"Right," he agreed. "Sal."

"Risk." She turned to the pale man. "Why the secret?"

"It's me," Tilso said. "My sister's the assistant manager now, and we moved Ma up into the loft with us. She keeps hoping that one day I'll carry on the family name."

"And you haven't told her you have no interest in women," Sal realized. "I get it. Your sister knows?"

The young man's eyes hit the ground. "Nah. It isn't tolerated well in our kind."

"Well, it's none of my business either way, but," she looked at Risk pointedly, "he is the barn manager for the Black Blades. I'm pretty sure no one would find it strange if he spent more time with us. Pretty sure your cabin has a door that locks, too."

"You don't think that would get out?" Risk asked.

"Not outside the Blades," Sal assured him. "Kinda like Blaec and me."

"Thanks, Sal. You have a point," Risk said. "The guys going to be upset?"

She looked at him, confused. "By what?"

Risk gestured at Tilso. "Me bringing home a man."

She still didn't really understand, but tried her best to answer. "No. They already know. They'll be happy for you. Just be nice to the kid, ok?"

Tilso blushed and busied himself with finding Sal's saddle. "He's pretty nice to me," he mumbled.

She pointed over his shoulder. "I need a pad too, if you could? And if this lasts more than a week, tell your family? Ok?"

"Why?" Tilso asked.

"Because if you wait longer, it'll only get easier to put it off," she explained. "It's your life, Ahn. You can't be someone you're not. You can't hide it forever and live a lie."

"Yeah," Tilso said. "You're right."

"And we got your back," she assured him. "Or a round at the pub and about eight shoulders to lean on. Deal?"

"Deal. Thanks, Sal," Tilso said, passing the tack to her.

Risk grabbed her arm, stopping her before she could retreat

from their intimate moment. "Sal? Say that again - and listen to it this time."

She thought back over her words - live a lie - and sighed. Wasn't that what she'd been doing when she tried to make herself human? Wasn't it just as pointless?

So she nodded, realizing she'd just given in. "I know, Risk. It's just not going to be easy to give him up."

"Easier than what you've been doing," he countered.

"Maybe," she admitted, "but Arden needs to stretch her legs, and I need room to think about it."

He nodded. "I understand. I owe you one, ok? And the offer holds for you too: a round and a shoulder."

Sal thanked him and returned to her mare. She brushed Arden thoroughly, losing herself in the simple task of caring for her own horse, then tacked her up. That simple sentence echoed in her head. She couldn't be someone she wasn't. She didn't really know who she was, but it was true. She couldn't make herself a human.

Leading her horse on a loose rein, Sal made her way through the barn. When she stepped into the daylight, she collided with Zep's broad chest.

"I know you're distracted when you run into something as big and black as me," he teased, gesturing to his fatigues.

"I am," she admitted. "I just kinda got smacked upside the head by my own words. What are you doing here?"

He glanced around quickly, looking for something. With a sigh, he gave up. "Don't kill me? I came to make sure you were ok."

She smiled at him and shook her head. "No death and mayhem today, big brother. I just need to stop wallowing in self-pity so I planned to take Arden out. Wanna join me?"

"I'd love to," he said, "but I can't." He glanced up to the arena balcony.

Sal's eyes followed his, and she saw Blaec leaning over the rail. Their eyes met for a moment, then Sal glanced away, quickly.

Everything she loved about him was still there, calling to her from his eyes.

"I'm pretty sure you're not getting a lesson," she said.

"Nah. Just need to have a chat with an old friend. You good with that?"

Sal reached up and grabbed Zep's hand, holding it for just a moment. "Yeah. Thanks, Zep. You're a good man, you know that?"

He kissed her forehead gently. "That's our secret then, ok? I can't risk my reputation. Go ride."

CHAPTER FORTY-FIVE

He'd been sleeping alone for over three weeks now, Blaec realized as he leaned over the railing, watching the barns below. Sal's white hair stood out against Zep's black uniform. He should go back to work. He was expected to report to Command in the morning, and his report wasn't close to finished, but he couldn't bring himself to look away from her. It had been weeks, and she still hadn't come back.

When he'd ended things between them, he expected her to simply move on. Cyno was always right there and willing. She hadn't slept with him since, either. Blaec sighed, resting his chin on his hands. She'd changed. She was no longer the bright, vibrant thing he remembered. She sulked through rooms now rather than stormed through them.

He moved back inside to the viewing room but found himself pouring a drink instead. He sipped at the liquor and walked to the balcony again. She was still there.

When the Blades had returned, they'd been met like a conquering army, but he wasn't the only one that couldn't feel the excitement. His men had become serious. They trained more and drank less. He rarely saw them in the pub. They just waited for something to happen.

He watched Sal across the distance. She leaned against Zep, and he knew they were talking, even if he couldn't quite hear it. He hadn't expected her to choose him. Of all the men, she spent her time with the human. He felt a spark of anger at that and smothered it with a long drink. When he looked back, he saw Zep staring at him. Their eyes met across the distance.

Thought you had a report due, Zep's voice whispered.

I did, too.

Below him, he watched his oldest friend look down at Sal. She glanced up to the balcony he was on but turned her eyes away from his quickly. Then she left, trailing her horse behind her. When she was gone, Zep looked back up.

We need to talk.

Blaec nodded, gesturing for Zep to come up, and turned inside once more. While Zep climbed the stairs, Blaec told himself that it wasn't his place to care who Sal spent her time with. This was better for her. It was better for all of them.

The door barely closed behind him before Zep spoke up. "I don't know what is going on with you two -"

"It's none of your business, Zep," Blaec said.

"Sorry, LT, but it is. I'm not gonna just sit here and watch you tear down their morale while you wallow in your self-pity. Either get over her or get her back, but stop dragging us all through the shit with you."

Blaec nodded, watching Zep's eyes. "I see you've taken up with her."

"Yeah, as a friend. I'm not sleeping with her if that's what you're asking."

"It's not my business anymore," Blaec reminded him.

"Like hell, it isn't. C'mon, man, what the fuck is going on? You can't be that mad about Arctic kissing her."

"She told you that?"

"No. She told me you want her to be human. *You* screamed that in front of the entire unit."

Blaec found a chair and let his body drop into it. With a wave of his hand, he gestured to the bottles on the shelf beside him. "Might as well grab one."

"Thanks, man," Zep said, doing just that. With a full glass and the open bottle, he sank into the chair across from his commander. "So what's going on?" he asked.

"I've been commanded to arrange an assassination. I'm to give the orders as soon as the Anglian bribe is secured," Blaec said, without a trace of emotion.

"What does this have to do with you and Sal?" Zep asked.

"In Anglia," he replied.

"Oh."

"It's three months there, by horse. The mission isn't a simple slasher either. Zep," he paused. "It's a political assassination and replacement. We're to eliminate the king and replace him with a Conglomerate sympathizer."

"Ok, so that's three months there, three months back, and probably another month for the job. I can only assume you're sending Sal," Zep said, immediately understanding his line of thought.

"I'm sending both of them. And it's more than that. I need them to protect the new king. I'm going to need them to gain his confidence. I need them to convince him to ally with us against Terric and if he will, then offer him military advice."

Zep tilted his glass up and drained it, refilling it before he continued, "Fuck, that's damned near an impossible mission. No wonder they wanted a Blade to do it. So, this is a long embed then. What, a year? More?"

"As long as it takes."

"And that's what this is about?" Zep brought the conversation back full circle.

"Yeah. No." Blaec shook his head, "I don't know, man. She

makes me crazy sometimes. When I'm around her, I stop thinking like a human. I feel her tugging at something inside me, and I don't know how to control it. I watch her with Cyno. They're so at ease, and I want that -"

"Then stop pushing her away."

"I can't," Blaec admitted. "I can't let her in like he does. Not with everything that's running around in here." He tapped his head, then sighed. "I told myself that if she came back, I'd make it work. If she doesn't, then this is what's best for her with what's coming."

"She won't crawl back this time," Zep warned. "You told her she was too iliri for you. She keeps asking me how to be human."

"Yeah. I don't know how to make up for that."

"I don't think you understand. Blaec, she's torturing herself trying to be what you want. She won't come to you because you made it clear you don't want her. She won't go to Cyno because she wants to be human." Zep shook his head. "Blaec, she can't cry, did you know that?"

Blaec looked up at him.

"Iliri eyes. They won't weep." Zep watched his commander, waiting for that to sink in. "She's not human. She chooses her meals by what a human eats, then spends the next hour vomiting because it isn't meat. She won't smile because it'll show her teeth. She barely meets anyone's eyes at all. She's trying, but she's destined to fail."

"Damn it," Blaec swore.

"Blaec?" Zep asked, waiting until he had his full attention before continuing. "What happened? What started this? You trying to bend the future again?"

Blaec felt his jaw clench, holding back the rant he wanted to let out. Instead, he gave the simple answer. "She challenged my orders."

"Ya think?" Zep laughed ironically. "Her idea was better - and it worked."

Blaec replied with the only thing he could. "You asked."

"So, why is it still going on?" Zep pressed. "Why haven't you just apologized to her? Is this another one of those iliri things I'm missing?"

Blaec huffed, proving he wasn't amused. "I'm only a half breed. Stop acting like I'm so different from you."

Zep chuckled and leaned forward, resting his arms on his knees. "Trust me, man. You're nothing like me. None of you are. Even Shift has it."

"Has what? Iliri breeding? We don't exactly hide it from each other."

"Nah, not that. I mean what comes with that. Damn, man. You should know by now." Zep sighed and leaned back again. "Why do you think we're so damned good? It's cuz we're iliri. Sal says I'm a freak of nature, which I take as a pretty high compliment from her. We move faster. We kill better. You all have these amazing things you can just *do*, and that's good and all, but that's not what it is. That's not what it is to be iliri."

"Ok, Zep. I'll bite. What is it?"

"We're a fuckin' pack, man," Zep told him. "Trust me, the other units don't have a bond like this. Hell, not even the elites. We spend all day crawling around in each other's heads, and it's like we're part of the same being half the time. Haven't you wondered why I refused to be reassigned so long ago? This shit's like an addiction. I can't get it as a human, not without your help. I just keep hoping I die in the field one day, so I don't ever have to retire. I don't think I could live without it. So stop being so damned ashamed of who you are and be like Sal. Embrace it. Use it. Put on a polite face in public, but with us..." Zep smiled. "We're a pack. We need an iliri leader."

"I thought that's what I'd been doing."

"Nah. You're playing politics," Zep said. "Fuck that shit, man. We're predators. Be fuckin' iliri already."

"I can't. I'm not like that," Blaec insisted.

"Well, you sure as hell aren't human," Zep told him. "Trust me. You don't wanna be, either. It ain't all it's cracked up to be."

Silence hung between them. Blaec looked at Zep, refusing the urge to stare into his eyes, even when Zep gazed into his, holding him. Finally, Blaec sighed. He leaned forward and poured himself another drink, downing half of it before refilling it.

"You felt it, right?" Blaec asked. "In the link, when Sal..."

"Which part?" Zep asked. "When she embraced the fact that your iliri natures gave you the advantage? When she took our fear with her bloodlust? When she located their position by nothing more than sound? When she risked her own neck to draw the Widows into a trap that left the rest of the unit safe? Or was it when Sal drew out the primal nature within us, even you?"

Blaec's lip twitched. "You forgot the part where she was making out with Arctic."

Zep laughed. "Yeah, and the part where she took the pain of my healing so I wouldn't have to suffer. Human, right?"

Blaec's head snapped up. "She did what?"

"Yeah, I didn't really want to say anything, but she did it and never thought twice about it."

"Fuck," Blaec whispered.

"Thanks, but you're not really my type, man."

Blaec laughed at that, the timing perfect to relieve a little of the tension in the room. "Not quite what I meant, and you know it." Then he sighed. "I was pissed because she was all over Arctic. Shit. I was annoyed with it at first, but then when she challenged me? I kept thinking - " he stopped.

"Might as well spill it now. You got this far."

"I kept thinking she'd replace me. I've already gotten in too deep with her to just go back, and she was just replacing me like none of it mattered. If she chooses Arctic, then it's still too late for me, and all of this will be wasted."

Zep pushed his hand across his mouth, then nodded to himself. "You're an idiot. You know that, right?"

Blaec let his head drop to his chest. "It's not just that. Ever since that day, you know, when Llyr was given command?"

"I remember it," Zep agreed.

"He said I needed to keep control of my iliri or we'd be disbanded. I don't know... I mean, everything depends on us staying together. It got me thinking, and it's like I notice how feral she really is now. If she snaps, then what? I can feel her begging me to bite her, or how she challenges me when she's intense about something. She's..."

"Amazing?" Zep supplied. "And I think a lot of that is you, not her. Trust me, man, being around her when she's in the lust? It's pretty potent. I almost took a blade from Cyno so I didn't have to let her go. I could see how it could make you want to fall into that part of yourself."

"You could be right." His reply was just a little too bland, and intentionally so.

"Yeah, because Sal's still just little Sal. If anything, she's been pretty human lately. That's why it shocked me so much when you lost it on her," Zep said. "Think maybe it has more to do with the fact that she's supposed to be our leader?"

"Probably." Blaec dragged his hands across his face. "Or because I know how much prejudice humans have for us, and just how far they'll go to keep us in line. Zep, if Sal goes feral, she won't be the only one paying for it. We all will. Don't you see how dangerous she is?"

"So yeah, I'm on the right track. Now here's a big question for ya." Zep looked him in the eye. "Why Cyno?"

"I have no idea. Maybe it's because I saw it, before that first assassination?" Blaec guessed. "He gives her something she needs, and I can't see him doing more than taking care of her. I dunno. Maybe it's because *I* can't give her what she needs when the lust is on her? He makes up for what I lack, I think."

"So, what if she ends up in bed with me?" Zep asked softly.

"You trying?" Blaec made sure his voice stayed neutral.

"I dunno, man. She's not ready yet. But you know the type of girl I've always gone for."

Blaec smiled at the truth of that. "Yeah. Running around with skin the color most of us would kill to have, and you're bedding the palest women you can find. Guess it doesn't get much more iliri than Sal."

Zep watched Blaec's face intently. "Yeah. She's pretty much the type of girl I've always wanted. Hell, ever since that day she got jacked, I can't really look at her the same. I don't wanna mess up anything between you and me, though."

Blaec shrugged. "If it happens, it happens. I screwed things up pretty bad. I guess it's best to know that she's with someone who really cares about her. You'd be good for her." He sighed. "Have to say, I thought it'd be Cyno."

Zep laughed. He didn't chuckle, he roared. Blaec looked across at his friend, trying to understand what he'd missed while Zep wiped tears from the edges of his eyes.

"Human!" Zep managed around his gasping laughs. "Oh. Oh, man. Ok. LT, you're a fucking idiot!" And he began laughing again.

"What the fuck? I missed the joke," Blaec said as Zep got control over himself.

"Sal. I love her, man, but not like you do. She's like," Zep looked at the ceiling. "She's the most honest friend I've ever had. She's pretty shitty for my love life, though. About the only way I could stick my dick in her is if she needed me to, cuz of the lust. Pretty sure there's enough people willing to volunteer that it'll never happen. That's it, Blaec. That's the only way I'm getting in her bed. Sal's one of my brothers, that's *it*."

With a lost look on his face, Blaec tried to understand the conflicting smells coming from his friend. "So... why did you just ask..."

"If I could fuck her?" Zep finished, and Blaec nodded. "Because you're sitting here claiming to be all human and shit, and when I ask my alpha male's permission for a piece of the pie, he gives it, and it's ok. But if I hadn't asked, you'd'a ripped me a new one for trying to steal a taste like you did Arctic." Zep grinned at him. "Trust me, that's not how it works for humans. If you were human, none of us would be allowed to touch her. *Ever*."

Blaec just looked at him, confusion apparent on his face. "No, that's not -"

"Seriously, LT," Zep interrupted. "When I was a kid, my best bud was gettin' it on with this girl. I had a crush on her real bad before they got together. He got tired of her and stopped seeing her and all, but wasn't anything that would make me even talk to her again. It kinda feels like if I spit on your food. You suddenly have no interest in it anymore. Same shit. That's what it's like to be human."

"Is that why you never really tried with her?" Now Blaec had to know.

"Yeah, kinda. I mean, I'm learning to think like you all do, now, but sometimes I just can't. That, and the fact that she thinks I taste good. That's just a bit more freaky than I want to try, but Sal and I have it worked out. We're friends. That's it." Zep smirked at Blaec. "But it does explain why you were so upset. She didn't ask first."

"For which?" Blaec was getting exasperated.

"For kissing Arctic, for taking over the mission. None of it. She didn't try to hide it, which may make it worse, I dunno. But you didn't give her to him. She did it on her own, right after she already stood up to you once, and your damned human alpha-male pride kicked in. Am I right?"

"Probably." Definitely.

"Are ya still pissed about it?"

"No," Blaec replied. It was the truth. "I feel like a fucking idiot, and I'm scared of what this will do to our unit, but I'm not pissed." He sighed and tilted his head back. "Now what? I fucked up. I think I fucked up bad. How the hell do I fix this?"

Zep just smiled at him before answering. "I know you've probably never seen them, but your men are bunked down on the other side of the stables, in the south wing. Sal has a cabin there. If it was me, I'd try begging for forgiveness. You can't afford to let your pride screw this one up, my friend."

Blaec nodded slowly, aware that Zep was the guy who knew what Sal was thinking right now. "I'll probably never find a way to repay you for this, you know. Damn it, Zep. I owe ya. If nothing else, for kicking me in the ass, but I'm hoping I'll owe ya for Sal, too."

"It's all good, man. Next time I won't wait so long to see if you're gonna grow a brain." Zep smiled and pulled himself to his feet. "And your chances are pretty good, but it's not going to be pretty. She's out for a ride. You might wanna catch her when she gets back."

"What do I say?"

"Tell her she should never try to be a human," Zep said seriously. "*Never*, LT. You hear me?"

"I know, Zep. It's just that we have to be careful, you know?"

Zep grabbed his glass and slammed back a drink. "No, I don't. You don't say shit when Cyno does his thing. And it's not like being polite will make Sal's skin any darker."

"I know," Blaec mumbled.

"I don't think you quite get it. Why do you train the horses the way you do?"

Blaec looked at him, confused. "We start them gently to keep their spirit and natural movement."

"Same shit, man. You give your damned colt more respect than you do your girl." Zep shook his head and sank back into the chair. "I'm fucking disappointed in you right now, but we've been friends a long time, so I'm trying to let it go, ok?"

Blaec was not keeping up. He was listening, but Zep's mind wandered too much to follow easily. "What do you mean?"

"You tried to break her. You hit her where it hurt her the most, and your damned pride stopped you from sucking up. You hit her with the one thing that's been bothering her for her *entire* life. She's not fucking human. She can't *be* human, but you told her she *had* to be human. The *one* damned thing she can't do, and that's what you told her it would take to get you back."

"Ah, fuck," Blaec whispered, finally understanding. "*Fuck.*"

"Yeah," Zep agreed. "And you sent away the only man who could convince her you're wrong."

The truth of Zep's words felt like a bucket of ice water over his head. "Cyno," Blaec realized.

Zep nodded slowly. "She went four days playing human, eating only human meals, before I caught her. She collapsed shortly after. I spent last night making sure she ate and slept, terrified she'd stop breathing in the middle of the night. I'm not fucking around, LT. If you want to kill her, there are easier ways."

"I never thought – "

"No," Zep interrupted, "you *didn't*. Your own amma was iliri. You should fucking know better."

"Yeah," Blaec said, grabbing the bottle and topping off their glasses. "I've been around humans too long, I think."

"When did you start hating what you are?" Zep took a long drink but watched LT over the top of his glass.

"I don't!"

"Then why do you keep trying to hide it?"

"Because they'd split us up, disband the Blades, and put us back in blues." Blaec thrust a hand out in the direction of their cabins. "Do you know what that would be like for them? Do you have any idea what it's like for iliri in the regular army?"

Zep shrugged that away, clearly waiting for the rest.

"That's it," Blaec said. "This is our family, our little haven. We're damned good, but we're still hiding from them."

"What can they really do to us, LT?" Zep countered.

"I just said..."

"And if they put Cyno in blue? What do you think would happen? Risk? Arctic? Razor? Hell, even Shift!"

"They'd defect," Blaec whispered.

"And I'd be right there with them," Zep almost snarled.

Blaec laughed and tilted his glass. "You'd just get reassigned into another unit."

"Doesn't mean I'd stay. We're a fucking pack. We leave when we die."

Which sounded great, but there was one big problem with that. "Where would we go, Zep? Really. Where would eight rogue iliri go?"

"Unavi Rebellion?" Zep suggested. "Myrosica? Hell, most of ya could probably get into Viraenova."

Which was when Blaec realized where their loyalty really lay. "You're serious?"

Zep nodded. "I'm not the only one that thinks it, either. You have what you need. It's time to make this country respect what you are."

Blaec set his glass carefully on the table and looked up at his friend. "It's been twelve years, Zep. Twelve *long* years. I remember what you were like back then. Never thought I'd see the day when you're more iliri than me."

CHAPTER FORTY-SIX

Sal kept her ears folded close to her head, protected from the wind. Standing in the irons with her calves against the mare's side, she watched the ground rush past. Her cheek was pressed close to Arden's neck, just to the side to stay out of the horse's way. Sounds faded under the pounding of hooves and scents mingled into a familiar taste of nature. Cantering across the rolling hills, her senses no longer trapped her in her misery.

When they reached the valley, she pulled Arden in, bringing her to an easy walk and giving the mare the reins with a friendly slap on the neck. Leaning back in the saddle, Sal felt her muscles stretch. The Conglomerate spring was fading into an early summer, and the flowers were withering on their stalks. The trees above them whispered in the breeze, taunting Sal with all the things she didn't understand. She couldn't make her mind stop. She couldn't just relax. Her thoughts were torturing her, trying to find the answer to a problem she couldn't fix.

"I can't be human," she whispered to her mare, leaning over to hug her neck. "I tried. It just doesn't work that way."

Before she became a Black Blade, Sal had learned to submit to the authority of humans. She'd been trained from an early age to ignore her aggressive urges, but with the Blades that was rarely an option. She couldn't stand quietly while her friends died around her. She couldn't refuse to use her teeth if it meant making the kill. Blaec appreciated her iliri abilities when she used them for assassinations, but not when she used it in typical combat?

Or could it just be when humans were watching?

She thought about that. It seemed he only worried about her iliri nature when humans might think less of her. He only wanted her to act human when it would affect how people saw his unit. She couldn't hide her species – her white skin and hair made that impossible – but she could help him prove that iliri could be controlled and used. She was one of the few purebreds to serve in elite ops, which made how she acted even more important.

But she couldn't be human. She couldn't even control her own urges! She was an assassin, and her job was to kill, but each time she did, the bloodlust took control. She kept screwing her partner then crawling back to her lover in between. That certainly was *not* something humans would ever understand. She shoved her face into Arden's mane and breathed in the musky scent of the horse to calm herself. She might be a damned good soldier, but she still couldn't control her instincts. Humans were right. She was just a beast that walked on two legs.

She couldn't stop her desire to kill. Humans smelled too sweet and moved like they wanted to be trapped. They were so predictable, traveling in groups, clustering together, just begging for her to pick them off. After the fight in those caves, she knew they tasted as good as they smelled. They were her prey.

The histories proved that, too. The more generations iliri were bred down, the easier they were to control. That was what made Blaec an excellent commander; he was human enough to get the iliri benefits without the consequences. She and Cyno, though, didn't get the control part. They had the desire to kill, the skills to kill, and the abilities to kill efficiently, but none of the control to understand when they shouldn't. Like with the hunting hounds, the handlers looked for dogs with a strong drive to track the prey, but a weak drive to kill.

And hounds that were too aggressive were put down.

She couldn't change who she was. She couldn't be anyone but herself. She could fake it for a few moments, but she was who she was. She was iliri. She was made to be a predator – a very good predator. Cyno hid in the shadows of others, never drawing attention to himself, but that wouldn't work for Sal. She was too pale, too female, and too obvious to be overlooked. Time and time again, humans noticed her, even when she did nothing to ask for it.

And now, that attention caused problems. She was ruining everything the Black Blades had worked for! If she had to resign, then that was what she'd do. She loved her brothers in arms, but she loved them enough to leave them.

Sal sucked in a breath and blinked at the sky when she realized what she was telling herself. Her only option was to leave the Blades. She didn't know what she would do or where she would go, but she had to do it. Maybe she could be reassigned to the stables? That would let her see them occasionally, and maybe they'd be able to remain friends. Over time, they'd forget her. That was just how things worked, but without her, the Blades wouldn't have the threat of being disbanded hanging over their heads.

Sal lifted Arden's reins and gently turned her back to the barns. She patted the mare's spotted neck one last time. For a few months, she'd had her dream. She'd tried. She may have failed, but at least she'd tried. She'd had her own horse, her own room, and even her own armor. It didn't sound like much when she thought about it like that, but she'd rarely had anything meant just for her. And she'd known love. Blaec's love, the love of her unit brothers, and the love of her job. For these last few months, it had felt so perfect. She'd thrown herself into life with a passion.

A passion that had ruined everything.

Step by step, she walked Arden back. She wouldn't be able to keep the mare. As a Private, she wouldn't have the wages to afford the care of a fully trained warhorse. She definitely wouldn't need one. Arden would serve the Blades well, and it would be a good life for the horse. All Sal owned was an entire wardrobe of clothes – most of it bought for her by Zep, Razor, and Shift. That was more than she'd had when she'd arrived. She had her clothes and a scar. It wasn't much to show for the life she'd led.

Sal! Jase's mind burst into her head. *Maast, Sal, please hear me.*

She sat up straighter, wondering if he'd somehow overheard her thoughts. *I hear you.*

We're fucked, kitten, he sent, panic tinting the tone of his mental voice. *It was an ambush. We're fucked.*

She stopped Arden without realizing it, all of her own problems forgotten. *Can you get out? Fuck the mission, Jase, get out!*

Na gonna happen. She could feel a part of his mind was preoccupied. *They already got me, kitten. We're gonna lose the link in a sec when they catch Arctic. I'm sorry, but can ya take this? I do na have time ta package it right, so ya'll have ta sort through it.*

She felt him offering his memories. The bright flame was raging out of control, larger than anything she'd handled before, but Sal reached for it. He passed the jumble of thoughts into her mind, and she grabbed at her saddle, trying to hold them.

Ever'thing's in there. Ever'thing. Sal, oh, Sal. I never got ta tell ya, ok? But ya'll know.

Where are you, Jase? Can you hold on long enough for me to make it?

I do na know. Just a little town called Yager's Crossing. Arctic's trying for LT. I know where the steel is, Sal. Ya have ta stop it. More than anything, ya have ta stop the damned steel or they'll kill all a us. They wanna cleanse the world of our kind. Yer the only one that is strong enough ta catch the memories.

I got them, Jase. I'm coming. Just hang on, killer. I'm coming for you. She put her heels into Arden's sides, making her words into truth.

Ya can na. It's the Black Widows, Sal. Just stop the steel. He broke off for a moment, and her heart lurched. *Fuck. They got him. Oh, maast. Sal...*

She didn't even pause for the gate, encouraging the mare to jump it, heading for the cabins and her gear.

Jase? she begged into the silence. A surge of fury hit her just before the link went dead.

She rode hard through the compound, humans leaping from under Arden's feet, not stopping until she reached her rooms. In a shower of dust, the horse slid to a halt and Sal slipped off, dropping the reins to the ground. Zep burst from his rooms behind her. They'd all felt the link fall silent.

"Sal!" he yelled.

"They got him," she called back, her feet never slowing.

She shoved open her door and didn't bother to close it, moving to her armor. She snagged the cuirass, fumbling to buckle it on when Zep grabbed the next strap.

"I buckle, you talk," he said simply.

"Jase said it was an ambush. He's caught, and they were about to get Arctic. I think they did, which is why the link's down. He sent me his memories, but he couldn't tie them up. Zep, they're burning in my head, and when I look at them, it's going to knock me off my feet."

"Stop wasting time and look," he said, pushing her back onto her bed. "I can put you in armor while you're out cold." He grabbed a greave and demonstrated.

Sal nodded and closed her eyes, looking at the fires in her mind. The surge of information hit her hard, and she dug her fingers into the covers, gasping. Cyno and Arctic had been sent to a small town just north of Fort Landing. A group of farmers there supposedly had been hired to assist with the transport of the steel into Unav. They were willing to talk in exchange for money. The Blades had taken the bait and sent Cyno in to make the deal, but he'd been met with the Black Widow Company instead of honest men. The Black

Widows knew the Blades never worked alone and went searching for his partner. That was when Jase reached out to her. Trussed in a farmhouse, the Terrans were only keeping him alive because they wanted more information.

His cold logic clouded the memories, except for his thoughts about her. Warm and bright, his longing ran at the edge of each one. It was his only regret. Sal made herself look past it. The feeling was too personal. He knew she'd see it, but he hadn't known that when he'd felt it. She repackaged the memories, keeping only the facts the Black Blades would need, and tried to sit up – failing the first time. Her head felt too light.

"I know where he is," she gasped.

Zep helped her up. "Ok, what are we doing?"

A scrape in the dirt outside her door told Sal that they weren't alone. Looking over, she saw Shift and Razor leaning through the frame. She looked back to Zep. "You're getting the Blades together. I'm going to save my partner."

Shift nodded, accepting that, and ran, intent on some mission of his own. Razor pushed into the room.

"We work in pairs," he said.

"Not this time." Sal grabbed her weapons and started strapping them on. "Black Widows know that. Guys, I can get places you can't. I can do this. I need you to get the unit mobilized."

"No." Blaec stood in the door, sadness and anger clear on his face. "We need to stop the steel. I have the location."

"Yes, sir," Sal agreed. "You do. I need to get my brothers."

"You can't, Sal. You go in there, and you'll give us away. The Black Widows have no idea we have this knowledge. We have to stop the damned bribe."

She looked up at him and snarled. "You were right about one thing, Blaec. I'm a damned beast. You don't *fuck* with a beast." She grabbed at her neck and yanked at the delicate resin chain hanging there. It snapped, leaving her holding the large opal. "I think there are a few things you forgot, Lieutenant," she said, tossing it at his feet. "I won't lose my brothers."

He growled, moving toward her, but Sal stood her ground. She stared deep into his eyes, her lip pulled away from her sharp teeth, and waited for him to get closer. He took the last step and she reached out, slapping her hand against him, her palm on his jaw. Then she shoved the information Jase had given her deep into Blaec's mind.

He gasped and stepped back, the force of the transfer so intense it rocked him on his feet.

"I quit," she said softly, then pushed him aside as she made for her mare.

"Sal!" Blaec called after her. "Stop!"

She grabbed her reins and swung onto Arden's back, catching his eye. "No, sir. We don't have time for politics. Act like a human all you want, but I'm done. Court-martial me when I get back."

She turned her mare and caught Shift coming out of Arctic's rooms. "You'll need this," he yelled, throwing something her way.

She caught the leather bag easily, feeling the tubes clank inside it. "A jakentron?"

"Yeah, his best." Shift hurried to Arden's side. "How many blades you got?"

"Four."

He began unbuckling his belt. "Guys, we need a pair of short swords, and... just, more blades."

Blaec wrenched at his own belt, looking at the men around him. "I want her covered in an arsenal, men. Pikes, halberds, make sure they're her size. Move!"

"Thanks," Sal said when she accepted the sword Blaec passed up to her.

"You're right, Sal. I'll get the army moving; you bring them back, ok?" He rested his hand on her leg. "I was wrong, love. You're better when you're a beast. Come back to me?"

She buckled his sword across her back and nodded. "I'll bring them home, Blaec. We'll talk then."

"Black Widows have twelve men there, two are wounded. Arctic thinks three of them are snipers. They'll be looking for a pair. Move fast." He squeezed her leg gently. "Be feral."

She nodded as the men returned, passing daggers and polearms up to her. Halberd in hand, a bladed staff behind her, two swords hanging on each side of Arden's saddle, and about fifteen daggers placed across her and her mount, she couldn't fit any more weapons. When she waved them off, the men stepped back.

"Be safe, kid," Zep whispered.

Sal didn't answer; she just turned Arden and kicked.

CHAPTER FORTY-SEVEN

Blaec stormed into the Command Room, the door slamming against the wall from the force of his entrance. The Generals looked up, shocked and speechless when he grabbed a map from the wall.

"It's here," he said, throwing the map on the table and stabbing a finger at it. "I need two units of heavy, one light, one of mounted archers, and fuck... make that three heavy. Infantry will never get there in time."

"What are you talking about?" an aged man asked, offended at the interruption.

"The metal bribe," General Sturmgren said softly, moving to Blaec's side. "How'd you get it?"

Blaec shot a warning look at Sturmgren. "My men were ambushed, but they got the intel out. Black Widows are busy right now, so we have to move quick."

"Five units of mounted?" General Gabik asked. "Ok, I'll send the orders down. This intel good, Lieutenant?"

"It had better be," Blaec growled. "I might lose two men over it."

"Ok then," Gabik agreed. "We'll run some background and get

the orders out. I'll have the Captains report to you the day after tomorrow."

Blaec slammed his fist onto the map. "I need them *now!*"

General Sturmgren rested his hand on Blaec's shoulder, gently. "Lieutenant, the military doesn't move that fast. 112th is out east. Devil Dogs are in the north. You're down two in the Blades. Think Azure can take it?"

Blaec shook his head. "Mounted skirmishers, maybe. Azure is foot. Shadow Company?"

Sturmgren shook his head. "With Lightning Brigade in Eastern Escea."

"Fuck."

The men in the room watched the exchange, hanging on each word. Ran Sturmgren patted the Lieutenant's shoulder again.

"We may have been outplayed, Blaec. Tell me what you know. Let's come at this a different way."

Blaec shook his head. "I don't have time, Ran. I have two men held by the Widows. I have to get them out. We need to start mobilizing before I get back."

"We need your intel, Lieutenant," General Maklan said. "That's an order. I know you hate losing men, but we need this intel."

"Who's out there?" Ran asked.

"Arctic and Cyno. Sal's moving for extraction as we speak."

"Aren't those your iliri?" General Zorion asked him.

"Yes, sir."

Zorion waved it away. "Then we need the intel more. I'm sorry, Lieutenant, but you'll need to replace them." He looked at Maklan beside him. "Not like we don't have enough conscripts to give him more."

"We're all fucking iliri!" Blaec snapped. "Haven't you figured that out by now? That's why the Black Blades get shit done! Because we're faster, stronger, and smarter than humans! Now get me five mounted units by the time I get back – I don't care how you do it –

and my iliri will save the Conglomerate again. Don't, and we can't. Clear enough?"

He shoved the map away from him and stormed out of the room.

"Blaec!" Ran called after him, jogging through the swinging door.

Blaec turned, a snarl on his lips. "Ran, don't fucking try to stop me. I won't leave my men to die out there."

"Not what I'm gonna do," Sturmgren said. "Lieutenant Doll, I order you to retrieve your men, in any way you deem necessary, and report to me when the mission is complete. Understood?"

Blaec sighed and nodded, his gratitude clear on his face. "I owe you, sir."

"Yeah, you do. I'll try to fix the mess you just made in there, but I make no promises. You just told the officer's council that your entire unit is iliri, you realize that?"

Blaec smiled coldly. "I do. It's about time they figured it out. She was right."

"Good luck," Ran said. "And I want to meet this new one you got. She's put a little steel back in your spine."

It took a couple hours to reach Yager's Crossing from Stonewater Stables, and each step of the trip felt like an eternity while Sal wondered if her friends still lived. Her mind stayed silent. Arctic hadn't even made an attempt to reestablish the link. Naturally, she feared the worst. Her instincts told her to rush in, to see if they lived, to rip apart the men who tried to hold them captive, but Sal knew better. When the road grew wider, she pulled Arden into the hills, circling around the cluster of farmsteads. From the top of the highest rise, she could see the roofs below.

Yager's Crossing was quiet. Too quiet. No children played near the houses. No dogs rummaged through the compost. Every door and window was closed tightly even as the day grew warmer. Inside, it would be stifling.

She moved away from the hilltop, not wanting her silhouette to be seen by the Black Widow Company. They weren't fools, Sal reminded herself. They may have been humans, but they weren't fools.

She found a cluster of trees and dismounted, looping a rein over a low branch to allow the mare to graze. Working fast, she assembled the jakentron and buckled on two belts full of daggers. Risk's fit her, but Shift's hung low across her hips on the tightest notch. It would have to do.

Holding the jackentron's pressure valve open, she made her way to the edge of the rise, falling to her knees before she could see over it. When the hissing stopped, she dropped in a simple glass needle filled with a quick-acting toxin. Her gun loaded and ready, she crawled the last few paces to peer over the edge. The hill dropped away into the backyard of someone's small cottage, offering a clear view of the three streets through town.

Letting her ears swivel, seeking any hint of her enemy, Sal waited. Her slit eyes caught each movement, from the sheets blowing on the line to the hummingbird flicking around a flower bed. The town felt deserted, but she refused to move.

Her patience paid off. She heard the creak of old hinges first, and her eyes darted to the sound. The door cracked, and a dark man peered through the gap into the empty streets. From where she waited, she could shoot through the door, hitting him easily, but Arctic had drilled her long enough that while she could make the shot, she waited. She wanted them outside, in the open, not hiding in the houses.

Seeing nothing, the Terran stepped out, moving slowly. He kept his body in line with the building, limiting the angles of attack and watched his openings. Step by step, he moved toward the center of town, his head looking between two buildings.

So now I know where they are, Sal thought. *Has to be one of those two.*

When he moved to cross the street, she took the shot. Leading her target slightly, the way she'd been taught, Sal adjusted for the wind and the man's movement, giving plenty of room for the needle to drop. The Terran soldier paused in the open to slap at the side of his face. He found the glass shard, pulled it from his skin, and looked at it. She saw his shoulders sag as the realization hit him, then the toxin took effect. His body began to convulse, and he screamed. Loudly.

On the hill above, Sal moved, a cruel smile playing on her lips. *That's for my brother,* she thought.

She opened the valve again. The jakentron was an amazing weapon, but pressurizing it was slow and cumbersome. She listened to the man scream while the gun filled and she relocated, unwilling to make two shots from the same perch. Halfway around the next hill, the hissing stopped, and Sal grabbed another dart, loaded it, then crawled toward the ridge. A large evergreen tree offered her a perfect vantage point.

Her first victim was nearly dead, twitching and frothing in the street. A second man crept toward him, trying to hurry, but unwilling to rush into the open. Sal waited. He reached the dead man and glanced around quickly before bending to check for a pulse. She exhaled and pulled the trigger. The needle hit and her prey stood, trying to rush back toward the larger house. He didn't make it to the edge of the street before he, too, screamed and writhed.

She moved again, wondering how many she could pick off like this before they'd change tactics. Circling back toward her mare, she hurried, trying to visualize the layout of the town from the backside of the rolling hills. When the second man stopped screaming, she looked for cover.

This time, there wasn't much. A single jagged tree stump was the only thing breaking the ridgeline. The smaller house lay directly below her, the larger just to her right but further back. The two dead men lay framed between someone's home and what looked to be a store. She couldn't be sure of her prey's approach from this angle, so she forced herself to breathe slowly and listen. In the house below, voices murmured quietly, unaware she was able to hear them.

"Robson! Looks like they sent a rescue party. They're darting us as we cross the street!"

"That means they have snipers in the hills. Take two and come up behind them. If they're watching the crossroads, they won't be watching their backs."

"What about the damned scrubbers, Sergeant?"

"Four of you stay here," the man called Robson ordered. "Fucking beasts are known to be unpredictable."

"Gotcha. You two, with me."

The back door to the house beneath her opened, and Sal pressed herself into the ground. The Terran gestured, and two men darted off, circling her, moving as silently as she would expect of an elite soldier. She began to pull away from the hill when movement caught her eye. A third man made an attempt to rescue his companions. Sal aimed quickly and pulled the trigger, then crawled backward from the ridge.

Gaining her feet, she ran to her mare, disassembling the gun as she went, storing it in the leather bag on the horse's hip. Arden barely flicked an ear at her return, grabbing greedily at the grass while Sal shoved the jakentron into a saddle bag and gathered her reins. Mounted, she pulled the horse away from the cluster of trees, putting distance between her and Yager's Crossing.

Her mind worked furiously while she made her way to another secluded grove. She had assassins stalking her. They would assume she was working with a partner, which would make them more cautious. She preferred to think of it as timid. They'd be looking for well-armed soldiers, gaps in armor, and properly placed snipers. What they wouldn't expect was her. Twining Arden's reins around the mare's neck, Sal stripped out of her armor, thankful for the warm weather. She hung the swords on her saddle, stored her gear, then removed her clothing, as well. All she needed was her steel blade. Her ceramic dagger, the double-bladed staff, and the two weapon belts she tossed over her shoulder. Then, tucking her clothing under her arm, she moved back toward the small town, leaving her mare protected by distance.

Naked, Sal shifted her skin to match the land around her and rushed forward, moving from cover to cover, heading toward the back of that small farmhouse. The sweet scent of her prey led her on, but she wouldn't be foolish. In the shadows under some scrub bushes, she hid her supplies and the long staff, then moved again. Reaching a large tree, she pressed into the trunk, changing her skin to match. On the other side, a breath gave away her enemy.

Sal waited for the man to take just one more step.

He moved around the tree and she pounced. Her steel blade pierced the resin across his chest, the other sliced at his sword arm while her teeth closed on his throat. Sweet, hot blood rushed into her mouth when she pulled back, and the soldier died with a wet sound. The bloodlust hit her, erasing her fears and replacing them with a desire for more while sharpening every sense she had. Sal could feel the edges of the grass under her feet and the gentle breeze lifting her hair away from her back, but most of all, she could smell men. There were two more, and she wanted to watch them bleed.

She licked the blood from her lips and moved.

CHAPTER FORTY-EIGHT

She skirted the trees, keeping the last two men in sight. They were intent on the ridgeline, scanning each bush for signs of her passage, unaware that she wasn't the prey, but the predator. The smaller of the two shoved his sword into a shrub quickly, glancing over at the other when it encountered nothing more than branches. The larger man glared and held his finger to his lips, his other hand gesturing in signals only the Black Widows knew.

They split up. The smaller man moved to the right, and Sal paced him quietly from the shadows. Keeping well back, she used the terrain to her advantage. When the scent of the other no longer filled her nose, she made her move. After coloring her skin to match the grass, she crawled toward him, pausing each time he stopped. Like a cat stalking a mouse, she crept ever closer, her knives pressed close to the ground, their blades hidden in the weeds. She flicked an ear back the way she'd come, checking to be sure they were truly alone, and then she struck.

Rushing forward, Sal covered the distance in four strides. At the sound of running feet, the man turned. She snarled when she swung. The steel blade dove deep into his chest, and the ceramic sliced at his face, cutting his mouth open. He tried to scream, but Sal shoved her hand over his mouth, muffling the sound.

"Just fucking die already," she snarled, yanking the steel blade out, just to shove it back in. This time she hit his heart.

With a strangled gasp, he lay still. Her ears flicked again, and she moved.

Sal circled back, breathing deeply. She wondered if the last man realized why the army put so much emphasis on hygiene. The pungent scent of stale sweat and moldy cloth led her right to him. He stared at the ground beneath the large evergreen tree she'd used for cover. Bending lower, he touched the dirt, a scuff in the leaves the only sign of her time there.

"So, they teach you how to track in the Widows?" she asked.

He jumped like a startled mouse, spinning in place. Sal stood before him, naked, her skin its true white. Lazily, she flipped the steel dagger in her hand and smiled. His eyes widened at the sight of her teeth.

"Yeah," he said, leaning against the tree, glancing across the ridgeline before looking back at her. "Terric gives us some pretty good training. You?"

She smiled. "I hear about twice as well as you and I can smell you a kilometer away." She scratched at the tip of her ear with the point of the blade, taunting him. "So, you kill my brothers yet?"

He shrugged. "Dunno. The one's pretty bad off. Guess they don't sedate so well. We know you beasts have tricks, though, and it all links back to him. Arctic, I think is his call sign?"

Sal nodded. "Yeah. What about the other?"

"He's being good. Gave us some intel so we wouldn't kill his friend. Only problem is that I'm not real sure how your partner is gonna sneak in there. We got 'em covered."

She laughed. "Yeah, see, that's the thing. The 'good' one? That's my partner. You kinda got it all wrong. It isn't that we work in pairs, it's that we never work alone. Kinda thought the Widows would know about being able to count to three, though."

He stiffened ever so slightly, and she nodded.

"I got three out there in the street. Got your two friends as well." She leaned slowly toward him. "And you just served your purpose. You'll make another third."

"Come get me, bitch," he said, pulling the sword at his back.

She laughed and flipped the steel blade again. "I'm a fucking animal, you shit, not an idiot."

As his eyes watched the steel spin in the air, Sal flicked her other wrist, sending the ceramic blade at his throat. He dodged, but the white knife lodged in his collarbone. Sal was on him before he could take a second step.

"Scream," she told him. "It worked well enough last time."

"Fuck you." He spat in her face.

"Fine, then I will. My brothers need to know I'm coming."

Sal shoved the dagger deeper, resting her hand on it to hold herself above his body. He clenched his teeth against the cry that wanted to break free, and Sal lifted her right hand, the steel dagger twice the length of the ceramic one lodged in his body. She pinned her ears close and yelled a primal roar, then shoved the steel into his chest. He gasped and writhed. Sal moaned softly, watching him die.

Just six more, and four of them would be in the small house below. She jogged back to her weapons stash and dug beneath the shrub for her gear. Arden was too far away for her to retrieve her armor, but Sal hoped she wouldn't need it. She got dressed, buckled on the belts, shoved her daggers into empty sheaths, and grabbed the resin staff. Her mind inspected the layout of the town as she made her way back to the last man's body. From this vantage, she could see every building. Below her, an old shed and a barn sat alone. It wasn't likely that the Black Widows would be taking shelter in such open buildings, so she slipped over the edge.

The drop was steep. She used the staff for balance when she made the staggering run down the slope. When she reached the bottom, she ducked behind the shed, seeking any hint of the Terrans. Silence greeted her.

She wanted to be nowhere near the bodies of her prey. That was the first place to look for the enemy. With one last flick of her ears, she darted to the next building, moving further from the small house that would be her final destination. The shadows against the walls made her black uniform the perfect cover, and unlike the Terrans, she had no need to move slowly. Sal darted, ducked, and ran from hiding place to hiding place until she pressed herself against the back wall of the large house that the first man had been so intent on. The scent of humans oozed from it.

She slunk around the edge, looking for an opening, and paused at a small window into the cellar. The glare of sunlight on the glass made it impossible for her to see through it, and she didn't dare risk pushing her face closer. Carefully, she leaned down, but jumped back when a small face looked back at her.

The boy smiled. Sal raised her finger to her lips, and he nodded, then twisted the latch. She heard it click, and grabbed her knife harder when the kid pushed it open.

"They're upstairs," he whispered. "You're one of the good guys, right? Terrans don't like iliri much."

"Yeah, kid," Sal said softly. "I'm a Black Blade. I need to get in there."

"Ok. It's a good drop though," he warned before jumping back to the floor.

Sal listened intently. With the scent of humans so strong, she knew there were more than just Terrans here. She'd never smell the scent of their weapons over this many bodies, but she had no other option. She stuck her head through the opening and looked around. The eyes of children were all that met her.

Wedging herself through the small window, she grabbed the sill and eased herself to the ground, pulling her weapons in behind her.

Six kids watched her, wide-eyed. An older boy glanced across her body.

"Don't think it," she warned him.

He shook his head. "Just wondering how you're going to get us out without armor."

"Don't need armor unless you plan to get hit. Now, I need to be briefed." She looked between the kids.

"What's that mean?" a young girl asked.

"Means she needs to know what is going on," the teen said. "There was a squad of them. Like ten or twelve came in yesterday. They locked us up in here. Our parents are upstairs. I'm pretty sure they separated the women and are using that to keep the men in line. They got a couple of prisoners a few houses over, too."

Sal nodded. "Yeah. That's why I'm here. How many were upstairs, say, an hour ago?"

"Like five?"

"Four," the young boy said. "There was four there earlier when Ma brought down lunch."

"Ok. Then there's only two up there now. Makes this easier." She looked at the older boy, "You ever dream of being a soldier?"

He smiled shyly and shrugged. "Yeah, I guess."

"Then I'm gonna need your help. For this to work, I need the rest of you to do exactly what I say, ok?" Sal glanced around the room, making her plans quickly. "I need someone to play the victim. All you have to do is scream and cry like you're hurt. One of you willing to do that?"

"I can," a girl, maybe ten, offered.

"Ok. Make it loud, and make it seem like you just cut your hand off or something." She turned to the younger boy. "You're going to have to stand in front of her like you're helping. Make sure they can't see that she's ok."

"Got it!" he said, beaming.

"Now this is the part I need to be sure I can trust you with. You have to stay in that corner." Sal pointed at the one spot in the room where the stairs wouldn't be visible. "No matter what happens, I need you to stay there and not move. I have to have room to work. If you get in my way, it could get us all killed. Ok?"

The five youngest nodded seriously. Sal hoped she'd scared them enough for them to obey. The older boy watched her, his nervousness showing.

"What am I supposed to do, ma'am?"

Sal smiled at him kindly, keeping her teeth hidden. "It's sir, and you need to pound on the door to get someone to open it." Confused, he nodded, and Sal pulled him away from the younger kids. Glancing back to be sure they couldn't hear, she leaned closer and whispered, "It's not fair of me to ask you to do this, but I think you're the only one that can take it, ok?"

"You gonna kill them?"

"Yeah. You'll probably see it, too."

He gulped. "Ok."

"All you need to do is bang on the door and run back down the stairs, telling them the girl is hurt. Close your eyes or don't, that's your call. I just need them to see *you* when the door opens – and not me. Ok?"

"Yeah. I've never seen a dead man before."

"I know. This stairwell is probably going to get really messy. Keep the younger ones down there. They don't need to see it."

"Ok. And thanks," he said, smiling weakly at her.

"For what?"

"For trusting me not to flip out."

"How old are you?" she asked.

"Thirteen."

"Then I'll see ya in the ranks in about five years. Deal?"

He stood a little straighter. "Thank you, sir," he said.

There was only one thing left. "We ready?" she asked the kids.

"Soon as you are," the precocious girl answered.

The teen nodded. "Yeah."

"Ok, when he's in the stairwell, give it all you got."

Sal grabbed the teen's arm and pulled him close. "I can move faster than them. I will not let you get caught in the middle of this. As long as you trust me, you'll be fine."

"Yeah," the boy agreed nervously.

"Then let's do this."

Together, they moved into the stairwell and made their way up to the door. With each step, Sal pressed against the wall until she became little more than a shadow behind the door, the resin staff tucked close to her body. Behind them, the girl put on a convincing performance.

Sal nodded, and the boy pounded. "Lona's hurt!" he yelled. "She's hurt bad. Cut herself and it won't stop bleeding! Please! We need some help down here!"

He glanced back. Sal smiled at him proudly, then tilted her head at the door, asking him to do it again.

He did. Pounding, his voice growing more and more worried, he yelled and begged for help while Lona screamed like only a young girl could. Her ear-splitting shrieks caused movement upstairs, and Sal could hear the voices of adults each time she gasped for air. Finally, the lock clicked, and the knob slowly turned.

When the door opened, Sal was invisible behind it. The teen looked at someone and begged, "She's hurt bad, she cut herself on an old lantern. We tried to stop it, but she's still bleeding. You gotta do something, mister!" Then he turned and darted halfway down the stairs. "Please?" he begged.

"Fucking kids," the man grumbled and pushed the door further open. "Fine!"

He never even checked behind him when he trotted two paces down the staircase. The teen glanced back, and Sal pointed down the stairs. The boy's eyes widened slightly, and he looked away as Sal swung. The lower blade of the staff hacked at the Terran's waist. Blood splattered the narrow space when she followed with a backhanded slice at his neck. The man spun in place at the force of the blows and crumpled as Sal speared the end of the blade through the door.

"Don't look back," she told the kid, "just keep them down there."

He nodded and ran to be with his friends. Sal rushed in the opposite direction, shoving through the door and into the chest of the second soldier.

The impact knocked her staff away, but her hands immediately moved to her waist to find knives to fill them. The right moved faster. She buried that blade in the Black Widow's back, the one in her left hitting his chest, while her leg swept out to knock him from his feet. When his body hit the floor, she finally stopped growling.

Shocked gasps were the first thanks she got, followed by fearful stares. On the main floor of the house, dozens of townsfolk had been detained – and she'd just made a very impressive entrance.

"There's a group of kids down in the cellar, and blood in the stairwell." When that got her no response, she tried again. "I'm pretty sure an elite soldier is the last thing any of you need to worry about."

"Are they ok?" a woman asked.

"They're perfect," Sal assured her. "We need to get these bodies out of their way, though. You," she said, pointing to a large man, "take this one. Drag him, carry him, I don't care. You and you," she picked out two more, "get the one from the stairwell. Throw them in a closet or something. We'll deal with it later."

The townsfolk nodded but didn't move.

"As soon as you get the bodies out of sight, bring the kids up. They don't need to see that shit. The older boy is keeping them around the corner. He knows what's going on, and I'm sorry for that, but he'll make sure the littler ones don't see."

"Thank you," a mother said. "Oh, thank you. I didn't think an iliri would understand."

Sal tried not to be offended. "I need to go save my brothers now.

I'll be back, but it may take a bit. Stay inside and keep the kids quiet until either myself or another CFC soldier is back."

When they nodded, Sal grabbed her staff, heading to the door. She looked at the dead men in the street and sighed. Nothing she could do about that now, but a hostage would have been useful.

CHAPTER FORTY-NINE

Sal closed the door carefully behind her and jogged across the street, making for the smaller house. She never crossed in direct sight of the building, well aware that there could be a couple of snipers waiting to pick her off. She wished she'd brought her armor, knowing leather and cloth would do her little good against four men, but she had enough weapons to make up for it. Her bloodlust begged her for another death.

Slipping beside the next building, her eyes and ears searched for any sign that the enemy realized they were under attack. There wasn't one. So long as that held, she could make it across the street in one piece. It wasn't far to her destination.

Her mind whirled, trying to think of a way to ensure her success. Reaching the door would be easy; it was what came afterward that would be the problem. Breathing deeply, she checked her weapons and knelt, rubbing her hands in the dirt to absorb any sweat that could cause her grip to slip. She'd just started to move when she heard the door.

Throwing herself around the corner, she pressed against the white wall while her ear swiveled to follow the sounds. A man walked out and stood on the hollow porch, his steps thudding clearly. He stepped again, away from her, and she dared to peek around the edge.

A shrill whistle pierced the air, making the Terran look up. From the ridgeline above, a dark man waved. Sal paused in shock. Dressed in black - his uniform nearly identical to that of the Black Widow Company - with the sun at his back, Zep was begging the man to see him.

The Terran stared, unable to make out the person, and Sal wasted no more time. She rushed the last steps, pulling her steel blade as she went, and hit him from behind. The staff pressed against his chest, the dagger in her other hand along his neck.

"Do not struggle," she told him. "Let's go inside, and if you're lucky, you'll live through this."

"Fuck you, bitch," he said – then struggled.

Sal growled and jabbed the dagger into his thigh. The point hit bone. "I mean it. I kinda like torturing your kind, but my commander says I shouldn't. I'm trying real hard to obey, get me?"

He nodded. When Sal pushed him to the door, he limped in the direction she desired.

"Open it."

He reached forward and yanked the door open. Sal, pressed tight behind his bulk, forced him inside. Three men waited, armed and ready.

"Looks like it's a stand-off," the man in the middle said. Sal glanced at his shoulder. He was a Sergeant, so probably the leader.

She tilted her head. "Yeah, kinda seems that way."

"So what do we do now? There's four of us against just you."

"You could give me back my brothers. I mean, if you haven't managed to kill them yet."

"Na yet," Cyno said softly.

"Ya feeling it, killer?" she asked, unwilling to take her eyes from the men before her.

"Yeh, a bit. Arctic's out cold. Still breathin', though."

"Gotcha." She flicked her eyes across the men before her. "Here's the thing. We're pretty evenly matched right now, right?"

The Sergeant chuckled. "Sure, if you say so."

"I mean, I already took out, what... eight of you? I think it was eight. Give or take."

"Fuck," the man on her right whispered.

"Yeah." She tossed the staff on the ground and watched it roll against the wall toward Cyno's voice. Then, she grabbed another blade from her waist. "You're pretty good though. I give you credit for that."

She pressed the dagger into the man's ribs on the other side and shoved her steel blade into the belt at her waist, trading it for another ceramic one.

"Well, you got balls coming in here," the Sergeant told her.

Sal chuckled. "I just got lonely back at home. Killer?"

"I'm watchin'."

"I don't know what it is you think you're up to, bitch," the apparent leader warned, "but you make me too nervous, and we won't care what happens to your hostage."

Sal chuckled. "See, that's why we're better than you. You know that, right?" She glanced quickly toward Jase and saw him tied to a support beam. His hands were bound together, waist high.

"Why?" asked the man she held, sounding nervous.

"Because we'd die to protect our own. We're a family. I'm sorry you never got to know that."

She shoved him away from her, flicked the ceramic blade toward Jase's waist – careful to make it a slow and predictable arc – and rushed the man to her left. Jase caught the blade as Sal ran her man through. Reaching for her steel blade, she slashed wildly, snarling as she spun. Flesh tore. Unfortunately, it was her own. The Sergeant slashed at her hip and his sword cut deep.

Jase cut himself free and rushed the man before him, burying the blade deep in his back. He rolled for the staff Sal had tossed to the floor. The blades whirled, cutting the legs out from under her former hostage, then Jase turned to the only man still standing. The Sergeant grinned at the little assassin.

"It's a strange trade-off you beasts make," he said, tilting his head at Sal's crumpled body.

She snarled, her anger pushing the pain away, but her damned body wouldn't listen. "He's worth it."

She and Cyno moved at the same time. Sal surged up from the floor and buried her steel knife in the man's stomach, while Cyno sliced at his chest. They both struck true. The Terran's face looked shocked. His blood smelled so sweet, spilling across the wood floor as he collapsed, not quite dead. Sal sank back to the ground, exhausted, wishing she could just lick it off him.

"Fuck, Sal, how bad is it?" Jase asked, rushing to her side.

"I can't walk." She tried to shrug it off. "The guys are on the ridge. I saw Zep up there."

He nodded and darted out the door. She heard a shrill whistle, then a long pause. "I got two down. Widows are done," he yelled, then stepped back inside. "They're coming, kitten."

"Ok. How's Arctic?" she asked.

"Stoned. He's fine, he just does na know it yet," Jase promised. "They were usin' us as bait."

"Yeah. Then help me sit up."

Jase grabbed her shoulders, dragging her back toward the wall. "Ya were na supposed ta come fer us, Sal."

"I couldn't leave you." She looked up at his eyes.

He glanced down quickly. "Yeh. Did na really expect ta make it outta this one, ya know?" He blushed slightly and shook his head. "Prolly woulda been a bit more careful of what I sent ya."

"Hey." She waited until he looked at her before she continued. "Fair's fair. You get enough shit off me each time you touch me, right?"

"Yeh, but I try na ta look too hard."

Sal nodded and grabbed his hand. "I know. I tried not to look too hard, either. I cleaned it up before I passed it on, too."

"Thanks." He paused as the sound of horses drifted through the door. "Can we talk about this later?"

"Yeah," Sal said. "But you should know, I kinda quit the Blades."

"Is that why yer here?"

"Was the only way to get Blaec to let me come. He'll probably court-martial me when we get back, but I thought you were worth it."

He lifted his eyes to hers. "Still rough tween ya?"

"Yeah." Sal looked away as the Black Blades stormed into the little farmhouse. Blaec entered first, sword drawn, but paused when he saw Cyno sitting so close to her.

"You both good?"

"Yeh," Cyno said. Sal just nodded.

"We lose Arctic?" he asked, his voice too calm.

Cyno shook his head. "Nah, ya woulda felt it, even with the link down. He just needs Shift. They drugged him up pretty good. They're sure he's got somethan to do with how we organize."

The tension drained from Blaec's body. He wiped at his eyes, but couldn't say anything. The smell of relief wafted from him.

Shift pushed past the Lieutenant and grabbed Sal. Without warning, she felt her world spin and closed her eyes. Breathing deeply, she waited until the vertigo passed. When she opened them again, Zep knelt before her.

"You made a mess out there, kid." He was grinning. "Where's your gear?"

"With Arden, southwest of here in a cluster of trees."

"Ok. We found a few bodies up there, too. How many did you take out?"

"Twelve," Jase said.

"Nine," Sal corrected. "Jase got two, and we left one to question. He'll need to be fixed up, though."

Zep chuckled and patted his friend's shoulder. "She's showing you up, man. Gimme a location when Arctic's up, babe, and I'll find your mare."

"Thanks, big brother."

Her wounds gone, she stood and pulled off the weapons belts, then passed them back to their owners. One last time, she looked at the faces of each Black Blade around her before walking out of the little house, onto the porch. The small town was still too quiet. She'd remember this place for a long time. Her last mission as a Black Blade. She'd won, but in the end, she'd lost it all.

"We need to talk, Sal," Blaec said, walking up behind her.

"You court-martialing me?" she asked.

"No. Never." He leaned beside her. "I'm also not accepting your resignation or approving your transfer."

"It won't work, Blaec. I can't be a human. I'm no good as a human!"

"I know."

"I don't think you do." She turned to face him. "I killed nine men today because I did it my way."

He nodded. "Jakentron to snipe three, pretty nice ambush for three, and three more in there. That's good work for a Blade."

"One in there, two more in the large house with the civilians. I got the kids out."

"Doesn't sound very beastly, saving kids," he pointed out.

She laughed once. "I tried to paint the walls with blood."

Blaec tried to hide his grin but failed. "Ok, that's better."

"I'm serious, Blaec," she continued. "I won't stop being iliri. I can't. I can't make you happy no matter how hard I try, so I'm done."

"No." He turned to her and caught her eyes. "You're not."

Sal held his gaze, unwilling to look away. He tilted his head slightly, and she set her jaw.

"Finish it," Jase said, from the door. "Just fucking finish it."

"I won't back down, Sal," Blaec told her.

She said nothing. Her resentment from the last few weeks suddenly surged inside her, enhanced by the bloodlust she had yet to slake. Her ears slowly tilted back, moving closer and tighter to her skull until they were pinned. A deep growl rumbled from Blaec and Sal's higher pitched one matched it.

"They gonna finish it this time?" Arctic asked, staggering to the door.

"Yeh," Jase said. "Sal's not backing down."

"She will," Blaec assured them.

"Make me," she snarled back.

"Fine."

For all that Blaec had urged them to be more human, he held the most rage. The Lieutenant rushed at Sal, expecting her to back off. Instead, she lunged at him. Snarling and snapping, he threw her over the porch railing, but she pulled him with her. Together, they crashed into the dirt, hard. Blaec tried to pin her to the ground, but she writhed and slipped from his grasp, only to come at him again.

She sank her teeth into his shoulder, trying to hold him, but he was stronger. Blaec threw her off, her sharp canines tearing gouges in his flesh. The sound of his shirt tearing was audible even over their snarls. She tried again. Blaec grabbed her shoulders and shoved her to the ground, pinning her beneath him. Sal snapped at him, but he held her too well. Her teeth found nothing. Unable to do anything else, she stared into his eyes, growling.

"Finish it," Arctic said softly. Beside him, the entire pack watched. This could change their future.

With his hands holding her, unable to move them without releasing her, Blaec only had one option left. He darted forward, avoiding her bites, and pressed his teeth against the side of Sal's neck, slowly increasing the pressure. She struggled again and tried to throw him off, but he only bit harder. When his teeth broke her skin, her growl stopped and a soft moan escaped. Sal closed her eyes and sucked in a long deep breath.

"I submit," she whispered.

Blaec kissed her neck gently, his way of easing the damage he'd done, then said, "You're not leaving the Blades, Sal."

"I understand."

"You're not leaving me, either," he told her. Leaning back, he watched her reaction.

Her eyes widened and met his for a second, before dropping to his mouth. She nodded. "Fine, but I won't be your human."

"No. You can't be, love. I may outrank you, but that doesn't mean I was right, ok?"

She nodded again.

"I told them, Sal. I told Command that the Black Blades are all iliri. I fucked up back in the caverns, and you were right, but I'm still in charge."

A smile made its way to her mouth. "Does this mean we're gonna show them what it means to be iliri?"

"Yeah," he breathed. "I think you kinda just did. We good?"

Sal nodded. "Yes, sir. We're good."

"I do love you, Sal."

Behind him, Jase slipped back into the house. He couldn't bear to hear the words she said next.

"I know, Blaec. I will never stop loving you. I can't."

"Iliri never do," Jase whispered.

EPILOGUE

Blaec tapped softly at General Sturmgren's door. He glanced down at his chest and brushed away a few specks of dust while he listened to footsteps cross the room inside. The handle turned, and the door opened. Ran Sturmgren waited on the other side, his face stoic.

"My orders were to report when the mission was complete, sir?"

"Yeah," Ran said. "Come in, Lieutenant."

He opened the door wider, and Blaec walked in proudly, well aware of the mess he'd left for the General to clean up.

"Take a seat." Ran gestured at a pair of chairs before his large wooden desk.

"Thank you, sir."

The General walked behind him, moving to the shelf at the side. He grabbed two glasses and a bottle of dark amber liquid before easing himself into the padded chair behind the desk. Without a word, he pulled the stopper and poured.

"Casualties?" he asked.

"No, sir. Both of my men were recovered with minimal injuries."

"Happens a lot to the Blades, doesn't it?" Ran didn't give Blaec time to answer before continuing. "You caused a stir before you left, Lieutenant."

"Yes, sir."

"We couldn't get the units together, either. We're going to miss the delivery."

Blaec smiled. "We brought back a prisoner, sir. Pretty sure we can figure out the route it'll be taking."

Ran smiled. "Yeah, that'll get you out of a lot of shit. How long will it take?"

"Couple of days at most."

"Ok," Ran said, nodding. "Do it."

"Yes, sir," Blaec answered, reaching out for Arctic. *We got the go. Find out everything that fucker knows.*

"So..." The General sighed, pushing the glass across the desk to rest beside Blaec's hand. "All of them?"

"Iliri? Zep's human."

He chuckled and nodded his head. "And it's pretty well known that he's an iliri lover. What about you, Blaec?"

"Sir?"

Ran waved that away. "I said Blaec, so you say Ran. That's how this works between us, remember?"

"Yeah. I don't understand your question, though."

"You an iliri lover, too?"

Blaec grinned and shook his head. "Take off the lover part, and you got it, Ran."

The General's eyebrows shot up. "Iliri? Really? But your coloring is normal."

"Yeah, half. My amma was pure."

"Never would have guessed."

"Most don't, that's how we pulled it off for so long. I immigrated from Unav when I was eleven, when the war started."

"So now that the secret's out, what are we going to do about it?"

Blaec took a long sip and sighed at the taste of quality whiskey. "Not a damned thing."

"It's gonna spread pretty damned fast. You know that, right?"

"Yeah. I'm counting on it."

"So why now? After nine years, why'd you decide to tell us *now?*" The General lifted his own glass and took a swallow, then a second, before looking back at his friend.

"Because I have the right group. I thought we were good before, but now? Nothing can stop us. It's time the iliri start to get a little respect, and I've got the soldiers to do it."

"Ah." He leaned back toward the table. "It's the girl, isn't it?"

"Corporal Salryc Luxx," Blaec corrected. "She's not just 'the girl.'"

"Yeah. I think you normally call her Sal?"

Blaec nodded, wondering where Ran was going with this. The General was rarely curious without a good reason. "Yeah. She's my newest."

"Changed things up having a pure-bred around?"

"A bit."

"You gonna be able to control her?"

Blaec couldn't hide the smile. Sal had submitted to him completely in Yager's Crossing and then again when they made it back. Visions of her pale form sprawled in his bed came to mind when he thought of it, but all he said was, "I can control her."

"You know about the females, I assume? I hear they get pretty headstrong."

"They do."

"You sleeping with her?" Ran pointed at the drink in Blaec's hand.

Blaec tilted his head and met his eyes. "You do realize that would be a breach of military protocol, right, General?"

"I do. Do you, Lieutenant?"

"Oh, I'm well aware of it."

Ran took another drink, this time a long one. "Just so we're on the same page, then. We both know that's the story that's going to start spreading."

"It started as soon as she was promoted, actually."

"Wait." Ran looked at Blaec with confusion on his face. "Which are we talking about, this time?"

"Just the rumors," Blaec said, laughing. "You're slacking, you realize that, right?"

"Yeah. Comes with age. That, and I always had trouble keeping up with the way iliri minds work. Everything makes a lot more sense now, though. I wish you'd told me sooner, but I get it."

"I was worried we'd end up disbanded if it got out, truth be told."

"So what changed?"

Blaec tossed back the last of his drink and rested his elbows on the table. "The girl."

"Ok, cut the double talk and give this to me straight. Doors are closed, and I'll take off the damned clusters on my shoulders if you want, but I need to know what is going on with my best unit."

"No, I trust you, Ran. When I accepted Sal, I had no idea what it would do to the Blades. She made us more. This won't make any sense to you, yet, but she's a Kaisae, the kind of female that we don't see very often."

"Ok?"

"Thing is, I haven't seen a true Kaisae since I was a kid. I thought we'd lost them all in Unav. The Emperor has been hunting them down. Sal doesn't know it yet, and none of us want to be the one to explain it, but she's something like you humans have never seen. She's a pack leader."

"So how's that work in the Blades?" Ran asked.

Blaec smiled. "Took us a bit, but we sorted it out."

"She running the show, then?"

Blaec's lips slowly spread wide enough to prove his teeth weren't quite like a human's. The edges were serrated. "No. She's the third in charge, and I want to promote her to Sergeant, but she's not running the show. I am. She thinks Arctic is a better balance for my temper than she is, so he's staying my First Officer."

"How you gonna keep it secret that you're sleeping with her?"

"She's having a pretty public affair with Cyno."

Ran's brow creased in confusion. "So you're really not sleeping with her?"

"I didn't say that." Blaec tapped his glass and Ran poured more whiskey into it. "Iliri women choose their lovers, not the men. They take as many as they want."

"That's going to get awkward."

"Nah. We don't tend to get jealous about it either, so long as it's handled right."

"Shit," Ran grumbled. "I couldn't do it."

Blaec shrugged, a smile playing on his mouth. "You're human."

"And you're not. That's gonna take some getting used to," Ran admitted. "You still going to be able to handle what we need?"

"Oh yeah," Blaec promised. "Yeah, and probably better than you'd expect. If we don't have to keep it a secret, we'll be even more effective than anything you've seen before."

"Good. Because I have a mission for you, Lieutenant."

GLOSSARY

The Iliran language is a constantly evolving one. The letters p, j, q, and the combinations of th, ch, sh, and ph are not native to the original language but have slowly become used through the association with humans. Due to the inability of humans to understand pack hierarchy, many new titles have been created to aid in interspecies and international relations.

ahnam: first
ahnor: first mate; also a title for the Kaisae's husband (capitalized when used as a title)
ahvir: eternally
aitae: help
akerna: dam or birthmother, does not imply a relationship nor exclude one
alous: always
amma: mother or mom
ankan: spread
arhha: north
Arhhawen: North Wind

GLOSSARY

arn: and
arzionah: evening
ast: are
aufrio: grey, typically used to describe a color pattern on grauori
aussah: thank you
auxec: save
avixa: tell
ayamae: help me
ayati: the nature of things, fate, and used as slang to mean joy/happiness
bax: earn
berrn: leave
brerror: loner or outcast from society
ca: with
canzara: distance (away)
cenla: slate
cessivi: soulmate; and a title for a partner bonded in such a manner
corvae: love
dargo: dominate
dava: father
denn: home
denwar: blocks
derc: two
dernor: second mate; also a title for the Kaisae's husband (capitalized when used as a title)
derza: right
dregor: sire or birthfather, does not imply a relationship nor exclude one
dru: you (plural)
e: the or to, depending on how used
ed: be
edst: is
einay: they
gan: does

GLOSSARY

gar: my
gara: most often translated as "uncle", but refers to a male pack member or caretaker, not related to the child. Used as a term of endearment.
garn: mine
gavwor: father-in-law; can be used as a title of respect
gehwah: show
genause: soul or direction of one's life path
gern: do
gerus: those grauori deemed successful enough to contribute to the species and allowed to breed; implies respect
grae: know
gru: babies
grunae: pup
ihrend: word
il: you
ilnae: an iliri child
ilus: derived from the grauori idea of proving one's worth, now used as a title of respect similar to sir or ma'am
inurga: wrong
Kaeen: female leader of Viraenova
kai: her
kaisae: leader (female); one of the four genders of iliri, when capitalized it refers to the chosen female ruler of the species
kaisor: leader (male); a title created to show respect to Blaec Doll
kaizen: leaders or rulers (plural)
kalargi: brother
kanae: his
kanna: name
kano: he
kauvwae: grandmother
khemma: daughter
kierna: she
koleri: sister

GLOSSARY

laetus: reverence
lannae (lannar): emotional sex, to make love
liall: dog
lor: for
loura: missed
lursarati: devil or demon, a personification of evil
lyrva: revenge
maargra: grauori soldier, literally means "one who protects"
maast: bloodlust, can be used as a profanity
maerte: the meat derived from humans
moxero: bravery
nacione: white, often used to describe a color pattern on grauori
nas: not
nee: please
nieur: die
novi: new
onsa: same
onsyc: homosexual or pansexual gender of iliri
Orassae: grauori queen, literally means "leader of the people"
ortas: intelligence
raergah: respect
raewar: strength of the pack, recently made into a title for military leadership
rafrezzi: gold, typically used to describe a color pattern on grauori
rahdreg: pride
raz: stop
rocrra: force
rornnae (rornnar): carnal sex for physical pleasure, to fuck
sadava: adopted father
sae: I
sahn: us
sahna: we
settivo: place
sevic: hunt

sinna: this
sivex: friend, not to be confused with acquaintance which has no specific word
suma: that
sussa: need
taunor: third mate; also a title for the Kaisae's husband (capitalized when used as a title)
tola: all
umso: submit
unes: where
va: am
vaera: life
van: will
vargwar: voice, recently made into a title for an official translator
vau: have
vau: was
vaun: are (plural)
verg: freeze
wen: wind
wohanna: honor
wona: true
xie: ridge
za: of
za: what
zan na: slang equivalent to "of course"
zar: in

BOOKS BY AURYN HADLEY

Contemporary Romance: *Standalone Book*

One More Day

End of Days - Auryn Hadley & Kitty Cox writing as Cerise Cole **(Paranormal RH):** *Completed Series*

Still of the Night

Tainted Love

Enter Sandman

Highway to Hell

Gamer Girls - co-written w/ Kitty Cox **(Contemporary Romance):** *Completed Series*

Flawed

Challenge Accepted

Virtual Reality

Fragged

Collateral Damage

For The Win

Game Over

Rise of the Iliri (Epic Science Fantasy):

Completed Series

BloodLust

Instinctual

Defiance

Inseparable

Tenacity

Resilience

Dissent

Upheaval

Havoc

Risen

Hope

The Dark Orchid (Fantasy RH / Poly):

Completed Series

Power of Lies

Magic of Lust

Spell of Love

The Demons' Muse (Paranormal RH):

Completed Series

The Kiss of Death

For Love of Evil

The Sins of Desire

The Lure of the Devil

The Wrath of Angels

The Eidolon Chronicles (Paranormal Poly):

In Progress

Not A Vampire

Not A Ghost

Not A Succubus

The Path of Temptation (Fantasy RH / Poly):

Completed Series

The Price We Pay

The Paths We Lay

The Games We Play

The Ways We Betray

The Prayers We Pray

The Gods We Obey

The Wolf of Oberhame (Fantasy):

Completed Series

When We Were Kings

When We Were Dancing

When We Were Crowned

Wolves Next Door (Paranormal RH / Poly):

Completed Series

Wolf's Bane

Wolf's Call

Wolf's Pack

ABOUT THE AUTHOR

Auryn Hadley is happily married with three canine children and a herd of feral cats that her husband keeps feeding. Between her love for animals, video games, and a good book, she has enough ideas to spend the rest of her life trying to get them out. They all live in Texas, land of the blistering sun, where she spends her days feeding her addictions – including drinking way too much coffee.

For a complete list of books by Auryn Hadley, visit:

My website -
aurynhadley.com

Amazon Author Page -
amazon.com/author/aurynhadley

Books2Read Reading List -
books2read.com/rl/AurynHadley

You can also join the fun on Discord -
https://discord.gg/Auryn-Kitty

Visit our Patreon site
www.patreon.com/Auryn_Kitty

Facebook readers group -
www.facebook.com/groups/TheLiteraryArmy/

Merchandise is available from -
Etsy Shop (signed books) - The Book Muse -
www.etsy.com/shop/TheBookMuse

Threadless (clothes, etc) - The Book Muse -
https://thebookmuse.threadless.com/

Also visit any of the other sites below:

facebook.com/AurynHadleyAuthor
twitter.com/AurynHadley
amazon.com/author/aurynhadley
goodreads.com/AurynHadley
bookbub.com/profile/auryn-hadley
patreon.com/Auryn_Kitty

Made in United States
Troutdale, OR
10/17/2023